Take three single dads,
three sets of motherless children,
three women who've already lost their hearts,
mix them up with a dash of special Christmas
magic and lots of love, and you have a recipe for

A MUM FOR CHRISTMAS

Enjoy!

*First published in Great Britain 1999
Silhouette Books, Eton House, 18-24 Paradise Road,
Richmond, Surrey TW9 1SR*

A MUM FOR CHRISTMAS © Harlequin Books S.A. 1999

A KISS, A KID AND A MISTLETOE BRIDE © Jimmie Morel 1998
DADDY'S ANGEL © Annette Broadrick 1993
THE MERRY MATCHMAKERS © Helen R. Myers 1995

ISBN 0 373 04645 6

102-9910

*Printed and bound in Spain
by Litografía Rosés S.A., Barcelona*

A MUM FOR CHRISTMAS

LINDSAY LONGFORD
ANNETTE BROADRICK
HELEN R. MYERS

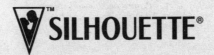

CONTENTS

A Kiss, A Kid and a Mistletoe Bride

Lindsay Longford

To my very own 'scullery wenches' who gave of their time and of themselves on a difficult day: Suzette Edelen, Patty Copeland, Myrna Topol and Margaret Watson. You worked like *dawgs*, you were sunshine through the clouds and you gave me the greatest gift of all: yourselves. I don't have words eloquent enough to thank you.

Chapter One

"You can't have that Christmas tree. It's mine."

The voice came at Gabrielle from between two low-slung branches. A foot stomped down, hard, on her instep. Startled, she tightened her grip on the scratchy bark.

Chin jutting out, a pint-size male face scowled at Gabrielle. "So put it back, you hear?" He wrapped stubby fingers around the branch nearest him and jiggled impatiently.

Needles spattered onto the soggy ground. "Me and my dad already chose *this* tree. It's *ours*. You gotta find another tree."

Not wanting to encourage the scamp, Gabrielle bit back her laughter and surveyed the small bundle of determination.

His shirt was carefully tucked into new blue jeans, his face was clean, and his eyes, dark brown and anxious, glared back at her. Someone had made a valiant attempt to slick down the cowlick at the crown of his head. The shoelaces on pricey new athletic shoes were double-tied.

Someone had taken pains to spiffy the boy up. Clearly, he didn't need her pity, but some thin edge of desperation or loneliness underneath his tenacity called to her.

Maybe it was only Christmas, the lights and smells of hope reaching out to her, making her vulnerable to this belligerent, wide-eyed waif. Or maybe it was her own loneliness and need for a perfect Christmas that shone back at her from this boy's eyes.

"So, lady, you understand? Right? You gotta find yourself another tree, okay?"

She heard the aggression, heard the rudeness. And in the soft darkness of a Florida night sweet-scented with pine and cinnamon and broken only by the glow of twinkling lights strung high from utility poles, she saw the bone-deep anxiety deepen in those eyes frowning up at her.

It was that anxiety and his dogged insistence that got to her. Bam. Like a hand reaching right into her chest, his need squeezed her heart.

But it was her damnable curiosity, which had been a besetting sin all her life, and maybe amusement that kept her interest as she watched him stiffen his shoulders and glower at her, waiting for her answer.

He was a pistol, he was, this tough little guy who wasn't about to give an inch just because she was bigger than he was. She took a deep breath. Somewhere in happy song land, elves were shrieking in glee because Santa had asked Rudolph to lead his sleigh. But here in Tibo's tree lot, as she stared at the pugnacious urchin, Gabrielle felt like the Grinch who was about to steal Christmas.

Wanting to erase that dread from his face, she dropped her hand. The tree wobbled, and she reached out to steady it. The boy's face scrunched in alarm as she grasped the tree again, and she released it as soon as she saw he was able to keep it upright. "How do you know I didn't see it first?" she asked, curious to see what he'd say.

"'Cause I was standing here guarding it. That's why." His not-Southern voice dripped with disbelief that she could be so dumb. He let part of the tree's weight rest against him. "My daddy's over there." Keeping his grip on the tree, the child jerked his chin toward the front of the lot. "He went to get Tibo. Tibo's gonna saw off the bottom so the tree can get enough water and last a-a-all Christmas," he said, finishing on a drawn-out hiss of excitement. "And in case you got any ideas, lady, you better not mess with my tree or with me 'cause my daddy's real tough. You'll be sorry," the boy said, never blinking. "You don't want to tangle with me and my daddy 'cause we're a team and we're tougher 'n a piece of old dried shoe leather."

"I see." Hearing the adult's voice in the childish treble, Gabrielle bit her lip to keep from smiling. "That's tough, all right."

"Da-*darned* straight." The square chin bobbed once, hard. "Nobody tangles with us. Not with me and my daddy, they don't, not if they know what's good for 'em." Sticking out his chest, he pulled his shoulders so far back that Gabrielle was afraid he'd pop a tendon.

This boy was definitely used to taking care of himself. His sturdy, small body fairly quivered with don't-mess-with-me attitude. Still, in spite of his conviction that he could handle anything, Gabrielle wasn't comfortable leaving him by himself. He couldn't be more than five, if that. Well, perhaps older, she thought, reconsidering the look in his eyes, but innocent for all his streetwise sass. And it was a scary world out there, even in Bayou Bend.

How could the father have walked off and left this child alone in the dark tree lot—in this day and age? It was none of her business, she knew, but she wouldn't be able to keep from telling the father that little guys shouldn't be left alone, not even in Tibo's tree lot.

"I'm sorry, but I really think I saw the tree first," she said, not caring about the tree, only trying to keep his attention while she scanned the empty aisles, looking for one tough daddy.

"Nope." He tipped his head consideringly but didn't move a hairbreadth from where he was standing.

"What, exactly, would your daddy do?" she asked, prolonging the moment and hoping the urchin's daddy would appear. "If I'd messed with—your tree?"

"Somethin'," her argumentative angel assured her. "Anyways, I know we seen it first. You was nowhere around."

"I saw this tree right away. I liked the shape of it." She fluffed a branch but made sure she didn't let her grasp linger as the boy's gaze followed her movement. "And it's big. I wanted a big tree this year." Her gaze lingered on the truly awful ugliness and bigness of the tree, and her voice caught. "I wanted a special tree."

He shifted, frowned and finally looked away from her, sighing as he glanced up at the tree. "Yeah. Me, too."

Again Gabrielle imagined she heard an underlying note of wistfulness in his froggy voice.

This stray had his reasons for choosing Tibo's sucker tree. She had hers.

The singing elves gave way to a jazzed-up "Jingle Bells," which boomed over her, and Gabrielle sighed. She and her dad had always made a point of dragging home the neediest tree they could find just to hear her mama rip loose with one of her musical giggles.

Last year, dazed and in a stupor, they had let Christmas become spring before either one of them climbed out of the pit they'd fallen into with her mama's death.

Christmas had always been Mary Kathleen O'Shea's favorite day.

Gabrielle and her dad hadn't been able to wrap their minds around the vision of that empty chair at the foot of the big dining room table. No way for either of them to fake a celebration, not with that image burned into their brains.

And so, in spite of a sixty-degree, bright blue Florida day that enticed Yankee tourists to dip a toe into the flat blue Gulf of Mexico, Christmas last year had been a cold, dark day in the O'Shea house.

This year, the giggles might once again be only a memory, but everything else was going to be the way it used to be. They'd have the right tree, the brightest lights strung on all the bushes around the old house, the flakiest mincemeat pie. Everything would be perfect. They'd find a way to deal with the empty chair, with all that it meant. In hindsight, she wondered if they shouldn't have forced themselves to face that emptiness last year, get past it. They hadn't, though, and the ache was as fresh as it had been barely a year ago.

But this Christmas, one way or another, was going to be perfect. Whatever perfect was, under the circumstances.

She sighed again and saw the boy's gaze flash to her face.

He shifted uneasily. "I'm sorry," he muttered, so softly she almost missed it. "But this is my special tree for me and my daddy."

She wanted to hug him, to wrap him in her arms and comfort him. Instead, knowing little boys, she tried for matter-of-fact.

"Well, that's life." Gabrielle thought she'd never heard a kid invoke daddy powers so often in so short a space of time. "Win some. Lose some," she said, hoping to erase the frown that still remained.

"Yeah. That's life," he repeated glumly before brightening. "Except at Christmas."

She heard the hope in his gruff treble. Well, why shouldn't it be there? All these Christmas lights strung up created a longing even in adults for magic, for *something* in this season when the world, even in Florida, seemed forever suspended in cold and darkness.

Her throat tightened, but she plunged ahead, desperate to change the direction of her thoughts. All this sighing and reminiscing weren't going to help her create her perfect Christmas.

"You didn't see me over by the fence? I was there, scoping out this very tree."

With his too-wise eyes, the boy examined her face, then shook his head with certainty. "Nah. You're trying to pull a fast one on me."

"Really?" The kid was too smart by half. "I might be telling the truth," she said thoughtfully, watching as he continued to study her face.

"Nope." He grinned, a flash of teeth showing in the twilight of the tree lot. "You're funning with me now."

Intrigued, she kneeled, going nose to nose with him. "How do you know?"

"I can tell." He shifted from one foot to the next, his attention wandering anxiously now from her to the front of the lot. "Grown-ups don't tell kids the truth. Not a lot, anyways."

"Oh." Gabrielle wrapped her arms around her knees to steady herself as she absorbed this truth from a kid who shouldn't have had time to learn it. "That's what you think I'm doing?"

"Sure." His mouth formed an upside-down U. "You're teasing me now, that's all."

This child had learned that his survival depended on knowing when the adults in his life were lying to him. She sensed he'd learned this truth in a hard school, that survival *had* depended on it. "You can tell when grown-ups are—funning with you?" She made her tone teasing.

"Funning's different from not telling the truth," he said matter-of-factly, his gaze drifting once more to the front of the lot. He, like her, was seeking the tough-but-absent daddy. "Funning's okay. No harm in funning. Most of the time."

"I see." Again that squeeze of her heart, that sharp pinch that made her catch her breath. "Want to draw straws for the tree?"

"No way," he scoffed. "You're still funning with me."

Suddenly delight washed over his face. "I remember! My daddy took the sticker off the tree, so we got proof."

"Ah. My loss, then." She smiled at him easily, letting him know their game was over.

In back of her, a foot scraped against one of the boards that formed narrow pathways between the aisles of trees. An elongated shadow slanted across her, and, still kneeling, still smiling back at the boy who'd shot her a quick grin, she pivoted, looking up at the silhouette looming above her.

"Daddy!" The boy wriggled from head to toe and launched himself at the silhouette, dragging the tree with him. "Daddy!"

Relieved, Gabrielle lifted her chin toward the tough daddy who'd finally shown up. Words formed on her lips—pleasant, instructive words designed to let this man know he should keep a closer eye on his son.

And then she saw the man's face.

Her heart lurched in her chest. Her throat closed, and her face flushed, with a heat so sudden and fierce she wondered she didn't burst into flames.

In front of her, Joe Carpenter, a lean, rangy male who'd been born with attitude to spare, attitude he'd apparently passed on to his son, rested his hand on the boy's shoulder and smiled gently down at the child who'd wrapped himself around his leg. "So, Oliver, reckon you're still determined to have this tree, huh?"

"Yeah." Clutching tree and man, the boy fastened one arm around Joe's waist and leaned against him. "This is the biggest tree. The best. A humdinger. *Our* tree. Right, huh?" He slanted a quick look at Gabrielle and before smiling blissfully at his father.

Gabrielle wondered if she could simply walk away, invisible, into the darkness, disappear behind tree branches, vanish. Anything so he wouldn't see her.

And then Joe Carpenter looked right at her, wicked amusement gleaming in weary brown eyes. "We've got to quit meeting like this, Gabby." He didn't smile, but the bayou brown of his eyes flashed with light and mischief.

As memory spun spiderwebs between them, she wished she were anywhere but kneeling at the feet of Joe Carpenter.

Knuckling his son's brown hair, hair only a few shades lighter than his own, Joe wrinkled his forehead. "Let me see. It's been what…?" One corner of his mouth gave a teeny-tiny twitch she almost missed in her embarrassment.

In spite of the past, a past embodied in Joe's son, a past made up of eleven years of creating her own life, she knew to the day and the month how long it had been. And he remembered, too, she decided as she watched his face and willed her own to fade from Christmas red to boring beige.

May 17. Saturday. Prom night. Out of place and miserable, she was fifteen years old and younger than her date's senior friends.

"Hey, pretty Gabby," he'd said that night, edging his motorcycle right up to the break wall behind the country club.

Water slapped against the dock while he surveyed her, the rumble of his cycle throbbing between them in the humid spring night.

"What are you doing out here? The dance is inside."

He motioned to the club behind them, with its faint bass beat and blaze of lights.

"I know." She turned her head and swiped away angry tears.

"So, you going to tell me why the prettiest girl is out here all by her lonesome? Or you going to make me guess?"

Gabrielle knew she wasn't the prettiest girl. She knew exactly who and what she was. She was the *good* girl, the one who chaired school committees, worked on the homecoming floats, went to church every Sunday. The girl everybody could count on. The girl who took everything too seriously.

Oh, she knew what she was. She wasn't the prettiest girl, not by anybody's definition, but she liked being precisely who she was, and now Joe Carpenter was teasing her, or making fun of her, or flirting with her. Whatever he was doing, she didn't know how to respond, and she wanted him to stop.

But she wanted even more for him to keep talking to her in that deliciously husky voice that raised the hairs on her arms.

That deep voice vibrated inside her, creating a hunger so unfamiliar that she felt like someone else, not a bit like Gabrielle O'Shea.

Joe Carpenter made her feel—wild.

And curious.

So she drew up her knees under the pale chiffon of her slim skirt, tried not to sniff too loudly and stared out at the shimmer of moonlight on the water. Better to watch the glisten of the water than to think about what Joe Carpenter might mean, because good girls knew better than to be alone with Joe. Even if they wanted to.

Even when their bodies hummed to the tuning fork of Joe Carpenter's voice.

Especially then, she decided, and wrapped herself tighter in her own arms.

He waited for a moment, but when she stayed silent, he kicked down the motorcycle stand, turned off the engine and walked over to her, his boots squeaking against the wet grass. "The prettiest girl should be inside, dancing the last dance. The one where they finally turn down the lights real low and everybody snuggles up and pretends all that touchin' is accidental."

Thinking about the kind of touching he meant, she shivered, and her barely there breasts tingled interestingly.

His voice burred with a kind of teasing she wasn't able to return, and he stepped nearer. "You know what I mean, Gabby. The kissing dance. That's what you're missing. I bet

Johnny Ray's looking all over for you. He'd want to dance real slow, real close, and see if your hair smells as pretty as it looks.''

He flicked his half-smoked cigarette into the bay and took one more step closer, his thighs bumping her stockinged toes. ''Because I've been wondering. Does it, Gabby? Does it smell like rain shine and night jasmine?'' With the tip of his finger, he brushed the top of her head, and her toes curled hard against the cement break wall.

She didn't say a word. Couldn't. Not even when he ran one callused finger down her shoulder, slipping under the cap sleeve of her dress and tracing the veins of her inner arm. She didn't speak even when he touched her wrist, gently, lightly, a butterfly touch that made her pulse skip and stutter. With a half smile she would wonder about for years, he lifted her arm, holding it up. Moonlight glinted on the thin band of her bracelet, on her skin, turning everything silver.

''Aw, what the hell,'' he muttered. ''Johnny Ray's not here, but I am. Too bad for ol' Johnny Ray,'' he said, and tucked her arm around his neck. ''Damned if I'm not going to find out for myself what rain shine smells and tastes like.'' His gaze never leaving hers, he lifted one of the curls that had cost her thirty-five dollars at Sally Lynn's salon and, shutting his eyes, stroked the curl against his mouth. ''Delicious, that's what,'' he whispered, his dark eyes filling her sight. ''Who could have guessed?''

And then the baddest of the bad boys kissed her, and she kissed him right back, a great big smooch of a kiss, tongues and lips and bodies touching in that silvery light. Oh, Lord, the touching. All down the stretch of his tough, hard body, her fifteen-year-old self melted, and there had been touching.

She liked feeling wild and wicked and out of control. She liked the hum of her body against his, liked the powerful drumming of his heart against her hand.

But just when she felt like soda pop fizzing out of control, his breath buzzing into her ear and making her insides quiver, he'd murmured, "You may be jailbait, sweet pea, but I swear to God it would be worthwhile. Except—"

He pushed her away from him, leaving her skin cold and hot and aching all at the same time. Stepping away with a grin that promised heaven or hell—she'd never been able to decide—he straddled his cycle and left her in a squeal of tires against pavement while she tried to decide if she wanted to call her daddy to come and pick her up or steal the car keys from her football-hero, drunk-as-a-skunk prom date.

For the rest of that night, her mouth, her body, her skin—*everything*—had ached and burned with that cold heat, and for the next two years she'd dreamed about Joe Carpenter.

Of course, she hadn't seen him again after that night.

He'd vanished, leaving Bayou Bend with its own kind of buzz as rumors floated, eddied and finally died away, leaving unexplained the mystery of nineteen-year-old Joe Carpenter's disappearance one month shy of graduation.

Now, staring up the length of his legs and thighs, Gabrielle swallowed. Even in the darkness of this Christmas tree lot, eleven years later, her entire body flushed with that memory.

No wonder he'd been the town's bad boy.

Well, she didn't want those disturbing dreams haunting her again. It had taken too many sleepless nights, too many confused days for her to erase Joe Carpenter from her dreams, her memories.

"So how long *has* it been?" he asked, his voice low and rumbly, goading, baiting her. "Let me think if I can remember the last time I saw you, Gabby. It must have been—"

"A while," she said grimly, struggling to her feet and catching one flat-heeled shoe on slippery needles and mud. "That's how long. A while." Her foot skidded forward and her arms windmilled crazily. Flailing, she saw her purse sail into the darkness.

"Whoa, sweet pea." Joe's warm hand closed around her elbow and braced her, his still-calloused fingers sliding down her wrist as she balanced.

Even through the silk of her blouse, Gabrielle felt that warm, rough slide. His hand had been warm that night, too, warm against her bare skin. She shivered.

"Cold?" Amusement glittered in his eyes. Heat was in the depths, too, as he watched her.

He knew what he was doing, as he had eleven years ago, eleven years that had vanished like smoke with his touch. He knew, but she was darned if she'd give him the satisfaction of going all giddy and girlish.

She was twenty-six years old, too old for girlish. Giddy and girlish had never been her style, not even at fifteen. "It's the damp. That's all," she muttered. "I'm not used to it anymore."

"Sure that's all it is?" His question, below the raucous rendition of the chipmunks and their version of "Jingle Bells," tickled the edge of her cheek where he bent over her, still supporting her.

"Absolutely."

"You moved away from Bayou Bend?" He clamped a hand under her elbow and steadied her.

"I've been living in Arizona. Same rattlesnakes. Less humid." She dusted off her red velour skirt, shot Oliver a smile and a "so long" and slung her shoulder strap over her arm. "Nice to see you again, Joe. Merry Christmas to you and your son."

She was almost safe. One second more, and she would have been up the walkway and gone, out to her car, away from the slamming of her heart against her chest, away from memory and the sizzle of his touch. One second. That's all she needed.

Out of the darkness of the next aisle, Moon Tibo lumbered, bumping into her and pitching her straight into Joe Carpenter's arms. "Okay, folks, let's haul this tree up front and get you on your way. I mean, you only got twenty-four days to the big event. Y'all gonna want time to hang up them ornaments before this year's over, right?''

"Right." Joe's laugh gusted against her ear, and Gabrielle felt her toes curl in memory. "Give me a minute, Moon. Got a damsel in distress here."

"Oh, yeah. Sure. How ya doin', Gabrielle? Your dad feelin' better?''

"Much." She was all tied up with her purse strap and Joe's arms, and she twisted, pushed, while Joe's chest shook with laughter against her. Over its broad slope, she finally angled her face in Moon's direction. "Dad's cooking jambalaya tomorrow night, in fact. For after we decorate the tree. Come on over. He'd enjoy seeing you."

Six foot five and built like a mountain, Moon gifted her with one of his rare smiles. "Might do that. Sure like your dad, I do."

She tugged again at her strap, which had flicked over Joe's head and bound them together. Mumbling under her breath to Joe, whose only help so far had been to keep her from landing face first in pine needles and mud, she said, "Give me a hand, will you? I can't do this alone."

"You got it, sweet pea. Lots of things aren't any fun done alone. I like lending a helping hand." His half smile could have lit up the town of Bayou Bend for a couple of blocks, and even Gabrielle's forehead blazed with heat. Lifting the strap, he ducked under it, his thick hair brushing up against her mouth, and stepped back. "I'm ready to help out. When I can." His palm was flat and firm against the hollow of her spine. "How's that?"

"Peachy. Thanks." Gabrielle untangled herself from Joe's clasp and brushed back her hair. Joe Carpenter would flirt if he were wrapped up like an Egyptian mummy. "This has been—special."

"Absolutely." He plucked a pine needle twig from her hair

and handed it to her. "A memento, Gabby. For old times' sake." His voice was light, amused, and his eyes teased her.

But behind the gleam, deep in their shadowy depths, she thought—no, imagined—she saw regret, a regret that made no sense, and so, surely, she must be imagining that rueful glint.

"We never had old times, Joe." She mustered a smile and let the twig fall to the ground.

"No?"

She shook her head and hoped her own regret didn't break through. "Not me. You must be thinking of someone else." Anyone else, she reminded herself. Joe's track record with adolescent hearts in high school had been gold-medal worthy.

But if she were honest with herself, and she tried to be, she knew her regret ran ocean deep because she'd never, ever felt that wildness with anyone since. She wasn't fifteen anymore, and she could handle Joe Carpenter's teasing. Sure she could, she thought as his eyes narrowed intently for a moment.

"Well. If you say so. Must not have been you I was re-membering outside the country club." He shrugged and let his hand rest on Oliver's head. "It was real good seeing you again." His gaze sharpened as he gave her a last glance. "Nice, that red skirt and silky blouse." He smiled, and again that flicker of regret appeared in his eyes. "You look like a shiny Christmas present, Gabby."

The weariness unraveling his voice and slumping his shoulders was real, and she hesitated, knowing she was making a mistake, knowing she'd be a fool to open her mouth when she had her exit line handed to her on a plate. Say goodbye and walk away. That's all she had to do.

She opened her mouth, then closed it. She would be asking for more trouble than she wanted, needed. And then, looking down at the boy, Joe's son, she spoke. "Come for supper. Tomorrow night." Joe's sudden stillness told her the invitation surprised him as much as it did her.

She would have taken the words back, but they hung in the

air, an invitation she hadn't intended, an invitation she wished she could take back the minute she spoke.

"Why doncha, Joe? Milo sure wouldn't care. You know how he is. More the merrier, that's what ol' Milo says." Moon hoisted the tree up with one hand and strode up the aisle toward the shed where the trees were trimmed and netted.

Gabrielle stared after him. She might have known, Moon being Moon, he would stick his two cents in. Trapped, she added politely for appearances' sake, "Dad makes a big pot. He wouldn't mind."

"Jambalaya, huh?" Joe rubbed his chin. "Milo makes good jambalaya."

"How would you know?" She closed her mouth, stunned. To the best of her knowledge, despite Moon's blithe assertion, Joe Carpenter had never met her father.

"Oh, I've had a plate or two of your pa's cooking." Running a hand through his hair, Joe glanced at Oliver, back to her, and then said, so slowly she couldn't believe what she was hearing, "Thanks. I reckon we'll take you up on your offer. It's a good idea."

Oliver, who'd been strangely silent throughout the whole incident, glared up at her, his face as fierce as it had been the first time she'd seen him, but he didn't say anything. Taking a sideways step, he plastered himself against his father and stayed there, a scowling barnacle to Joe's anchor.

Uneasiness rippled through Gabrielle as she saw the boy's hostility return, and she wished, not for the first time in her life, that she'd counted to ten before speaking. She was trapped, though, caught by Moon's interference.

Judging by the expression on his face, Oliver was trapped, too. As she looked away from his frown, her words tumbled out. "Good. Company will be great. That's what the season is all about. Family, friends. Get-togethers. Eggnog." Mumbling, Gabrielle scrabbled through her purse for a piece of paper and a pen.

"Right." The corner of Joe's mouth twitched. "Eggnog's always sort of summed up Christmas for me." He ruffled his son's hair. "Eggnog do it for you, Oliver?"

"No." Oliver worked his scowl into a truly awesome twist of mouth and nose. "Eggnog stinks."

Joe's hand stilled on the boy's head. "Mind your manners, Oliver," he said softly and then spoke to Gabrielle. "We'll be there."

Restraining her impulsive nature, she bit her bottom lip. Her instinct was to reassure Oliver, but faced with his ferocious grimace, she stopped. Oliver's likes and dislikes were Joe's concern, not hers.

Even though the boy's anger was clearly directed toward her, she knew enough about kids not to take it personally. She didn't know anything about this particular child. Whatever was going on between him and his father would have to be settled between them. She wasn't involved.

She pulled out a small cork-covered pad and flipped it open. "All right, then. Let me write out the address."

"I know where you live, Gabby." Joe's hand covered hers, and yearning pierced her, as sweet and poignant as the smell of pine on the cool evening air.

It was all she could do not to turn up her palm and link her fingers with his.

"Unless you've moved?"

"No." Her voice sounded strangled even to her own ears. "Dad hasn't moved." Unnerved by the thought that he knew where she lived, she flicked the notebook shut, open. "Oh," she said, dismayed as a sudden thought struck her. She looked up, made herself meet his gaze straight on. "And bring your wife, too. As Moon said, Dad likes a crowd."

"I'm not married, Gabby." Joe's bare ring finger passed in front of her. He closed her notebook, his hand resting against the brown cork. "What time?"

"What?" Her mind went blank. Nothing made sense. Joe

Carpenter, the Harley-Davidson-riding outlaw who could seduce with a look, had a son. Joe Carpenter knew her dad.

Joe Carpenter, whose kiss could melt steel and a young girl's heart, was coming to her house for jambalaya and tree trimming.

And eggnog.

Sometime when she wasn't paying attention, hell must have frozen over.

Even in Bayou Bend, Florida.

Chapter Two

"The time, Gabby?" The tip of Joe's finger tapped gently against her chin, snapping her out of her bemusement.

"What time shall Oliver and I come caroling at your door?"

"Eight, I suppose. That might be late for your son, though." She hoped Joe would pick up the hint and let her off the hook.

Joe Carpenter, of course, didn't. "Not a problem. Oliver doesn't start school until after the holidays."

Gabby sighed, a tiny exhalation. Joe had a plan. She couldn't imagine what was possessing him to take her up on her invitation, an invitation offered only out of politeness, not for any other reason.

Liar, liar. You like being around Joe.

With a jerk of her head, she silenced the snide little voice and dislodged Joe's finger. Her chin tingled, as if that phantom touch lingered warm against her skin.

Bearlike in his red-and-green plaid shirt, Moon waited for them to join him. "Well, then, you folks ready to check out?"

He held up a red plastic ball made of two hoops and topped with mistletoe and a green yarn bow. "Free kissing ball with each tree.'' Moon wagged the kissing ball in front of her until she thought her eyes would cross.

Resolutely, she kept her gaze fixed on the tip of Moon's Santa hat and told herself she was merely imagining the heat lapping at her, washing from Joe to her, and wrapping her in warmth and thoughts of more than kissing.

''Somethin' special for old Moon's customers, this is. And we got treats in the shed. Cookies. Apple cider. The boy can have a cup of hot chocolate while I bundle up this beauty. So come along, y'all.'' A trail of brown needles followed Moon's progress as he herded them forward. ''Good stuff, cocoa. You'd like that, wouldn't you, young fella?''

Oliver ducked before Moon's beefy hand landed on his head. ''Maybe. Maybe not.'' He trudged after Moon and the tree.

Moon grinned back. ''Shucks, kid. Everybody likes hot chocolate.''

Oliver planted one new shoe after the other, following Moon and hanging one hand tight to the edge of Joe's pocket. ''I only like it the way my daddy makes it. Out of the brown can and stirred on the stove. And only with little marshmallows.'' Head down, ignoring Moon, Oliver adjusted his shorter stride to Joe's, matching left foot to left.

The boy needed physical contact with his father. Gabrielle slowed and let the two of them walk slightly ahead of her, a team, just as the boy had stressed. Everybody else on the outside.

Her curiosity stirred again as she watched the two, one rangy and dark, a lean length of man, the other, short and dark, a stubby child with eyes only for his father.

''Where's your tree, Gabby?'' Joe stopped and looked over his shoulder at her. ''Oliver and I'll give you a hand with it while Moon bundles ours.''

''Umm.'' She saw something tall and green from the corner of her eye and pointed. ''That one.''

"That one?" Not believing her, Joe stared at the ratty tree. The one Oliver had insisted on was three good shakes away from mulch, but Gabby's tree— "You sure?" He frowned at her. "This one is, uh, well—"

"It's a terrific tree. It'll look wonderful with all the old ornaments." Gabby tilted her face up at him. Her off-center smile filled her face. Christmas lights sparkled in her mist-dampened soft brown hair, and he wanted to touch that one spot near her cheek where a strand fluttered with the breeze against her neck.

The look of her at that moment, all shiny and sweet and innocently hopeful, symbolized everything he'd come back to find in Bayou Bend, a town he'd hated and couldn't wait to leave. Like the star at the top of a Christmas tree, Gabby sparkled like a beacon in the darkness of Moon's tree lot.

"Come on, Daddy. We got to go." Oliver pulled anxiously on his hand.

Still watching the glisten of lights in the mass of her brown hair, Joe cleared his suddenly thick throat. "Right. But we'll help Gabby first, Oliver. Because we're stronger."

"She don't need our help. Moon can wrap her tree."

"Mr. Tibo to you, squirt."

"She looks strong enough to me." Oliver scowled and kicked at the ground.

Joe scanned Gabby's slight form, the gentle curves of her hips under some red, touch-me, feel-me material, the soft slope of her breasts beneath her blouse, breasts that trembled with her breath as she caught his glance. His gaze lingering on her, he spoke to his son. "Well, maybe she is strong in spite of the fact that she looks like a good sneeze would tip her over. Let's say helping out's a neighborly kind of thing to do, okay?"

"Neighbors?"

He would have sworn her breathy voice feathered right down each vertebra under his naked skin. Even as a teenager, her voice had had that just-climbed-out-of-bed sigh. He wondered if she knew its effect on males.

Her voice was the first thing he'd noticed about her back when he'd moved to Bayou Bend as a surly high school troublemaker.

Even then, the soft breathiness of Gabby O'Shea's voice held something sweet and kind that soothed the savage creature raging inside him.

Seeing him on the sidewalk outside the grocery store where he'd lied his way into a part-time job, she'd smiled at him in his black leather jacket and tight jeans and said, "Hi, Joe Carpenter. Welcome to Bayou Bend." Her voice slid over the syllables and held him entranced even as he folded his arms and gave her a distant, disinterested nod.

At seventeen, a year older than his classmates and new to this small community, cool Joe Carpenter didn't have time to waste on thirteen-year-old skinny girls with kind voices, not when high school girls fell all over one another offering to give him anything he wanted. Thirteen-year-old junior high girls were off-limits, not worth wasting time on.

But, touching that bitter, angry place he'd closed off to the world, her voice made him remember her over the next two years as she grew into a young woman, made him lift his head in baffled awareness whenever he heard that soft voice reminding him all the world wasn't hard and mean and nasty.

And now, even years after he'd fled Bayou Bend, her voice sent his pulse into overdrive with its just-got-out-of-bed breathiness.

"We're going to be neighbors?"

He shook his head, clearing his thoughts as she repeated her question. "Yeah, Gabby. All of us. You. Me. Oliver. We're going to be neighbors. I bought the Chandlers' house. Down the block from your place."

"Oh." Her hair whipped against his shoulder, tangled in the fabric of his jacket, pulled free as she turned toward the tree she'd chosen. "I hadn't heard." With two hands, she lifted her tree and thumped it up and down on the ground a couple of times.

He could have driven a pickup truck through the spaces between the branches, but at least her tree didn't drop needles like a cry for help.

"We're living in a hotel." Oliver tugged him toward Gabby's tree and checked it out critically. "For now. With a indoor swimming pool. I like the hotel."

"You're going to have a tree in the hotel?" Gabby's quick glance at him was puzzled. "That's nice, but—"

"A friend's letting us store the tree for a day or two.We're moving into our house on Tuesday." Joe watched as her eyes widened, flicked away from his.

"Ah." She touched the branch. "Tuesday. You'll be busy. Do you need some—" She stopped, just as she had before she'd issued her invitation.

Help was what he thought she almost offered before she caught herself.

She was uneasy with him. Edgy. Aware of him.

He took a deep breath. Nice, that awareness.

With one hand still wrapped around Joe's, Oliver poked his head under one of the branches. "This is a okay tree. Not as good as ours, though."

Joe inhaled, ready to scold Oliver, to say something, anything, because the kid had a mouth on him. But then Gabby's laughing hazel eyes stopped him. Her mouth was all pursed up as if she was about to bust out laughing. He shrugged.

"No problem. And Oliver's right." She gasped as his son glowered at her. "His tree *is* better. In fact, a few minutes earlier, we were negotiating which one of us was going to walk away with it." Her expression told him not to sweat the small stuff.

At least that's what he thought it meant.

"Right, Oliver?"

"We didn't nogosh—didn't do that thing you said," his son, stubborn as ever, insisted. "It was my tree 'cause I seen it first. Me and her settled that."

"Yes, we did," Gabby confirmed, smiling down at Oliver.

Joe ran a hand through his hair. Should he make Oliver give up their tree to Gabby? Was that the right thing to do? Hell, what did he know? He was the last person to try and teach a kid about manners and being a good neighbor and—

This daddy business didn't come with instructions. Wasn't like putting a bicycle together. More like flying by the seat of your pants, he was beginning to see. He didn't think he'd ever get the hang of it.

And he wasn't used to having a small recorder around, copying his words, imitating his ways, watching everything he did.

The responsibility made him lie awake at night, his blood running cold with the sure knowledge that he wasn't father material, while Oliver's warm neck rested against the crook of his arm.

"I like this tree, Joe," Gabby said gently, as if she could read his thoughts.

Her voice warmed the chill creeping through him. Scrubbing his scalp hard, he stopped his spinning thoughts. "Fine, Gabby. If that's the one you want."

"Oh, it definitely is." Her laugh rippled through the air. "It will be absolutely perfect for Dad and me."

"Whatever you say. Come on, Oliver. You take that branch and haul it up to your shoulder."

"'Course." His son puffed out a biceps you could almost see without a microscope. "Because I'm strong."

"I can see you really are," Gabby said admiringly, her expression tender as she looked down at his grumpy son.

God. His son.

Once more that weight settled over him. The responsibility. The constant fear that he'd mess up. But he'd asked for this responsibility, gone looking for it, in fact. He would do what he had to do.

"Ready, Oliver?" Joe heaved the tree off its temporary stand.

"Sure." Oliver clamped onto the assigned branch with both hands. "This is easy." His whole body was hidden by the branch held tightly in his grip.

"Can you see?" Gabby's question brought Oliver's attention back to her.

"I can see my daddy's behind."

"A guiding light, huh? So to speak."

This time Joe was sure he heard a strangled laugh underneath her words.

"Watch it, smarty-pants," he muttered to her as she walked beside Oliver. "Nothing good happens to smart alecks."

"Who? Me?" Her hair glittered and glistened, shimmered with her movements in the damp air.

"Oh, sure. You have that butter-won't-melt-in-your-mouth look to you, Gabby. Even in eighth grade, you looked as if you were headed straight for the convent. Still do, in fact." He lifted one eyebrow and felt satisfaction as her face flamed pink. "But I know better. That nifty red skirt gives you away, you know. That skirt's an invitation to sin, sweet pea."

She sped up her steps, trying to pass him.

"You're wicked, Gabby, that's what you are." He liked the flustered look she threw him. "Wicked Gabby with the innocent eyes and bedroom voice."

Her mouth fell open even as she danced to his other side.

He liked keeping her off balance. One of these days, if he ever had the time, he'd have to figure out why he liked pushing her buttons. Always had. "You're a bad girl, Gabby." He waggled a finger in a mock scold. "Santa's not coming down your chimney this year, I'll bet."

"Oh, stop it, you fool," she sputtered, finally darting past him with a laugh. "You're incorrigible, Joe, that's what *you* are."

"Shoot, everybody knows that."

"What's corgibull?" Oliver planted his feet firmly in place, stopping the procession. He stuck his head up from behind the branch. "And why are you and her laughing? What's so funny?"

"Your daddy is funning with me. He's making *very* inappropriate jokes," Gabby said primly, digging in her wallet and sending Joe a sideways scolding look as she dragged out money for the tree.

"Yeah?" Oliver stuck his fist on a nonexistent hip and rushed to Joe's defense. "My daddy's 'propriate."

"Oliver's right, Gabby." Joe tightened his mouth. "I'm very appropriate. Especially—"

"Uncle," she said, her eyes gleaming with laughter and something else that made Joe want to step closer and see for himself what shifted in the depths of those changeable eyes.

But he didn't.

Getting too close to Gabrielle O'Shea would be one of the stupidest moves in a lifetime filled with mistakes.

"I give up, Joe. Let me pay for this dratted tree and get home. Dad's probably wondering what sinkhole opened up and swallowed me."

Joe stood the tree against a pole.

Pine needles in his hair and all over his clothes, Oliver stomped up beside him.

"Stay with Gabby, Oliver, while I lug this tree over to Moon."

Mutiny glowered back at him.

"It's polite, son. To provide ladies with an escort." Feeling like a fool, Joe didn't dare look at Gabby. She'd be laughing her head off at him. Him. Giving etiquette lessons to a kid. What on earth was the world coming to?

When he turned around, though, she wasn't laughing. Her

face had gone all blurry and kissable, and he couldn't figure out what he'd done to make her look at him the way she was.

If they'd been alone, he would have kissed her for sure. Would have stepped right up to her, wrapped his arms around her narrow waist and given in to the itch to see what that shiny blouse felt like under his hands.

No question about it. He wanted to kiss her more than he'd wanted anything for himself in a long while.

Instead, ignoring the warning alarms in his brain, the voice screeching *Stupid! Stupid!* he gave in to the lesser temptation and slicked back the curl of hair that had been tantalizing him for the last fifteen minutes.

Against the back of his hand, her hair was slippery like the silk of her blouse. Against his palm, the slim column of her neck was night-and-mist cool. For a long moment she stood there, not moving, just breathing, hazel eyes turning a rich, deep green, jewels shining in the darkness as she stared at him. He curled his palm around her nape and dipped his head.

Well, he'd never laid claim to sainthood.

Against the end of his finger, her pulse fluttered and sang to him, a siren call.

And beside him, clinging like a limpet, his son leaned, small and cranky and utterly dependent on him.

The strains of "O Holy Night" drifted to him. Heated by her body and nearness, the scent of Gabby, so close, so close, rose to him. Surrounded by scent and sound, he forgot everything except the woman in front of him.

Forgot the silenced alarms in his brain.

Forgot responsibility.

Forgot *everything*.

Oliver pulled at the edge of Joe's pocket. "I want to go, Daddy. I'm tired."

Joe stepped back and let his hand fall to his side. He wasn't about to tell sweet Gabby he was sorry, because he wasn't, not at all. If it wasn't for Oliver, well, mistake or not, he'd have Gabby O'Shea wrapped up against him tighter than plastic wrap.

But Oliver was in his life with needs and fears Joe was only beginning to glimpse.

His son had taken up permanent residence in the cold, lonely recesses of Joe's heart.

No one else had ever found the key to that cramped room. But Oliver had, that first time three weeks ago when Joe had taken his small hand in his and walked with Oliver out of the apartment where he'd been left.

Not hesitating, Oliver had picked up a raggedy blanket, latched onto Joe's hand and said only, "I told Suzie you'd come. I told her I had a daddy who would find me." He'd smiled at Joe, a funky, trusting, gap-toothed smile. "I knowed you would. You did."

That had been that.

Next to that power, even Gabby in Christmas mist and glittery lights could be resisted.

He hoped. And maybe only because she backed away at the same time he did, both of them knowing better than to yield to that sizzle.

So when his son's gruff voice came again, Joe knew the choice was easy. Whatever he wanted wasn't a drop in the bucket compared with what Oliver needed.

It couldn't be.

He wouldn't let anybody, not even himself, cause this tiny scrap of humanity one more second's worth of pain.

"Okay, squirt. You're right. It's late. But first we have to drop off Gabby's tree with Moon. Then we'll hit the highway. We'll decide what to do about the party later."

Oliver's sigh was heavy enough to crush rocks. "I want to go home. *Now.* And I don't want to go to a party."

Joe was torn. What was he supposed to do? Yell at the kid for being mouthy? Is that what a good parent would do? It didn't feel right, though, not with Oliver looking up at him like a damned scared puppy who'd just peed on the rug. Hell. Strangled, Joe tugged at his shirt collar.

Gabby curled her fingers around Joe's arm. "No problem, Joe. You and Oliver decide after you get back to the hotel whether you want to stop at the house tomorrow night. Right now, Oliver's tired and probably hungry." Not crowding his son, she added casually, "Maybe having some of Moon's cocoa and doughnuts would be a good idea."

Her skirt pulled tight across the delicate curves of her fanny as she stooped to Oliver's level, her manner easy and relaxed. Joe admired the way she gave Oliver space.

He admired her tidy curves, too, and decided a man could be forgiven for appreciating a work of nature. Looking didn't hurt anyone. Be a shame not to admire Gabby's behind. After all, she'd checked out his.

She caught his faint grin and yanked her skirt free where it had tightened against her.

"Turnabout's fair play," he drawled. "And the view is swell."

Being a woman of good sense, she ignored him. "Oliver, I understand you're particular about your cocoa. Anybody would be, but Moon makes a killer cup of chocolate. The older guys like it. But maybe it's an acquired taste." She stood up, shrugged. "You'd make Moon feel good if you gave his cocoa the Oliver taste test."

His son hesitated, reluctant to give in. Stubborn little squirt. "Maybe I'll take a sip. If it'll make Moon feel better."

Bless her. Oliver *was* probably hungry. Joe kept forgetting how fast a six-year-old ran out of gas.

"I was thinking—" Gabby wrinkled up her face "—that you look like a guy with discriminating taste buds."

Intrigued, Oliver quit scuffing the ground.

"Doughnuts might not be your thing. Want to try some trail mix?" Gabby pulled out a plastic bag with chips of dried fruit and nuts. Opening the closure, she pulled out a couple of raisins and offered the bag to Joe.

"Trail mix sounds good. Raisins, huh?" Joe hated raisins, hated dried fruit. Prissy stuff. But he took a handful and handed the bag to Oliver, who, imitating him, grabbed a fistful and shoveled it into his mouth.

"Lots of raisins." A sly smile tugged at Gabby's mouth, curving her full bottom lip up. "You like raisins, don't you, Joe?"

"Yum. My favorite—" Dubiously he looked at the wrinkled speck he held between two fingers.

"Fruit, Joe. Filled with nutrition." Her eyes sparkled up at him.

"Yeah. I know." He ate a raisin and figured he'd learned another lesson. Carry food. He reckoned his jackets would start looking like chipmunk cheeks before the kid grew up.

No wonder kids needed two parents. His respect for single parents shot up five hundred notches. How did they do it, day after day? How could *he* be this kid's only adult? Day after day.

Impossible.

He scowled.

"Hope your face doesn't freeze like that, Joe." Gabby poked him in the stomach.

"I was just thinking."

"Oh?" The sweetness in her voice almost undid him.

"Nothing." Grimly, he picked up the tree and walked to the shed, Gabby slightly ahead of him. Clamped at his side, Oliver chomped happily on trail mix.

The kid deserved better than a selfish thirty-year-old loner who didn't have a clue what he was supposed to do now that he'd become a parent literally overnight.

You couldn't return a child like a piece of merchandise.

A kid was for life.

The kid hadn't asked for Joe, either, not really. Oliver had wished on a star for a dad, and a whimsical fate had thrown him Joe.

So, the kid was stuck with him as a dad. Joe was all the kid had. Where was the fairness in that? The justice?

Coming to the end of the aisle of trees, Joe tipped his head up to the velvet blackness of night in Bayou Bend. Nothing in the star-spangled darkness answered him. Sighing, he glanced back down at his son.

And in that moment, as he watched Oliver manfully chew on trail mix while checking out Joe's reaction, wonder settled over Joe. Nobody had ever looked at him like that, like he'd hung the moon and stars, like their whole world was filled with him.

He might be all the kid had, he might not be worth a tinker's damn as a father, but, by heaven, he had one thing working for him.

He wanted to do right by this boy more than he'd ever wanted anything in his life. That ought to count for something.

Taking a deep breath, Joe grinned at Oliver. "Come on. Hitch a ride on an old hoss." Holding the tree with one hand, he swung Oliver up onto his shoulders and settled him. "Been a long day, huh, partner?" He patted Oliver's foot.

Oliver rested his chin on top of Joe's head as they approached the shed. "Yeah." Oliver's chin ground into Joe's head with each munch of trail mix. "I like it up here." He folded both arms on top of Joe's head and wrapped his legs around Joe's neck.

Hell, nobody was born knowing how to be a parent. There were plenty of books on the subject. Joe could learn. He'd make mistakes, but he could keep from making the same mistake twice. With a little luck.

And a lot of work.

He could do this daddy business.

"I'll find Moon, Joe. If you don't mind, just lean the tree against the shed and you two go have that cup of cocoa."

Gabby reached up and wiggled Oliver's toe. "Nice meeting you, Oliver. Let me know what you think of Moon's cocoa, hear?" She pivoted and whisked behind the corner of the shed so fast Joe didn't have a chance to stop her.

He thought the night seemed darker and colder without the glow of Gabby's face.

"Let's go, Daddy." Leaning forward, Oliver peered into Joe's face. "We don't need anybody else, do we?"

"Duck, son. The shed door's low." He didn't see Gabby again. By the time he and Oliver drank cocoa, checked out the baskets of ornaments and made their way to the van, Gabby was nowhere in sight.

"Gabby leave yet?" Joe slammed the van door shut.

"Right after I tied down her trunk. She was in a hurry. Worried about her dad, I guess."

"Milo looked fine when I saw him. But that was from a distance." Joe lifted Oliver into the passenger side and motioned for him to fasten the seat belt. "What's the problem?"

"Damned if I know. Milo's complaining about Gabrielle coming home, swearing she's making a fuss over nothing, that's all I know. He's worked up a head of steam about Gabrielle threatening to sell her Arizona condo and come back to Bayou Bend on a permanent basis." Moon leaned over confidentially. "You ask me—and I notice you didn't—that's the problem."

"I don't get it. What do you mean?" Sticking the key into the ignition switch, Joe paused. "She's back for good?"

"That's what's making Milo crazy. He's ranting and raving that she would be making a mistake, that he doesn't need any help—"

"Does he?" Joe straightened out Oliver's twisted seat belt and snapped it into the slot.

"I don't know." Moon rolled his shoulders. "He was in the hospital for three weeks back around Halloween, but you know Milo."

"No, actually, I don't. Not well, anyway."

"Huh." Moon raised his eyebrows. "Funny. I thought you knew the old man. Don't know where I got that idea."

"Neither do I." Joe kept his face empty of expression. What Moon might know or might guess wasn't important. Joe wasn't about to fill him in on any details.

He'd told Moon the truth. He didn't know Milo well.

Not in the usual meaning, at least.

Moon nodded. "Anyway, if Milo's got a health problem, he sure wouldn't broadcast it. He'd make a joke out of it, but he'd keep any problem to himself. Milo's good at keeping secrets."

Joe didn't have to be a rocket scientist to read between the lines. Moon knew something, after all, about that night years ago, but, like Milo, he could keep a secret. "Thanks for your help, Moon." Joe reached out to shake Moon's ham-size hand.

Moon's face split into a grin. "Sure. Any old time." His squeeze of Joe's hand was hard enough to discourage circulation for a few minutes. As Joe started to pull the driver's door shut, Moon rested his hand on it, stopping Joe's movement. All the folksy drawl disappeared from Moon's rumble of a voice as he gave Joe a keen look and said, "Merry Christmas to you and your boy." He slammed the van door shut. "And, Joe…"

"Yeah?"

"Welcome home."

Looking at Moon's large, sincere face, where understanding lay beneath the good-old-boy mask, Joe felt his throat close up.

He'd felt the same way years ago when Gabby welcomed him to Bayou Bend, a place he'd never called home.

A place he couldn't wait to run from as fast as he could.

A place he'd returned to because of Oliver.

And if it killed him, he was going to make this town home for his son.

Staying away from Gabrielle O'Shea would be part of that price, no matter how drawn he was to her sweetness.

In the hotel later, Joe watched shadows dance across the wall. Shifting, changing, like his life, the shadows passed one after another, each blurring into the other until the original pattern was no longer visible.

Beside him, snoring gently, small bubbles popping with each breath, his son slept. Peacefully. Securely.

Safely.

For the first time since he'd heard about his son, a son he didn't even know he had, Joe slept soundly, too.

In his dreams, pine scent and Christmas carols mingled, and he followed the glow of Gabby's smile, like a star leading him through the darkness.

Chapter Three

"Here. Taste." Milo handed Gabrielle a wooden spoon dripping with broth and rice. "What do you think?"

Gabrielle thought her dad's face was too gray and too exhausted-looking, that's what she thought. She kept her opinion to herself and took the spoon. Tasted. A complex mix of flavors burst on her tongue, and she sighed with pleasure. Her dad's version of jambalaya might not be authentic New Orleans, but it was a feast for the senses. "I think it's perfect, Pa. Best you've ever made."

"Good." Milo snatched the spoon from her and stirred the huge pot of rice, tomatoes, chicken, broth and sausage. Pale green celery dotted the red and white. Next to the stove, piles of translucent shrimp shimmered in a heap on a bright green ceramic platter. "But it needs a touch more red pepper."

"Maybe," she agreed. "But don't make it too spicy, Pa."

Not looking at her, he sprinkled pepper flakes carefully over the simmering mixture. "The boy. Oliver."

"Oliver." Gabby nodded. She didn't know whether to hope that Joe and his son would ring the doorbell or hope they wouldn't.

Every time she thought of Joe, her tummy fluttered, her pulse raced and she felt—agitated.

All this internal turmoil must mean she'd be disappointed if they canceled.

Or maybe it meant she didn't want to face the knowing glint in Joe Carpenter's brown eyes again.

What did she want?

She sensed that it was crucial that she figure out for herself what she'd wanted for herself in returning to Bayou Bend.

She looked around the homey kitchen with its worn wood cabinets and old linoleum floor. Milo's banged-up copper-bottomed pots hung from stainless steel hooks fixed into ceiling beams. On the counter over the double sink, the deep pink buds of a Christmas cactus hinted of the promise of the season, a reminder that darkness would end in light.

Spicy scents of past and present mingled with memories in a mixture as rich as Milo's jambalaya, scents evoking joy and laughter and warmth from earlier years.

Like the cactus, happiness was a prickly-leaved plant waiting to bloom.

That was why she'd come home. To find that joy she'd lost, the joy she believed in her heart Milo needed.

What *did* she want?

And where did Joe Carpenter and his son fit into the new life she was shaping?

She wanted the best Christmas she could make, and being around Joe made her sparkle and feel alive. Made her look forward to the next hour or day, when she hadn't looked forward to anything since her mother's death.

Being around Joe made her feel like the Christmas cactus, all tight pink buds waiting to burst forth.

If he decided to take a pass on an impulsively issued invitation, she couldn't blame him.

But as her attention focused on the cactus buds, the truth slapped her in the face.

She wanted him and Oliver to ring her doorbell. She wanted them in this old house, sharing the tradition of arranging ornaments to hide the bare spots on the tree. She wanted to see them spoon out heaping bowls of jambalaya and hear them sing carols around the ancient upright piano.

She wanted all the corny, traditional trappings of the holiday, all the gaudy color and glitter and sound. She longed to surround herself with heaps of packages wrapped in shiny red-and-gold paper and elaborately tied bows.

For whatever reason, she wanted Joe and Oliver to be part of that richness, not left by themselves to celebrate Christmas in a hotel on the highway.

"Hope these damn shrimp taste as good as they look." Milo held a glistening shrimp up to the light and examined it critically before adding so casually that Gabrielle was immediately alerted, "Didn't know you know Joe Carpenter?"

She knew what he was doing. Joe Carpenter wasn't the real issue. Her dad wanted to talk. Like a cat stalking a bird, he'd sneak up on what he really wanted to talk about and, sooner or later, pounce.

That's when the feathers would fly.

She could wait.

Because Milo wasn't happy with her. She was pretty sure he was ready to launch into a lecture about her return to Bayou Bend, and she was in no hurry to tangle over this particular subject with a stubborn Irishman.

Double dose of hardheaded, is what she called him.

"So how do you happen to know Carpenter?" He plopped a shrimp back onto the heap.

"It's a small town, Pa. Why wouldn't I know him?"

"Bayou Bend's small, all right. Folks know everybody's business more than they should. Seems funny, though, you knowing Joe. He's older than you, and he left town before you were in high school."

"No, he left his senior year. I was in tenth grade. I used to see him around town. That's all." She wasn't about to tell her dad about that long-ago night. Harmless as it had been, it felt private. Special.

"That's right. You were only a sophomore. I'd forgotten." His frown disappeared. "So you saw him at Tibo's and invited him? That's all?"

Puzzled, Gabrielle glanced at her dad. "Sure. Why? Is inviting him a problem?"

"No." Milo poked at the shrimp, cleared his throat. "Just—oh, Joe Carpenter's had a hard life, least that's what I've heard. I wouldn't want you getting hurt, that's all."

Gabrielle avoided addressing the implied question. "It was a friendly invitation to new neighbors, nothing more. Is there a problem?"

"Nope. Not at all. Joe's welcome in my house."

"Maybe not in other houses?"

"Probably not in a lot of houses," Milo agreed.

Joe's tough, don't-give-a-damn exterior made it difficult to see him as vulnerable to the town's opinion, but her heart ached as she imagined Joe with his son, seeking shelter from Bayou Bend's coldness. He needed a friend.

She could be a friend.

"Here, Pa. Your scalpel." Gabrielle handed him the deveining knife. Poking her father lightly on the shoulder, she studied him surreptitiously.

Usually thin, he'd lost even more weight since she'd last visited.

"Thanks, honey." He ran the knife down the back spine of the shrimp, discarding the vein on a paper.

"Want help?"

"Nope."

Thinking of the conversation the day before at the tree lot, Gabrielle added, "Didn't know you'd had Joe Carpenter to dinner."

"Not recently." Milo pitched the shrimp into the colander,

picked up another. "And it wasn't exactly a dinner party, for your information, missy."

"You're making me curious, Pa."

"Well, we know what curiosity did to the cat."

Gabrielle opened the refrigerator and found the mushrooms and red onions she'd sliced earlier. Digging around the overloaded interior, she plucked out bags of lettuces and endive. "I can't help being interested."

"Be interested. That's fine." He ignored her whuff of exasperation.

"You're not going to tell me, are you?" Gabby tilted her head.

"Not my place to. If you're so interested, ask Joe. It's his business. If he wants you to know, he can tell you. I already told you Joe and his son were welcome here." Holding up the knife and using it as a pointer, he stopped her midsyllable. "And that's all I'm going to say about *that,* Gabrielle, so don't go poking around trying to make me tell you, hear?"

"We'll see." From under lowered lashes, she glanced at her dad.

He groaned. "I know what that means. You're going to pester me until you winkle out what you want to know, aren't you?"

"Probably. After all, I learned from the master. I didn't grow up a lawyer's daughter without picking up a few tricks."

He shook his head, grinning back at her. "My sins are coming back to haunt me. And speaking of coming back—"

Interrupting him, a tiger-striped cat thudded onto the counter.

"Down, Cletis!" Flapping her hand, Gabrielle made frantic shoo-shoo motions at him. "Take your greedy self off this counter this instant. If you know what's good for you."

Cocking a hind leg and licking it, Cletis mewed inquisitively, "Mrrrr?"

"Yes, you, mister. I mean it. Down. Now."

Working his head under a paper bag lying on the counter, he made himself as invisible as twenty pounds of fur-covered creature could.

"Sorry, buster, I can see you." Gabrielle hoisted the cat off the counter and took out a saucer from the cabinet.

His attempt to hide from her was no more successful than hers had been as she knelt at Joe Carpenter's well-shod feet yesterday. An errant sympathy for Cletis moved her to swipe a piece of sausage from the jambalaya.

Chopping up bits of sausage, she used her hip and leg to keep him on the floor even as he chirped and twined himself around her legs. "Here, beast." She placed the saucer on the floor and stooped to scratch him between the ears. "You are one spoiled fat boy."

Cletis slurped and gnawed enthusiastically.

Milo was suspiciously quiet.

Kneading the cat's head, Gabrielle glanced up at her dad. "You've been letting him on the counter, haven't you, Pa?"

"Once in a while."

Cletis nibbled her thumb as she started to stand up. "Hah. Every night is my guess." She could understand. The cat was company for her dad. "Lord, he's gained weight while you've lost at least ten pounds. You're feeding him and not making meals for yourself, just nibbling from the refrigerator and counter, not sitting down for a real dinner, right? It's a good thing I came home to take care of you."

Milo thwacked the spoon on the edge of the pot. "That's what I want to talk to you about, missy."

"And what's that?" Gabrielle rested her arms gently around her dad's bony shoulders. As she'd thought, the discussion about Joe was a red herring. Push had finally come to shove.

"This damn fool notion you have. That you have to look after me. What makes you think I need any help? I have most of my hair, my hearing and, with bifocals, I see pretty damn well." He slapped the spoon on the counter.

Cletis looked up hopefully.

"You're not taking care of yourself, Pa. I can see that. You look worse than when I came home when you were in the hospital. You haven't bounced back from your surgery."

"It was minor surgery, and Doc Padgett says I'm fine. I feel fine. So I'm fine, Gabrielle. This nonsense about selling your business and moving back to Bayou Bend is—" He frowned, twirled the spoon between his fingers. Rice grains speckled the counter. "Honey, I love you. You know that. And I'm pleased as punch you're home. For a while."

A sharp pang whipped through her. She went motionless, stunned by the unexpected pain and sense of rejection.

"Now, don't look at me like that." He patted her hand. "I'm doing fine. We should have talked over this decision of yours before you leaped headfirst into this kind of change."

Gabrielle decided to be as blunt as he had been. "Pa, I don't like the way you look. Your face has all the color of a banker's suit. I think you're sick—"

"Damn it, missy. I was in the hospital for three weeks before Thanksgiving. I lost my appetite, that's all." He scowled at her. "I was a skinny guy even before my surgery."

"And I wouldn't have known you were having surgery if Taylor Padgett hadn't called me."

"I'm right annoyed with that boy, too."

Taylor Padgett was thirty-six years old and had been practicing in Bayou Bend ever since he'd finished medical school. "Why?" she asked with exaggerated patience.

"I didn't want him bothering you."

"Bothering me? *Bothering* me?" Pacing in a circle, she waved her arms in frustration. "Heaven forbid that my aged father should *bother* me. I certainly wouldn't want to miss out on my busy social schedule because my *father* was in the *hospital.*"

He picked up another shrimp and sliced it down the back. "You're worrying too much, Gabrielle. And I may be sixty-four years old, but I'm not *aged,* so don't get sassy." Head down, his fists balancing him on the counter, he stopped, sighed. "Somehow you got it in your head that I can't manage alone since your mama died."

"Pa, I didn't mean to upset you." Gabrielle rested her cheek against his paper-thin one. She remembered too well her panic at the sight of her strong, bullheaded dad surrounded by tubes and IVs. "I want you to get well, to be your old ornery self."

He snapped his head up and went back to deveining shrimp with a vengeance. "Then don't worry me any more with this idiotic plan of sacrificing your life to look after me, Gabrielle Marie. You're a good girl, and you mean well, but, honey, I'm fine. I don't need you here to baby-sit me."

Again that slice of pain. "Pa—"

He gestured her quiet. "Go back to Arizona after New Year's and get on with your life. I don't want you giving up your life because of some dopey idea that I'm headed into a decline."

"Dopey, Pa? Thanks a lot." His word made her laugh out loud. Her dad was trying too hard.

"Gabrielle Marie, I fully intend to live another twenty or thirty years, and I'm going to have myself one hell of a terrific old age. You're making a big fuss out of nothing. I'd tell you if I were ill. Trust me."

She didn't. And he wouldn't. He would try to protect her with his last breath, that's what Milo O'Shea would do. "I'm here, Pa. I'm staying."

Smelling of brine and cayenne, he hugged her tightly. "Not that I don't appreciate the offer, honey, but I'm not looking for a keeper. Not yet."

"Pa, it's too late. I sold the house-sitting agency. I sold my condo. Yes—" she forestalled his inevitable question "—I made money on both." She tapped his forehead, enumerating. "I gave away my plants. My aquarium. I'm home. You're not going to be alone anymore. I'll keep you company in the evening. I'm going to make you nutritious meals.''

Exasperation tightened his mouth into a line. ''And I reckon you're going to keep Cletis off the counter.''

She nodded.

''Sounds like the seventh circle of hell.''

''I've made my decision. It's a done deal.''

''Hell's bells, Gabrielle. You really sold everything?'' His voice was dismayed.

She sat down abruptly, shaken by his insistence. Suddenly she wondered if she'd misread all the signs that had sent her to the Realty office. ''Except the car.''

Her dad blew an explosive raspberry of annoyance, a sound she knew all too well. ''Missy, didn't you hear a word I said?''

Standing up, she walked over to him. ''I heard you, Pa.'' She kissed the top of his head. When had he shrunken so much that she could easily plant a kiss on that saucer-size bald spot? He did need her, no matter what he pretended. She'd done the right thing. For him.

For herself.

''Gabrielle, honey,'' her dad said slowly, patiently, ''I'm not lonely. The old coots and I haven't given up our Saturday morning coffee at Bell's Diner. I'm not sitting around waiting for the Grim Reaper. I miss your mama, that will never change, but I'm making friends, going on field trips.'' He laughed. ''Sixty-four years old and going on field trips for the first time in my life.''

''You gave up driving?'' She was truly worried now. Milo would never give up driving. Driving was in his blood. He loved cars.

''Lord, honey, I still drive. I got talked into these overnight field trips around the state, and I kind of like them. Interesting folks going to interesting places. People I wouldn't have met if I hadn't stepped out and taken a chance on this program.''

"I don't understand what you're talking about. A program?"

"Oh…" His voice was lawyer-smooth and Gabrielle's antennae rose. "One of the hospital candy stripers told me about these outings the park district arranged."

Gabrielle was mystified. Milo was up to something, the fox. She'd find out—when Milo was ready for her to. "You go on field trips to tourist attractions?"

"Sure. Up to Tampa. To Atlanta. To shop."

"You go *shopping?* You hate shopping."

"Thought I did, honey, but life has a funny way of springing surprises on you. At the very moment you think you have everything figured out and you have a clear vision of what the rest of your life will be, well, darn if life doesn't pitch a high, hard fast ball your way. I've had calm and serene for most of my life. I'm ready for wild and woolly. Anyway, who said you can't teach an old dog new tricks?" Throwing his head back, he laughed, and the sound was so natural and warm that she would have believed him if she couldn't see his gray skin and fatigue.

"Sure, Pa." She wondered why shopping seemed like a wild-and-woolly adventure, but if it worked for him, that was good enough for her. "Whatever you say. But you're still stuck with me."

"We'll see, missy. We'll see." Something in his chuckle made her lift her head and stare at him.

The clanging of the old-style bell ringer startled them both. They gaped at each other, then at the clock.

"Good grief, where did the time go?" Gabrielle's heart did double-time, and her cheeks flushed hot. *Joe.*

"I see we can't cook and have a serious conversation at the same time. Now *that,* honey, *is* a sign of old age." He scraped the pile of garbage off the counter and into the trash. "Get the door. I have to wash up." Moving rapidly, he poured lemon juice over his hands and then stuck them under the faucet.

Gabrielle blinked. What on earth? Her dad's mottled cheeks were as pink as hers felt. The gray she'd seen earlier had vanished with the rush of blood to his face. "You okay?"

She wasn't about to walk out of the room and leave him to have a heart attack on the floor.

"What?" Distracted, he glanced at her over his shoulder and continued scrubbing his hands. Drying them, he checked his appearance in the miniature mirror next to the fridge. "I look okay?" He flattened his hair with still-damp hands.

"Sure, Pa." Gabrielle had never seen her father flustered like this. He must be too tired. Having a bunch of people over for a meal was apparently a bigger drain on his energy than either one of them had figured. She shouldn't have let him—

"Uh, Gabrielle." He hesitated. The deep breath he took left his belted pants sliding toward his hips. "There's something you and I need to discuss."

"Yes, Pa?" She spoke in a pleasant monotone designed to soothe him. He was upset. She didn't want to upset him any more.

He frowned. "Why are you talking so funny, missy? Like I've gone deaf or crazy." Before she could answer, he was scanning his appearance in the mirror again.

The doorbell clanged, a prolonged, raucous shriek.

"Go, go. Somebody's here. Get the door: Don't want to keep anyone waiting."

Strolling to the door, Gabrielle sorted out her impressions. Without a question, her dad was up to something.

She opened the door to cool darkness and Joe Carpenter leaning against her doorjamb. Her heart stuttered and galloped as he smiled at her. Oh, yes, all that heart-thumping and face-flushing meant she wanted to see Joe Carpenter again.

Wary and on the verge of a frown, Oliver stepped out from

behind the safety of his dad. The cowlick was nowhere in existence. Joe must have smashed Oliver's hair down with industrial-strength hair control.

She wanted to hug them both. Oliver, because the boy needed hugging. Joe? Well, just because. Her mouth curved in sudden happiness, everything inside her blazing with expectation and—*lightness*.

She felt as if a skyful of stars had taken residence inside her tummy, burning and tumbling and glowing.

The screen door squeaked as she swung it wider. "Hi, guys. Come on in. Hungry?"

Clutching a mangled paper cone of flowers, Oliver plopped one foot over her threshold, hesitated, turned toward Joe, who nudged him forward.

"Here." Oliver thrust the flowers at her. "Hostess gift."

"Thank you very much." Taking the offering, Gabrielle sniffed at the roses and white orchids surrounded by long-needled pine and baby's breath. Cold and sweet, their faint fragrance floated to her. "They're beautiful, Oliver."

Freed of the flowers, he grabbed Joe's hand. "I didn't pick 'em out."

"That's all right. It's the thought that counts."

The look that crossed their faces at the same time could only be described as desperate. They looked equally uncomfortable.

"We weren't sure what to bring." Joe raised his hand as if he were going to touch her, as if he didn't quite know whether to shake her hand or—

Gabrielle motioned them in, the thought of the *or* sending another wave of flame through her. "Pa's in the kitchen finishing up the jambalaya."

Behind her a pot lid clattered to the floor.

"Damn, Cletis. Now look what you've done!"

"Milo making a guest feel at home?" Joe's eyebrow angled skyward in amusement.

"Whoops!" Gabrielle pulled at Joe's arm and slammed the screen door behind him.

A weight of fur collapsed onto her feet and rolled off, panting.

Looking down at the cat lying belly-up in front of him, Joe drawled, "Cletis, I take it?"

The cat's legs sprawled in abandon, his belly flattening against the floor like a pancake.

"He's an insider kitty, but he has a yen for the forbidden, so we have to watch him. He's faster than he looks, but that's not saying much."

"A cat! I like cats." Oliver dropped to his knees. "Can I touch him?"

"Sure. He won't bite. Or scratch. Takes too much energy. He just wants to be worshiped and adored." In an aside, she murmured sweetly to Joe, "Like most guys."

"Cruel." Joe flicked her chin. "Whatever happened to peace on earth and good will to men?"

"Oh, golly, men don't like to be adored?"

"Of course we do. Nothin' like a pretty woman making goo-goo eyes to make us feel all manly and studly, ma'am." His drawl was pure provocation as he tipped an imaginary cowboy hat in her direction.

Cradling the flowers, she laughed at him, her heart thumping like crazy. "I don't think you ever needed anyone's goo-goo eyes, Carpenter, to make you feel studly."

"Ah, you noticed, huh?"

She motioned for him to follow her to the kitchen. "Didn't everyone?"

"Good to know all that effort wasn't wasted. You going to stay with the cat, Oliver, or come with us?"

With his chin resting against Cletis's neck, Oliver considered them, hesitated, then finally decided as Cletis batted a paw against his face. "Maybe I'll stay with him so he has company. He wants me to."

"Looks that way to me." Joe stooped and rubbed his knuckles along the cat's belly.

Watching his long, lean fingers work into the fur of the cat's stomach, Gabrielle swallowed. Like Cletis, she felt the urge to purr.

Instead, she bent to Oliver and directed his attention to the chest near the door. "If you open this drawer, you'll find some kitty treats. We keep them here so we have a better chance of luring him back inside if he goes for a walk on the wild side."

"Okay." Oliver grabbed a treat and held it in his palm, waiting for Cletis to roll upright.

Cletis, however, merely turned his head, watching expectantly until Oliver held the mouse-shaped munchy close enough so that the cat only had to stick out a rough tongue and lap Oliver's hand.

"Another guy habit?" Leaning in close to her, Joe murmured in her ear, and his breath eased its way inside her, into her lungs, her blood.

"Probably."

"Think I'll go through my next life as a Cletis clone, then." Joe stood up, holding a hand to her. "Wait for the munchies to come your way. No hunting, no effort. He has the right idea."

The glance he shot her way made her decide that the kind of munchies Joe meant didn't come prepackaged. She rose at the same time and her hip bumped his, his hand slid along her side, and her whole body went soft and boneless. Her breath hitched in her throat, and she wanted to say something clever, something to lighten that terrible awareness, to make it unimportant.

She couldn't let it be important.

Oliver chortled, "Tickles!" as Cletis scoured his face with a lazy tongue. Joe turned to his son, and Gabrielle's lungs expanded, inhaled, releasing her.

"The kitchen's this way." Her breathing shallow, Gabrielle

brushed her hair away from her blazing cheeks and hurried toward the sound of slamming pots and rushing water.

"Going to put me to work?" Leading her forward, Joe rested his hand at the waist of her dress.

"Of course. The devil makes work for idle hands."

"Too easy, Gabby," he murmured, and the creases around his eyes deepened with laughter, the brown turning almost golden as he turned his head.

"I'll let that one pass."

Under the pressure of his fingers, the brushed rayon fabric of her dress slithered under his palm as she moved, stroked against her skin. The touch of cool, slick material over her body and the press of his warm hand created an unbearable tension in her. She wanted to lean back against his hand, move against it. Her belly, her breasts, *everything* ached, tightened as he flexed his hand.

A simple touch. A polite gesture.

Nothing more.

But his palm might as well have been flat against her naked skin, and politeness and good manners had nothing at all to do with the spritz and sizzle inside her.

Gabrielle quickly stepped ahead of him, and under her thin dress, the curve of her waist where he'd touched her felt chilled as his hand fell away. Oddly bereft.

She shivered.

She'd liked the touch of his hand on her.

She might be as essentially inexperienced as that girl she'd been when he first kissed her, but she was old enough to know what was happening to her body.

No wonder she'd resisted making love, having sex.

All these years of dating and kissing, and she'd had no idea of the power of need. Of desire.

In the most essential way, Joe Carpenter had imprinted that adolescent girl she'd been with the scent and feel of him, imprinted her for life.

No wonder she'd never found anyone who made her feel as if her very breath were his, his heartbeat hers.

Like a chick imprinted, her body followed Joe, obeying some primitive, brain-deep command of scent and touch, some primal command over which she had no control.

She was in trouble.

Because, no matter how she figured the numbers, Joe Carpenter and Gabrielle O'Shea didn't add up in anybody's math equation.

Chapter Four

"Gabrielle, who's at the door?" A dish towel tucked into the waistband of his navy slacks, Milo came into the hall. His gaze passed over Joe, focused on the front door, returned to Gabby.

"Joe and Oliver."

"Oh?" Slightly formal, a bit distant, Milo's question sent Joe's heart rate into second gear. "I don't see the boy."

"Oliver's still in the front hall. With Cletis." Pausing in the bough-and-ribbon-draped alcove between dining room and living room, she looked over her shoulder.

Her smile came slowly, gently, all tipped corners and softness, a miracle of its own slowing his pulse to molasses. Joe didn't understand the reassurance in her greeny-brown eyes, but he welcomed it, luxuriated in the warmth of that smile that sneaked through the chill icing his heart.

With that smile, she made him feel as if he had an ally. She'd smiled at him the same way she had that day he'd first seen her outside Forester's Fresh Foods.

This time she wasn't thirteen, though.

This time he was smart enough to know what a gift a smile like that was.

And, seeing Milo O'Shea again, Joe conceded he liked having Milo's daughter in his corner.

For a moment he wondered what Milo intended—wondered, too, what Milo had told Gabby. Joe tightened his mouth, preparing for anything that might happen. If Milo had told Gabby about that night long ago when Joe had run from Bayou Bend, would she still look at him with eyes wide and dark with flirtation? Or would her eyes hold the contempt he'd sensed in everyone else's eyes all those years ago even before that last night?

He didn't think Milo would have said anything to her, but Milo held all the cards. Joe was on Milo's turf. Whatever was said, not said, was Milo's decision.

Looking back down the hall toward his son, Joe hated the sense of helplessness that washed through him.

He liked being in control of his life, and nothing except the decision to return to Bayou Bend had been in his control since he'd gone to find the boy.

The boy who *might* be his son.

Or *might not* be.

There were questions there, too, questions he'd have to decide how to handle. For himself. For Oliver.

Tricky, that little question.

He'd chosen to return to Bayou Bend because he thought it offered a stable, safe environment for a child who'd never had either. This town could be good for Oliver. While folks didn't leave their doors unlocked at night anymore, even here, Bayou Bend offered the benefits of small-town life, a place where Oliver could ride his bicycle down the sidewalk, and Joe wouldn't have nightmares about drug pushers and kidnappers. In this town, if everything worked out, Oliver would be safe.

Truth to tell, Joe thought as Milo's gaze fixed on him,

Bayou Bend was the only place he had any attachment to. And maybe a negative attachment was better than nothing.

At seventeen, with a chip on his shoulder, maybe he wouldn't have liked any place his old man had dragged him to. At least in Bayou Bend, he was familiar with what would be expected of him as he tried to make a family for Oliver and him.

And if Joe Carpenter was the last person anyone in the town would have expected to come back as a sedate family man, the town could take its opinions and—

Midthought, Joe stopped.

Places changed. People changed.

He had to give the town a chance if he expected it to return the favor. He'd strolled down its streets with that chip on his shoulder once before. That attitude had brought him nothing but trouble and a fast ticket out of town.

He would do whatever he had to, to make this work.

He just hoped he hadn't made a mistake.

Narrowing his eyes, he met Milo's gaze straight on. What would be, would be.

"Joe." Milo stuck out a wide-palmed hand and grasped Joe's. "Good to see you, son."

"You, too." Joe nodded. He ignored the lump in his throat. Milo had called him *son*. He was going to make the situation easy for Oliver. For Joe.

They'd taken the first hurdle.

"I hear you make a killer jambalaya, Milo. Thanks for including us."

"The more the merrier."

Gabby's laugh was a silvery chime that slipped along Joe's skin, tightening it. "Moon told Joe you'd say that."

"Did he, now?" Milo shrugged.

Joe wondered if he'd been mistaken. Was he going to have to collect his son and bolt for the door after all? "Not that it matters," he said evenly, "but it was Moon who actually invited us to your party."

"Son of a gun." Milo laughed. "That boy's a friendly cuss, even with somebody else's hospitality."

"Pa, *I* invited Joe and Oliver, too." Facing her dad, posture rigid, head up, Gabby reminded Joe of a kitten facing off with the head tomcat. All she needed was claws and a good loud hiss. Once again, her defense of him eased a tightness in his chest, warmed him in the glow of her kindness.

"Shoot, honey, you already told me that. Joe's welcome, and so's his boy, no matter *who* invited them. Don't go getting your hackles up, hear me?"

Not sure who Milo was directing that final comment to, Joe felt his own hackles lie right back down and relief flow through his tensed muscles. He hadn't realized until that moment how keyed up he'd been about this encounter.

Milo was cool about the situation.

He'd welcomed Joe.

But as he shook hands with the man who had changed his life, Joe wondered how Milo would have reacted if he'd seen Joe about to plant a kiss on Milo's darling daughter at Moon's yesterday.

Knowing that, would Milo have been quite so cool about having Joe Carpenter in his home?

Not likely.

One more reason to keep his distance from Gabby.

Too much at stake.

"Come on into the kitchen, Joe. Everybody hangs out there."

"Don't know what we need a living room for, Gabrielle. Nobody uses it," Milo grumbled. "We'll find a job for you, Joe. Let you get messy with the rest of us."

"Fine."

The ringer on the door clamored for attention, and Milo did

a brisk about-face. "I'll see who this is. You all go on. Gabby, take care of Joe. Set him to work, hear?"

"I hear you, Pa." Gabby half turned to look at Milo as he scurried toward the front door. "It's probably Moon."

"Could be." Not stopping, Milo called back, "Or it might be some of my friends from the bus trips."

The concern that flashed over Gabby's face before she shuttered it with politeness caught Joe's attention and puzzled him. As she turned to him, her red-banded hem slithering over his slacks, he filed away the memory of her expression. He'd think about it another time. Later, when she wasn't right in front of him, distracting him with her voice, her *self*.

"I told you we'd make you sing for your supper, didn't I?"

Resisting the urge to take two fingers and smooth away the line between her eyebrows, he stuck a hand in his pocket. "In fact, what you said was that you'd put Oliver and me to work. Singing's an entirely different matter."

"We might make you sing. Later."

"Don't want to go there." He leaned against the wall. "You've never heard me sing."

"Can't sing, poor baby?"

"I can sing." Joe liked the way her clingy gold dress with the red bands at the bottom and around the sleeves burnished her skin with reflected gold.

She shimmered in front of him, her dress shifting, shining, slipping over her hipbones, drawing his attention with her every move. Like the red bands on her dress, her cheeks bloomed with color as she teased him. "If you can sing, what's the problem?"

"I sing like a frog with indigestion."

She sputtered with laughter. "I see. In that case, you're safe." She turned to push open the kitchen door. "Umm, Joe?"

"Yes, Gabby?" He hesitated. One step more would bring

him so close to her that her elusive fragrance would wrap around him once more.

A smart man wouldn't take that step. He pushed himself free of the wall, anticipation thrumming inside him.

A man who had a child dependent on him absolutely would not take that single, dangerous step closer to Gabby and her gold dress.

He relaxed against the wall again. ''You had a question, sweet pea?''

''What *does* a frog in gastric distress sound like?''

Following Gabby past the alcove and into the kitchen, Joe reminded himself one more time that he couldn't let himself slip again the way he had yesterday. He'd have to keep his guard up around her.

For a man like him, Gabrielle should erect a Keep Away sign that was billboard high and neon bright.

He wished he could understand his yearning for her. Not exactly lust, something different, something *more*. His need to be around her distracted him. Yielding to distraction could destroy everything if he didn't watch himself.

But damned if the little distraction herself didn't walk right up to him, put her arms around his waist. Her hands moved, flattened, turned against him.

Her light scent was a teasing sweetness in his brain, and he wanted to bend closer to her, breathe more deeply of that sweetness that flowed through him and sang in his blood. Where had this need come from, this need to breathe her essence, this need to taste her?

He tipped his head.

She stepped back with satisfaction. ''There, Joe.''

''What?''

Hands on her hips, she surveyed him, mischief lighting up her eyes. ''Don't want you getting shrimp juice and tomato sauce on your elegant slacks.''

Joe glanced down. Like Milo, he now wore a dishcloth

apron around his waist. She'd tucked the cloth neatly into his belt loops and waistband so quickly he hadn't even realized what she was up to. Taking a breath, he pitched his voice so low that only she could hear. "You're a sly boots, Gabby O'Shea, aren't you?"

"Me?" Reaching behind her, she removed a red apron from a hook on the wall. Festooned with silver bells and painted packages, the apron swallowed her. Its bells jingled as she moved with rapid, dancelike steps to the massive round table in the middle of the kitchen. "Nah. I'm only being thoughtful. A good hostess takes care of her guests," she said primly, flicking a bell out of the way as she tied the wide sash around her waist.

"I'll keep that in mind." He reached out and set one of the bells to jingling. "In case I need any—care."

Her face flushed, and she looked away from him, frowning.

His frown came on the shadow of hers. He cleared his throat. Looking for a task, he picked up a platter of plastic-covered hors d'oeuvres. Shifted it from hand to hand. Put it back down.

Flirting with Gabby was stupid.

It was the season, that was all.

A pretty woman, carols in the air and the warmth of this house seeped into him and made him feel as if he belonged— somewhere.

And flirting with Gabby was so easy, so pleasurable, so *right*.

Returning to Bayou Bend was bringing back too many of his bad habits. He *liked* women. This thing with Gabby, though, this went beyond his experience. *Liking* he understood. He didn't understand this mix of emotions he was experiencing around her, this amalgam of past and present, of Christmas and loneliness and hope all linking together and making him *want*.

Silently he went to work on the salad she pointed out to

him, and as streams of people threaded in and out of the kitchen, Joe watched her, saw her easy teasing of the guests, watched her fetch and carry glasses of wine, watched her kiss Moon, who dangled a sprig of mistletoe over her head and demanded a kiss.

She made it all seem effortless, all the work and bustle fueling her until the air around her seemed to shine with the gold of her dress.

He couldn't take his eyes off the shine and glitter that was Gabby O'Shea.

Gradually the kitchen emptied as she directed people to the boxes of ornaments. "Pick one and hang it on the tree, Taylor," she said to the man she'd introduced as Milo's doctor. "Moon, you have to do the lights because you're the tallest."

Grumbling and laughing, they followed her directions until Joe was the only one left.

"Heads up." Gabby's bells alerted him, and he ducked as she passed him with a platter.

"That phrase has never made sense to me. It's guaranteed to make you look up."

"It's one of those warnings we ignore in spite of good sense, I suppose." She stuffed a shrimp in his mouth and jingled away in a swirl of red and gold. The kitchen door swung shut behind her.

"Damn right," he muttered through a mouthful of spicy shrimp. "Any fool with an ounce of brains would know better than to stick his head in harms's way." He chewed slowly. "And yet we keep sticking our heads up. Serves us right when we get beaned."

The kitchen door slammed open against the wall. Gabby danced by him, a whirl of bells and bright red fabric. "Sorry. I didn't hear you, Joe. What did you say?"

"Nothing important. A reminder to myself, that's all." He leaned against the counter. How could this slip of a girl, this *woman*, make him ignore all the warnings of his own brain?

"Give me another job, Gabby." Even with the warning still echoing in his brain, he extended his arms slowly, bracketing her waist between them. The heat of her body warmed his wrists. The shape of her enticed him as if he could feel her beneath his hands. His palms curved the air between them.

He didn't touch her.

"Right. Those idle hands the devil's looking for." Breathy, her voice rubbed against his nerve endings. Her gaze dropped to the floor and she stepped back, away from him. Her face matched her apron as she grabbed a wooden spoon from a poinsettia-shaped ceramic dish near the stove. Handle first, she handed the spoon to him. Rice grains dripped to the floor. "How are you at stirring?" Still not looking at him, she stooped to scrape up the rice.

"I've been accused of stirring up trouble a few times."

Standing slowly, she said softly, so softly that he had to lean forward to hear her, "Is that what you're doing now, Joe? Stirring up trouble?"

He rotated the spoon between his fingers, studying its spinning bowl, which held no answers, before he finally sighed and said, "I don't know, Gabby. Maybe flirting with you a little."

"Flirting's as natural to you as breathing. This—" her hand fluttered in front of him "—seems different. I don't know how—" she stopped, continued "—to react. You make me feel—"

Again she stopped, and he stared into her troubled face, stung by the uneasiness he sensed in her.

"How do I make you feel, Gabby?"

She straightened her shoulders, looked around the kitchen as the words rushed out so fast he figured she hadn't meant to say them. "Female. Fluttery. And I don't know whether I like feeling this way."

His unreliable conscience, long dormant, struggled to the surface and made him offer. "Do you want me to leave,

Gabby? I will." He placed the spoon carefully on the counter behind him.

Not answering, she looked everywhere except at him.

He smelled the spicy richness of the jambalaya, heard the muffled sounds of laughter from the hall and living room, felt the weight of the air in the room heavy on his skin, and waited, feeling oddly like a man about to be sentenced. Until he'd offered to leave, he hadn't known how much he wanted to stay. "Say the word. I'll go."

On a long exhalation, she said, "Stay." The word hovered between them.

"Why?" he asked baldly, everything in him poised to leave this place that felt like a sanctuary.

"I want you to."

"Why?"

Her words came slowly, measured out as if with an eyedropper. "I don't know."

His lungs expanded, filled with air. He hadn't realized he'd been holding his breath until that moment. He felt light-headed, dizzy. "I'm making you uncomfortable."

"Oh, yes." She nodded hard, the bells on her apron jingling, and one strand of hair flipping against her cheek. "You do."

He lifted the strand up, twined it around his finger and tucked it behind her ear. "I kind of like knowing I make you—fluttery. But I don't mean to make you uncomfortable, Gabrielle Marie."

Her laugh burbled up, shakily, her breath fluttering against his hand as it stilled in front of her face. "Joe Carpenter, I don't think you could help making me uncomfortable, no matter how hard you tried."

He didn't pretend not to know what she meant. Meeting her honesty with his own, he said, "There's something going on between us, isn't there? Some electricity neither of us wants?"

She dipped her chin, hesitated. "There's something, yes."

Lifting her chin, she waited for a moment while his heart drummed heavily inside him. "I'm not good at flirting, Joe." She stuck her hands into the pockets of her apron and tiny bells chimed. "You are."

He didn't miss that she'd skirted his second question. "I like women, Gabby. I like to tease, to flirt."

"I know." Something he didn't quite understand shivered underneath her admission.

"Flirting doesn't mean anything." Trying to keep the mood light because that inexplicable note he'd heard in her voice disturbed him, he shot her a shuck-and-jive grin. The words felt like a lie. The attitude had begun to feel like a lie for a long time now, and being around Gabby made it worse. But he thought he could defuse the intensity and turn the situation into something casual that would relieve her anxiety. "Flirting's not important. No harm in it. It's only playing around, that's all."

"I know."

He tapped her chin, the supple skin creamy soft beneath his touch. "Gettin' in a rut, Gabby. You're repeating yourself, sweet pea."

"I—" She laughed, and the shadow he'd seen moments ago in her eyes vanished with the laughter. "I almost said it again, didn't I?"

"Almost."

"Party nerves."

"Think so?" Because she'd retreated further than he intended, contrariness seized him, and he wanted to push her, to break through this brittleness and make her admit— What? That she liked the sizzle between them? Was that what he wanted from her? That admission she'd avoided earlier? "Sure it's not that…*something* popping between us?"

"Joe," she said, holding her hands out to him, palm up, warding him off, or warning him away, he wasn't altogether sure, "you can't help flirting any more than you can stop yourself from breathing. I'm not in your league. You need to play with someone who's up to your speed.''

"Suppose I want to play with you, Gabby? What then?" He didn't want her to retreat into polite distance. He wanted her to look at him again as if she were on his side, in his corner. As if he were special to her.

Abruptly, she turned away from him, and the column of thin gold fabric showing in the gap at the back of her red apron was like a golden flame drawing him nearer, to see if its heat was real.

He remained slouched against the counter. Fire burned.

When she turned back to face him, her eyes were guarded, her face pale. "Joe, I like being around you. I like *you*. I like Oliver.''

"He's a tough little nut. Sometimes he's not easy to like. And I'm not, either. Truth to tell, Gabby, I'm not an easy man.''

"No, you're not." At the base of her neck, her skin flushed. "And if we're into truth telling, yes, that *something* between us makes me nervous. Because I'm not good at games, not the kind you're talking about playing, anyway." Her smile wavered, but she plunged on, and he was touched by her courage. "You throw me off balance." She looked up at him, her eyes dark, the tiny flame of himself in their center. "I don't know what the rules are. That's all." Her hands fell to her sides. "I don't know what you expect from me. In your game.''

"Nothing. That's what, Gabby. And there aren't any rules." He wanted to touch her, he wanted to comfort her, he wanted to ease his mouth over hers and drink from the well of her sweetness. He took another step closer, trying to make sense for himself, for her, of the confusion roiling inside him. "I came back to this town because of my son. I have to figure out the best way to give him the kind of life I didn't have.''

"Yes, you do. He needs you." Her attention was intent upon him.

"I know how to play the male-female game, Gabby. I don't know how to play the daddy game. In my own way, I'm struggling to sort out what's going on in my life, and you were there at Tibo's, all shiny and sparkly, and I wanted to spend a little time with you. I like being around you." He ran a hand through his hair, trying to explain the need he had to hear her laugh, the need to see her, to be near her. He shrugged, giving up. He didn't have the right words. He bent his knees so that he could look her straight in the eyes. "I don't want to hurt you, that's all I know."

"Are you afraid I'll expect something from you, Joe? Is that what you're trying to tell me?"

"We're real different, you and me, Gabby. I've always been an outsider in this town, and you're not. You'd have a right to expect—" He frowned as a smile blazed across her face.

Her attention sharpened as if a thought had occurred to her. "You're trying to be noble, aren't you? You're worried that I might misinterpret flirting as something else." She gave a strangled laugh. "You only want to *play* with me."

In spite of himself, he grinned, "Well, sweet pea, when you put it that way, it sounds kind of rascally, doesn't it?"

"But you *are* a rascal, Joe." She reached around him and retrieved the spoon he'd put down earlier. Handing it to him, she said, "Here. Stir the jambalaya so the rice doesn't stick. Add some of that chicken broth from the jar if you need to. Or the tomato juice. Either one's fine."

Not taking his eyes from hers, he stuck the spoon into the pot. "Uh, what's going on? I think you changed directions on me."

"Did I?" Her apron jingled merrily as she moved to the kitchen table for a platter. As if she'd reached a decision, her face was serene, the confusion gone.

"Yeah."

With the platter balanced in her hands, she said, "Everything's clear to me now. I needed the ground rules clarified, that's all. If you flirt with me, it's only a game. If I flirt with you, you're not going to expect anything from me." Shallow lines made dimple creases in her cheeks. "Like sex, for instance."

"Sex?" The heat that rioted through him right down to his groin had nothing to do with the word and everything to do with the prim purse of her mouth as she said it. If he kissed her, her mouth would purse up in that same way. At least with the first touch— "Sex?" he repeated, staggered by the thoughts rioting through his brain.

"Sure, sex. I only wanted to have everything out in the open. Cards on the table. No misunderstandings. You know." Her smile blazed like a comet through the air as she flipped past him. "So now we can flirt to our hearts' content."

Sex? Sex? Joe scrambled to clarify his overheated thoughts. Since she'd mentioned sex, he couldn't think of anything except the cling of her dress along her back, the clean line of her calves under the red hem of that slinky fabric. "Whoa, sweet pea. Who said anything about sex? Who asked? Who offered?"

Once more she danced through the kitchen door, letting it swing shut behind her.

"I'll be damned." Bits of sausage fell from his spoon back into the pot.

"Probably." Milo ambled through the door.

"Don't be rude, Milo." Beside him, a stunning, trim woman who looked to be close to Milo's age placed her hand in the crook of Milo's arm.

Clipping their heels, Gabby sailed back into view, red apron sails flapping at her side. Joe wondered if she saw the easy press of Milo's hand against the woman's arm.

"Meet Nettie Drew, Joe." Under Milo's bushy eyebrows,

his faded blue eyes brightened as his gaze returned to the woman.

"Hello." The hand Nettie extended was cool, lightly dotted with age spots. "I've already met your son. He and Cletis are currently under the tent of the dining room table. Occasionally they venture out for—" She looked up at Milo. "What did Oliver call it? Fodder?"

Milo nodded.

"That's an unusual word for a child his age. I was terribly impressed. He explained to me that it was a game he played with you. Weird words, he called it. We talked for quite a while before he retreated to the tent. He said he was observing feet."

"Is he making a pest of himself?" Sticking the spoon back on the poinsettia spoon rest, Joe prepared to go rescue Milo's guests from Oliver. And Cletis.

"Not at all. He's a charming boy." Nettie opened a drawer across from the table and took out a large serving spoon. "You should be proud of him."

"I am." Joe felt more than saw Gabby's movement toward his side. Again that sly warmth crept through him. A protective creature, she had a loyalty that wouldn't vanish like spit in the wind. But, sex? Gabby thinking about sex with him? Heat shot through him, a searing column of flame.

Nettie patted him on the arm. "Clearly you're a good father. The boy adores you."

Joe tried not to look at Milo. Milo would know better than anyone how unfit Joe was to be a parent. Milo would know what a joke it was, that Joe Carpenter could pretend to be a father, a responsible citizen of Bayou Bend.

"Got what you need, Nettie?" Milo draped his arm lightly around the woman's shoulders.

"Yes." The private smile she gave him would have gone unnoticed, but Joe saw Gabby turn at that exact moment, saw her go stick-stiff as Milo's hand slid over the curve of Nettie's hip.

"We can eat in a few minutes." Enveloped in her gaudy apron, Gabby looked forlorn as she observed her father. "We can finish decorating while we have supper. There's plenty of glogg still out on the buffet. Do you want some, Joe?"

Joe had had one cup of the hot Swedish drink with its combination of whisky, grain alcohol and brandy. And raisins. One was enough if he wanted to be able to walk straight for the rest of the night. "No, thanks."

"Pa? Nettie?" Brittleness turned her voice tight.

"No more for me, honey."

"I've had my limit, but thank you, Gabrielle. Milo told me it's Mary Kathleen's recipe that she made every year?" Nettie Drew's face was warmly sympathetic.

"Yes."

"How lovely that you would make it this year. You must have beautiful memories of her."

"Yes."

Joe couldn't stand the way Gabby's brightness dimmed with each second Nettie talked. "I need some help over here, sweet pea." He motioned to the pot. With his other hand, he waved Milo and Nettie out of the kitchen. "Go ahead. Gabby can show me what to do."

In the silence after Milo and Nettie left, Joe stirred and waited for Gabby to speak.

The bewilderment in her face touched him. The spark that usually lit her from the inside had vanished as if someone had blown out the candle. She looked pale and terribly fragile. He managed to resist the wayward impulse to gather her into his arms.

"You saw? Pa and Nettie?"

"Yeah." Giving her time to collect herself, he dug at the bottom of the pot, scraping loose the sticking rice. "Tough, huh?"

She nodded, a jerky wobble of her head. "I don't understand. Pa never told me." She slid along the wall into a sitting position. "This is…a surprise."

"You didn't know he was seeing anyone?"

"Oh." Stricken, she stared up at him. "You think it's serious?"

Joe turned off the burner and went to stoop beside her. Taking one of her hands, he unclenched the tight fist. "Yes, sweet pea, I think your dad is very serious about this woman. And I think she's crazy about him. In a very ladylike way, of course—subtle, nothing pushy or overt. She'd be a stunner at any age, and she's a very nice lady."

Gabby gulped. "Yes. You're right. She's nice."

"But?"

"She's not mama."

"Ah." Joe cupped her shoulder with his hands and rocked her back and forth gently. "You're jealous?"

She swiped her eyes with an abrupt movement, and he thought he saw a glint of moisture. "Jealous? You think I'd be so selfish I wouldn't want Pa to have a friend? You think I would begrudge him any comfort he could find?" She pushed Joe's hands away and struggled to her feet. "I'd be ashamed to behave like that."

"If you're not jealous, why are you so shaken, Gabby? Your dad's in his sixties. These days that's not so old. Why do you look like your world's caved in on top of you?"

Crossing her arms around herself, she stayed still for a long moment before saying, "I came back home because I thought Pa needed me. I wanted to believe that. I wanted it to be true. I told myself he was lonely." Her laugh was ragged. "I thought he was ill. And hiding the truth from me." A hiccuping sob rose from her throat.

"And now you don't know whether it was his need or your own that made your decision."

Her face crumpled, but she didn't cry. "I had a business,

friends, a place to live, but I wanted to come home, to be with Pa. I guess I misread the signs.''

''Because you wanted to.''

''Because I wanted to.'' Turning her back to him, she laid her forehead against the wall. ''Because I needed to.''

Joe slipped his arm around her waist and turned her toward him. Pushing her head to his chest, he said, ''We all look for someone to need us. Being needed, having someone to worry over, having someone to worry about us when we don't show up—that's one of the most basic human needs. Why should you be any different?''

Lying still in his arms, all her bright sassiness muted, she seemed infinitely vulnerable, and he wanted to shield her. He knew he couldn't. Gabby would have to come to terms with her decision and figure out for herself where she fit into her father's life now. What her own life would be.

Joe tightened his hold. Like Gabby, he couldn't see the terrifying future clearly. Like her, he would have to chart a new course for his life. Made with the best intentions, his decision to return to Bayou Bend, like hers, had far-reaching consequences.

Standing in the corner of her dad's kitchen with Joe Carpenter holding her as if she were a priceless vase, Gabrielle clung to him, her lifeline to safety on a rough sea.

Against her cheek, the steady, reassuring thump of Joe's heart anchored her.

Chapter Five

Gabrielle moved her hot cheek slowly against the cool, slick finish of Joe's shirt. She breathed in the clean, starchy fragrance, breathed in the clean smell of *him*. Joe Carpenter, offering her comfort in a dark moment.

The thump of his heart steadied her. He could make her feel dithery and fluttery and totally unlike herself. Now, with her heart aching, his touch calmed her and gave her a chance to pull herself together. Odd that it should be Joe Carpenter who had the power to soothe this pain inside her.

She had no tears, only this dislocation yawning like a chasm inside. Joe's touch was a bridge for her, a way back over the emptiness that opened beneath her. Clutching her fingers against his cotton shirt, she thanked heaven that he was there. Too hard to pretend in front of her dad and his Nettie. Too hard to hide all the hurt that rolled up like a tidal wave and crashed over her as she saw him with Nettie, the two of them with her on the outside.

"You okay?" Joe's hand cupped her nape, warm and comforting.

"I'm fine." She allowed herself the luxury of remaining within the circle of his arms, protected and safe. *Safe*. The word struck her as unexpected in the context of what she knew about Joe Carpenter. Or at least what she believed she knew about him. "No big deal. I overreacted, that's all."

"You weren't prepared, were you?" He shifted, and her cheek slipped against one of his shirt buttons. "For Milo and Nettie?"

"No." She wanted to sink into the strength of Joe's chest, stay there, not think about her dad and the kind woman he'd curled his arm around. "I think Pa started to warn me right before the party started, but we were sidetracked. The situation is probably as awkward for him as it is for me. Maybe more."

She lifted her head. "I'm being silly. I was surprised, that's all. I wasn't expecting Pa to have a—significant other." Her laugh felt rusty in her throat. "Gosh, that sounds so funny. My pa *dating*."

"How long ago did your mom pass away, Gabby?"

At the back of her head, his fingers massaged her neck and she rested against their power, shutting her eyes.

"Over a year ago."

"I'm sorry. That must have been difficult."

"It was." She tightened her grip on his shirt. "Oh, Joe, I miss her every day. So much. I thought it would get easier. It doesn't. It only gets—different. A phrase I overhear while I'm shopping will remind me of her. I think I see her out of the corner of my eyes. I'll see a shadow in the corner, and I'll think she's there." She hesitated, continued. "I turn, ready to share the joke with her, a glitch in my brain making me forget that she's dead, and I *believe* she's right behind me." Memory stung her, a sharp pain that never seemed to vanish. "But she never is."

"Aw, sweet pea."

Gabrielle swallowed. "Mom would want Pa to be happy, to have someone to share his life with. I do, too." Her head tilted to each side as Joe worked out the stiffness in her neck. She hadn't realized she'd become so tense during the evening. "I must have realized something the minute Nettie arrived. Pa kept watching the door, but I thought he was excited about having the party again. Getting back to normal. Whatever normal is."

"This must be very tough for you. Missing your mom. And, in a way, losing your dad."

She went still. Seeing her dad with Nettie *had* felt like loss. That was the source of her pain. Another loss. Opening her eyes, she met Joe's, their golden brown depths wryly compassionate. "You're right. I don't know how you understand this, but you've nailed it. You must think I'm a selfish brat."

"I think you love your dad." Again his nimble fingers kneaded the muscles in her neck. "Hold still." He placed both thumbs along her jawbone and tipped her head back and forth, touching her chin to her chest and back, working out the last of the kinks. "And I think you're wired tighter than a Slinky toy."

"What?" With her head down, she focused on the tips of his glossy shoes. Nice shoes. Expensive shoes. "Slinky?"

He rolled her head back, resting it on his open palms and pressing against her temples with his busy fingers. "Didn't you have a Slinky when you were a bitty girl?"

"I don't remember. Maybe."

Once more he tipped her head forward. His shoes came into view as he moved his fingers to her shoulders, digging and smoothing until she thought she'd whimper with pleasure, her body relaxing and melting under his touch, her eyelids drifting closed. "You must have had a Slinky. Milo would have given you anything, I'll bet."

"Does Oliver have a Slinky?"

Joe checked the movement of his hands against her shoulders. "Beats me."

"You haven't been busy packing toys and finding Lego

pieces under your bare feet?" Raising her head, she stepped back, curious.

"No." Joe walked to the sink, looked out at the yard.

Under his shirt, the long muscles of his back defined his spine. "No, I haven't found Lego pieces underfoot. I wish to God I had." Turning abruptly toward her, he braced himself on the counter. "Gabby, I don't know much about my son."

"Why not?" She wondered at the intensity in Joe's expression. This was more serious than a man experiencing pangs of incompetency as a father. "Were you traveling a lot while he was growing up?"

"Oliver comes with a lot of baggage, but not a lot of possessions. No Lego. No stacks of books. No robot monsters. He has a blanket and a banged-up scrapbook with three pictures."

"I'm sorry, Joe. I don't understand." Gabrielle thought about the child who'd been so territorial about his tree, so possessive of his dad. "How could he not have *stuff*? Kids are pack rats. They all have stuff. They collect junk from the road. All kinds of gross things."

"Oliver doesn't. And, until three weeks ago, I was a man who had no idea he had a son." His knuckles were white as he clenched the sink rim. "An early Christmas present, you might say."

Delicately, picking her way through what she sensed was a difficult situation, and her heart going out to the pain she saw in Joe's face, Gabrielle asked, "You didn't know what? That Oliver existed? That he'd been born? What?"

"All of the above. He was living in an apartment in Chicago with a distant relative of his mother's."

"Your ex-wife?" She recalled that Joe had told her he wasn't married, but he hadn't said anything else.

"A woman I lived with seven years ago. She never told me about Oliver. I was careful, so I wouldn't have expected her to become pregnant."

"Oh." Gabrielle wondered about the woman who'd been with Joe, borne his child. Had Joe loved her? She must have loved him. Surely she had. "What happened?"

"His mother had left Oliver with the relative-by-marriage four years earlier. Walked out. Never came back. Oh, Jana called from time to time, enough to keep her relatives from calling the authorities. She sent the occasional check, too, and Suzie, the sort-of relative, liked kids, liked Oliver, and time passed. But Jana walked out on Oliver the same way she walked out of my life. The difference was that I wasn't a two-year-old baby. And I didn't care."

"You must have cared. A little."

"Lust. Propinquity. Opportunity. A seven-month version of a one-night stand, I reckon. Nothing more."

Gabrielle wasn't sure she believed him. Either way, his version of the story was bleak. No matter what anyone said about sex for sex's sake being fun, it was an emotional desert. She couldn't comprehend removing all emotion from an act that personal, that intense. "That's sad, Joe. Empty. For you. And I'd guess for Jana. But she must have loved Oliver in her own way. She sent checks to…Suzie? That means *something*."

"Really?" His drawl was bitter. "Not much in Jana's case, that's for sure."

"Joe—" she shook his arm "—she was his *mother*. I'm sure she loved him. In her own way. How could she not?"

"Well, Gabby, it's your nature to look on the bright side, to expect the best out of people. But you didn't know Jana."

"True. Look, I'm no Pollyanna. I know that there's evil in the world. Don't sell me short. You may think I'm a naive, small-town girl still, but I'm not. I read the newspapers. I understand what can happen. It seems more credible to me that Jana had a compelling reason to walk away from Oliver."

Breaking loose in a sudden bark, his laugh was harsh. "Pleasure? Lack of interest?"

"Ah, Joe, that's so cynical. You knew her. If you didn't love her, you must have liked her, at least."

"Fair enough." Joe scrubbed his face hard, as if he were punishing himself. "The situation wasn't all her fault. I'll cop to that. I wasn't a man who was living up to anyone's expectations at that point in my life. Jana was—available. I was, too." He sighed heavily, the sound loud in the quiet kitchen. "And she made me laugh. Yes, I liked her. Until I found out about Oliver."

Gabrielle waited, thinking hard before she asked her next question. She didn't know Jana, but she knew Joe, knew him at some elemental level. He'd hinted he wasn't a candidate for Good Citizen of the Year, but every instinct in her body told her he wouldn't have abandoned a woman he was involved with. Not Joe. There were some facts missing. As carefully as she could phrase her question, she asked, "Why do you think she didn't tell you about Oliver?"

There was a long pause before Joe answered, his words coming slowly as if he were sifting through possibilities. "I can't answer that. Her behavior is a mystery to me. But I'm looking for answers. I would have married her, given her support money. Anything she needed. For the boy."

Gabrielle would bet a thousand dollars Joe had left something out, some fact he wasn't prepared to share. "So you'd never heard of him or seen him?"

"The day I strolled into that apartment was the first time I saw him." Joe's gaze was blazingly fierce as it fixed on her. "My son."

"How did you find him?" Gabrielle yearned to say something that would ease the tightness in his face. She couldn't imagine what that moment had been like. For both of them.

"Suzie had kept Oliver for four years, waiting for Jana to come back for him. She didn't. Once in a while a check arrived, but after Suzie hadn't had any money from Jana for almost a year, she couldn't afford to keep Oliver any longer.

It boggles my mind that she played mother for as long as she did. She has four kids of her own and no husband. Suzie has a kind heart, and she's a sucker for a sad tale. Jana must have played her along. At any rate, not hearing from Jana, Suzie was desperate. Going through some boxes of papers Jana had left in storage, she found my name and tracked me down. Jana had put my name on Oliver's birth certificate.'' His mouth thinned. ''At least Jana had enough sense of responsibility to do that. But I'm amazed Suzie found me. That address was seven years old. The apartment where Jana and I had lived for a while.''

''What if Suzie hadn't found you?''

''She'd planned to call the Department of Child Welfare after Christmas. Oliver would have gone into the system.'' Joe slowly lifted his shoulders, as if moving them took all his strength. ''I would never have found him. That's what almost happened.''

''How horrible.'' In one quick step, Gabrielle was at his side, her hand curling over his hand that still gripped the sink rim with such force she wondered the porcelain didn't shatter. ''He's with you permanently? His mother surrendered custody?''

''I hired a private investigator. He found Jana. She'd been killed in a drive-by shooting down in Gary, Indiana. She was living with some man under a different name. Nobody connected Jane Stakowski from Gary with Jana Stanley, who'd abandoned a small boy in Chicago.''

''Oh, Joe. Poor Oliver. No wonder he clings to you the way he does. I'm amazed he hasn't been at your side this whole evening, in fact.''

''He's attached himself to Cletis and your dad, but he keeps his eye on the kitchen door. He checks to see that I'm in here. That I haven't gone strolling out the back door. He and Cletis poke a finger and a paw through the door on a regular basis. Haven't you seen it crack open?''

"I missed that. After all that's happened, he must be terrified you'll disappear, too." Gabrielle rubbed her cheek against the sleeve of his shirt.

"He trusts me. For some crazy, illogical reason, the little guy trusts *me*. Never saw me before, and he strolled out of that apartment as if he'd been with me all his life. Didn't even blink. Nuts, huh?"

"Sure. Silly kid. Trusting you like that. What's the matter with him, anyway?" A tear slipped from her eye and dampened his sleeve. She rubbed her eyes dry on the smooth cotton. She didn't have the right to inflict her distress on Joe. Not after what Oliver had endured. Surreptitiously, she wiped her eyes again. She wasn't involved. She was a bystander in Joe and Oliver's lives, on the fringes. As she now was in her dad's life. Her dad had moved on. She hadn't.

Through the lustrous fabric of his shirt, she felt the hard muscles of Joe's arm bunching and tensing. Like a string drawn tight on a bow, his whole body leaned forward, only the most enormous discipline keeping him from lashing out with his fist and smashing something.

Someone.

But there was no one to smash, no way to change the past, to *fix* the terrible wrong. No villains, at least none that she saw.

Still, thinking of Oliver cast adrift on the seas of chance, Gabrielle wanted to smash something herself. No child should be tossed out like tissue. Oliver deserved more from life. His stubborn independence and sturdiness demanded recognition. Against all odds, he'd survived. Oh, not merely physically, but emotionally. The scars were there, sure, but he'd survived. And so had Joe.

Like father, like son. Two peas in a pod, as her mama used to say.

For a long moment she and Joe stayed silent, side by side,

the rhythm of his breathing matching hers, breath for slow, even breath.

The oddly tranquil moment had a rightness to it that confused her, comforted her, made her yearn for something she couldn't quite identify.

The door slammed against the wall. "Are we going to starve out here, or what?" Moon's big face preceded the bulk of his body as he leaned through the door and stopped as he saw them side by side, her arm resting on Joe's. "What's going on, folks? Spreading a little Christmas cheer of your own?"

"Mind your business, Moon." Joe straightened slowly, an alertness in the muscles under her hand, his stance that of an animal ready to attack. Or defend.

He was worried about *her,* about her reputation.

"Actually, Moon, for your information, I was flirting with Joe. You've interrupted us in the throes of passion. I confess. You caught us." She batted her eyelashes theatrically at Joe and felt the tension in him ease.

"Oh, right, Gabrielle. You and Joe. Sure. And you have that swell piece of property along the gulf that you're willing to sell me for next to nothing. Like I'd believe that story." Moon's laugh was full-bellied. "Good one. Anyway, when are we going to eat, girl?" His face turned pitiful. "I'm starving. I need food. I'm a growing boy."

"Lord, I hope not." Joe strolled over to him, punched him on the shoulder. "If you grew any more, you'd shake the house to pieces with every step, old son."

"Don't 'old son' me, you cycle-riding hooligan." Laughing, Moon punched him back, a playful swipe at Joe's arm and shoulder, but a bearlike thwack all the same.

Joe didn't flinch.

Gabrielle was impressed. The punch had been hard enough, even in fun, to rock most men back on their heels. She'd been aware of Joe's muscled body under his civilized suit and shirt, but she was amazed by his toughness in the face of Moon's enthusiastic whomp on the shoulder.

Seeing her astonishment, Joe said, "Relax. Moon and I like each other."

"Yeah." Moon nodded vigorously. "Joe's not half bad. For a short, underfed specimen."

Gabrielle's gaze drifted to Joe's sinewy six feet, then returned to Moon. "Gosh, I really enjoy the way guys express affection. All that pounding and whacking at each other. So what do you do when you're ticked off with each other?"

Moon and Joe exchanged glances.

"Women. They don't get it, do they, Moon?"

"Nope," Moon added agreeably. "But I *really* need to get some food, Gabrielle. I'm not fooling."

"All right, Moon. I suppose I ought to have pity on you. Carry the news back to the troops. The next round of food is on the way."

"Damn, it sure smells good." Moon lifted the lid on the pot, reaching in with one thick finger. "Did Milo make enough?"

"For you, or for everyone else?" She smacked his hand with the wooden spoon. "There's this pot, and the one staying warm in the oven. Think that will be enough? One pot for you, one for the rest of the guests?" Behind her, Joe cleared his throat with amusement.

"Aw, Gabrielle, don't be mean. I can't help myself. I love Milo's cooking." Moon threw a heavy arm around her shoulder, and she staggered momentarily under the weight.

"Come on, Moon. You and I can haul out the jambalaya. Okay, Gabby?" Joe lifted Moon's arm off her shoulders and handed him a pair of Santa Claus pot holders. "Grab the handles, Moon. I'll get the door and the other batch. Heads up, sweet pea." Joe's grin whipped across his face, a blaze of white teeth and satisfaction.

In an exaggerated bend and stoop, she dodged as Moon

swung the massive pot off the stove and headed for the door. "I'll bring the salad bowl." She poked Joe in the ribs as he opened the oven door and lifted out the second pot. "And behave yourself."

"More fun not to."

"You're a bad boy, Joe Carpenter."

"Of course," he said smugly.

"But only some of the time," she added softly.

As Moon backed through the door and out of hearing range, Joe murmured, "Thanks. For listening." His eyes didn't meet hers, and a narrow flush touched his cheekbones.

"Anytime." She hit him on the shoulder. "There. Guy-style communication." She regarded her fist thoughtfully. "Hey, there might be something to this. Efficient, at least. Once you get the hang of it. A kind of one-style-fits-all communication."

"Better ways of communicating. Between a man and a woman, that is." His grin was all masculine provocation. "And, Gabby?"

"Yes?" She gave him the prissiest look she could muster.

"In case you're wondering, I'm flirting with you."

"I know. And, Joe?"

"Yes, sweet pea?"

"I'm flirting back." She swished her skirt at him.

"Okay." The door shut quietly as he, too, backed out, following Moon.

Everything inside her loosened and relaxed. All the questions about Milo and Nettie, the distress over Oliver's situation, her confusion about the way she felt around Joe—everything smoothed out as she thought about the look on Joe's face as he'd teased her. An inexplicable affection there, underneath the gleam, an affection that reached right down inside her, fluttering her tummy.

In the dining room, the sideboard and dining table were loaded with bowls and platters of food. Under the dangling edge of the tablecloth, she saw a furry gray paw reach out to slap at Taylor Padgett's ankle as he leaned over the table to spear a smoked oyster.

"Watch it, Taylor. You're being stalked." The salad bowl in her hands, Gabrielle pointed with her elbow.

"You scared the heck out of me for a moment. Surgeons don't like to hear that word." He shuddered. "These days that could mean a dissatisfied patient."

"I hear you do good work, Taylor." Gabrielle set the bowl on the buffet across from the sideboard. Moon and Joe had already placed the white pots of jambalaya at each end. Earlier in the day, she'd arranged the red-and-white Christmas dishes on the buffet, their faded trees and tinted gold stars giving her pleasure.

"I like to believe that. But you've heard the rap on us surgeons. We think we're one miracle away from God." He raised his eyebrows, offering her the chance to make fun at his expense. "And sometimes it's true."

"But remember, Taylor, I knew you back when." She stuck her tongue out at him. "Hard to create God-like awe in someone who's seen you skinny-dipping with your college girlfriend."

He grimaced. "Oh, yes. I remember. Bad day at Black Rock, so to speak. And not nice of you to remind me. Alas, a prophet without honor in his own country. Maybe I should think about that offer from Atlanta Medical. *They* think I'm hot stuff."

"Having seen you 'buck-nekkid,' as Pa would say, I have trouble agreeing with them." She laughed as he sputtered cracker crumbs tableward. "But don't expect me to apologize. Heck, you paid off in soda pop for the rest of the summer. Anyway, Taylor, reminiscences aside, I haven't had a chance to talk with you since I came home. I haven't heard any complaints from Pa, but he's not saying much about his surgery."

Crunching an oyster-laden cracker, Taylor ambled over to

her. He brushed cracker crumbs off the lapels of his brown jacket. "Milo did quite well."

"You don't think he looks tired?" She brushed away a crumb that had caught on his sleeve. "Because I do."

Taylor swiveled his head until he located Milo in the midst of a group in the living room, Nettie Drew beside him. Taylor watched for a minute. "He looks one hundred per cent to me, Gabrielle. That infection he developed after he left the hospital—"

"Pa didn't mention an infection."

"No?" Cracker crumbs dribbled into his mustache.

She shook her head. She'd been right to come home. Milo *was* ill. "This is the first I've heard of an infection."

"It wasn't serious. I stay on top of complicating factors like postoperative infection. Milo called as soon as he popped a fever, and we caught it early. Milo's fine."

"I worry about him, Taylor." Gabrielle took his hand and held it. "He's not telling me everything. I'm scared that something else is wrong with him. That you didn't get all the tumor. I worry."

Taylor covered her hand reassuringly. "Hey, kiddo, don't insult my work. I've got ten years on you, and remember, I kid-sat you for a spell while you were in diapers, so you have to show me proper respect. I'm good. Best in the area, in fact. Milo is fine, Gabrielle. Trust me." He patted her hand. "You don't have to worry about him. Enjoy Christmas. Have a cup of glogg. You won't worry about anything after half a cup of that brew."

"Doctor's orders?"

"You bet. Drink up, kiddo. The night's still young." Giving her a hug, he wandered toward the crowd in the living room.

She would have a cup, too. Maybe even two.

This was what she'd wanted when she left Arizona. Everybody around her, the house loud with merriment.

Tradition.

This was the way Christmas was supposed to be. She could let the richness of being home envelop her. She wouldn't give in to this nagging worry about her dad.

Taylor would have given her a hint, a clue, if anything were wrong with Milo.

She frowned. Wouldn't he?

In the living room, the tree, no longer ugly, shone with tiny Italian lights and ornaments, some of which had come down from her great-grandparents. The salt-dough angel she'd made with her mother years ago and sprinkled extravagantly with blue glitter hung heavily from one skinny branch.

After supper, her dad would hang the crystal star. It symbolized the magic of Christmas for her, its crystal glinting softly in the dark. Old and fragile, the star had come from Ireland, a souvenir of her grandmother, her mother's mother, whose powdery scent clung to Gabrielle whenever she cuddled on her grandmother's lap.

A link from the past to the present, rich with memories.

Gabrielle remembered taking the star down from the tree that last time with her mother and wrapping it carefully in tissue. Sipping orange tea, they'd laughed about the holidays and toasted each other, "To next Christmas!" Christmas over for another year, her mother had laid the star gently in its own special box and rubbed her head.

It was their last Christmas together.

The lights on the tree blurred into a shimmer of white.

Suddenly, a claw snagged her ankle, catching her nylons. "Hey, Cletis." She stooped and scratched the cat's ears. "Where's your buddy?"

The tablecloth pooched, billowed out.

"Here." The edge of the tablecloth framed Oliver's face. His cheeks were bright red and he was slightly sweaty. His hair had thrown off the constraints of whatever Joe had put on it.

"Hungry?" Picking up Cletis and tucking his chunky head

under her chin, Gabrielle wandered slowly in Oliver's direction, stopping to collect a rolled-up sliver of smoked mullet Moon had brought. Cletis poked his head into her face and kept pushing at her chin until she shared a nibble with him.

"Me and Cletis have been eating."

"I can tell," she said seriously.

Inch by inch, Oliver crept out from the protection of the tablecloth. "And drinking."

"Oh? What did you have?" She put Cletis down as he head-butted her again. "Sorry, mister, the mullet's gone."

"Milo gave me punch. It's red. With frozen strawberries. He said that other stuff is bitter. He let me lick the spoon. I didn't like it. But the red stuff's okay."

"Good." She breathed a sigh of relief. For an instant she'd been afraid Oliver had been nipping glogg. "Want to come with me to the living room? We'll tell everybody soup's on."

"I don't like soup."

"It's not really soup. That's an expression that means it's time to eat."

He stood, rear end angling skyward as he wiped his hands down his pants. On the bottom of his dangling shirttails, red stains sent a festive message. "I can tell everyone?"

"Sure. Can you speak loudly enough so everyone can hear you?"

He rolled his eyes. "Of course." He reached for Cletis, who had waddled under his own steam beneath the table toward safety.

Gabrielle suspected Cletis—and Oliver—had their own stash of munchies hidden under the table.

The cat's belly hung in folds as Oliver hoisted him up, grunting. "Me and Cletis will tell everybody soup's on. Even if it's not soup." He marched toward the living room and stood in the archway between the two rooms. "Soup's on!" he bellowed, and then led the parade to the dining room.

Joe stood aside, letting people tromp past him. Everyone

was pairing up, couples, friends, lining up for food and making their way to corners and end tables where they could eat and visit.

He didn't know anyone except Moon and Gabby. And Milo, of course.

Maybe this would be a good time to leave. He and Oliver, who'd clearly been stuffing himself all evening, could slip out the door.

No one would even know they'd gone.

No one would miss them.

Milo waved his hands, directing people to both sides of the table. "Y'all come on. Moon, help me shag this crew toward the food. All this sudden bashfulness sure seems suspicious to me. Y'all sure you're the same group I see around town every day?" Laughter greeted Milo's words as he placed a hand at Nettie Drew's waist and led her in, while Moon was at the back of the line of guests.

"What do you expect, Milo? We're all squashed into our party duds. Have to behave when you have a tie choking you."

"Hell's bells, Dial. We've seen your damned tie. Stick it in your pocket and eat," Moon groused. "Don't hold up the line, man. Some of us are desperate back here."

"Right, folks. And you sure don't want to be in Moon's way when the notion takes him to eat." Milo motioned for them to make a path for Moon.

Joe watched Gabrielle walk over to Taylor Padgett and tuck his arm into hers, leading him toward the dining room. He was the surgeon, a man she'd grown up with. A family friend. Why wouldn't she make a point of ushering him in first? Well, not first. Oliver and Cletis had taken care of that. Joe could understand Gabby's interest in the doctor.

After all, he had standing in the community, respect. He was the perfect man for Gabby. Unencumbered with burdens from the past, Taylor Padgett could give her the kind of life she was used to.

The kind of life Gabrielle O'Shea deserved.

Joe wished the idea gave him more satisfaction. Surprised, he looked down to see his clenched fist. Slowly unclenching his fingers, he stuck his hand in his pocket and reminded himself once more of Padgett's sterling qualities.

Much better to think of those sterling qualities than to imagine smashing in the doctor's carefully groomed, mustached face.

Unfortunately, Padgett's sterling qualities were all too easy to find. The man was the next best thing to a saint. Everyone in town had made a point of mentioning how wonderful Doc Padgett was.

Sourly, he had to admit Taylor Padgett did seem like an all-around, hell of a fine fellow. Shoot, he even liked Padgett himself. What wasn't to like?

The only problem with Padgett was that he was next to Gabby and Joe wasn't.

She sure seemed enthralled by the man.

If Padgett stepped any closer, the man would be wearing her for his very own lapel pin.

At some intellectual level, Joe found his very primal reaction to the doctor amusing. This visceral urge to pin the man's ears back was unexpected. He couldn't ever recall feeling so— protective about a woman. So possessive.

And that thought shocked him most of all.

Because he wanted to be Gabby's friend, not her lover.

He hadn't realized how much he'd needed a friend until she stood at his side and listened as he sorted out the crazy mess of his feelings. There had been no one before her he'd wanted to tell about Oliver, and how Joe had found the boy.

Sometimes a man needed a woman friend, someone he could talk with about confusing thoughts and feelings. Sex complicated things between a man and a woman.

Every damned time.

He didn't want the complication of sex in his life, not sex with Gabby, anyway.

She was different.

Sex would destroy the fragile bonds of friendship they were developing. That awareness was what they'd both danced around with their discussion about flirting. They could flirt and be friends. They couldn't have sex and remain friends.

He knew Gabby wasn't the type of woman who could separate sex from her emotions.

Flirting was one thing. Sex another.

Being ticked off with Padgett went beyond the boundaries of friendship. Coiling inside Joe, that emotion had to do with sex, not friendship.

He wanted friendship.

But, hell, he still wished he was the man standing that close to Gabby, not Padgett.

That was the way of the world. Water sought its own level.

He knew that, had accepted it long before he moved to Bayou Bend, but he'd never before been so ticked off at a really nice guy, a swell fellow who didn't have a clue that Joe was happily fantasizing ways to get rid of him.

As the very wonderful doc leaned and spoke into Gabby's ear, she laughed, a light, lovely sound that came to him and left him feeling as alone as he'd ever been in his life.

Outside, looking in.

Where he'd always been.

Then, at the exact second Joe felt like a kid with his nose pressed up against the toy shop window, Gabby turned and smiled at him, strolling back through the crowd to stand next to him.

"Hey, Joe, come join the party. Oliver has a head start on you. I think he's staked out his spot under the table with the cat. We'll find you a place." Slipping her arm through Joe's, her palm sliding over his forearm, she led him into the dining room.

Funny, the word she'd used, he thought as she tugged him forward, making room in the crowd for him.

His *place*.

He wished he knew what his place was in Bayou Bend. Once upon a time he'd understood exactly what his place here was and had run away like a wild child. But now, could he find a *place* for himself and Oliver?

Gabby seemed determined to find one for him.

He wasn't used to having someone look after him.

Her concern tickled him, warmed him faster than the glogg Moon pressed into his hand.

Maybe Doc Padgett didn't hold all the cards.

Question was, though, could a man be friends with Gabby O'Shea and keep sex out of his thoughts?

Maybe.

Maybe not.

Joe let his fingers slip down to close around hers.

Together, they entered the dining room.

Chapter Six

Joe knew exactly how he came to be seated with Milo, Nettie and Gabby.

With her skill at maneuvering people, she could have been a general. Padgett wound up with Moon and three nurses Milo had invited from the hospital, Oliver and Cletis lay stretched out on their overstuffed bellies under the table, and Joe, miracle of miracles, found himself with Gabby curled up on the floor next to him, her hair clinging to the fabric of his slacks.

"You like Pa's cooking, Joe?" she asked drowsily, placing the mug of glogg on the floor beside her. Lifting out the cinnamon stick, she licked off the last drops and let the curled twig fall back into the mug. Her cheeks were pink-tinged, and her eyes all soft and dreamy. "He does a pretty good job, doesn't he, this old man of mine?"

Hearing her, Milo turned to them. "Only one correct answer, Carpenter. This is a test, you know. Wrong answer, you don't get dessert."

"I usually get my just deserts, Milo. You know that." It was the closest Joe would allow himself to touch the subject of that night years ago. He wanted Milo to know he remembered, that he hadn't forgotten what Milo had done.

Placing her hand on Joe's knee to steady her, Gabby shifted. Her touch burned right through the fabric. "Joe," she repeated sleepily, "you didn't answer."

"Milo's jambalaya is fit for a king."

"Joe, why don't you and I have coffee one morning soon?" Not looking in Joe's direction, Milo handed Nettie a shrimp from his own plate. Offhand, casual, the question attracted no attention.

But Joe heard the message in the invitation and was relieved. He and Milo needed to air out the past. "Good idea. I'll have to work out sitter arrangements for Oliver and get back to you."

Gabby yawned, the pink tip of her tongue catching his attention. "Oliver can stay with me. I'm planning on making cookies tomorrow. Maybe he'd like that. He can help me. If not, we'll go shopping." She stretched her arms and yawned again. "We'll figure out something. An adventure. After I clean up whatever mess is left from tonight." She shook her head, and a feathery strand of hair floated against his hand.

Such power in that light touch, power to make him want. To hope for impossible things.

But reality was built, brick by brick, from what was possible.

He stirred, and her hair settled against her cheek, a shiny brown line against pink.

"Sounds like a plan," Milo said. "We can meet tomorrow. Nine o'clock too early, honey?"

"Pa, usually I've done half a day's work by nine. I believe I can drag myself to the flour canister by that time of day." Resting her hand again on Joe's knee, her breath puffing warm and damp against his leg, she added, "Check with Oliver first, though, all right?"

A less-controlled man would have hauled her straight into

his lap. Joe didn't. Without making an issue of Oliver's situation, she'd solved it. Gabby knew how Oliver might react to Joe's heading off somewhere. That was why he'd waited to return to work until after Christmas. His business could be put on hold for a little while.

Longer if Oliver had trouble settling in to this new school.

"You not working tomorrow, Joe?" Milo's casual question shouldn't have pushed a button, but it did.

Joe knew what Milo was after. Details. Milo's lawyerly instincts, picking and nailing everything down. "Nope."

"No time clock to punch?"

"Nope." Joe didn't think it would hurt Milo to wait for information until they had their meeting. He didn't want to explain everything in front of Gabby, not unless he had to. Eventually he would tell her everything.

But not yet.

Not until he'd settled Oliver in.

"Speaking of Oliver, honey, what would you think if we let Oliver stick the star on top of the tree?" Milo's voice was low, almost as if he didn't see Oliver and Cletis crawling on their bellies toward them. "Okay with you, Joe?"

The question had a weight to it he didn't quite catch, but he understood that for the O'Sheas, topping the tree with this star was an important moment. If the star was that important, maybe Oliver shouldn't be involved. Uncomfortable, feeling like an outsider suddenly thrust into the spotlight, Joe started to stop the snowball before it rolled downhill. "I don't—"

"Sure, Pa. I think that would be a wonderful idea." Gabby's voice trembled as she interrupted Joe.

Looking sharply at her, he felt his uneasiness increase. This star thing was significant. A low profile seemed much more appealing to him as father and daughter waited for his answer.

"I think Oliver would like that, Joe," Gabby murmured huskily. "Ask him." Tucking her legs under her, yoga-style, she bent forward, her back stretching out all gold and slippery as she rested her elbows on the floor. Her hair fanned around her shoulders, light brown against gold shimmer as she spoke to Oliver. "Wouldn't you?"

Facing her, nose to nose, his son gazed steadily at Gabrielle. "I don't know."

"Putting up the star is a tradition for us. It means—oh, Oliver, it means Christmas is around the corner. It means we're all together. Family. Friends. Together."

"Does it mean Santa Claus will know how to find you?"

"Yes," she answered, solemnly, drowsily, "it means that, too. It shines so everyone can find their way home, Oliver."

"I want to hang the star." Oliver tugged on Joe's hand. "Okay?"

Glancing at Milo and Gabby, Joe tried to read their expressions, to see if there were any reason his son shouldn't participate in this small ceremony.

Finding no clues to help him, he yielded to the second, imperceptible tug. "Please, Daddy?"

Gabby caught Oliver's attention. "I'll get the star, and tomorrow, Oliver, if you help me make cookies, I'll tell you the story about the woman who brought this crystal star all the way from Ireland."

"Crystal? Magic? Like with the robots on TV?"

"Crystal, yes. Magic, definitely. But I don't know about the TV robots."

"'Cause you're too old, probably," he said matter-of-factly, and trotted to the living room, Cletis lumbering behind him.

"I think your cat has adopted my son."

"Or vice versa."

"You don't know about TV robots, huh? Even I know that much." He tsk-tsked. "I feel awful bad for you, age creeping up on you like this."

"I know. I'm a pitiful case. I can hear the creaking joints right now." Gabby stood up, swayed, and Joe caught her elbow, steadying her. Looking down at his hand cradling her arm, she said, "This is turning into a habit."

"Not one that has to be broken," he said as she leaned into him.

"What habit's that?" Milo stood up and held out a helping hand to Nettie. "Who needs to break bad habits?"

"We all do, Milo." Nettie's gentle comment had Gabby turning to her.

"Not a bad habit. I ran into Oliver and Joe at Moon's tree lot yesterday. Joe kept me from falling flat on my face in the mud."

"A good man to have around," Nettie said, following them. "When there's heavy-going."

Joe hesitated. Where had Nettie's kindness come from? Did she have any idea what that casual comment meant to him? She couldn't, of course, but her easy words smoothed some rough, raw spot inside him.

"Where's the star?" Oliver stood by the tree, ragtag and the worse for wear.

Joe groaned as Gabby retrieved a camera from a shelf and squinted through it.

Pictures.

Would this be a memory Oliver would want to keep in that scrapbook with his three pictures? Would it, too, curl and dim under the pressure of his son's fingers tracing the faces?

"Here's the O'Shea star." Milo sat on the sun-faded couch and motioned for Oliver to come over. "Listen," Milo whispered, and flicked his finger against the crystal.

The clear, pure *ping* made Oliver inhale. "Oh," he murmured, and leaned against Milo, enthralled.

"See, Oliver, how this hollow center will go over the point of the tree top?" The crystal shone, catching the reflection of the lights in the room, shooting rays of light back.

Oliver nodded, his eyes huge and dark. "And it will shine and anybody can find you."

"Right. Joe, you want to lift your boy up so he can stick the star up there? Right on the tippy-top."

Joe lifted his little son. Body shaking, Oliver clipped an arm around Joe's neck. "I'm going to put the *star* on the tree, Daddy," he whispered in awe. "I *never* done that before. The *Christmas* star."

Milo handed Joe the ornament, Gabby squinted through the camera, and Joe handed the crystal star to Oliver, who leaned forward and reached with both hands for the lovely piece of Irish workmanship.

A flash popped, Nettie laughed, and then, so fast Joe could only stretch out his hand, the crystal slipped through Oliver's hands and tumbled, end over end, sparkles of light flashing and shining as it fell.

Shards of crystal twinkled at Joe's feet.

The stunned silence in the room was the loudest sound he'd ever heard.

His son's cry was the most wrenching.

"Daddy!" Oliver screamed, and buried his head in the crook of Joe's neck. "I killed it, I killed the star!" His sobs were wrenching, deep and horrible.

Sorrow filling him, Joe clutched his son and whispered, "It's okay, Oliver. It's all right. You didn't kill it." As Oliver's sobs subsided to a steady, quiet racking of his small body, Joe lifted his head and glared at the assembled adults, daring them to—what?

Say something?

React with outrage?

Call the cops?

He didn't know, but no one was going to hurt his son with careless words, not over some damned trinket, even if it was the O'Shea Irish star and cost the earth.

Her scent came to him first, and suddenly Gabrielle stood beside him. Wrapping her arms around Oliver, she pressed her face against his shaking shoulder. "Shh, sweetie. Your daddy's right. You didn't kill it. It's only glass.'' Her eyes were shining with tears as she clung to his son, but she kept murmuring to Oliver, telling him over and over that no one was angry with him, that everything would be okay. "It was an accident, sweetie. Accidents happen to everybody.''

"But I killed the star!'' Oliver hiccuped and sobbed uncontrollably, tears smearing his cheeks. "I ruined Christmas!''

"No, you didn't,'' Gabby whispered, her voice catching. "You couldn't. Christmas is people. People make the magic, Oliver. Not things. Listen, sweetie, we'll find something else to put on top of the tree. You and I can talk about that tomorrow when we're baking cookies. If you decide that's what you want to do.''

"I want the star back,'' he wailed. "I want Christmas.''

"Milo, Gabby, I think it's time for us to leave. It's late. Oliver's overtired.'' Sweat pouring down his back, Joe ached to get Oliver safely away, ached to make his son's world right again.

He wondered if he could.

He had no magic to heal a little boy's heart.

And there was Gabby, tears trembling in her eyes, her face pale and devastated.

Damage here, serious damage, to both Gabrielle and his son.

"Gabby, I'll call you about—well, you know." Joe gestured vaguely toward the glass glittering against the hardwood floor. "I'm—sorry.''

"Joe, it's nothing. Please, don't worry about it.'' Still tear-filled, her eyes met his. "I don't want Oliver to lose any sleep over—over a bauble, hear me? And that's *all* it is. Was. A bauble.''

As she spoke, everyone moved, scattered, leaving them alone. Over Oliver's shoulder, Joe saw the back of Milo's head.

Stopping under the arch between the two rooms, Milo

looked back, his face gray, his eyes as devastated as Gabby's. "Hey, squirt?"

Oliver burrowed his face into Joe. Joe braced himself, ready to do battle for his child, even with an old man, his host.

Cracking, Milo's voice carried into the stillness. "You listen to me, Oliver, because I'm a whole lot older. I'm supposed to be wiser, too. Sometimes. You listening, young man?"

The burrowing halted.

"You're a good boy. I was honored to have you put our star on the tree. If I had it to do over, I'd hand that star right back to you. *You,* no one else. Got it?"

Oliver's nod was imperceptible. Joe didn't know if Milo could see the tiny movement.

"Now, you go on back to the hotel with your dad. Get a good night's sleep. Tomorrow, you'll see. Christmas hasn't been ruined." Milo's shoulders were stooped, and the energy that had driven him throughout the evening seemed dimmed as Joe watched him try to console the small boy. "See you in the morning, Oliver."

"I'll walk you and Oliver to your car, Joe. Give me a minute, okay?" Gabby patted Oliver on the back once more and hurried after her father, her narrow shoulders slumped.

"Fine." In Joe's arms, Oliver went limp with a shudder, laying his head on Joe's tear-damp shoulder. Calling after her, Joe said, "My suit coat's in the kitchen. I threw it on one of the chairs. I'll get Oliver's jacket."

Striding to the closet near the front door, Joe shifted Oliver to a dry shoulder. "How you doing, my man? You okay?"

"'Kay."

Joe worked Oliver's arms into the sleeves of his new jacket and grabbed his own suit coat from Gabby, stuffing it under his arm as he headed for the door.

"Joe, slow down." She tagged the back of his shirt.

He didn't want to look at Gabby, didn't want to talk to her. Even though she and Milo had minimized the situation, it was clear that the star had been more to her family than a piece of crystal. Through him, harm had come to Oliver. To Milo. To Gabby.

He should have heeded that initial sense of discomfort.

Should have known better than to come here. Should have known better than to let his guard down and forget. He didn't belong here, and neither did his son. No matter how Gabrielle O'Shea pretended otherwise.

"Really, Joe, everything is fine." Forcing him to halt, she pushed at his side until he faced her. "You and Oliver are *not* to give this a second thought," she said fiercely, poking him in the side. "And if you don't get that gloom-and-doom expression off your face, I'll never speak to you again."

Another solid jab between his ribs.

Hand on the doorknob, Joe said, "I hear you, Gabrielle. And my ribs are going to be bruised for a week." Twisting the knob, he sought for words. "I understand what you're trying to do, believe me. I appreciate the effort and the intent. But—" He stopped as Oliver's foot twitched against his waist. "This was a mistake. Anyway, thanks. We'll head to my car now. Better if you stay with your guests." He opened the door and stepped out into the night, grateful for the darkness and the cool air. Behind him, the screen door clattered shut.

He had one foot on the porch step.

"Don't run away, Joe." Quiet as star music, her voice came to him. "You don't have to. I want you to stay." Blurred by the screen mesh, her face, drawn and serene, was backlit by the lights from inside the house. Lumped at her feet, Cletis watched lazily as she touched the mesh. "You were our guest, too."

"Yeah. Thanks."

Her smile wobbled. "And you don't have to keep saying 'thanks.' Repeating yourself, you are. Picking up my bad habits, Joe."

"I don't know what else to say, Gabrielle." Helpless to

explain the evening's impact, he shrugged. "Go back inside. Where you belong." Softening the bluntness, he added, "It's chilly. You'll catch your death."

Her laugh was nothing more than a sigh of sound, wistful and lonely, and her hair floated like the clouds around the moon, all gauzy and lit with light. "My mama used to say that to me all the time."

"Go inside, sweet pea." He took the two steps in one stride and placed his free hand flat against the screen over hers. Through the scratchy mesh her skin was warm under his.

Her fingernails scrabbled against his palm. "Good night, Joe."

"Good night, Gabrielle."

"See you in the morning, Oliver." Her palm slipped past Joe's.

"'Kay" came the muffled answer.

During the drive back to the hotel, Oliver fell asleep, his head slumping onto the car door, the car seat keeping him upright. Joe pressed the button to lower the window slightly on the driver's side. Like a tranquil touch from an unseen hand, the cool, damp air blew against his face.

He would find some way to salvage Gabby's heirloom star. Hell, he had an importer friend in New York who made regular trips to Ireland. They could find a duplicate. A replacement. She would feel better.

And Oliver would see that problems could be solved, that the world didn't end with a mistake, with an accident.

The scent of oranges, pungent and sharp, drifted in with the damp air.

The replacement wouldn't be the star that had broken.

That was gone. Even Tommy Boyle couldn't possibly find a substitute for that lovely thing before Christmas.

Gabrielle swept up the bits of glass onto the dustpan. Tilting it, she let the chips and shards flow in a rainbow of colors into the original cardboard box.

"Honey, I'm sorrier than I can tell you," Milo said as he watched her. "Because I came up with a damn fool idea, I made you and Oliver miserable. The kid got to me, though, the way he and Cletis hid out and watched all of us, the little guy noticing everything with those big brown eyes and not bothering a soul. Every now and then, he'd check on Joe, then scoot back under the table. I thought the boy would enjoy having a special moment. Something to remember. I made a terrible misjudgment. Can you forgive a damn fool old man?"

"Pa, I'll survive." She blew her nose in the tissue he handed her. "It's a wonder the star lasted as long as it did. Any kind of bump could have shattered it. I'm surprised no one's dropped it before. I mean, sixty-three years. It's—it *was* almost as old as you." She couldn't find a smile, no matter how she struggled. "But, oh, Pa, I sure wish it had been one of us who'd dropped it instead of that poor child. What a burden for him. His sobs broke my heart. No matter what we said, he kept blaming himself. He took it so hard." She blew her nose again.

"I know, honey, I know. My heart went out to him, too. And to Joe. He looked like someone had hit him with a sledge-hammer. I know what that star meant to you, Gabrielle. It's a tough loss for you. And for me. Mary Kathleen's—"

Her lip trembled and she worked to gain control. "Yes," she whispered.

Her dad took the cardboard box from her slack hands, saying reluctantly, "You want me to pitch this in the trash?"

"No." Gabrielle carefully closed the lid and took back the box. "I can't do that. You couldn't, either."

"Sure doesn't seem right, but I don't know what else to do with all this glass." He let his hand linger against the burgundy box, stroking the smooth surface.

"It's not repairable, but I couldn't toss it out with the garbage. Holding it earlier tonight, I thought for a moment I felt Mama brushing her hand against mine.''

''Aw, honey.'' Milo bumped his forehead against hers as he gripped her hand. His eyes, like hers, were moist.

''Maybe I'll find a pretty jar and put the splinters and fragments in it. Turn it into a piece of modern art. What do you think?'' Clutching the box, she reached for another tissue.

''Whatever you want to do, honey, is fine with me. We can't change what happened, so if that's your attempt to make lemonade, go for it.''

She rattled the box and listened to the flat, scratching sound of broken glass, the *ping* gone forever. ''I'll clean up the kitchen and put the food away after everyone leaves. You're going to take Nettie home?'' Opening the drawer near the front door, she tucked the box inside. Packages of Cletis's treats were squashed around it.

''She came in a taxi. All right with you if I chauffeur her back to her place?'' Unsaid, but acknowledged now, the fact that her dad should have prepared her for Nettie Drew.

''Sure, Pa.'' She kissed him on the cheek. ''I think that would be a great idea.''

''Might take a while. She lives on the island.''

''Party on, Pa. I'm not going to wallow in melancholy.'' She swallowed the last of her tears and pitched the tissue in the trash. ''Don't worry about me. I suppose I should warn you not to stay out too late and remind you to check the gas before you leave, right?''

''Mouthy brat.'' He hugged her. ''You're my own special star, Gabrielle Marie, always.''

At his words, her eyes welled up abruptly, but she opened them wide so that tears wouldn't fall. No more tears tonight, at least not in front of her dad. If she had any tears left, she would save them for later, when she was alone.

With Joe and Oliver's departure, the party lost energy.

Shortly, people began filing out the door to choruses of "Great party, Milo" and "Good to have you home again, Gabrielle."

"Merry Christmas, everyone," she said brightly, waving farewell. "Thanks for coming." With every farewell, she thought of Oliver's face as the star had slipped through his childish hands, thought of Joe's posture, so fierce and protective as he'd held Oliver, and she thought, too, of Oliver and Joe, alone, in the sterile atmosphere of their hotel room.

And with every farewell, she heard her mother's voice.

Outside at midnight, saying her final goodbyes, Gabrielle lingered on the front porch, listening to the distant, deep chiming of church bells.

She'd forgotten this part of Christmas.

The scents, the flavors. The bells, that great, peaceful rolling-out of a sound that seemed to come from heaven itself.

Every night at midnight from December first through New Year's Eve, the church would ring its bells. How could she have forgotten this gift of Christmas?

Gabrielle stayed until the last sonorous gong died away, leaving the night quiet and serene under distant stars, real stars, not crystal symbols.

She stood for a long time in the silence with her face tipped up to those stars, letting the night seep into her and calm the storm of unhappiness inside her.

In that still, quiet sparkle of star shine, she knew that somewhere, in this universe or some other space and time, her mother's spirit watched over her.

Returning to the house, she grabbed a garbage bag and began collecting the debris from the party. In the living room, her dad and Nettie sat on the couch, talking, their faces serious. Nettie's shoulders angled toward Milo's, and his left arm lay along the back of the couch, millimeters away from Nettie.

"May I help you, Gabrielle?" Nettie rose.

"No, but thanks. There's not a lot left to clean up in the

kitchen. I cleaned as I went. Once I find room in the fridge for the leftovers, I'll call it a night."

"Four hands can carry faster than two." Nettie followed her into the dining room and picked up two platters.

"Six are better." Milo grabbed the empty jambalaya pot. "The three of us can make short work of this mess. Good thing you sent some leftovers home with Moon, honey. Think they'll last until morning?"

"Doubt it."

"Me, too. Moon's fairly passionate about his food."

Scraping salvageable leftovers into plastic bags and containers, Gabrielle moved swiftly from counter to sink and back as her dad and Nettie brought in the rest of the serving dishes.

Gabrielle, her mother and Milo had worked together after the tree-decorating parties as long as Gabrielle could remember, the cleanup sometimes more fun than the festivities.

She expected pangs of memories, that soreness around her heart to return, but the moments with her dad and Nettie were peculiarly comforting. Different, a reminder of loss, but—comforting.

Milo disappeared, saying he had to see a man about a dog, but Nettie remained, wiping the counters and table.

With the dishrag in her hand, Nettie faced Gabrielle. "I'm so sorry you were caught off guard. I wish Milo had told you that he and I are—"

"Dating?"

"I suppose that's the word. I can't think of a better one, but *dating* is not a word I'm comfortable with, not at my age." Behind Nettie's stylish, silver-rimmed glasses, her uncertain eyes met Gabrielle's. "I wish Milo had explained things first. So that you weren't surprised. That wasn't fair to you."

"Nor to you," Gabrielle admitted, grateful that the tightness around her heart had disappeared. Nettie Drew didn't deserve a cold shoulder from Milo's daughter. She was a good woman. Cultured, sensitive. *Nice*. Joe was right. "Pa didn't know how to tell me. So he avoided facing the issue, and it was too late. You were here.'' She took the dishrag, rinsed it and draped it over the spigot. Pressing it against the stainless steel, she said, ''I have to admit I was—surprised. Maybe hurt, a little. Not your fault,'' she said, waving Nettie silent. ''It was difficult at first, but Pa's happy around you. His happiness is important to me.''

''That's very generous of you.'' Nettie rubbed her hands along the edge of the counter hesitantly. ''But I realize how— how terribly awkward this situation has to be for you.'' Her index fingertips met in the center of the counter.

Gabrielle smiled and, reaching out, gave the woman a hug. ''As strange as it seems for my dad to be *dating,* I'm getting used to the idea. Give me time, that's all.''

''Time.'' Thoughtfully, Nettie took off her glasses and clipped the stems together. She held the glasses for a moment before saying, ''You're a lovely girl, Gabrielle. Mary Kathleen must have been so proud of you. I'm sorry I didn't know her. Milo loved your mother immensely. He still does.'' Her smile was rueful. ''I'm not Mary Kathleen, and I don't want to take her place with your father. I couldn't.''

''Pa's lonely, Nettie. I'm glad he met you.'' Gabrielle meant every word. She would find a way to handle the emptiness inside herself, this forlorn voice that cried out for someone to *need* her. ''This is hard to say, but I understand he needs more in his life than a grown-up daughter. A daughter isn't enough. You see, I decided he needed me, and I made decisions that affected him without listening carefully to what he was saying. I didn't really give him a chance to tell me about you.''

Nettie reached out, and her glasses bumped Gabrielle's wrist. ''But you haven't said what *you* need, Gabrielle. Did you see yourself taking care of Milo forever? Living here, letting your youth vanish year by year? Your intentions were admirable.'' Concern crumpled her face. ''But in the long run, would your plan have been good for you? Or, ultimately, for

Milo? No one welcomes becoming the altar of someone else's martyrdom.''

''Is that what I was doing?''

''I don't know. But your father might have believed that.'' Nettie tapped her wrist gently. ''You wouldn't have wanted him to think that. I don't imagine you saw yourself as a martyr.''

''No, I only wanted to help.''

''It's been my observation, Gabrielle, that sometimes the best way to help someone is to step back and let him help himself. Or herself.'' She unfolded the stems of her glasses and slid them over her ears and back into place. Behind the lenses, her bright blue eyes were shrewd and compassionate.

''Were you a counselor, Nettie?'' Gabrielle opened the refrigerator and moved the mayonnaise jar and a bottle of wine to make room for the last container of jambalaya.

''Oh, I still am. Part-time, though, but I love what I do. And work keeps my brain functioning. That and Ginkoba.'' Her smile was self-mocking. ''But I hope what I said didn't come across as interference. Or giving advice where none was sought?''

''No.'' Gabrielle leaned her forehead against the refrigerator. Had her dad seen her actions as martyrdom, as taking away his independence? Lifting her head, she smiled brightly in spite of the lump in her throat. ''I'm glad we had a chance to talk, to get to know each other a bit.''

''Me, too. I like you, Gabrielle. Milo is very special to me. I think we both want him to be happy. But your happiness is equally as important to Milo.'' She looked around the kitchen. ''Is there anything else I can do before your father drives me home? No?'' She gave Gabrielle a hug and a light kiss on the cheek. ''Good night. Thank you for your kindness to a stranger who came uninvited into your life.''

''You're easy to be kind to, Nettie.''

''Thank you, Gabrielle.'' Hesitantly, Nettie moved a plate

of fudge, frosted with green-and-red flowers, back and forth. "What do you know about Joe Carpenter?"

Astonished by the question, Gabrielle could only stare at her. Nettie had been on her way out the kitchen door, yet she'd stayed around to ask this completely out-of-the-blue question. "He moved here in high school, but he left before his senior year was over. I never heard why, though. He had a—reputation as a troublemaker, but I thought a lot of that reputation depended on smoke and mirrors. People talking and spreading gossip, but no one having the facts. That's about it. Why?"

Nettie's gaze was direct, the blue eyes piercing. "Because I think he's a man who hasn't had much kindness in his life. He stands on the edge of a group and watches, like a stranger. An outsider. He interests me. He and that boy of his. I like them both."

"So do I," Gabrielle whispered.

"Good." Nettie nodded as if something Gabrielle had said answered some unasked question. "Well." She paused. "And, Gabrielle, don't worry about your father. Good night again." And she was gone, the faint scent of lemony flowers remaining behind her, floating in on the cool air from the front of the house.

Nettie Drew left more than her scent behind—she left her friendship.

Outside, the low rumble of a car engine being started broke the stillness of the midnight hour. Milo, taking Nettie home.

As Gabrielle wiped the stove down and emptied the dishwasher, she considered Nettie's astonishing comments. An interesting woman, to spot Joe's stranger-in-a-strange-land aura so quickly.

Joe had never seemed at home in Bayou Bend.

Equally astonishing that he'd chosen to return here to raise his son.

Pushing her way through the kitchen door into the darkened hall, she headed toward the living room to check on the tree lights before going upstairs to bed. She walked through the hushed house, the glow of the Christmas lights pulling her forward, magic even without the star.

In the dim glow, she saw two figures and stopped suddenly, not entering the room. After starting the car, her dad had come back in to get Nettie. They stood close together in the archway between the living room and the front hall.

They were under the kissing bough Moon had hung there, their bodies forming one silhouette, moving together even as she watched.

The baggy sag of her dad's pants was that of an old man. But the passion in his embrace was that of a young man, vital, intense. It was the tenderness in his voice, though, that held Gabrielle motionless.

"Ah, Nettie, sweetheart," he said, the shadows shifting, moving as Gabrielle watched. "You make me want to wake up in the morning. You fill my life with sunshine. So much darkness. And now you. With me."

"Milo, Milo," Nettie murmured, her arms slipping around his neck to hold him closer. "You're my treasure, the best, best thing in my life. Ever."

Quietly, scarcely breathing, Gabrielle backed out of the hall into the kitchen, her heart drumming in her chest.

Letting the kitchen door swing silently closed behind her and making no noise, she dipped out a cup of the still-warm glogg. Sinking into one of the kitchen chairs, she dragged another closer. Lifting her feet onto the second chair and leaning her head back, she wiggled her toes luxuriously and stared at the ceiling.

Thoughts and feelings moved through her like a river current, lapping here, there, at her consciousness.

An exhaustion beyond the physical drained her of her last ounce of energy or will. She tasted the spicy glogg, breathed in its warm vapors.

As she sipped, she let her mind wander, let the events of

the evening swirl around, sort themselves out. Looked for the flow.

All in all, what a strange, unsettling night it had been.

Nettie and Milo.

Oliver.

Joe, the town's bad boy with a chip on his shoulder and attitude to burn.

Joe Carpenter, a man with a polished edge and a wary toughness lurking in the depths of his teasing brown eyes, a man who could make her heart pound like wild surf in a storm.

A man with a son who broke her heart.

Chapter Seven

"**D**addy!" Oliver streaked to Joe and glommed onto his leg.

"Hey there, squirt. Missed you."

"Me one, me too." Oliver rubbed his face against Joe's jeans. "I have to finish my cookie." He trotted back to the O'Sheas' kitchen table, and Joe followed, one hand on his son's flour-stiff hair, relief flooding him.

Earlier, he'd been reluctant to leave Oliver, but, pinch-faced and withdrawn, Oliver had insisted he wanted to see Cletis and make cookies. Even if he did have to stay with Gabrielle.

"Gabby's one of the good guys, Oliver."

"Maybe. Maybe not. But I'll stay. Cletis wants to see me," Oliver had said, sighing heavily. "So I gotta go."

But the boy had stayed at the screen door, pressing his face against the mesh, Cletis on his feet. As Joe drove away, his son's reflection remained in the car's side mirror until the end of the driveway curved and Oliver was out of sight.

Now, obviously Gabby had worked some kind of magic on Oliver in the meantime, and Joe was grateful. Nothing he'd

said last night as he tucked Oliver into bed had helped. Whatever Gabby had said to the boy or done with him today had
worked, and Joe felt an enormous load lift from his spirits.

As he entered the kitchen, she looked up, arrested in the
middle of plopping a spoonful of manila-colored dough onto
a cookie sheet.

"Nice makeup, sweet pea." Joe traced the line of white
flour down her cheek, over her chin and to the curved neck
of her sleeveless dark green T-shirt. Streaks of flour decorated
her faded navy shorts, collected in the cuffs. "In a Kabuki
mood today?" Her skin was soft, yielding under the dusting
of flour. "Hmm. What's this?" He touched his fingertip to a
sparkly grain and licked. "Sweet. Sugar."

"Me?" Gabby batted his hand away.

"You? Nah." He licked his finger again. "The sugar, of
course. What did you think I meant?" He had meant her, of
course, the taste of her sugared skin lingering in his mouth.
He should have resisted that tiny indulgence. But he hadn't
expected the taste of her skin under the sweetness of the sugar.
He'd meant only to tease, but the joke had turned on him,
leaving him with a hunger sugar wouldn't begin to satisfy.

Shining brilliantly through the open windows, the sun
washed the planks of the floor with gold, chased shadows into
the far corners.

On a day like this, small indulgences could be forgiven, he
decided, because some hungers were destined to go unfed.
That was okay. He'd plotted his course. He could live with
his decisions.

At least in the warm sunshine of Gabby's kitchen, he could.

Loneliness hit harder in the cold night, though. Made it
harder for a man to remember what he knew he had to do.

"Me and Gabby made cookies." Oliver held up a heavily
frosted sugar cookie tree. Colored sprinkles dotted the floor
and crunched under his sneakers as he bounced up and down.
"Here, Daddy. I made this one special for you."

"Delicious." Joe choked down the thick cookie. Actually, underneath the six feet of icing and decorations, the cookie was good. If you wanted to commit suicide by sugar, that is. He lifted Oliver into his arms. Sugary hands planted themselves on each side of his face, and Oliver smacked a kiss on his cheek. "How was the morning?"

"'Kay." Oliver settled against his hip.

"'Kay," Gabby said, half a beat behind Oliver. Lingering at the table, she rested one bare, tanned foot on the rung of the chair beside her. Her pink toenails and feet sparkled with sugar bits. "We melted crayons and ironed paper over them. Christmas wrapping paper," she explained seriously. "For presents. Oliver and I were doing a Martha Stewart day." Gabby held up a waxy purple-and-pink piece of tissue paper. Gold glitter poured off it onto the floor.

"Festive." One of the purple blobs looked a lot like a Christmas tree.

"We thought so. Right?" She laid the paper off to the side, away from flour and sugar but near Oliver and Joe.

"Yeah." Leaning forward in Joe's arms, Oliver swooped to the floor and smashed his hand against the glitter. He brushed his hands clean over the tissue with a happy sigh. "There."

"We baked half a million cookies, and we kept Cletis off the counter," Gabrielle added.

"Mostly," Oliver confided in a whisper to Joe. "But not always. And I gave him munchies. Lots."

"Cletis throw up much?" Joe nudged the collapsed fur heap under the table with his foot.

"Once or twice." Flour puffed in a cloud as she dropped a scoop back into a container. "We coped."

"I'll bet." Joe liked the way the sunlight gilded her skin and touched the hair along her temples with gold. "Milo and I ate lunch."

She paused, the rolling pin in her hand, as if she was about to ask him about their conversation. Instead, she said, "Coffee? Lunch? Gee, you guys know how to make a day-long feast." Rolling pin and flour container in hand, she danced by him, her topknot of hair flopping with each step. "Wild men. Layabouts." Dusting her hands over the sink, she said sternly, "We, however, have worked all day like dogs and have not eaten. Oliver and I expect high-class cuisine for our efforts, right, sweetie?"

Oliver nodded. "Def'nitely."

Joe smiled. At some point Oliver had picked up Gabby's *definitely* and made it his own.

He squirmed, and Joe swung him down to the floor. Circling Joe's thigh with an arm, Oliver leaned against him companionably, saying, "Hamburgers. Apple pie. Milk shakes. High-class—stuff."

"Where's Pa?" Gabby asked, making another round trip from sink to table and back. Opening the oven door, she shoved in the dough-spotted aluminum sheet and set a timer. "Did he come home with you?"

"He said he had errands."

"Nettie."

"That would be my guess. He took off like a bat out of—"

"A cave?" Gabby's smile melted over him like hot fudge, beguiling and seductive and completely unselfconscious.

"Yeah. I saw him slicking back a strand of hair to cover that kind-of-thin spot at the top of his head, so I figured he was off to see the lovely Nettie. Since he was so interested in his appearance."

"Mean, Joe." Gabby slapped him on the arm. "Pa prides himself on his manly mane. What if your hair started thinning?"

"I'd buy a whole new collection of baseball caps. Or I'd do the Michael Jordan look." He mashed his hair back with both hands. "What do you think?"

"If you could slam dunk, it might work for you, but, gee,

Joe, it's not quite you.'' She wrinkled her nose. ''Good luck. I hope you inherited good, hairy genes.''

''Hairy jeans?'' Oliver covered his mouth and hooted. ''You'd have to get your jeans cut and your hair cut and you'd have to shampoo your jeans. That's silly, Gabby.''

Strolling to the sink with the last of the containers, Gabby laughed and thumped him cordially on the head. ''Show some respect, youngster, for those of us one step away from Medicare.''

Oliver's solemn eyes searched her face. ''You're old, but not as old as Milo. Are you?''

Joe sputtered, Gabby laughed.

''No, sweetie, not as old as my dad, thank you very much.''

''I didn't think so. Milo's *very* old, older than anybody.''

''Oh, if Pa could hear little pictures speaking.'' Turning on the water, she said, ''Of course, it would kill his image of himself. And, speaking of Pa, he's interested in Nettie.'' Not looking at Joe, she asked, ''Did you know? Did Moon or Milo tell you?''

''About Nettie?'' Joe had picked up the vibrations from the two and found the idea of Milo and Nettie rather touching. A winter love, a Christmas love between two people who hadn't expected passion to enter their lives again and had, unexpectedly, found each other. ''No, Gabby, neither Moon nor Milo said anything to me about Nettie.''

''Doesn't matter. I saw them last night. Milo and Nettie. Mistletoe. Kissing.''

''I get the picture.''

''Probably not, Joe.'' Her expression as she scrubbed her hands under the running water was contemplative. ''It was quite—touching.''

''You okay with it, sweet pea? Senior citizen romance?''

''I think I am. But, let me tell you, there was nothing senior citizenish about them, Joe.'' Her voice turned wistful. ''I stayed awake a long time last night, thinking.''

"Me, too. Not that all that brain-straining did me any good," he muttered, watching the silvery spray of water and the movement of her hands under it, reminded once again of his resolution that seemed to last only as long as he wasn't around Gabby. "How about you?"

"I believe I have some things sorted out. Maybe." She turned off the faucet and lifted her dripping arms up. Water slid in a glistening rivulet down the inner sides of her arms and she shivered. "Life's full of curve balls, isn't it?"

With Oliver clamped onto his leg, Joe followed her to the sink, handed her a paper towel. "Want to go Christmas shopping?"

"Me?" She turned so suddenly that his hand slid along her hip, settled against her fanny, the linen fabric of her shorts nubby against his touch.

He wanted to cup the sweet, slight curve of her hip where it sloped into her rear, draw her up against him, thigh to thigh.

Stepping back abruptly, he bumped into Oliver. Joe cleared his throat. He thought he'd settled that argument between his libido and his brain during the late-night hours after he and Oliver had returned to the hotel. Looked like that had only been round three of what apparently was going to be a hell-raiser of a battle.

Gabby followed him. "You're inviting me to lunch?"

"Hey, I can recognize a hint when I hear one."

"I'll remember that you can take a hint. In case I ever need that information." Again that slow, soft smile.

She was flirting with him. He caught that hint, too. They had agreed flirting was okay. But that was before his hormones and his good sense had struggled to the death. He and Gabby could be friends.

But no matter what he and Gabby had decided, Joe knew friends couldn't flirt. And last night he'd made that brutally plain to that feisty maverick romping through his blood and hog-tying his conscience and reason.

As he kept stepping back, she kept following, and Joe felt a line of sweat build up along his hairline.

Sweet, innocent Gabby couldn't realize what she was doing to him.

"Come on, squirt, let's get you out of harm's way." Lifting Oliver again, using his son as a shield between a shorts-clad, bare-legged Gabby who made his mouth water, Joe answered, "Sure. Lunch. You. Me. Squirt, here. Payback for a morning spent kid-sitting, okay?" Friends needed to pay back favors. Everything equal, balanced. That was how friendship worked, especially if he was going to make this man-woman friendship work with Gabby. "Lunch at some fine dining establishment with arches and fries."

"And hamburgers." Oliver leaned over backward, his head not far from the floor. "I love hamburgers and fries and cola and pie and—"

"Sure this child isn't related to Moon?" Gabby giggled and caught Oliver's arms as he swung them in mad circles.

That, of course, was the sixty-four-thousand-dollar question. Did Joe really want to know who Oliver was related to? And would it matter if he left that question unanswered?

To Oliver?

To himself?

What if, as he suspected, Oliver wasn't his son, not by birth, anyway. What if Jana had merely put Joe's name on the birth certificate for convenience, or for some perverse reason of her own?

If she had been that cruel, how would her decision alter his and Oliver's lives? Because it would. Wheels within wheels, but he'd die before he'd let any more hurt come to this boy.

As the silence lengthened, Gabby glanced at him, puzzled. "You know, Joe. Moon and his voracious appetite for anything animal, vegetable or even mineral?"

"Yeah. I'd forgotten about Moon's primary passion in life." Joe swung Oliver upright. The kid was like a rubber monkey, bending and contorting his small frame in Joe's arms. "You that hungry, guy? Hungry as old Moon man?"

"More hungry, a gazillion times more hungry," chanted an upside-down-again Oliver.

"That's that. We're going on an adventure." Whirling out of the room, Gabby left them.

Joe scarcely had time to wipe Oliver's face and hands before she reappeared. Some kind of pin scooped her hair back on one side. Every time she moved, the bells on the pin jingled. Slim stretchy black pants shaped her thighs and calves. He liked the snowflake cutouts sprinkled on the red sweatshirt hanging past her hips. When she bent over to slip into her shoes, the sweatshirt rode up and treated him to the sight of Gabby's very tidily curved rear end. Stretchy black pants might turn out to be his favorite female fashion.

In the gap between her black shoes and pants, white reindeer pranced across the ankles of her black socks. The lead reindeer sported a shiny red nose. Gabby was literally throwing herself head over heels into the spirit of the season. He gestured ankleward. "St. Patrick's Day socks, too?"

"And Halloween and Valentine's Day."

"I'm speechless."

"I noticed," she said dryly. "What's wrong with celebrating? I like holidays. I like celebrating." Slinging a black purse embroidered with three elf angels over her shoulder, she said, "Who's driving?"

"Since I can all too easily picture your car with a miniature Santa Claus and reindeer leaping across your dashboard, I'll drive."

"When did you become so conservative, Joe Carpenter?" She fluffed her hair free of the neck of her sweatshirt.

"Guess I'm not into the season the way you are. If it doesn't move, I swear you'd put a bow on it."

"Golly, until you brought the idea up, though, I hadn't

thought about the car,'' she mused. "Maybe I'll put a wreath on the front bumper. What do you think, Oliver?''

"Cool,'' he breathed.

Joe figured Oliver would be insisting on a wreath and dash decorations before the day was over.

An hour later in the washroom at Bayou Bend's local hamburger palace, Oliver hitched up his pants. "Guess what else I did today?''

Joe helped him cram his shirt inside his jeans and buckle up. "Damned if I know. Made a Santa Claus hat for Cletis?''

"Cletis would not like that. He would feel silly.''

"Yeah, well, I can understand that. Wash your hands, squirt.''

"I don't see handles.'' Oliver rested his chin on the side of the sink.

"Stand here. Right in front of this round circle in the wall. It's a sensor. To turn the water on and off.''

"Cool.'' Standing on tiptoe, Oliver stuck his hands under the spray of water, moving back and forth as the water stopped and started.

"That's enough. We don't want Florida to turn into a desert.'' Joe took the rough brown paper and dried Oliver's obediently outthrust hands. "So you didn't make Santa Claus hats. What did you make?''

Oliver bent at the waist to peer under the stalls. Seeing no one, he whispered, "A present. For Gabby and Milo and Cletis.''

"Did Gabby help?''

"No. It's a surprise. But she will like it,'' Oliver confided as Joe pushed the door open and they exited. "You can't tell Gabby I made a present. Christmas is for secrets. And this is a bi-i-ig secret.'' He stretched his arms as far out as they would go. "Promise?''

"I promise.'' Joe wondered what glitter-sprinkled, flour-dusted creation his son had come up with. "You're feeling better, squirt? About last night? And about me going off with Milo this morning?''

''Def'nitely.''

''Because I wouldn't have left you at Gabby's if you hadn't been okay with it.''

'''Course not.'' Oliver trotted by his side back to the wrapper-strewn table where Gabby waited for them. ''Now I want to go into the ball cage. You come with me. Gabby, too,'' he offered.

Gabrielle watched the Carpenter men approach her. Joe's head was bent toward his son, Oliver's face was uplifted to his father. Joe had slowed his long stride to match the boy's hop, skip and jump. Joe's oatmeal beige, long-sleeved shirt was folded at the cuffs, and water spots marked the front. Hard to be a *GQ* guy with a six-year-old.

Interesting that the jeans-clad, leather-jacketed Joe had become this man in conservative, expensive clothes. She recognized the cut and fit of expensive tailoring when she saw it, and Joe's slacks and shirt made her long to touch their beautiful fabric, see how it felt against her skin.

Clothes like that made a woman think about the man beneath them.

But long ago, she'd dreamed about Joe in his leather jacket and tight jeans, too.

Joe and Oliver both looked at her as they stood beside the table, their expressions so similar she almost laughed. ''That was fast.''

''Unlike the females of our species, men don't take a lot of time lollygagging. We're efficient.'' Joe didn't look down at Oliver, who'd clamped his hands over his mouth.

''Ah. Getting even with me for my layabout accusation, are you?'' She wadded up wrappers and stuck them on the tray. ''Plus leaving cleanup duty for me. You don't think that's carrying revenge too far?'' She dumped the tray's contents into a nearby bin, then placed the tray on top.

"Revenge?" Joe opened his eyes wide and looked innocently down at Oliver, who was hopping from foot to foot, his hands still clamped over his mouth. "Would two gentlemen like us be interested in revenge?"

"Yeah!" Oliver exploded. "But *you* was the layabout, not me. I worked."

"Go play in the ball cage, squirt. You've betrayed me. I'm crushed. Where's the loyalty these days?"

Oliver hooked onto Joe's hand.

"And gentlemen would help clean up." Gabrielle handed Joe a cardboard pie container. "Pitch it, buster."

He did. "Gosh, I sure do like a bossy woman. Something mighty appealing about a woman who knows her own mind. Makes a man start to fantasize—"

"Hush up." That dratted red flushed her skin again with his sly look, and she swatted him with her purse.

"I hear and obey."

"Right," she muttered under her breath. "Like I'd believe that."

He smoothed the wide strap of her purse where it had twisted over her shoulder. "Hey, I know my place."

She might have believed him if his touch hadn't lingered underneath the fabric strap, might have believed him if he hadn't been standing right within her space. She might have believed him if she hadn't seen the hunger flickering like eddies in the deep currents of his dark eyes.

Even with her inexperience, she recognized that expression.

Abruptly, breaking their linked gazes, Joe gave his son a slight nudge toward the tall wire cage before turning to her. "Coming? Or do you want to meet us later? Do some shopping?"

"I'll watch."

Bending down, he murmured, "You don't have to. You've earned your angel's wings for this morning." His breath slid against the curve of her ear and sent shivers down the length of her spine. "You and Cletis. I reckon we shouldn't leave him out." Laughter moved in his brown eyes as he watched her. Thin and elegant, his mouth lifted at one corner in amusement, and she wanted to smooth her fingers over the supple line of his upper lip.

"Oliver and Cletis have bonded. Cletis sold his loyalty for munchies. He follows Oliver around with this mournful, hopeful expression on his face and his tail in a question mark. But I think a winged Cletis would have as much chance of going airborne as a penguin would."

"That's an image that could give me nightmares. Cletis with wings and a halo." Holding Oliver with one hand, Joe placed his other hand against her waist, palm flat, just as he'd done the night before while guiding her through the throng of holiday-merrymakers.

And, exactly as before, her tummy fluttered, sensations curling through her, and her knees went slack. All these lovely feelings running riot in her blood, and she'd lived all her life without experiencing them before. Oh, a tingle every now and then, but nothing like this awareness of her skin, of her breasts, of every part of her. Like a parched flower, her body thirsted for his touch, for him.

But last night she'd understood the between-the-lines message, loudly and clearly. He'd said flirting didn't mean anything, not from his point of view, anyway.

Hard not to understand then that he was warning her off, letting her know he didn't mean anything with his teasing, sexually charged behavior, and so she'd fallen back on pride and zipped her own message back, her very own little devil making her say that Joe shouldn't expect anything from her, either—like sex.

She would have loved a photograph of his face when she'd tossed that into the conversation. She'd known that would stop his foolishly noble attempt to make sure she understood the difference between the town's very bad boy and its good girl.

Well, he'd changed during the last eleven years, and so had she.

Life could pass a woman by while she was waiting for it to begin.

Sometimes a woman had to know when she'd wasted enough time.

And maybe even reformed bad boys could learn a thing or two from a good girl who was looking to be a little bad.

With him.

Even good girls who weren't skilled at flirting could yearn to be naughty.

The idea intrigued her and slowed her steps. If Joe could rock her world with a touch, a look, not even trying, what would happen if she turned the tables on him?

A spark of mischief prompted her to slide her arm around his waist.

He stopped midstride, looked at her, frowning. "Gabby?"

A few yards ahead of them, Oliver shed socks and tennis shoes, tucking them into one of the cubbyholes in a row of blue shelves. With a determined look on his face, he climbed the two steps to the cage and silently pitched himself face first into the pool of multicolored balls.

"Yes, Joe?" She smiled brightly and held on for dear life, every nonaggressive cell in her body shrieking with terror. "What were you saying?"

"Nothing." Contemplating her, obviously thinking the situation through, he continued to frown. "Whoa," he said suddenly, pulling her out of the way of a careering tot chugging gaily forward. Joe's arm stayed, lightly, carelessly, though, around Gabrielle's shoulders.

"Thanks." That her voice was calm was an act of will and maturity, because her pulse skidded and leaped like grease on a hot skillet. Her body flushed from head to toe, and she stepped closer, again surprising a frown from him. She smiled.

"The barbarian hordes," she said, gesturing to the rampaging children swarming around them.

"Yeah. Uh, Gabby?"

"Yes, Joe?" She tipped her head back, brushed her hair off her cheek. Her silver angel earrings swung in a cool sweep along her jaw.

His frown creased a vee in his forehead, drawing his dark eyebrows together as he regarded her. He finally shrugged. "Nothing, I reckon." But his expression as he glanced away remained puzzled.

She liked this unexpected sense of power over him, liked the novelty of throwing him off balance.

Moth to the candle, exhilarated, she dipped and floated, aware with every second of the candle's heat, the danger. And with every passing second, her damnable curiosity urged her to hover ever closer to that bright flame, to see if it really burned as hot as it shone.

"Oops." She brushed her hand across the front of his shirt, scraped her fingernail near the pocket. "Ketchup," she explained as he jerked under her touch. "You'll have to soak the spot in cold water."

"Yeah." He watched her grimly.

"Or you could send it to the cleaners," she offered helpfully. His chest had been hard, the muscles tight to her touch.

"I could do that." He took a step back, propping himself against the edge of one of the round tables, and crossed his arms.

Something gleamed in his eyes, and Gabrielle caught the tail end of a second thought, hung on and stayed where she was. That gleam was pure, undiluted trouble.

"Send a lot of your stuff to the cleaners, do you, Joe?"

"That's what single guys do. Unless they have time to do their own laundry."

"You don't?" Keeping her distance, she let the conversation drift where it would while she collected her courage for another swoop toward the flame. "Have time?" Her tongue tangled over the simple syllables as his glance, intense and amused, speared her. "I mean, your job keeps you busy?"

"Milo asked the same question." A slight edge iced his voice. "About my livelihood."

"Right." She plucked at the hem of her sweatshirt, dug at one of the appliqués, trying to identify the exact moment he'd left the state of bewilderment and entered the county of back-in-control. She crossed her arms, aware with each movement of his gaze. Everything puckered to a delicious tightness and she shifted uncomfortably. "And what did you tell Pa?"

"That my job keeps me busy. That I've taken time off to be with Oliver." He leaned forward, cupped her chin and lifted it. "And, sweet pea, if you're interested, I work for myself."

"Oh. That's—nice." She'd never thought of the chin as an erogenous zone. Not until this moment, at least. "What kind of work is that, Joe?"

"I started a computer hacker company."

"Hacking's illegal. Isn't it?"

A slight, unexpected hostility replaced the amusement in his face. "You checking me out, too, Gabby? Like Milo?"

"What do you mean?" Gabrielle tried to see beneath the edginess. Like an old wound, pain was still there in Joe Carpenter, a pain she'd never understood, still didn't. Whatever the burdens of the past were, they needed to be put down. "You thought Pa wanted to check up on you?"

"Milo had legitimate questions. I answered them."

"And because he wanted to visit with you, you saw it as an interrogation? Pa's a lawyer. Asking questions is as natural to him as—as *breathing*. It's not personal. It's not interrogation, for heaven's sake."

"But isn't that what Bayou Bend would expect? That I'd be mixed up in something illegal? Something shady? Isn't that what everyone would predict for Hank Carpenter's troublemaking son?'' His mouth a tight line, he angled for a better view of Oliver.

"So you advise companies on how to keep hackers out of their systems?"

"Bingo, sweet pea. Got it in one."

"Well, why didn't you say so at the beginning? So when did you start this company?" Exasperated, she scowled at him. She was missing something. "I mean, asking someone about his business is not the equivalent of taking a deposition, even from Pa."

His shrug was tense, controlled. "But I doubt anyone but you would opt for that interpretation right off. I suspect most everyone else would expect me to be breaking into computers. Or heisting them. And for anyone who's interested, I started my business six years ago, and it's been successful. Any other questions?"

Distressed by the shadow of bitterness that moved over him, she smoothed her hand down his arm. The emotion emanating from him swamped her and made everything else unimportant. "Joe, I don't know what drove you away from this town. Over and over you tell me that Bayou Bend is where you want to raise your son, but I don't get it. Why would you come back here if you believe everyone mistrusts you and thinks the worst of you? You wouldn't put Oliver in that kind of situation, not if you truly believed that this town has turned its collective back on you. Something, *some* memory brought you back here. Nothing else makes sense to me."

"What a good girl you are, Gabrielle. First Jana. Now me. You'd give the devil himself the benefit of the doubt, wouldn't you?" His mouth twitched in a semblance of a smile, but there was no humor in it.

In front of them, solemnly leaping out of the pool of balls, Oliver waved to them, dived back under.

She gripped Joe's shirt, crumpling the smooth fabric in her fist. "Listen to me, Carpenter. I told you once before, but you didn't hear me. Or didn't listen. Contrary to whatever you think of me, I'm *not* naive. I'm not stupid.''

"I never said you were stupid," he drawled, unfolding her fingers one by one. "Never believed you were, either."

"But you've locked onto this idiotic idea that I'm naive, and that being naive, I err when I look for a positive interpretation of an event, don't you?'' Her sweetness was acid-etched.

"You're innocent as a fresh-hatched baby turtle, Gabby. No more ability to protect yourself against the evil and nastiness in the world than those poor baby hatchlings scrabbling for the safety of the ocean.''

"Lovely image you have of me, Joe." Funny, too, because that's how she had pictured Jana for an instant, leaving her infant as unprotected as those fragile turtles. Well, Gabrielle didn't care one bit for Joe's vision of her as naive and child-like. "A real ego-booster that you see me as this fragile, 'barely one step away from a fainting couch,' pathetic, help-less little female who's too naive and innocent to be respon-sible for herself? That about cover it, bub?'' She gave him a good shake for the sake of principle.

"Gabby, look, you haven't lived in the same world I have. All my life. You've been raised in a nice town with nice par-ents and nothing nasty lurking in the closets of your bedroom. If you saw monsters in the night, why, I expect both your parents tripped over themselves to get to you and shoo away the scaries."

"Yes, I've been lucky. I wouldn't deny it for all the money in the world. And maybe what you imply is true. If I hadn't had the kind of family that I did, well, maybe I'd see life through darker glasses. But maybe I wouldn't. Because life gives us choices." She wadded his shirt even tighter and jerked. "Smarter, more sophisticated to look for the hidden agenda? Is that how you choose to live? Because that's one of the choices, Carpenter. How we see the world around us.

Is that your view of the world? The one you want Oliver to pick up from you?''

Joe tightened his mouth, but she had his full attention.

"You want your son to think that everybody's an enemy? That every time you turn the corner, the first person you see will have a contract out on you? Is that your world view?'' she repeated, shaking him hard, anger ripping through her that he could be so blind to all the goodness and kindness out there waiting for him if he'd only take a chance and come out from behind the wall he put between himself and everyone but Oliver. "Because it's not mine."

"I know it isn't, Gabrielle. And that's quite a speech. Are you thinking of taking up the pulpit?'' His voice was gentle as he tucked a strand of her hair behind her ear.

"Don't you dare make fun of me.'' She glared at him. "You don't have the right. You haven't walked in my shoes. And because I haven't walked in yours, I'm willing to cut you some slack. Think you could do the same?''

"You're fiercely loyal, you *choose*—'' his smile almost broke her heart "—to believe the best, even of me, and you see the world as rich with possibilities and happy endings.''

"I know life isn't a fairy tale.'' Fury licked through her, singeing every nerve ending. How could he reduce her life to such a simplistic interpretation?

"Do you, sweet pea?''

She nodded so hard, her forehead slapped against his chest.

"See, I don't.'' As if he were comforting her, Joe continued stroking her hair, tidying up the strands that had flown wildly as she'd tried to make him see that life didn't have to be lived with suspicions and behind walls. "Because the only happy endings I've ever seen were in books and movies. Not in real life. Life experience has taught me that truth. And I'm a good student.''

"This is what you'll teach Oliver, too, Joe.'' She trapped his wrists. "What a sad, lonely legacy to leave your son. Because that's the legacy he will carry with him long after you're gone.''

Joe's head turned toward the ball cage. His eyes narrowed as he watched Oliver bounce up and down, flop back under the balls, leap back up. All alone, Oliver bounced and dived, bounced. Dived.

Alone.

Once more that sharp pain sliced through Gabrielle. She couldn't fix Joe's problems, no matter how much she yearned to.

Only he could.

And if he didn't? Couldn't? If the past couldn't be forgotten, forgiven?

Ah, she thought, clasping his strong wrists, there would be the real tragedy.

Dimly, she grasped that his tragedy could become hers, too.

Chapter Eight

Gabrielle expected that the rest of the day would be ruined after her outburst. She should have known Joe wouldn't let the atmosphere remain supercharged with tension. That wasn't his way. Lightly, good-naturedly, keeping away from emotional deep waters, he stayed behind his mask of charm.

There were moments years ago when she'd glimpsed the bitterness and pain he usually kept hidden. She'd witnessed accidental ruptures in the facade he'd created.

Had that long-lost nineteen-year-old man, with his leather jacket and attitude, been only a facade, too? One she'd sensed but had never gotten to know because he kept everyone at arm's length with aggression and flippant sexuality?

Like Oliver, when she'd first met him, staking out territory, had Joe claimed his own domain over the years, a place where he felt safe? Easier to keep folks at arm's length than to risk rejection.

Easier to reject them first.

Putting yourself at risk was opening yourself to enormous pain.

At thirteen, when she'd first seen him, she'd sensed that, sensed the shadows in him, but at fifteen, on the cusp of understanding, she'd been overwhelmed by the pure, raw power of Joe Carpenter's masculinity. And then he'd disappeared, taking his shadows and mystery with him and leaving her with this sense of some other land faintly seen, a land that called to her in dreams, her arms outstretched in a futile search, the shores of that distant place receding with daylight and business.

Christmas was a time to step away from the shadows, to rejoice in the light and promise of the season. No matter what he said, Joe had returned to Bayou Bend to close a circle. He'd come home.

Like her, he'd come back in search of a missing piece at the core of himself. She'd arrived at a crossroads in her life. Because looking after her dad had seemed like an answer, she'd grabbed at the excuse. Joe's excuse had been Oliver's need for small-town values. She was determined to find out what Joe's own need was.

They shopped. They snacked again in the food court. They shopped. Finally, when she thought she'd fall in a heap, to heck with the shop-till-you-drop mantra, Oliver asked in a mumbled aside for her help picking out a present for Joe. Still keeping a cautious reserve, though, Oliver didn't take her hand.

"Will you help me? 'Cause daddy can't be with me. Or it won't be a secret."

"Do you need money?" she whispered, stooping down. "I can loan you some. You can pay the loan back by brushing and feeding Cletis."

"I have five dollars." Oliver unzipped the wallet hanging by a cord around his neck. "See?"

Peering inside, she inspected the wad of singles, coins and a picture with ragged edges. "That should be enough." She patted the wallet. "Zip up your money bag and tuck it back under your shirt. Nice picture,'' she added casually, standing up.

Oliver regarded her warily. "It's mine."

"Of course it is, sweetie. Maybe sometime you'll show it to me. I'd like to know who the baby is. You?"

"Maybe." Oliver snicked the plastic zipper shut.

She'd caught a quick impression of a pale-haired woman pushing a baby stroller. If the baby was Oliver, the woman most certainly was Jana. Even though Gabrielle doubted that he remembered his mother, the picture meant something to him. A treasure.

"Joe," she said, turning to him and tugging at the hem of her sweatshirt, "Oliver and I are going on a scouting mission. We have important business ahead of us. See you later."

Joe squatted beside Oliver, said something Gabrielle didn't hear and gave his son a hug. "Sure?"

"Yeah."

"All right, then. Meet y'all at the exit in an hour?"

Gabrielle nodded. She hoped Oliver would find what he wanted in an hour. From what she'd observed of him so far, he was very deliberate about his decisions. Which tree, what sprinkles to put on cookies—the boy thought situations through at his own pace. She didn't want to hurry him, not on this particular decision, so she said to Joe, "If we're not there, call me on the cell phone. There's a pay phone near the exit. That way you won't worry, and Oliver won't feel rushed. Shopping's serious business, in case you didn't know." She scribbled out the number on a paper napkin.

Joe gave Oliver a slow wink. "I might do some shopping of my own."

Oliver studied him and then said, "You don't have to get me any presents. Santa Claus will bring everything this year."

"Yeah. But since I kind of like you, maybe I want to give you a present, too. Your first present from me."

"You bought me my shoes." Oliver stuck out a foot. Clots

of cookie dough and dirt spotted the less-than-spanking-new white.

"That was a dad present. Not an under-the-tree present." Joe's palm curved over his son's head, lingered. "This will be a special present from me to you, because this is a special Christmas. We'll be spending it together. We've never done that before. We need to celebrate." Joe glanced at Gabrielle. "I've been told celebrations are important."

"'Kay." Oliver hopped forward, backward. "A present for under the tree. Cool."

The poignancy of Joe's efforts to make his son's world perfect moved Gabrielle to press her hand against Joe's chest, smooth out the wrinkles she'd put in his shirt. "So you did hear what I said. When I leaped up onto my soap box."

"I pay attention to everything you say, sweet pea. I listen closely to what you tell me, to the words you use. And to the ones you don't use." His tone was nonchalant, his body language relaxed, but the rueful sincerity in his slight smile moved her in a way none of his sexy teasing had. This admission was one more crack in his diligently guarded mask. A gift, in a way, to her. "As a result of listening to excellent advice, I decided my son needed an exceptional present."

"Big job you're taking on, trying to find that kind of present. Whole lot of pressure you're putting on yourself, cowboy. Good luck." Impulsively, she raised herself on her tiptoes and pressed a kiss against his cheek. "You're something special, Joe Carpenter."

His cheek was scratchy under her lips, and before she stepped away, he turned and met her mouth with his, briefly, a brush of lips, firm, sculpted, turning hers softer and more yielding than she'd intended, transforming a friendly kiss into something else.

If she'd been in a movie, she would have heard bells, swelling music.

What she heard was her own swift intake of air, the leap of

her heart as Joe's mouth covered hers. She heard the sound of Christmas sparkling through her with every beat of her wayward heart.

In the middle of a crowded mall, she heard magic.

Her legs trembled. Her heels snapped against the tile floor. She opened her eyes and stepped back. "Um. Oliver and I should, hmm—" Her brain went blank. Her mouth still felt the shape of Joe Carpenter's mouth against hers.

"Go shopping?" Nothing simple in the dark depths of his eyes this time as he spoke, only a swirl of confusion. He lifted a hand toward her, let it fall to his side. Frowned. "I'll, uh, see you. Later." He didn't move.

Neither did she.

Possibilities hummed, sang between them, and she felt for the first time in a very, very long while as though she saw through a glass clearly, saw what might be if a person acted with courage and faith.

"Come on, Oliver. Time's wasting." She remembered not to take his hand. If he wanted to take hers, he could. She wouldn't step into his space uninvited, though. "Ready, sweetie?"

"Yeah." He unwound himself from Joe and froghopped to Gabrielle's side. "And I want a present for Suzie. She'll think I've forgotten her. And Cletis." He stopped, wrinkled his nose. "What would Cletis like?"

"Food?" Joe laughed as she and Oliver turned in sync to him. "Sorry. But if it's the thought that counts, Cletis doesn't seem to think of anything else, does he?"

"You have a real streak of cruel, don't you, Joe?" Mock-scolding, Gabrielle waggled her finger at him.

"No, no. But think about Cletis." Snickering, Joe captured her finger, stilling it, and curled her hand into his. "What else does he yearn for?"

"I know what I'm getting him," Oliver said. "And it's not food. But he would like snacks…" he trailed off. "I'll get him two presents." He patted his wallet-on-a-string happily. "That's it."

"We'll see you when we see you." Not about to risk another swoop toward the candle that was Joe, Gabrielle ushered Oliver toward the melee of the mall. Her mouth still burned.

Only a kiss. Barely a kiss.

But, oh, what a kiss from the right man could do.

Oliver settled on a shiny red vinyl food mat for Cletis. And a big bag of munchies. He found a pad of sticky notes for Suzie. "Because she leaves notes on the cabinets, on the front door," Oliver told Gabrielle with amazement. "Everywhere. Suzie says it's good to be organized. These will help," he said, sighing with satisfaction.

He couldn't find a present for Joe. Nothing was special enough.

"Do you want to make your dad a present, sweetie?" Gabrielle asked finally when Oliver seemed on the verge of a total meltdown. They were seated on a bench outside Nature's Nest, where the display of colored liquids and rocks had drawn Oliver.

He swung his feet back and forth, clunking them on the inside of the bench. "Maybe."

"If you made him a present, did all the work yourself, you'd be giving him a part of you. Something that no one else could give him. And that would be the best present of all. I mean, I'm not a parent, but, gosh, Oliver, Pa still has ceramic pots and picture frames I made for him years ago. He wouldn't part with them for all the gold and diamonds in the whole world."

Oliver raised his head. His feet hung motionless. "Picture frames? You know how to make those?"

"Sure do." And if she couldn't remember exactly how, she'd make darned certain she had good instructions.

He fingered his wallet. "Maybe a picture frame, Gabby."

And then he smiled at her, a six-year-old killer smile that melted her.

She wanted to hug him.

She didn't.

Instead, folding her arms over her purse as she held it in her lap, she nodded thoughtfully. "Pictures are important. They're the past. A picture is a memory of a moment that will never come again."

"Like your star."

She sighed, but agreed. "Like the star, Oliver." She'd hoped that issue had been settled while they were baking cookies. Digging into her purse, she found a roll of Life Savers and offered it to him. "But I have the *memory* of the star, sweetie. I have pictures of it, from other Christmases. Those pictures are more precious to me now than ever. Pictures are memories frozen in time."

Her voice cracked a little at the end, and Oliver stretched out one chubby hand and patted her knee. "I have three pictures."

"Well, then, you understand."

He patted her knee again before retreating. "My daddy would like a picture in a frame."

"Want some help making one?"

For a moment she thought he might refuse.

"You could show me what colors and material you wanted, and we could spend a morning putting it together. If you're interested. You could wrap it and put the present under your own tree in your new home."

He slid off the bench and faced her. "A picture frame. Cletis can help, too."

She extended her hand to shake Oliver's, as close as she could come to a hug. "Done. We have a plan."

He shook her hand. "Def'nitely."

That easily, the problem was solved. Gabrielle felt as drained as if she'd run a marathon. Oliver's present for Joe had been a crucial decision. She wouldn't have left Oliver alone with that worry weighing down his narrow shoulders. Too important to leave to chance.

"We've done a good job shopping. But now I'm thirsty. Want a drink?"

Walking beside her, he shrugged. "'Kay." For an instant, she thought he would take her hand in his. He looked as if he would.

He didn't.

Surprised, she realized how much she wanted him to, though, wanted his trust more than she could have imagined wanting anything in the last year.

Like his father, the son had sneaked into her heart and made a place for himself.

When they returned to Joe and settled plans for supper, Gabrielle played up their shopping efforts, exaggerating for all she was worth. Putting the blarney on it, as her dad would say.

And with the memory of Joe's unexpected kiss still tingling on her lips, she flirted, moth once more to his candle, safe in the crowded mall and with Oliver an oblivious chaperon.

Close, close to the heat.

But safe.

Later, as they ate dinner in a family restaurant in the mall, she toyed with her earrings, fingering the smooth angel wings, her throat tipped up. Joe stopped abruptly, spaghetti strands dangling from his fork. He grinned across the table at her. "You're flirting with me, aren't you, sweet pea?"

"For a fellow with a reputation, it took you a long time to catch on." She dipped her chin and looked up at him through tangled lashes.

"Just checking, that's all." Meticulously, he twirled his fork in the spaghetti until all the strands were tightly looped around the tines. "Feeling pretty adventurous, aren't you?" Taking a bite, he gazed at her, his expression enigmatic, the planes of his face sharp and shadowy, mysterious in the dim light of the restaurant.

"Yeah," she said, mocking him with a grin of her own as she gave her earring one last flip and nudged his foot with hers. "Flirtin' like all get out."

"Careful, Gabby." His voice had a harshness she didn't recognize. Not anger. Not annoyance.

Something else.

Something enticingly dangerous.

The burred tightness pricked her curiosity, tempted her closer, moth wings fluttering.

She didn't want serious. She didn't want complicated. Not now. This was a day for exploration, for flirting, for trying out her wings.

She wanted to make Joe laugh, to chase away the shadows lurking in him.

And she wanted to see his son's killer smile again, that lighthearted, gap-toothed smile that would break hearts in ten years.

As his father's had.

Unlike his father, though, Oliver would have people in his life who cherished him, who would guide him through turbulence. Unlike Joe, Oliver wouldn't be labeled the town's bad boy.

It was late, the crescent moon shining silver in the dark sky, when Joe dropped her off at her house, Oliver's snores a faint whistle in the back of Joe's four-by-four.

Her father hadn't left a porch light on, and the house was dark. Either he had gone to bed, or he was still with Nettie. In the shadowy recesses of the porch, Joe placed one hand on either side of her face as she turned to him after unlocking the front door. The screen door wobbled against his hip. "Have you enjoyed flirting, sweet pea?" In the deep darkness, he was shadow in shadow, his voice lapping against her like an incoming tide.

Her back was pressed against the heavy wood of the front door. Her throat closed up, and for a moment she didn't think she could speak. "Yes." She moved restlessly, her feet scraping against the floorboards. "How about you?"

"Oh, yeah, Gabby. I enjoyed flirting with you. You've no idea how much." His voice turned thick and rough-edged.

She couldn't resist one last dart at the flame. "How much, Joe?" she whispered, sliding her arms around his waist.

At the skim of her arms around him, he moved his right hand, slid it through her hair. Her hair comb jingled and clattered to the porch, rolled silent. Lowering his head, he brushed his nose against hers, stroked it and waited. His breath, coffee-tinged and rich with the scent of him, stirred against her. She clenched her fists into her sweatshirt and fought the whimper of need rising, rising, from some deep, unknown place inside her.

Then, his movements slow and easy, molasses over warm pancakes, he took her mouth with his, fitting his mouth over hers and sealing their lips together. Over his shoulder, she saw the moon flicker into darkness as her eyelids drifted shut with the whimper that sighed from her to him.

His thighs nudged hers, and she stepped into the cradle of his body without even thinking, the urge to be close, closer, pulling her deeper into the mystery and wonder of his embrace. And with her movement, the kiss turned dark and hungry, urgent in a way her dreams had been.

Standing on tiptoe, she stretched herself against him, her breasts molding to the hardness of his chest, her thighs trembling against his, and she linked her arms around his neck, tugging him closer, the hunger in her leaping to meet the hunger she tasted in him.

This was what she had wanted, this merging of her self with someone else. No, she thought, dazed and lost in sensation as he curved his palm over her stomach, no, not *someone* else. Him. *His* touch, his lips. *Him.* Joe.

Since she was fifteen, this was the touch she'd waited for. No one else's.

This was the reason her curiosity hadn't tempted her since. Until now. Until Joe.

Her knees buckled, and she sagged against him, only the strength of his arms holding her upright as he moved forward, bracing her against the door as he bent, fitted their bodies tighter together, sealing them mouth to mouth, body to body.

Sliding both thumbs to her chin, he tipped her head back and kissed her throat, nipping at the base as his fingers stroked her cheeks and earlobes. "Joe," she said frantically, pulling him tighter. *"Joe."*

"Me, Gabrielle. It's me you're kissing." He kissed her again, his tongue sweeping inside her mouth, calling her tongue out to play, and she surrendered to the moment, to the sensations she'd known in her dreams of him.

Behind her closed lids, she glimpsed the shimmer of that distant land, clouds parting around it, the sun gleaming on its green shores and blue water.

And then Joe rested his head against the door, his hands supporting him, his body taut against hers. His breath was as ragged as hers, his chest heaving. She felt the thunder of his pulse throughout her body, her own heart pounding wildly to the beat of his.

He lifted his head and took her face between his hands. "And that wasn't flirting. In case you wondered."

And then he was gone, the taillights of his car a wink of red in the night.

Two days later, oddly formal and distant, as if that moment on her porch had never happened, Joe handed her a folded white paper. "Oliver and I are inviting you, Milo and Moon to a tree-trimming party at our house. No glogg."

"Wise decision," she said, opening the piece of paper. A

waterfall of miniature plastic trees, stars and reindeer shimmered into her lap. "Oliver made this, I gather?"

Stretching his arms wide, Joe lay back on the blanket they'd spread on the pine needles at the beach park. "No, smarty britches, I did." Dappled with sun-and-pine shade, his smile was lazy. "Hidden talents."

She looked at the letters straggling across the page. Lots of red. Green. Lots and lots of glitter. She glanced up at the dock where her dad and Oliver were wetting their lines. The picnic had been Oliver and Milo's idea. She and Joe had retreated into this amiable formality as if they were strangers.

Or people who knew each other too well.

In front of her, the gulf was a brilliant blue, the warm December sun gold in the sky. She read the painstakingly printed words and folded the paper along its creases.

Joe must have helped him. Every word was spelled correctly, the erasure marks showing under the bright colors. She tucked the invitation into the basket she'd brought. They would have labored over the invitation a long time. She cleared her throat. "Sounds like fun. What can I bring?"

He reached up and twined a strand of her hair around one finger, drawing her closer, almost as if he couldn't help himself. "Oh, yourself. In a pair of socks I haven't seen."

"I can manage that."

"You have more?"

"One or two pairs left." She had a drawerful of seasonal socks. If pushed, she could wear a different pair for the whole month of December. "If I can't bring food, can I help cook, set up?"

"Nope. This is a guy project."

"Notice I didn't offer cleanup services."

"I noticed. Oliver and I have it all planned out. Pizza and cola. Beer and wine for the old folks." Joe stroked the end of her hair against her throat. "For your information, that's you and me, too. He's been determined to have a party ever since he was at your house. Incidentally, thanks for helping him with the last of his shopping. And wrapping. The presents are in a bag, waiting to be unveiled at the big moment."

"Christmas Eve?"

"Nah. The moment we put the tree in its stand. I think the squirt can hold out until then. Possibly. He takes them out of the sack, turns them over and over, and then puts them back in." Joe rolled over onto his stomach and braced himself on one arm. "Gabrielle, we need to talk."

"I'm sure we do." As if she were back on the porch with him, her body constricted, flushed, blood pooling fast in her tummy.

"I've been thinking about what you said the other day when we were talking about my job and why I came back here."

She blinked. Readjusted her thinking. "Umm. All right."

He plucked a pine needle from the blanket, bent it, sniffed. "You need to know some things about me."

His comment took her from hot to cold, that fast. That was the line people used when they had bad news to tell, catastrophes they wanted to prepare you for. "What I need to know about you, I already do." Scooting down, she faced him. The breeze off the water was chilly against her bare feet. Her sandals weighted down one corner of the blanket.

"You never asked Milo what we talked about the other day at breakfast, did you?"

"Even if I'd asked, he wouldn't have told me. Lawyers are good at keeping secrets. Pa's *very* good." Not looking at Joe, she traced the line of the root-bumpy ground. "Your secrets are your own, Joe."

Her sun-washed face was half hidden by her hair. He wished she would look at him. Telling her would be easier if he could see her clear, truthful eyes. Looking at him, though, she wouldn't be able to hide her revulsion, her disgust at what she heard, and there would be no chance to pretend that this fragile friendship they were building could continue.

He didn't want to lose her friendship.

While he wasn't clear what, exactly, he wanted from her, he knew he didn't want her walking out of his life.

Now, watching her trace the ground beneath the blanket, Joe almost reconsidered. He didn't have to reveal this ugliness to her, not on this beautiful golden day. There would be other days. A better time.

There would always be a better time.

And he would be a coward if he didn't let her into his life enough to trust her with this truth about himself.

If she walked away, that would be her decision.

Something inside him curled up protectively against the idea of Gabby's turning her back on him.

But at least he would have given her the information she needed to make her decision. She deserved the truth about him. Fair was fair, especially between friends.

Staring out at the blue, blue gulf, its purity mocking him, he began. "Once upon a time—"

Laughing, she brushed her hair away and turned to him. "I thought you didn't believe in fairy tales, Joe."

"This is a true story, sweet pea."

"Does it have a happy ending?"

"I don't know how it ends."

"A never-ending story, then." She studied the ground again.

He'd been wrong. Better, much better if she hadn't looked at him with those innocent eyes that hadn't seen the world he had. Too hard to strip away everything he'd built up and go back to that nineteen-year-old punk he'd been. Doggedly, he started over. "Once upon a time there was a boy. A stupid, reckless boy. An angry boy."

Softly on the afternoon air, her words came to him. "I think I knew this boy. A long time ago."

"Could be, Gabby." He rolled to a sitting position and faced the water, his profile to her. "He hated everyone."

"Did he really?" She still lay beside him, facing away from the water. Her skirt draped in dark red folds against her bent leg.

"Yes, he really did. He hated himself, too, of course. Why wouldn't he? He had no reason to like who he was. No one else did. He was an outsider, on the fringes looking in the windows of other people's lives. All he wanted to do was smash his fist through—anything. Everything."

"Someone must have been concerned. For this angry boy." Lying flat, she dropped her head onto her arms.

"If you were writing this story, someone would have loved him. But not in this version."

"What happened to the angry boy?"

Joe heard Oliver's shriek of laughter as Milo whipped up his fishing pole and splashed water.

"He grew up."

"Did he stay angry?" Such gentleness in her husky voice, that he wanted to run, run as far away from her as he could before he had to finish the story.

He nodded slowly, remembering the anger that had lived with him. "The anger went underground, building like a pressure cooker inside him. Year by year. Until life taught him lessons he hadn't learned earlier. Until then he—"

"Was a troublemaker?" She stretched out her arm toward him, the sun glowing against her skin as she lay unmoving on the blanket, only her clear eyes watching him with understanding, an understanding that gave him courage to continue as she let her arm fall to the blanket. "A guy with an attitude?"

"You've heard this story?" He almost picked up her hand and covered it with his. But that would have been cheating.

"One like it." She sat up with a quick movement, her skirt flowing darkly red around her calves and thighs, like the crimson rush of the sun at the end of the day. "But in the one I know, the boy wasn't bad, not really. More a case of style and image, it seemed to me."

"Wrong story, sweet pea." He pleated the blanket between his fingers. "In this story, he was very bad. Oh, sure, he wasn't evil. Mixed-up, confused, no question. But, yes, he also did bad things."

In a movement so fast he wasn't prepared, she took his fists in her hands, forced them open. "Ever heard of forgiveness?"

"Sometimes a person can't forgive himself." He lifted her hands from his, placed them on the blanket, freed himself of the comfort of her nearness. "And that's what happened with this boy. He didn't mean to hurt anyone, but he was in the wrong place at, oh, I reckon you'd have to say it was the right time, and people got hurt."

"What did you do, Joe? You wouldn't have hurt anyone on purpose. Not you."

Watching his son, Joe rested his chin on his knees. "I hated my father. Over the years I've tried to understand him, and even now I can't. He was a mean drunk. He lied, he cheated, he stole. Nobody's candidate for Daddy of the Year. And he was fast with a fist. With me. With anyone who was in his way. Didn't matter. Fed up, my mom walked out on us when I was four, and I never heard from her again. Once my old man said she'd died. Years later I found a yellowed newspaper notice of her death. Said she was survived by three children. Daughters."

"Ah, Joe, Joe." Tears in the soft sound of his name.

He couldn't have borne her touch at this moment. Her pity would have unmanned him.

"She should have taken you with her. She should have, she should have." The sound of her tears was hushed, a counterpoint to the music of the breeze and water.

"It's only a story, sweet pea. And an old one at that. Nothing to fuss about."

He heard a sound from her, but he couldn't look at her. Not now. If he did, he'd never finish the damned story. She deserved to hear the rest of it, the worst.

A seagull flapped to a landing a few feet in front of them. Flinging the bits of torn-off bread high into the sky, Joe watched the circling white wings dip and soar, birds catching the bread airborne.

"Anyway, me and my old man moved every year or two, sometimes more often, keeping one step ahead of the bill collectors, the local sheriff. I never knew. By the time we landed belly-up in Bayou Bend, there must have been warrants out for my old man across half the country. I knew we wouldn't stay here. We never stayed anywhere. But I was tired of being that poor, snot-nosed Carpenter kid."

She stirred, and her bare feet flashed into his view, the toes shiny with alternating red-and-gold polish. "So you became Joe Carpenter, the boy who drove teachers crazy because he was so smart but never paid attention, the boy mothers warned their daughters to stay away from. And, of course, all the girls followed you around like bees after honey."

Even with his chest hurting with pain and regret, he smiled at her exasperation. "They weren't interested in me. They liked the thrill of being seen with the town's bad boy."

"You sell yourself short, Joe. I liked you. Other people did, too. Maybe you couldn't see that what drew people to you wasn't simply your 'cool' attitude, the lure of the forbidden. You made people laugh. And you charmed us all, Joe, one way or another." She was quiet, her sigh blending with the rising wind.

"The night I kissed you outside the country club was the night I left town."

"I remember."

He'd thought she did. All the sparks flying between them like fireflies that night at Moon's tree lot had been lit that crazy, sad night so long ago. "I left you and went home. My old man had boosted a car and stuck up a convenience store. Shoot, he didn't remember what he'd done. I saw the gun and the money and figured it out. For me that was the last straw.

I was so angry I couldn't think straight. All I knew was that I'd had enough of him, of his meanness and destruction.''

"What did you do?'' Her toes dug into the sand, their sparkle dusted with white.

"I wanted out, away from him. If he'd been awake, I don't know what I'd have done. Hit him back? Maybe. The anger was building in me like those volcanoes you see pictures of, everything collapsing and then spewing out and out, destroying everything in the way. Like a dope, I stuffed everything in the car and headed back to town, thinking I'd leave the car somewhere and everything would be all right.''

"Oh, no. Why, Joe, why? That was so—''

"Stupid? Reckless?'' He laughed, remembering the fury and the anger that had burned away reason. "Of course it was.''

"What were you thinking? That you could keep your father out of jail?''

"Don't see good motives where they didn't exist, sweet pea. I wasn't protecting *him*—'' the word was like acid in his mouth "—I didn't want one more scandal landing on top of me, one more reason for people to step off the sidewalk when I came walking down it. Town after town, move after move. The same. Settle in, try to put down roots, and then my old man would mess everything up. I'd see the pity in teachers' eyes, and I'd say something smart-mouthed, anything to erase that pity. And then the old man and I would skip town, start over. But the pity and the disgust always, always surfaced. Sooner or later. So I took the damned car and left. I didn't know where I'd dump it. Somewhere far away from Bayou Bend, that's for sure.''

As he watched Milo and Oliver, Joe finally comprehended something. The words coming out slowly, as if he were only now sorting out the emotions of that damning night, he said, "Because I wanted to come back. Bayou Bend was beginning to feel like home, and I was tired of running. I never understood that until this minute. I thought I hated the town. I didn't.''

"And that's why you came back after you'd run away?''

Joe held his hands out, palm up. ''The two years I lived here were the longest time I lived anywhere.''

''That's the reason you brought Oliver back here. This was home to you.''

''Sure didn't seem that way at the time, not when I was flying down the highway at a hundred miles an hour. All I could think about was running away. Putting as much space between me and this town as I could. I couldn't get that old junker of a car to go as fast as I wanted to.''

''You were stopped.'' She flung a chunk of bread skyward. The flash of her slim arm was a curve in the reddening sunset. ''I told you, this story is about a reckless, angry boy without a lick of good sense. No, I didn't stop when I saw the police in back of me. Two counties south of here, I crashed the car and, in a blind panic and rage, broke one cop's jaw and fought off the police until they cuffed me and hauled me to the station.''

''The news never made the papers here. Why didn't any of us ever hear anything about it?''

From the corner of his eye, he saw her tightly folded, shaking hands. He believed he sensed her withdrawal from him. That, after all, was what he'd expected. ''Because your daddy, Gabrielle, saved my soul.''

''What?'' In a whirl of dark red skirt, she jerked upright, facing him on her knees.

He looked for disgust in her face.

He saw bewilderment.

And something softened in her eyes as she steadily regarded him—acceptance, compassion, he didn't know what he saw, but in that moment, he knew he'd lay down his life for her.

For Oliver, because he was his son.

For her, for this woman who offered him friendship when he'd expected nothing.

Hoped for nothing.

Chapter Nine

Joe told her the rest. The humiliation a corrosive in his soul, he explained that Milo had persuaded the local police to reduce the charges, that Milo had put his own reputation on the line for Hank Carpenter's troublemaking brat, and that Joe had never understood why.

"Because Pa saw something good in you."

"If you'd seen him that night, you wouldn't think that. Your dad's eyes were the coldest, hardest eyes I'd ever seen in the face of any man, not even one whomping the living breath out of me. I called Milo because I didn't know any other lawyers. I didn't have anyone else to call."

"What about your dad?"

"If I'd been dying, sweet pea, I wouldn't have called him. Never. Not on this earth. Anyway, he was in an alcoholic stupor. A year later, cirrhosis of the liver finished what he couldn't accomplish on his own. Thus, my pappy played his last scam and avoided prison."

"I'm so sorry, Joe. I wish you knew how much. What a terrible burden for you." Her husky voice splintering, she reached out toward him once more, still on her knees in front of him, her skirt glowing against the darkening sand and pine needles.

Abruptly, awkwardly, he stood up, stuck his hands in his jeans pockets and paced back and forth, keeping his back to her, his gaze stretching to the horizon where the sun blazed in the darkening sky. "Because of your dad's intervention, I served six months, work-release time. I might have gotten off with probation without the resisting arrest charge, but Milo told me I needed to take responsibility for my own actions, regardless of what my father had done. I needed to get my life in order or I would wind up like my father, the way I was wasting my opportunities and talents."

"Never. You would never have turned out like your father." Her voice rang with a certainty that made his breath hitch in his chest.

All these years later, Joe couldn't believe that Milo had made everything so clear to him in the midst of all that turmoil and fear. "I was the one who'd gone off half-cocked. *I* was the one who hadn't thought the situation through. 'Consequences,' Milo said. 'Damages required reparation.'"

"That sounds like Pa."

"He was right, too, to take the hard road. I needed to step back and look at my life, get a handle on it, because at the rate I was going, I was headed nowhere good."

"You were young, Joe."

"Not that young. Truth to tell, I don't ever remember feeling *young,* not in the way you mean. No, I was responsible for what I did, and Milo helped me find a way through the darkness."

"How did Pa work his magic?" In back of her, red-gold water lapped at the shoreline in irregular curves.

"Oh, after he'd made it clear to me that he wasn't going to help me walk away scot-free, then Milo talked a blue streak, told the cops they had some discretion in how they reported the 'incident.'" Joe ran both hands through his hair, easing the ache in his head as the salt air blew over him, through him, a strange cleansing. "The 'incident,' Milo called it. Sheesh. The cops were licking their pencils to write up theft, robbery, traffic violations, resisting arrest, assault. I had visions of living the rest of my life *under* the jail. But in that calm, rational way he has, Milo kept saying the incident could be handled. Oh, he didn't try to excuse what I'd done, Gabby—"

"No, Pa's not into excuses. Face the music and learn from your mistakes." Bits of sand clung to her skirt as she rose and confronted him. In the failing light, her eyes were troubled. "I can't see him as being hard or cold, though."

"You weren't the one standing in front of him with your arms cuffed in back of you. He emphasized my stupidity, quite eloquently, in fact, but he said he knew me, could vouch for my essential character, and that the incident rose as much out of fear as stupidity."

"You *were* afraid, Joe. Of your father, of having your life collapse around you one more time. Pa understood that."

"Think so? He didn't know me. We hadn't spoken more than five words to each other before that night."

"Then why did you call him to act as your lawyer? What made you think of him? Why not let your fingers do the walking through the yellow pages?"

A gull shrieked in the red-gold sky. Streamers of pale clouds lay like whipped cream between the muted colors. He hadn't considered anyone but Milo. He knew Milo would come, no matter that he'd had to travel two counties down from Bayou Bend at ten o'clock at night. He'd known that as surely as he'd ever known anything in his life. Strange, now, thinking of that certainty.

"That summer your dad broke his leg—"

Her skirt frothing around her ankles like the incoming tide on the gold sand, she turned to him. "I remember. I'd turned fifteen and gone to camp for the month. I was looking forward to starting my sophomore year, being in high school, maybe getting to go to the Junior/Senior prom. Most of all, though—" she sighed "—I was excited about the chance to see you in the halls every day. From a distance, of course."

Her smile was rueful.

Doggedly he returned to his story. "Anyway, I saw your dad sitting on the porch with his leg in a cast and on a footstool. A few days in this humidity and heat and a yard can become a jungle. The lawn mower was sitting beside the car in the porte cochere, so I went over and fired up the mower. Never said a word. Mowed the yard, clipped bushes. Left. I showed up every week until I knew you were back."

"Pa told you I was home?" Her face was soft and puzzled, and he grasped that the complications of his life were so totally alien to her that she must feel as if she were listening to a story in a foreign language.

"No, sweet pea, I saw your itty-bitty bikini hanging on the clothesline in the backyard, so I didn't come back. And you know something? I pictured you in that scrap of cloth for the rest of that summer and into the fall. Pretty little Gabrielle in her bright pink bikini." Remembering, he started to touch her face, but didn't.

She blushed, a tide of her own suffusing her face as she ignored his comment and said, "That's how Pa knew you, then. You must have talked during those weeks, had an iced tea. He got to know you, what you were like. That's why he seemed so cold at the police station. He was worried for you. Worried *about* you. Don't you see?"

Joe thought back to those long, hot afternoons. The roar of the mower, the smell of the grass. Milo, sitting on the porch, watching through hooded eyes as Joe pushed through the heavy tangle of weeds and grass. "Gabrielle, your dad never said two words to me. I never spoke to him. Money was never discussed."

"Pa didn't pay you? That's strange. He's not cheap."

"I wasn't mowing his yard for the money."

"Why did you help, then? What did you want, if not

money? With your father's situation, you would have needed extra cash.''

''I had a job in Calhoun's garage, fixing engines. I made out all right.'' Joe frowned, thinking hard, his original impulse lost in the intervening years. ''Damned if I know why it seemed important to me to mow Milo O'Shea's yard that summer. I saw him. I started mowing. It seemed simple. No complications. Each Saturday afternoon, he left a thermos of tea by the mower. That was that. We never talked. And you know something?'' Stopping, Joe took a deep breath as the realization struck him. ''Those hot, sweat-drenched afternoons were the happiest times I'd ever known. Your dad. Me. Nobody talking. Nobody yelling. Everything *simple*. Just a normal summer afternoon mowing the yard. A Beaver Cleaver afternoon. Funny, huh?''

''Not so funny, I think.'' She touched him then, and he jerked away.

He couldn't let himself accept her sympathy. Sympathy was another form of pity. Whatever he wanted from her, and he was becoming increasingly confused about that, pity was nowhere on the list. ''Anyway, Gabrielle, the police found the spark plug my father used to break in the car window. My old man hadn't taken it out of his pants pocket. Splinters of glass in the cuffs of his pants matched up, so it was obvious he was the one who'd heisted the car. Nobody placed me at the scene. The clerk at the store indicated that the old guy was the single robber involved, the tapes from the outside surveillance camera at the store corroborated his account, and your dad made counseling part of the deal. Because I hadn't been drinking, there was some flexibility possible despite the fighting. My juvie escapades were sealed, so the cops agreed to the arrangement. Milo put up bail, took me to your house, fed me. That's how I knew about his cooking. He fixed red-eye gravy and biscuits. Best meal I'd ever had.''

''I didn't get home from the after-prom dinner and parties until daybreak. I can't believe I didn't see any signs that anyone had been at the house. Mama must not have known about it, either.''

"She didn't. Milo said she'd gone to the hospital to stay with a friend."

"I remember now. The Potter baby was ill. Mama didn't want Anna Potter to be alone." Frowning, she shrugged. "I'd forgotten."

"I didn't ask Milo to keep the incident secret—" he laughed "—I started calling it that, too, but to the best of my knowledge, Milo never told anyone about that night. Moon knows. I reckon one of his cousins down around Sarasota picked up rumors. I don't think Moon ever told anyone, either. The way he likes to talk, I'm surprised he kept his mouth shut. Would have been a swell piece of gossip to pass around."

"Moon wouldn't. He talks, but he's careful about not hurting people. A lot of big, tough guys are like that. All that strength makes them careful about using it against other people. Joe—" she laid her hand lightly on his arm, stopping him as he walked to the blanket "—what did Pa want to talk about the other morning?"

Looking down at the curl of her hand against him, Joe wished he were a different man, a man who could turn to this woman and— What? Offer her himself? A man like him with a woman like Gabrielle O'Shea? His darkness to the sunshine of her innocence and hopefulness? She deserved better.

Hard, though, at Christmas, not to think of what-ifs.

"Will you tell me about your talk with Pa?" she repeated softly.

"Sure. Milo asked me about my work. About Oliver. I answered. Small talk, nothing more." But Joe hadn't told Milo everything about the boy who, no matter what, was his son. "Milo offered to take Oliver fishing today, we shook hands and that was that."

"Nothing about that night?"

"Not a word."

Her hand tightened. "He wants you to know what happened in the past isn't important, Joe. Believe me. Let it go."

"Yeah. I suppose. The past shapes you, though, makes you who you are. You're sweetness and light." He lifted her hand from him as carefully as if it would break.

"And what are you, Joe? Because you're no longer that angry, confused nineteen-year-old boy."

Breaking free of her grip, Joe squatted to grab the edge of the blanket and shake the sand out of it. "I'm an unexpected father, Gabrielle."

"So you are." Stooping, her feet sinking into the sand, she lifted the other end of the blanket.

Joe glanced briefly at her solemn face as he handed her sandals to her. "With a son who desperately needs me. I'm all he has."

"Will you be enough, Joe?" Gentle, the words. Sharp, the sting.

"I don't know what you mean."

"Think about it," she advised, slipping into her sandals. Not looking at him, her face sun-flushed, she collected paper plates and cups, tidying up.

Her point eluded him.

The day was over. He'd done what he had to do. He'd told Gabrielle the worst about himself. What happened next would be entirely up to her.

He would have to live with whatever she decided.

And if she decided never to see him again?

It would be the smartest decision she could make. He had too many dark corners in his life, too many rough edges for someone like her to waste time on.

As for him, hell, he hadn't come back to Bayou Bend expecting anything. He'd already gotten more than he'd dreamed of. He could see a future now, for him and Oliver in this town. And if that picture of the two of them seemed incomplete, lonely, so be it.

Until Oliver, he'd been alone all his life.

As Gabby held one end of the blanket, Joe cracked the blanket hard. Sand gritted against his face.

Now his job was to protect Oliver. His biggest debt was to this boy. Step by step, Joe intended to pay his debts to the past. Birth son or not, Oliver was his, problems and all. He couldn't imagine a woman taking on that kind of uncertainty.

A clean slate.

He drew the air deep into his lungs. With his debts paid, a man could endure loneliness.

Matching blanket ends with Gabby, he halted, a thought snapping through his confusion. "Gabrielle, I think I know now the real reason I had to come back to Bayou Bend."

"Why's that, Joe?"

"To make the past whole. To fix it. Like Milo said, for reparation. I guess I felt I owed something here. Maybe to Milo. I don't know. I haven't figured everything out."

Her hand brushed his as she took the blanket from him. "Maybe you owed something to that boy who ran away."

For a long moment, he stood, her hand next to his, Gabrielle watching him steadily, her breasts moving gently up and down with her slow breathing. Stunned, he couldn't move. The moment acquired a clarity that stunned him. "Maybe," he said finally.

Sticking two fingers in his mouth, he gave a shrill whistle. "Hey, Oliver! Milo! Time to haul in the lines." Bait bucket in hand, Oliver trotted toward him, suntanned and grinning, Milo by his side.

Joe felt his heart constrict with emotion. *This* was his future. This child he'd sworn to make a life for, to provide the home Joe had never had with his own father. Strolling toward the dock, he waited for Oliver to reach him.

Thoughtfully, Gabrielle finished folding the blanket.

She'd accused Joe of being noble once before, thinking he was trying to let her down lightly. In her own insecurity and shyness, she'd missed too many clues. The man was too darned noble for his own good. He wouldn't see an elephant in front of his face if it bellowed at him.

So intent on explaining to her all the sins of the past, he couldn't see the forest for all the trees. Way she saw it, and she guessed Milo did, too, was that Joe Carpenter had been more sinned against than he'd sinned. Of course Joe didn't see that.

The ride across the bridge back to the mainland was quiet. One arm crooked on the door where the open window allowed the salt-and-flower-scented air to blow in, Joe didn't say anything. Weariness deepened the lines around his eyes, but each time he glanced at her, she believed she saw a peace in him that she'd never seen, the wariness gone, replaced by this acceptance.

From the back, Milo and Oliver's occasional comments mingled with the hiss of the tires on the road and the hum of the engine, lulling her to sleep. Her last conscious thought was a drowsy awareness that the four of them, together, felt good. Right, in some indefinable way. Nice, the four of them.

A family. The words drifted in as if spoken aloud. *Family.* On the sound of the word, Gabrielle slid into sleep.

The next two weeks collapsed on themselves with plans for Christmas. Bonded by their fishing expedition, Milo and Oliver went clamming, crabbing and fishing again. One crab, released. One bucket of coquinas, dug up from the sand. Mesmerized by the way the minute creatures in their iridescent shells dug themselves back under the sand, Oliver wanted to cart them home. Milo told him they would die away from the gulf, so Oliver upended the blue plastic bucket. "He was so fast, I had coquinas squirtin' through my toes, honey," Milo told her later. "The kid's got a good heart."

Joe and Oliver included Nettie in their tree-trimming party, and that felt right, too.

Walking into the hall of Joe's new home, Gabrielle was speechless. The wide staircase was looped awkwardly with ropes of pine branches; Christmas lights of every size and shape twinkled around doorways; and in the living room, the tree— "Oh, my lord," she gasped, seeing the tree again, "it's—"

"Beautiful," Oliver said happily.

With every step anyone took, the tree merrily shed needles. Straight in its stand, it rose majestically toward the ten-foot ceilings. Lights curled, drooped, swooped around it. Popcorn strands wrapped it like a package.

"Beautiful," Gabrielle agreed, with a lump in her throat. It was the perfect ugly tree. Beautiful in its transformation, its top, like that of the O'Shea tree, was bare.

"I broke your star, so it's not fair for me to have a star on my tree when you don't got one," Oliver informed her with a melancholy sigh. "Next year, me and daddy will have a star."

But it was the house that turned her quiet as Joe gave her the tour, showing her the renovation projects he and Oliver had already begun.

Joe had plans for his house.

Rooms empty of furniture and knickknacks were filled with plans, with possibilities. Permanence.

"See the grain of the wood under this cracked varnish, Gabrielle? It's beautiful oak. Think how it will look when I've sanded and refinished it."

"Big job." She ran her hand over the crazed-and-blackened varnish of the banister. "Who are you going to hire to do a project of this size?"

"Me." Chest stuck out like a Thanksgiving turkey's, Oliver pushed past her. "Me and my daddy are strong, and we are going to ren..ren..." He turned to Joe for help.

"Renovate," Joe said, and love rippled like a current in his voice as he spoke to his son. "We're going to—"

"Work like *dawgs* and paint and scrape and get dirty," Oliver explained in a whirl of words. "We are going to do all the work ourselves. Me. Daddy. We don't need nobody else."

Moving back to the living room, Joe ripped open the new

boxes of ornaments, handing a box to each person while Oliver unwrapped the ornaments her dad, Nettie, Moon and she had brought as tree gifts.

"I like this one." Oliver hung a ceramic crab on a branch at eye level. The branch bent toward the floor under the weight of the ornament. "Yeah," he said, moving back, "this is my favorite 'cause me and Milo went crabbing. But we didn't bring any home."

Gabrielle gave Oliver a tiny cat bell with wings and a halo. She thought it was a sign of progress that he didn't hang the ornament at the back of the tree. And when he thought she wasn't looking, she saw him stroke the cat's whiskery face gently, each stroke setting the bell to chiming.

She smiled. Oliver's feelings toward her were confused, mixed, sometimes hostile, sometimes friendly, but he was beginning to permit her into his world. In fits and starts, granted, but she figured nothing worthwhile was built in a day. Or week.

As she turned to hang another ornament, her eyes met Joe's. Pensively, he returned her gaze, almost as if he were trying to understand something, and as their gazes held, the room seemed to narrow, dim, until the two of them were left in candlelight and silence.

But he didn't say anything, nor did she, and the moment passed.

Later, Moon, Nettie, her dad and Oliver made a foray to the kitchen, looking for more pizza.

"Like what we've done with the place, sweet pea?" In the candlelight of the living room, Joe's eyes were serious, a question in them that went beyond the one he asked.

Pizza slice in one hand, wineglass in the other, and her mouth filled with cheese, Gabrielle nodded.

She grasped that the house was a symbol for Joe and for Oliver.

Joe had bought an old house when he could have bought one of the newer houses on stilts, one of the fancier houses in the new subdivisions that sprang up overnight in old pine forests and timberland. Stripping the growth down to the sandy soil and bulldozing ancient trees, the developers marched across the land, leaving concrete footprints and noise where there had been green trees and quiet.

Joe was making a home for Oliver, but Joe was making a home for himself, too. Watching the two of them tug at the balustrades and discuss what they were going to strip first, she wanted to weep for both of them.

She decided wine made her too sentimental.

Or maybe it was the pizza.

Shaking off the seriousness, she headed for the CD player, looking for music. Placing her wineglass on the shelf beside the system, she brushed her hands down her bronze velvet slacks and flipped through cassettes, records and CDs before saying, "We need music. Any requests?"

She recognized the presence at her back without turning around. In the corner of the candlelit room, shadows offered privacy as he lifted her hair with one hand and bent down to her neck, to the shallow indentation at the base of her skull. The kiss he placed there sent shivers down her spine, and she shuddered. His kiss was one quick, delicious prickling of her skin, and then he let her hair fall.

His finger stayed against the spot he'd kissed, a substitute for his lips. "Merry Christmas, Gabrielle," he whispered, and turned back to the others gathered around the tree.

After the tree-trimming party, as one day turned into the next, she felt on the verge of some momentous discovery.

Dropping Oliver off or picking him up, Joe lingered with her over coffee, eggnog and, one especially warm day, iced tea on the porch. Long silences punctuated their talk. She told him about her house-sitting company, how she'd gotten started. He explained that after his probation ended, he'd joined the army and learned about computers, deciding eventually to start his own business.

And in the words and silences between them, something

quivered, like a thin, fragile green stalk struggling through the darkness toward the sun, something that could bloom or be blasted by a sudden frost.

Keeping a careful distance, Joe flirted with her. She flirted back, sensing that they were walking carefully among emotional minefields, as if the wrong word, the wrong look, would trigger…*something*.

Clinging to Joe, to Milo, Oliver continued to keep the distance he'd established between himself and Gabrielle. No matter how carefully she approached him, he kept her at arms's length, frowning once when he saw Joe lean over her and cup her neck with a hand. Stepping back, freeing herself of Joe's light grasp, Gabrielle met Oliver's scowling, terrified eyes.

Moon invited all of them to crew on his boat during the annual Christmas Boat Parade.

"Do we gotta wear a costume?" Oliver asked hopefully.

"Damned straight you do," Moon answered. "Anything you want."

Moon's expression, where utter delight mixed with chagrin that he hadn't thought of the idea first, made Gabrielle laugh, a quickly smothered cough. No one had ever worn costumes, but Oliver had tapped into Moon's love of the theatrical. She wouldn't be surprised if Moon coerced the rest of the parade participants into costumes now that Oliver had presented the idea.

Gabrielle loved the boat parade. All the magic and mystery of the season were spun out over the cool darkness, night and river shimmering in an enchantment of color.

As far back as she could remember, every year on December 21, regardless of when the date fell, regardless of the weather, Bayou Bend boat owners decorated their boats, no matter what size or type, with strings of lights, turning the boats into floating displays of sound and sparkle against the dark water of the bayou. The boats would leave the creeks and bayou and head toward the wide bend of the river where it flowed through the center of town, boats drifting by in breathtaking beauty to the music of watchers along the way who sang carols back to the passing boats.

The parade ended at the luminaria-lined docks, where candles flickered in sand-weighted bags. As each boat arrived at the town center, it would turn off its lights, leaving nothing more than the golden glow of the luminaria in the darkness. One by one, the silent boats would slip into darkness, disappearing until only the lights of the final boat shone bravely on the river.

The crowd would grow quiet as the lights on the last boat winked out.

For a moment, joined in silent darkness, there would be a sense of community, of humankind, whatever the religion, joined together against the blackness of hate and anger and fear.

And then, at a signal from the lead boat, all the boat lights would come back on, blindingly, fiercely triumphant against the darkness. A sigh, as if everyone had been holding their breath, would rise up from the crowd, join the cheers and laughter and light.

Oh, she loved the parade of boats through the bayous and creeks, joining in a grand stream through the center of town. She loved the jostle and bustle of her neighbors, the wonder of that moment of darkness yielding to light.

In the depths of her soul, she was reminded in that moment of the fragility of life, of earth's majesty spinning through the darkness of eternity and space.

Sometimes the blaze of light moved her to tears.

Oliver allowed her to help him with his costume. Gabrielle knew better than to suggest an elf or angel costume. Wavering between a seal and a robot, he finally decided with Milo's help that he would be a red crab. Red for Christmas. "A crab, 'cause we're going on the water and I will be Sandy Claws."

The idea worked for Gabrielle. "Okay. But Pa has to help us with the padding for the crab's body."

"My daddy will make my claws. They will be sharp and scary."

Milo helped. Joe made the claws. Not sharp, but sufficiently scary to satisfy Oliver's bloodthirstiness. Gabrielle found red leggings and worked with Oliver to make a crab head.

Days later, costumes ready, the boat decorated, they headed to the bayou.

"Can't be Sandy Claws without a Santa hat," Moon offered, plopping his own hat on top of Oliver's headpiece as Joe swung Oliver aboard Moon's boat.

In a splash of red and pink, the sun melted into the creek water. A fish erupted from the water, twisting and turning in a gleam of shining scales, startling Oliver. He squealed with delight. Setting Oliver on deck, Joe reached back to Gabrielle to give her a hand on board.

"Hey, you forgot. I grew up around water." Gabrielle rolled up the bottoms of her jeans and took two steps back, preparing to launch herself forward.

"I like the socks, sweet pea." Joe closed her in his arms as she came flying over the gap between dock and boat. "The Santa seagulls are kind of cute, I have to admit. Gives us a theme for Moon's boat."

With Joe's arms tight around her and her body plastered against him like white on rice, she couldn't think of a comeback, not with his heart pounding like a snare drum against her own, and her breath caught somewhere south of her rib cage.

But Oliver looked toward them, his Santa hat drooping over one eye, and she smiled, took a shuddering breath, stepped away from the sound of Joe's heart calling her, and said, "C'mere, sweetie. Let's get your life jacket on you. You can take it off once you're on dry land again."

With everyone in life jackets and at their assigned stations, they set sail, catching the evening breeze. White against the blaze of sky, the sails flapped and filled with air in a great whoosh, moving back upriver toward town.

Earlier in the day, Moon and Joe had sailed the boat from its berth upriver down into Mosquito Creek, from which point they would start and join up with the other boats as their turn came to swing into the parade lineup.

While Moon and Joe moved the boat to its starting point, Milo and Oliver had followed in the car so Moon and Joe would have a ride home and back again after an early supper.

Left at home, Gabrielle had mock-complained that she was stuck once more with scullery duty. Nobody had paid any attention to her.

She hadn't really wanted them to.

She'd had Christmas plans of her own to complete in the early afternoon, and she didn't want anyone around while she set them in motion. Everybody deserved surprises at Christmas, and she'd finally decided what to give Joe.

Now, watching Oliver leap from one end of Moon's boat to the other, Gabrielle felt her heart leap with him, taking sail into the night.

The accident happened shortly after Moon slipped into line, about thirty boats back from the first one. Ahead of them, Gabrielle saw the shine and twinkle of electric reindeer and Santas. Tiny Italian lights outlined sails and spars. Some boats were outlined from bow to stern and up to the top of their sails. Smaller putt-putt boats were turned into water floats for elaborate figures shaped out of a myriad of lights. The chug of engines was muted by the hum of voices singing along the banks of the creek and river.

Entranced, Oliver stayed beside Joe near the bow of the boat. Gabrielle was halfway back on the port side, her life jacket bunching up her sweatshirt uncomfortably with each movement. Reaching for the buckle on her life jacket, she saw Oliver catch a glimpse of the boat behind them, saw his astonishment at the moving illuminations that moved from bow to stern, port to starboard. Joe had turned to catch the bowline Moon pitched his way.

One arm outstretched, Joe didn't see that slight shadow dart away toward the stern.

As Oliver bolted past on the starboard side of the boat, Gabrielle began moving, some instinct sending her into motion before she realized what she was doing. Her boat shoes gripped the deck as she ran flat out toward Oliver. "Joe," she called, her voice catching in the wind.

He turned in her direction.

Not quite at the stern, Oliver leaned over the side of the boat for a better look, his small rear end rising skyward.

Gabrielle vaulted over the anchor and grabbed. Her fingers scrabbled against the slick fabric of his life jacket as he disappeared into the water. Ripping off her jacket, she dug one foot into the railing, balanced herself and dived deep, stroking furiously as she plunged into the chilly water.

The last thing she saw was one crab claw flailing in the water. Downstream, Oliver's Santa hat floated, moved by the wake of the passing boat.

Oliver was nowhere in view.

"Damn, Moon, stop the damn boat!" Joe's frantic shout carried to Gabrielle as she pulled and kicked in the direction of the hat, terror lending her strength.

The darkness enveloped her, salt and brackish water filling her nose. She would later think how odd it was that she couldn't hear a sound, couldn't see anything except the waterlogged Santa hat. Somewhere a small boy with two claws had to be bobbing alone, safe in his life jacket.

Oliver had to be safe.

Why couldn't she see him? Had he hit his head on the boat as he pitched forward? Was he trapped underneath one of the boats? Anything was possible.

She inhaled, kicked hard and dived deep, searching in the blackness for movement, for the sight of a small, helpless boy. As she came up for air, thrusting against the water, her lungs burning, she flung her hair out of her way and trod water for an instant, scanning the water's surface for any movement, anything.

There, fifteen feet downstream and off to her side, she thought she saw a head. Kicking across the river's current, she stroked toward the pin dot that had to be a head.

Afterward, she would wonder why her throat was sore. When she heard nothing but silence around her, everyone else had heard her screaming Oliver's name with every stroke she took.

As she closed in on the dot, stroke by stroke, pulling with every ounce of energy so that she could intercept it, the dot bobbed, grew larger, turned into Oliver's head, his eyes wide and amazed as he floated serenely along.

"Hey, Gabby," he sputtered through a mouthful of water as she caught him in her arms and used her feet to keep them in one spot until Moon and Joe could turn the boat around. "This is neat, but I'm getting cold. Can we go back to the boat now?"

"You bet, sweetie." Sobs shook her as she rested her chin against his wet head. "Anything you want."

Holding the small, squirming boy tightly to her, Gabrielle swallowed her sobs. As Moon's boat circled near them and Joe reached out for both Oliver and her, she knew what was most important in her life.

With no warning, no clue, she'd fallen in love with Joe and his stubborn, terrified, wary son. She wanted them both in her life.

And she wanted to be part of their lives. She wanted to strip varnish and make Halloween costumes and wake up each morning to the sound of Joe's breath in her ear, to the snuffling snores of Oliver down the hall.

Chapter Ten

Joe grabbed Oliver from Gabby's arms and thrust him toward Nettie, reaching down again for Gabby, a bedraggled, stringy-haired Gabby, who at that moment was the most beautiful woman he'd ever seen. Retching creek water, she hung over the side for a moment before regaining her balance as Moon swung his boat clear of an oncoming motorboat.

"Oliver?" she gasped, clasping her cold hands on Joe's arms, her eyes smoky rings in her pale face.

"Oliver's fine. He thinks he's had an extra adventure. We need to get both of you dry." Her teeth chattered and her body shook against him. Or his shook against hers. He wasn't sure. All he knew was the sheer screaming panic that had taken him as he saw Oliver and then Gabby fall into darkness. "Come on, sweet pea, you're solid ice. Moon's going to turn the boat around and head back to the car." Trying to warm her, he rubbed her arms hard and turned to Nettie.

Nettie had brought towels. "I like to be prepared," she'd murmured. "Even for midnight swims."

Gabby went belowdecks to see if she could find something

for herself and Oliver to wear. Oliver didn't want to leave the flotilla of illuminated boats.

After the scare they'd all had, nobody had the heart to deny him this treat. Joe sure couldn't. The kid was a trouper, for damned sure. Clutching Oliver close, Joe clenched his teeth.

If he hadn't, he would have howled like a wounded dog, a terror he'd never known forcing its way up from his gut. Oliver. Gabby. He could have lost his son. Could have lost her.

Keeping his mouth clamped shut, Joe took Nettie's towel and wrapped it around Oliver, drying him off and stripping his crab costume off in soggy, heavy clumps.

Without the life jacket, Oliver would have drowned. He couldn't swim, and in the heavy costume he would have sunk like a stone to the bottom. Gabby wouldn't have seen him. It was a miracle she'd seen him, anyway, that small dot almost invisible in the noise and confusion.

As long as he lived, he would never forget the sight of her, her slim, sweatshirt-weighted figure cutting through the water, spotlights blinding her, her hair flat against her skull as she'd reached Oliver and held him so that they could see he was safe.

She'd given him his son back.

Moon's sweatshirt dangled around Gabby's ankles, but it was warm and dry. Gabby found a belt to tie around the waist of the sweatshirt she gave to Joe for Oliver. Even belted, the shirt dragged along the deck, but it didn't matter, because Joe had no intention of letting Oliver out of his arms.

He kept one arm around his son, the other around the woman who'd saved him, and each breath was labored, the knot of terror under his rib cage painfully constricting his breathing.

They wound up being the last boat in the parade, but Moon knew what to do, and he played the scene for all the drama he could wring from it, taking a bow as all the lights came back on.

Joe couldn't let anyone else hold Oliver. His arms had frozen around his son. And somewhere in the miracle of darkness and light as they floated toward the dock, he sent a silent thank you to Jana, for the gift she'd given him in spite of everything.

It no longer mattered to him why she'd put his name on the birth certificate, he no longer cared that she might have played him for a fool. As he breathed his thank you, he forgave her. Whatever had driven her no longer mattered.

It was in the past.

Whatever Oliver wanted to know about his mother, Joe would tell him, and he would give Jana the benefit of the doubt as Gabby had suggested.

With Oliver safe in his arms, and Gabby, wet and shivering, by his side, the pain he'd lived with all his life was suddenly set free, a balloon floating up and away in the dark.

Oliver fell asleep on the way home, his stiff hair scratching Joe's cheek.

Once he'd tucked Oliver into bed, creek-smell and all, Joe went to the shower. For a long time he stood under water so hot it stung his skin, tears streaming down his face and mixing with soap and water as he leaned his forehead against the steamy tiles and cried for the first time since he was five years old.

The next evening, Nettie and Milo asked Oliver to come for a B movie night. "Bad movies, the worse the better. And popcorn," he added. "We're planning on staying up until midnight. If you can stand to be with the old codgers, that is."

Joe hadn't wanted to let Oliver out of his sight. He did, though.

He had to, for Oliver's sake.

Alone in his own house, he sat in front of the tree, watching the lights twinkle and listening to the creaks and groans of the house.

The ring of the doorbell brought him out of his reverie, and somehow he wasn't surprised to find Gabby at his door. Shifting from foot to foot, she was clearly nervous. He'd never seen Gabby this fidgety. "Is everything all right on the home front?" He peered around her, half expecting to find Oliver.

"Umm. Yes. Everyone's fine."

"Good." He rested his hand on the door, suddenly ill at ease himself in the charged atmosphere.

"Are you going to invite me in, Joe?" She brushed a swath of hair back behind her ear and straightened her shoulders. "Because I'd like to come in."

"Sure," he said, puzzled. Gabby wasn't flirting, but the atmosphere was humming like an electrical field between them. "Come on in." He opened the door wider, and she stepped in sideways, not looking at him, her arms wrapped around her waist. "Can I get you something to drink? A glass of wine? Soda?" He shrugged. "Whatever you want, sweet pea."

At that, her head jerked up, and her eyes met his. "Good. That will make everything much easier." She squared her shoulders, looked around the hall. "Let's go to the living room, Joe."

"All right," he said slowly, intrigued by her determination and militant air. "The living room it is, then."

"Sit down, Joe. Please." With one hand, she pushed against his chest until he sat down on the couch.

Then she climbed into his lap and circled his neck with her arms. Her slight weight wriggled against his lap as she made herself comfortable. Resting her forehead on his, she tweaked the top button of his shirt free of its buttonhole, working her way steadily down to his waist. She took a deep breath and tugged his shirt free of his jeans.

He covered her hand with his. "What are you doing, Gabrielle?"

"Golly, Joe, I'd expect a man of your experience to know what I'm doing."

The lights were dim in the room, and he couldn't see her face clearly, but he thought she smiled. "Maybe you ought to spell it out for me. I've already had one glass of wine."

Her small, capable hands were tugging at his shirt and smoothing the skin of his chest, tugging at the tendrils of his chest hair until he couldn't think clearly. "That's good, Joe," she said earnestly. "Because this is a celebration."

"Is it?" Without even thinking, he twined his fingers in her hair, stroked the angle of her chin. "You're confusing me, Gabby."

She slipped her arms under his shirt and around to his back, tracing his ribs with her clever fingers. He shuddered.

"You like that, don't you, Joe?" she asked in a husky whisper that made him shiver again.

"Uh, yeah, sweet pea, I really do." He stood up, taking her with him and then reversing their positions until she was curled on the sofa and he was standing. And then he took a good look at her.

She was wearing some red, slinky outfit that clung and curved to her. High-necked and long-sleeved, the dress shifted and moved with her. He could swear he saw the outline of her panties. He knew he saw the small pooch of her nipples. Gabby wasn't wearing a bra. Joe blinked.

"Okay. I need an explanation. Fast."

"You're perspiring, Joe," she said sweetly, sliding her feet out of a pair of the highest heels he'd ever seen. Thin straps of shiny black, they thunked onto the floor.

"Damned right I am." He stuffed his shirt back into his jeans and scowled at her. "Does Milo know you're here?"

"Probably. Pa's not stupid." Curling her nyloned feet underneath her, she rose to her knees and slipped her index finger into the loop of his belt. And then she tugged, bringing him one step closer.

He hadn't expected that and he pitched forward, balancing himself with one hand against the couch.

"Ah, much better." She rose up and smoothed herself against him. "Yes. Definitely better."

Her kiss was sweet and innocent and hot, a need in the way she kissed him that almost shattered his good sense and his caution. He had just enough of both left to break her hold and take several giant steps away from her. Away from temptation and warmth.

"You don't know what you're doing, Gabrielle." He leaned against the window near the tree, trying to rein in the mad gallop of testosterone and lust. And that other emotion, too, the one he couldn't put a name to.

"Oh, Joe, you nincompoop. I know exactly what I'm doing. I'm seducing you. I'm propositioning you. I haven't waited this long not to know my own mind." She scrambled to her feet, her skirt inching up into the danger zone.

"That's very flattering, but believe me, you don't want to do that." He backed up flat against the cool glass as she moved in front of him, her stocking feet resting against his bare one. Her toes nudged his.

"Believe me, I do," she murmured, and stood on tiptoes, arching into him. "And I may lack experience in this area, but I read a lot. I know precisely what I want."

And she whispered something into his ear that seared every cell in his body.

He groaned. "Aw, Gabby. This is a mistake. You're not the kind of girl for cheap sex."

"Cheap sex isn't what I want from you, Joe Carpenter. I could have had cheap sex any time I wanted over these years. I'm not inexperienced because I haven't had the chance to lose—" she hesitated, nibbled at the base of his collarbone for a moment contemplatively before continuing "—my inexperience. I've had plenty of opportunities if cheap sex was all I wanted."

Joe cupped her shoulders, keeping her at a distance that didn't singe his nerves with flash fires. "So, what is it you're after here?" He cleared his throat. "If you don't mind telling me?"

"I'm after your heart and soul, tough guy, that's what. I'm offering you me, in marriage." Her gaze flicked away from his then, revealing her nervousness. "I'm offering to make an honest man of you, Carpenter.'' She tugged at his shirt, trying to pull him closer.

She'd managed to stun him immobile. ''Marriage?''

''Yeah,'' she said with satisfaction. ''You. Me. Oliver. Marriage. Family. I think it's a great idea. And so I'm proposing to you. Of course,'' she added earnestly, ''I'm also trying to seduce you, but that's a separate issue.''

He couldn't think. ''Gabrielle, this is craziness. You deserve someone like, what's his name? Padgett?'' He raked his hands through his hair. ''Right. Someone like that.''

''Nope.'' She trailed a finger along his mouth, distracting him. ''I deserve you. And you deserve me, too, Joe, if you'd think about it.''

''Damned if I can think of much of anything right now, sweet pea,'' he said, managing to laugh. ''You're making me crazy, you know.''

''Am I? Really?''

He heard the trepidation in her voice and was moved by it. ''Yeah,'' he admitted. ''You are.''

''Oh, good. I'm trying to, you know.''

''I figured that out.'' Deciding that the best defense was a well-maneuvered offense, he enclosed her in his arms and swept her up, carrying her back to the couch—no, not the couch, he decided with the last remaining bit of conscience still alert in his overheated brain—the straight-back chair. Once there, he held her still in his arms. ''Look, Gabrielle, you're not thinking clearly. This isn't what you want.'' He waved toward the room, himself.

Her face turned serious, its sweetness weakening him in spite of everything. ''Joe, I mean exactly what I'm saying. Oliver needs a woman in his life as well as a father. He needs the kind of stability I could offer him. As for you, I think I've loved—''

He covered her mouth. ''Don't say it, Gabby. You can't take back words once said.''

Holding his gaze with hers, she pushed his hand away. ''I

think I've loved you since I was fifteen and you kissed me. My first kiss. I never wanted anyone else but you, Joe. And I want you now. With every fiber of my being, I want you. This isn't a sudden impulse on my part. It's been a gradual dawning of the light, you might say. It took me a while to sort out my motives and feelings, but I want you and Oliver in my life. For good. I want us to be a family and to celebrate Christmas and all the other holidays." She placed her hands on his cheeks, and her hands were warm. Not thinking, he pressed his mouth to her palm. "This is the best offer you'll ever have in your life, Carpenter, and you'd be a fool to pass it up."

It was an offer he didn't deserve, shouldn't listen to. He knew it was wrong, knew it wasn't fair to her, and he desperately sought the words to make her see how wrong for her marriage to him would be. "You deserve better," he repeated.

"I know what I deserve, Joe. And I know it won't be easy. Oliver is mixed up about his feelings toward me, and this may be difficult for him. I don't know how hard it will be. But I'm a tough cookie, Joe." She smoothed her thumb across his mouth, and he couldn't help following that light touch, couldn't help taking a taste of her skin. "I'm stubborn enough to wear him down. And, Joe," she murmured into the crook of his neck, "I'm stubborn enough to wear you down, too. So surrender, cry uncle, and say you'll marry me. Christmas Eve."

He discovered he didn't have the words to convince her how bad an idea marriage to him was for her. She would be taking on more than she could imagine. In one, final, desperate attempt to convince her, he told her about his doubts concerning Oliver's parentage. He was sure that knowledge would dissuade her.

It didn't.

She paused, thinking. "That's a tough one, Joe. What are you going to do? Does he need to know? Does it make a difference to you? Because it sure doesn't make an ant hill's bit of difference to me. He's your son. It's your call, whatever you decide. Sure, I think he should know someday. Maybe not right now when he's had so many changes. But someday. And whatever you decide, I'd like to be there *with* you, by your side. Because I'm crazy about the little stinker. And one day, whether he knows it or not, he's going to be crazy about me.''

That easily it was done.

His conscience lay in shreds, demolished by the feel of her in his arms, defeated by the shining dream she held up to him, the dream that she kept telling him could be real.

He'd thought it would be impossible to schedule a church wedding. It wasn't. Gabby knew of a small church on the island. Quaint, rarely used, it was on the gulf side, its tall, old-fashioned windows opened to the tang of salt air.

It offered a midnight service and a Christmas morning prayer service. During the early part of the evening, the church would be empty. If they wanted, they could be married at eight o'clock Christmas Eve.

Gabby wanted. And Joe discovered that he wanted to give her what she so foolishly had decided was necessary to her.

On Christmas Eve, as he waited at the head of the church, Oliver beside him in a navy suit and white shirt, his small hand gripping Joe's, Joe felt the stirrings of his conscience. He looked down at Oliver and straightened the Christmas-theme tie Gabby had given him. ''You okay with this, squirt?''

''Maybe,'' Oliver said. ''Maybe not.'' He fingers tightened on Joe's. ''Milo will be my grandfather?''

Joe nodded.

''That's okay.'' Oliver scuffed the floor. ''And Cletis can visit?''

Joe nodded again.

''And all Gabby's going to do is live at our house for a while?''

''For good, son. Forever.'' And with that word, Joe finally understood that Gabrielle was the person he needed to fill the emptiness inside him. It was as if there were a spot inside his heart that had waited for her through all the ugliness and sadness and anger. She completed him.

The immensity of that knowledge filled him, pushed away the shadows and hate still lingering. Music swelled around him, and for a moment, he thought the music was playing only in his head.

But the whispers behind him told him otherwise, and he turned to face Gabrielle, the woman who'd proposed to him, the woman who'd insisted that, no matter how bad he'd been, she believed he was good enough for her.

A slim column of white moved toward him. Her hair lay loose and free on her shoulders, and the narrow fabric of her dress, some sliplike, silvery white thing, moved and shimmered in the candlelit shadows of the church. Every pew had been draped with evergreens and red bows. Thick white candles in heavy gold candelabra were at the aisle end of each pew, and tiny white flowers like stars made a waterfall down the sides.

Gabrielle carried a spray of glossy green leaves and more star-shaped flowers that draped down the front of her long dress. Floating from a wreath of flowers and gold stars, her veil covered her face, but he saw her eyes grow damp as Milo took her hand and gave it to him.

"I love you, Pa," she whispered to Milo before he took his seat beside Nettie in the front pew.

Gabby had told him earlier that Nettie wanted to do the flowers, and watching Milo take Nettie's hand in his, Joe wondered if Gabby might soon return the favor.

The fragrance of the flowers and candles and pine were an incense of the spirit, and Joe breathed in the sweetness as Gabrielle came to his side. Taking her hand in his, keeping Oliver's stubby hand clasped in his other, Joe faced her and took her, for better, for worse, in sickness and in health, to be his wife.

And he pledged himself to her, a promise that he would

give her the best of himself in every way, that he would care for her, too, in sickness and in health. That he would never betray her or harm her.

Oliver gave him the ring, and Joe slipped it onto her finger as her hand curled into his. Each moment seemed more and more unreal, a moment out of time where he was caught in a dream from which he didn't want to wake.

Lifting her veil, he stared at her. "Are you sure, sweet pea, really sure?"

"Of course I am."

Spoken with sweet certainty, her words pierced his soul, reverberated through him as he took her mouth with his.

All the guests, and there were more than Joe could have imagined, flocked back to Milo's. Milo, of course, had cooked. In her white dress, Gabby moved among their friends, Joe and Oliver at her side, until everyone, even Moon, had left.

Nettie and Milo had taken their wine into the kitchen, leaving Gabrielle, Oliver and Joe alone in the living room. The tree lights shone in the darkened room, and the three of them, suddenly quiet, sank onto the couch, Joe in the middle. Gabby leaned her head on his shoulder, and a faint, elusive fragrance rose to him from her skin, her hair.

On his other side, Oliver stirred. "Want your present, Gabby?"

She leaned forward, across Joe. Her breasts were a sweet, tempting weight against his thighs. "Sure, Oliver. I'd love to open a present."

"'Kay." Oliver raced toward the kitchen. "Come see! Presents!"

Gabrielle linked her fingers through Joe's. Everything she wanted was in this house. Everything she'd come home to find had been here, waiting for her. Pa. Nettie. Oliver.

Joe.

She'd wanted to make a perfect Christmas for her Pa. Instead, she'd stumbled on love. She'd taken a risk and tried to seduce Joe. *She'd* proposed to him. Because she loved him.

Oh, she knew her feelings toward him, and she knew, even in her inexperience, that she could arouse his passion. What his deeper feelings were, she could only hope and let her instincts guide her. If Joe came to love her, and she believed he would in time, believed in her most private heart that he would see how right their marriage was for all of them, well, then, she would truly have a miracle. She would have been given a Christmas gift that had no price.

Oliver handed her an awkwardly wrapped brown paper package. Glitter sprinkled onto her wedding dress as she opened the package carefully, spreading the decorated paper open. When she saw what lay on her lap, tears slid down her cheeks, tears that she couldn't stop, no matter how often she wiped them away.

"What's wrong, sweet pea?"

"You don't like it?" Oliver said softly, his voice cracking. "I wanted you to like it. I thought it would fix everything."

"Oh, sweetie, I *love* it. It's the most beautiful present anyone ever, ever gave me." She wanted to hug him close, but she didn't dare. She brushed his hair back from his face, and immediately it flopped back onto his forehead. "What a wonderful, clever idea." Then, with shaking hands, she held up the homemade star. The star was mounted on an aluminum-covered toilet paper roll. Glued to its front and back, shards of Irish crystal sparkled with rainbow reflections.

"I found the broken pieces in the drawer with Cletis's munchies. Is it okay?" Anxiety pinched Oliver's face.

"It's more than okay. It's, oh, Oliver, I can't believe that you thought of this." Tears slid down her face again, and Joe pulled her closer. She brushed Oliver's hair back once more, to let him know the wonder of his gift. "Joe, hold Oliver up to the tree. So he can put on the O'Shea star." Her hands still trembling, Gabrielle handed the star to Oliver.

Joe held Oliver up high, and, not saying a word, Oliver carefully settled the star at the top of the tree.

Milo snapped a picture of the three of them together by the

tree. Gabrielle held up the hem of her dress so that her snow-flake-flocked stockings would show in the picture.

"I might have known." Joe laughed. "My Christmas bride and her Christmas socks."

"*Stockings,* Joe," she said prissily. "Socks are cheaper. *These—*" she stuck one foot in his direction "—were very expensive."

"They look worth the cost." He encircled her ankle with his finger and thumb. "I'm developing quite a fondness for holiday socks."

She and Joe and Oliver curled up on the sofa, intending to watch the lights on the tree and the star while her dad drove Nettie home. Wanting Oliver to share every minute of Christmas Eve and to celebrate their marriage with them, she and Joe stayed at Milo's, waiting for him to return before they left for Joe's house and their wedding night. In the morning they would go back to Milo's for the rest of their Christmas celebration. Instead, tired and comfortable, drowsy with wine and emotion, they slumped together, Joe in the middle, and all three fell asleep.

Gabrielle woke to a splash of brilliant sunlight in her face. During the night someone had covered them with a blanket. She yawned, stretched and looked at Joe and Oliver. Both male Carpenters slept with their mouths slightly parted, Oliver making tiny snuffling noises.

She leaned over and kissed Joe. "Merry, merry Christmas, Joe. Want to stay here or go home and change? Christmas dinner will be much later. What would you like to do?"

As she climbed out from under the blanket, he stirred and turned to her. "What I'd like is my wedding night, sweet pea." He snaked his open palm up along her ribs, covered her breast. "I've been dreaming I got married. But I don't remember making love to my wife. And I'm hungry—for her, not for food."

She glanced quickly toward the sleeping child, blushed and said sternly, "Later. Tonight. If you're lucky."

"I plan on being very lucky," Joe said to her with a wicked, wicked gleam that woke up every ounce of her sleepy blood. "And so will you." He kissed her quickly, lightly. "Be." He kissed her again. "Lucky." He kissed her again, a long, lingering exploration that buckled her knees and left her wishing Christmas day were over.

With most of Gabrielle's clothes still at her father's house and in storage, she stayed at Milo's while Joe and Oliver left to shower and change before returning to the O'Shea household where everyone was coming for Christmas dinner.

With part of her mind on the turkey she was basting, Gabrielle tried to keep her thoughts away from the coming night. Her heart skittered and thumped every time she thought about herself and Joe, alone for the first time in the big bed he'd ordered for his—no, for *their* bedroom.

What if she disappointed Joe?

What if her inexperience bored him?

What if she couldn't—

"Darn!" She wiped gravy from the kitchen floor and washed her hands, letting the cold water run over her wrists and soothe her overheated self, even if it couldn't cool down her imagination. What would be, would be. She'd survive. Joe would, too.

Maybe, as Oliver was so fond of saying, she thought grimly and slapped the faucet off.

By the time Joe and Oliver returned to open the rest of the presents, she was a bundle of nerves and excitement and hope.

She'd changed into a green-and-burgundy-plaid taffeta dress that rustled satisfactorily when she walked, and as she answered the door she flushed as Joe's gaze moved slowly over her like the brush of his hands.

As Joe finally let his eyes leave her, he walked through the door, a lumpily wrapped package in his hands. Folding back the paper, he silently held out the object to her. Gold-painted macaroni covered a cardboard picture frame. Inside the frame, a chubby-faced three-year-old smiled back at her.

"Your idea, Mrs. Carpenter?"

Looking down, she touched the frame carefully, impossibly moved by the expression in Joe's eyes. "I helped. Oliver wanted to give you something special. I told him something he made would be part of himself, the best gift possible." She glanced at Joe. Made vulnerable by his love for his son, he was infinitely dear to her, and her heart almost cracked with the weight of her love for him. For his son. "You're a good man, Joe Carpenter. Your son loves you." Touching the frame again, she swallowed past the sudden lump in her throat.

"Thank you, Gabrielle." His hand slid to the back of her neck and he pulled her close for one fierce, tender, heart-dissolving kiss.

Oliver helped Cletis unwrap his presents, told Gabrielle about the bicycle Santa had left him at his own home and dug around under the tree, an expectant look on his face. He didn't say anything, though.

"Oliver, there's a special present for you, way to the back. It's that square package. See it?" Gabrielle held her breath as he pulled it out, dropped it and picked it up again.

"Mine?"

"Yours. From me." She waited, crossing mental fingers as he tore into the wrappings.

The star was Irish crystal. It hadn't been made by the same artisan that had made the O'Shea star. She'd had to drive to Tampa to have the star made in time for Christmas Day.

"You don't want the star I made you?"

"Oh, Oliver." She knelt and wrapped her arms around his tense body. "I love my star. It will always be on my tree. But this star? It's for you, for your children, for your trees in all the years to come. It's the *Carpenter* star. Yours, forever."

"Oh." He touched the edges carefully. "For me. Because you're marrying my daddy and going to live in my house." He laid the star carefully on the sofa. "Well, I don't want your old star," he sobbed, tiredness and frustration tearing through him as he wrapped his arms around Joe's leg. "He's *my* daddy. He wants *me,* not you."

"Of course he does," Gabrielle said. "I gave you your star because I love you. Because you deserve your own star. Because your daddy loves you more than anything in the whole, wide world. You're his son, and no one can take that away from you. No one can take your place. Not me, not anyone." She stooped next to him. "Do you understand how much your daddy loves you, Oliver? He would die for you. That's how much. A father's love can't be replaced. *Nobody* could ever take your place." Hugging him carefully, cautiously, she felt the tension seep from his small body. "Do you understand? Because it's important for you to know that, to know what a treasure you are. And *that's* why I gave you your crystal star."

"'Kay," he said, wrapping one chubby, sweaty arm around her neck. "Maybe I do."

He stayed with Joe for a while, and then Cletis galumphed by, Oliver took off after him, and Gabrielle wanted to waltz and sing carols and "eat Christmas cookies till I pop," she said, and nibbled on one of the cookies Oliver and she had decorated. "This is, without a doubt, my favorite Christmas of all."

And later, at Joe's house with Oliver sleeping down the hall, exactly as she'd dreamed, she unwrapped Joe's present to her. Joe had placed candles everywhere in the room, candles fragrant with the smells of Christmas. In the candlelight, the large, ungainly box sat at the edge of the bed. Pulling the sides of the box clear, Gabrielle gasped.

Inside the box was a narrow burled wooden chest with twelve thin drawers.

"Open the drawers, sweet pea." Lounging against the bedroom door, watching her alertly, Joe waited.

Each drawer was filled with neatly rolled-up socks. Thanksgiving, Halloween, Fourth of July, socks for each month of the year. And in each drawer, one pair of masculine socks, discreetly and seasonally patterned, lay next to the rest of the socks.

"Joe?"

"I thought I could get into this celebration thing. Maybe, maybe not," he said, echoing his son. "But I thought I'd give it a try."

She knew he was talking about more than socks. In the last drawer, a lumpy pair of Christmas socks wrapped a bulky object. Pulling the lump free of the candy-cane-patterned fabric, she gasped. In the darkness of the black material, light winked, something glittered.

"Oh, Joe," she whispered, holding up a crystal star. "Oh, Joe. You and Oliver, you both gave me Christmas back. My two stars."

He touched the star gently, ran his long finger over it, up her bare arm to her breast where her heart shuddered under her silk nightgown. He cupped his palm over her breast, and his expression was intent, focused on her, her face. "No, Gabby, you gave me Christmas. You gave me—"

Something she'd hoped to see stirred in his eyes, and she gathered her courage. "You love me, don't you?" Her throat closed.

"Yeah, sweet pea, I sure do. You're the gift I never expected in my life, wouldn't have known how to ask for. You're my very own Christmas miracle. Your goodness to me, to Oliver, to the people around you, leaves me speechless with awe. I don't deserve you, but I'll be double-damned if I won't go to bed every night for the rest of my life giving thanks for you." His voice turned dark and fierce. "I love you so much that it stuns me. It scares me, because if you walked away from me, I don't think I could survive."

"I'd never leave you, Joe. I've loved you all my life. I waited for you when I didn't even know I was looking for you." She tucked her finger in between two shirt buttons. And tugged. "Come to bed, Joe. Good girls can be bad, too, you know."

"Oh, I like the sound of that," he muttered into her ear as he lifted her into his arms. "Very promising idea. But did you know that bad boys can be very, very good? Given the right encouragement?"

He took the star off the bed and placed it on the nightstand, where it shimmered in the room, its light catching the flickering candle flames. Looking at it, he grinned. "Think we could have more than one Christmas tree?"

"Oh, Joe." With his shadowed face leaning over her, she couldn't think, couldn't breathe. "We'll have a houseful of trees and kids and celebrations."

She fumbled with the buttons of his shirt, love and passion making her clumsy. He helped her, guided her hands down the shirt to his belt. He helped her there, too, until they both lay skin to skin, his elbows supporting him as he moved in a rhythm she'd vaguely sensed long ago, that hunger as nothing compared to the need he created in her now with every touch and stroke. And, delighted, she began to see that she, too, was creating that same hunger in him.

This was what she'd waited for, this *togetherness,* this understanding that what he could make her feel, what she could make him feel, that what they were creating in this room where candles shimmered around them and their glow touched his face, hers, with light was a miracle of love and caring, a miracle worth waiting for.

Over his shoulder she saw a star blaze through the darkness of Christmas night, and as she took Joe to herself, his touch filled her with wonder. "Ah, Joe," she murmured into the curve of his neck as his hand curved over her and sent her into delicious shudders, "I'm *so* glad I'm not fifteen anymore."

"Me, too, sweetheart." His chuckle sent the loveliest shivers throughout her body. "Because I've waited too long already."

"So you have," she said primly, her skin prickling and tingling as he kissed his way up from her tummy. "And you

should be rewarded. I think I have just the reward for you.''
Lifting her arms, she wrapped them around his neck and pulled
his mouth to hers.

And by the light of the stars shining through the windows,
she proceeded to show him exactly, precisely what a good girl
could do when she loved the right man.

* * * * *

Daddy's Angel

Annette Broadrick

This book is dedicated to all those very special angels
who devote their valuable time to the loving,
nurturing and caring of a husband and/or children
365 days a year.

You know who you are. So does God.

Prologue

Noelle waited patiently.

Noelle St. Nichols had all the patience in the world. Of course, technically speaking, she wasn't part of the world.

Not exactly.

For several seasons now, she'd been a Christmas angel, the kind who presides at the very top of the Christmas tree each season.

Before accepting her present occupation, she'd enjoyed a multitude of varied assignments…all part of the training for novice angels. Not that people on earth understand the extensive training each and every angel willingly pursues. Many people have absolutely no conception that angels exist.

Of course most people have heard about them, particularly at Christmastime. Whenever the Christmas story is told, the listener hears about the time when the angels appeared to the shepherds, announcing the birth of the baby Jesus.

Because of the special sense of love and understanding that seems to fill the air around Christmastime, some people—if asked—might admit that quite possibly there really was a time when there were angels who actually talked to shepherds. If pressed, they might admit to believing that even in this day and age there are angels who protect small children.

Few people, however, want to admit that they could have a guardian angel, although they might joke about the possibility.

Noelle had never been able to understand how people could speak about guardian angels as though they were a joke. How could such an honorable profession be considered amusing?

At one point in her training, her highest aspiration had been to become a guardian angel. She had diligently studied for her proposed calling and had been given several assignments that had resulted in less than spectacular results. She'd discovered that attempting to guide and protect a person who was determined to ignore that quiet voice within could be difficult—not to mention downright frustrating!

Noelle sighed and thought back over her long and varied career, which had been filled with unexpected twists and turns.

One of her less admirable traits was her impulsiveness.

She wouldn't be where she was today if she hadn't

impulsively offered to fill in for a friend on this particular assignment.

How could she have known at the time the far-reaching effects her present occupation would have on her own goals and aspirations? Even if she could have foreseen the consequences, she wasn't certain she could have resisted the opportunity to be with children.

Children were her very special love. What better way for her to be around them than to become part of their annual celebration of Christmas?

Small children still had memories of the time when they lived with the angels. They recognized her immediately. Consequently she had no difficulty communicating with them.

She'd been filled with excitement by the thought that she might be placed in a child's home and be given the opportunity to offer one or more children a refresher course on love and all its many aspects— such as compassion ... and caring ... understanding ... and sharing ... empathy ... and acceptance.

As far as she was concerned, one of her most sacred duties was to remind children of the larger significance of Christmas, that it was a magical time when love could produce miracles.

Children came into the world filled with a wondrous knowledge of all things. Unfortunately many of them forgot about the wonder and the magic of Christmas as they grew older, which was why Noelle St. Nichols chose to come to earth as a reminder. So she became a Christmas tree angel.

And fell head over heels in love.

She sighed, thinking of the series of events that had taken place for her since she had become a Christmas tree angel. So much had happened, both joyous and sad.

Bret Bishop had had an extraordinary effect on her. He had stolen her heart as surely as a train robber successfully empties a safe.

She winced at her unfortunate choice of metaphor. The train robber had been one of her earlier assignments as a guardian angel. He hadn't been one of her successes.

Her record carried as many failures as it did triumphs, although her supervisor continued to remind her that there was no such thing as a failure in their dimension...only lessons to be learned.

Falling in love certainly hadn't been part of her particular curriculum, but it had happened, even though Bret Bishop was unaware of her existence.

While she waited for her annual liberation from the attic, Noelle reminisced, reliving that time in her history when she had believed she would be filling in as a Christmas tree angel for only a few weeks.

She wore a shimmery white gown with a long full skirt that stood stiffly in a full circle around her. Her white-blond hair fell in waves to her waist and framed her face. A twinkling halo of brilliants encircled her head and in her left hand she carried a tiny, star-tipped wand.

For several days she'd entertained herself by sending waves of loving energy to the children who walked through the aisles of the department store where she was displayed. Rarely did she notice the adults until the day she heard someone say, "Bret, would you look at this?"

A young woman with short black curls framing her face paused in front of the tree ornament section where Noelle was prominently displayed. The man beside her obligingly glanced at Noelle.

Noelle looked back...and was a goner.

The first thing she noticed about Bret Bishop was his happiness. He glowed with it, especially whenever he looked at the woman beside him.

He was young, Noelle noted. A very fine specimen of manhood—his body perfectly proportioned, his face filled with integrity.

Noelle was certain she knew him...or had known him from some other dimension in space and time. Her reaction was much too strong not to have been forged in an earlier reality.

"She's something, isn't she, Patti?" he responded. His deep voice caused shivers along Noelle's spine.

"Wouldn't she be beautiful on top of our tree?"

Bret smiled, his teasing filled with love. "Honey, I don't know quite how to tell you this," he drawled, "but that angel, small as she is, would dwarf our puny li'l ol' tree."

"Then let's get a bigger tree," Patti promptly suggested.

"You're the one who said a miniature fir tree was all the two of us needed this year."

Patti looked up at him with an impish grin. "I

know. I was thinking about this being our first Christmas.'' She touched his arm, her gaze imploring. ''Darling, someday we'll have a family. Can't you just picture that little angel sitting on top of a tree, with all our children gathered around?''

He slipped his arm around her waist and tugged her closer to his side, placing a light kiss on her nose.

''*A-a-l-ll* our children?'' he repeated, chuckling. ''Sounds like you're planning to have dozens.''

She tucked her fingers into the side belt loops of his snug-fitting jeans and peered up at him through her thick lashes. ''I have a hunch that we have so much love to share we're going to want a houseful of babies, honey.''

Bret's response to her throaty, deliberately provocative comment was laughter—rich, exuberant and filled with joy.

How could Noelle have resisted falling in love?

All right, so this couple didn't have children. So what? They were young, probably newlyweds and they understood what love and life and Christmas were truly about. Noelle hoped they would buy her, regardless of the size of their present tree. She wanted to be a part of their lives, to oversee a family that would grow and become an integral part of her present existence.

She also hoped to find a niche in the life of Bret Bishop. She would be content to see him each year, content to be a tiny part of his world.

Noelle got her wish. Bret and Patti took her home

that very day, to a two-room apartment near the campus where he was attending his last year of college.

During that first Christmas season with Bret and Patti, Noelle learned of their hopes and dreams as they sat in front of the lighted tree each night and discussed plans for their future.

She discovered that Bret had been born on a ranch in central Texas. Patti had grown up nearby. They had been friends all their lives. Neither one had ever considered living anywhere other than in the familiar hills of central Texas.

When Bret's grandfather died when Bret was eighteen, he left his ranching property to his grandson. However, Bret's father had insisted that Bret get his education—learn the latest about agriculture and livestock breeding—before taking over the actual running of the place. Bret had married Patti the summer before his senior year knowing that as soon as he graduated, they would move to the ranch and live there full-time.

Patti had finished a two-year course of her own and had found a job in the college town until her husband finished with his schooling. Their apartment was like a dollhouse. Life for them their first year seemed almost like playing and not at all like being married. The small apartment often rang with their laughter.

Noelle blessed their first Christmas together and patiently waited throughout the next year, and all the years that followed, to spend those few very special weeks with her newly expanding family.

First came Chris, a stocky little boy with his mother's gray eyes and his father's flashing smile.

Two years later Brenda appeared, full of bounce and seemingly unlimited energy. She had her father's light brown hair and golden eyes.

Eventually Sally arrived—tiny, but with a strong will and healthy lungs.

Noelle introduced herself to each one of the children and explained to them who she was and why she was a part of their household. As the years passed, each child came to her to share secret wishes and cherished dreams. She watched as each one grew older until first Chris, then eventually Brenda and Sally forgot how to speak with her...and how to listen for her voice.

Noelle would never forget the year when Bret and Patti were decorating the newest Christmas tree and Patti told Bret that, once again, she was pregnant....

Bret stared at Patti in dismay. "Pregnant? But you can't be! Didn't the doctor say—"

Patti went up on tiptoe, wrapping her arms around his neck. "What do you mean, I can't be?" she whispered with a smile. "Is your memory already slipping, cowboy? Do I have to go into detail exactly when and how this happened?" She kissed him in her very special way.

She managed to distract him, as usual, but only for a few moments. When he pulled away from her, he was frowning. "How can you joke about it, honey? How could you forget about the rough time you had when you carried Sally? The doctor told us then that—''

She covered his mouth with her hand. ''I know what the doctor said, Bret. But lots of things have changed. Sally is almost five, so my body's had plenty of time to rest and recuperate. Besides, there's been all kinds of medical advances since my last pregnancy. I'm not worried and I don't want you to be, either.'' She danced away from him, threw her arms wide and turned in a circle. ''I'm so excited. Just think! We're going to have another Bishop to love. Sally will start preschool in the spring. By fall she'll be ready for the first grade. The house will be so empty.''

She paused and looked around the room with all its boxes of decorations. ''Just think, Bret. This time next year we'll have a baby in our home once again, one who'll be dazzled by all the lights and color.'' She returned to Bret's side and brushed her fingers against his cheek. ''Please be happy, honey. I know it's a bit of a shock, but I didn't want to say anything to you until I found out for sure. I wanted my news to be a special Christmas surprise for everybody.'' Her voice dropped to a whisper and tears filled her eyes. ''I can't think of anything I want more than to have another one of your children to love.''

He took her hand and gently placed a kiss in her palm. ''Honey, if this is what you want, then I'm happy, too.'' He gathered her in his arms as though she were made of the most fragile porcelain. ''All I've ever wanted was for you to be happy.''

"How could I not be happy? I have everything I could possibly want in my life—you and the children. I feel truly blessed."

He shook his head, humbled by her courage and her determination. "I love you, Patti Bishop," he murmured, holding her close.

"I love you, too, Bret. More than I can possibly say."

Unfortunately their love for each other wasn't enough to keep Patti alive.

She was careful.

She followed the doctor's instructions.

She did everything she was supposed to do.

But her heart gave out without warning during the delivery of her second son. The skilled medical staff was unable to resuscitate her.

Noelle knew the events of that year despite the fact that she was packed carefully away with all the other decorations.

She felt Bret's pain at the loss of his beloved wife.

She felt his bewilderment when faced with the prospect of trying to raise four children on his own.

She felt his anger that God could have allowed such a thing to happen.

The newborn was a healthy little boy with his mother's black curls and gray eyes. Bret gave him the name Patti had picked for a boy—Travis.

Travis was four months old his first Christmas. If the older children hadn't insisted, Bret wouldn't have put up a tree that year. He found the season too pain-

ful a reminder of other years when Patti had been by
his side.

The children missed their mother with a heartbro-
ken intensity. Having the new baby to care for kept
them going. Travis became their focal point. Taking
care of him helped to heal their pain and ease their
loss.

Three more years had passed and it was Christmastime once again, the fourth Christmas the Bishop
family had spent without Patti. Noelle wanted to
weep at the harsh changes that had taken place in
Bret.

The laughing young man she'd first caught sight
of all those years ago was gone, never to be seen
again. In his place was a grim-faced rancher with
overwhelming duties and responsibilities.

Bret had adjusted to his new way of life in some
ways. He'd grown accustomed to being on his own
with the children. He made certain he was there
whenever they needed him. He planned his work
schedule around their school schedules. He watched
over them and supervised them.

What saddened Noelle the most was that over the
years Bret had lost more than his mate....

Bret had lost his belief in the goodness of life.

Bret had abandoned all his hopes and dreams.

Noelle knew that yet another upheaval was soon
to cause additional problems for the Bishop family.
Unfortunately, as a mere Christmas tree angel she
didn't have the jurisdiction to change certain events
that had already been set into motion. She understood

that every seemingly random event had a positive reason and result behind it. However, she knew that Bret wouldn't see the event in that light. He would see another burden placed on his shoulders.

She was afraid for him…afraid he would falter under his grim load of responsibilities because he'd lost sight of the very things that could lighten the burdens for him.

Somehow, someway, she wanted to be able to help him—to ease his load, to help him regain some of his beliefs about life, to help him to understand how things have a way of working out if we only give them a chance.

If we only believe.

Noelle contacted her supervisor to discuss the present situation in the Bishop household. She had a request to make—a very special request—one that was most unusual but because of the upcoming emergency, most necessary.

She knew the risks. As an angel she had never taken human form, never experienced human emotions, never been plagued by earthly considerations. She knew there would be limitations placed on her. She knew that, if she was given permission to take a more active role in the Bishop family, she would have to return to her original form no later than midnight on Christmas Eve.

She didn't know if that would give her enough time to help Bret. She only knew that she had to make the effort before he gave up on life completely.

She had to try.

Chapter One

Dark clouds rolled along the northern horizon, add-ing an urgency to Bret's movements. He gave the barbed wire an extra twist of his wrist, then wearily straightened and looked along the fence he'd recently mended.

No doubt a deer had pulled the top strand loose while bounding across the fence, causing the line to sag. He'd been checking all the fence lines of his ranch for the past several days. Some of the terrain was too rugged for him to use his pickup truck, his usual mode of conveyance. For the last two days he'd ridden Hercules.

Perhaps traveling around the ranch on horseback had prompted the recurrence of his memories of Patti. After all, Patti had given Hercules to him. She'd always enjoyed riding with him whenever she could get away for a few hours.

No doubt his saddling up Hercules and riding him yesterday had triggered the dreams he'd had last night.

He'd dreamed that Patti was alive. She'd been there next to him, holding him, talking to him, loving him.

His dream had seemed so real.

In it he told her that he thought she'd died. They laughed about such a silly idea. She'd held him in her arms and told him that she would never leave him. Not ever.

In the first seconds of awakening that morning he'd reached for her with joy in his heart, glad to be through with the nightmare of doing without her, only to find the other side of the bed empty.

He'd opened his eyes and realized the truth.

Patti was gone. She'd been gone for more than three years now.

No doubt his vivid dream the night before had caused the ache of missing her to be so strong today. He'd been feeling her loss all day in the same way he'd felt during those first black months when he hadn't believed he could go on without her.

A soft whine and the familiar weight leaning against his knee called Bret back to the present. He glanced down and rubbed his hand over Rex's head, glad for the German shepherd's company.

Even though the dog was getting up in years, he continued to follow Bret around the ranch, generally riding in the truck cab when it was raining or cold.

"Yeah, I know, old man," he murmured. "The

wind's picking up and we've got a ways to go before we're home, with no truck heater to take the chill off.''

Bret glanced around, seeing the gusts of wind create eddies of silt around them. He readjusted his broad-brimmed hat, pulling it low over his eyes, and headed over to where the horse waited.

The creak of the leather made a familiar sound as he mounted the horse and gathered the reins in his gloved hand. He glanced to the north, narrowing his eyes as he measured the swiftness of the clouds racing toward him.

Those clouds looked ominous, threatening cold wind and icy rain. He didn't want to get caught in the hills when the rain hit. The footing among the rocks and cacti was dangerous enough in the best of conditions. Hopefully they would make it to the ranch road before the threatened downpour reached them.

Bret started down through the heavy underbrush of the rock-strewn hillside. Rex followed close behind.

Now that he was headed home, Bret's thoughts raced on ahead to his family, his expression growing more grim.

Chris had reminded him over breakfast this morning that they needed to get a tree before the yearly shipment of firs were all picked over. Chris, especially, insisted on keeping all the family traditions Patti had started. Even to the point of dragging out the same decorations year after year.

Thinking about the decorations reminded Bret of the year he'd suggested to Patti that they should replace the bedraggled-looking Christmas tree angel they'd found the first Christmas they were married.

The tiny figure had lost the tip of one of her wings, her dress hung limp and the glitter had long since disappeared from her halo. Patti had been shocked and incensed that he would suggest such a thing. The angel was part of the Bishop Christmas tradition.

Now the children were just as bad about adhering to tradition. Christmas season didn't officially begin in the Bishop household until the tree was up, decorated and Bret had placed the angel with great ceremony at the top.

If Chris had his way, Bret would be up on the stepladder tonight, clutching the tiny ornament in his hand.

Bret had tried to explain that he didn't have time to go to town today, that he had too many other things to do. That's when Chris had asked if he could get Roy to take him to get the tree.

Bret didn't know what he would have done during the past three years without Roy Baker. The ranch hand originally had been a part of the crew that worked for Bret's father ever since Bret had been a teenager. When Patti died, Roy—with no commotion—had moved to Bret's ranch and taken over the daily chores around the place. He knew as much about ranching as anybody in the district, but had never wanted the responsibility of his own place.

Roy was exactly the kind of friend Bret had

needed during that black time after Patti's death, when Bret hadn't been certain he could survive without Patti by his side.

Roy had filled in wherever he was needed. A shy man only a few years older than Bret, Roy understood what needed to be done to keep the ranch in working order without Bret having to mention it.

Bret had been grateful for the help. They had never discussed whether the move would be temporary or permanent, but during the past three years Roy had settled into the small house that was part of the ranch buildings and become an integral part of the Bishop family circle.

Bringing a brand-new motherless child home from the hospital had been a painful and traumatic time for all of them. Bret hated to think what they would have done if fate, in the form of another lifelong friend, hadn't come to his rescue.

Freda Wilkenson had spent her early youth caring for her invalid mother and had never had time to develop a social life of her own. A few years older than Bret, Freda, timid and soft-spoken, approached him with a suggestion a few days after he'd brought Travis home.

Her mother had recently passed away and Freda felt lost with nothing to do to fill her empty days. She offered to move out to the ranch as housekeeper and to look after the children.

Accepting her offer of help had saved his sanity.

Bret knew that he couldn't have gotten through these past three years without the help of Roy and

Freda. They had been there for him, encouraging him to establish some kind of life for his children during those days when all he'd wanted to do was to saddle up and keep on riding until he fell off the edge of the world.

Eventually he'd learned a very important lesson—a person couldn't feel sorry for himself for long when he had four children who needed his attention and care.

He still saw Patti in the silvery-gray flash of Chris's eyes…and caught a glimpse of her sparkling mischievousness in Brenda and Sally. But it was Travis who repeatedly pulled at his heartstrings. As though to make up for her loss, Patti had somehow passed on to her youngest son not only her black curls and features, but her gentle and loving personality as well.

Travis didn't talk much. With three older siblings, he didn't have to, since all of them had a habit of anticipating his every want and need. Despite the attention, he wasn't spoiled. He was just a happy little boy who offered his unconditional love to everyone around him.

Travis had listened to the girls over breakfast that morning as they asked when they were going to go shopping. He had stopped them all by asking if he was going to get to see Santa at the mall again this year. No one had thought Travis could have remembered his visit last Christmas, but obviously he had.

In an effort to gain some time, Bret had agreed to let Chris ask Roy to take him to town today to buy a tree, but only if Roy didn't have something else he needed to do.

Bret knew he was being a coward. He knew he should have agreed to take Chris into town, himself. It was just that Christmas never seemed to get any easier for him. He wished he could disappear until all the fuss of the season was behind him for another year.

He hated having to go into town for supplies between Thanksgiving and New Year's. Shiny tinsel streamers and giant red bells arched across the main streets of the small ranching community where they did most of their shopping. Every store he entered had its own display, generally accompanied by Christmas music.

There was just no getting away from the music. Even the country music station he listened to in the truck interspersed the current hits being played with familiar voices singing traditional songs.

A person couldn't get away from the reminders, no matter how much he tried.

A strong gust of wind grabbing at his hat brought Bret jarringly back to the present. He reached up and once more tugged the brim down low over his eyes.

Looking around, he noticed that while he'd been lost in thought, they'd managed to reach the dirt road that led back to the ranch buildings. Bret signaled the horse by subtly shifting his weight. Hercules immediately responded with ground-eating strides and Rex loped along beside them.

They reached the ranch buildings minutes before

the storm hit. Safely inside the barn, Bret watched from the wide doorway as large hail bounced off the ground and the surrounding buildings. He breathed a thankful prayer that he'd gotten home when he did.

He took his time unsaddling Hercules and cooling him down before he wiped the horse dry and fed him. Although he could always explain to Freda and the kids that he'd been waiting for the first of the front to pass by, he knew the truth.

He dreaded going inside. If Roy hadn't taken Chris to town when he got home from school, then Bret knew he'd have to do so as soon as they ate.

If Roy had taken Chris to town, then Bret would have to help decorate the tree tonight. He knew he was putting off the inevitable. Sooner or later he would have to go into the house and face whatever festivities the family had planned for the evening.

By the time Bret sprinted across the wide expanse between the barn and house the hail had been replaced by pounding, icy rain splashing mud and turning the ground into a slippery quagmire.

He took the back-porch steps two at a time, then paused beneath the shelter of the roof to wipe off the bottoms of his boots before entering Freda's spotless kitchen. He removed his gloves and opened the door, already anticipating a cup of Freda's coffee to help remove the chill.

The first thing he noticed when he opened the door was the dark kitchen. The kitchen was the heart of their home, and its light generally came on first thing in the morning and stayed on until the last thing at night.

Today it was dark and deserted.

Bret absently brushed his hat off his head and hung it and his coat on a set of hooks beside the back door, next to the children's jackets. He noted that Chris's coat wasn't there, which probably meant that Chris and Roy hadn't returned from town, but didn't explain why Freda wasn't in the kitchen preparing supper.

"Hello?" he called. "Anybody home?"

Bret heard scrambling upstairs and the clattering of feet on the wooden stairs. At least somebody was here.

Eleven-year-old Brenda was the first to appear. Her golden eyes were wide with concern. Bret had a sudden sense of unease flash over him, which was confirmed with her first words.

"Dad! Thank goodness you're home! You'll never guess what happened this afternoon!"

Since his daughter was known for speaking in exclamations whenever she was excited, Bret tried not to let her delivery cause him to jump to premature conclusions before hearing some details. Obviously something had happened out of their normal routine.

Eight-year-old Sally arrived immediately behind her sister, looking worried. However, Bret felt a strong sense of unease when three-year-old Travis came in clutching his familiar stuffed giraffe by its long neck, his eyes red from crying and his face pale.

Bret knelt down on one knee and Travis ran into his arms, burying his face in Bret's neck.

Bret fought a surge of panic. The three younger children were obviously all right. It had to be...

"What happened? Is Chris—"

Brenda rushed into speech. "Chris and Roy had to take Freda to the hospital a while ago. She fell and Roy's afraid maybe she broke her leg or her hip or something. Oh, Dad! It was awful! She was in the kitchen and Roy thinks she must have stepped on some tree needles or something that dropped on the floor when they brought the tree inside and she didn't see it. Roy checked her as best as he could, then he called the doctor and the doctor said for him to get her to the hospital." She finally had to pause for a breath.

Bret stood, still holding Travis in his arms. In a quiet voice, which effectively disguised his growing sense of panic, he asked, "How long ago did this happen?"

Sally was the one who answered. "Almost two hours ago. We promised Freda we'd keep Travis entertained until you got back home and we did, but now he's saying he's hungry and we weren't sure what we should do."

Brenda responded. "Of course we knew what to do, Dad. It isn't like I don't know how to cook or anything. But you told us not to have any fire going when an adult wasn't here, so I've been waiting, thinking you'd be home soon."

Bret stroked her head with his hand. "Thanks, honey. I'm glad you remembered."

"We could have sandwiches, couldn't we?" Sally asked, glaring at her sister.

"That's a good idea," Bret said. "Why don't you make some while I call the hospital and see what I can find out about Freda?" He gave Travis a quick hug, then set him in his high chair. With quick strides Bret headed down the hallway to his office, where he could talk in private.

The closest hospital was almost fifty miles away. Although the facility was small, several doctors drove from the surrounding large cities—Austin and San Antonio—to provide additional services to the sparsely populated hill country. He knew that Freda would receive excellent care there. What he was concerned about at the moment was the seriousness of her injuries.

As soon as he got through to the hospital Bret had Roy paged. He drummed his fingers on the desk, waiting what seemed like hours before Roy finally came on the line.

"How is she?"

Roy laughed, which eased Bret's tension considerably. "That woman's too feisty for her own good, boss. She's insisting she's got to get back home tonight, that she's got too much to do and that the children shouldn't be left alone. You know what she's like."

"Can you tell me what happened? The girls were a little excited and I'm not sure I understood."

"She stepped on something slippery and her foot went out from under her. Me and Chris had been trailing back and forth through there, bringing in the tree and all, and it's my guess we tracked something inside the house and she didn't see it in time to avoid it. It wouldn't have been so bad but she fell wrong— all awkwardlike. From the pain she was in I pretty much figured she'd broke a bone."

"Is that what the doctors say?"

"Yep, her leg's definitely broken. They're ordering further tests, including more X rays, to look for anything else that might have been injured. I called Freda's sister in Austin to let her know about it, so she's on her way over here to sit with her."

"Did the doctor say how long she would need to stay in the hospital?"

"He wants to keep her for several days, which has got Freda all upset, let me tell you."

"You tell Freda that I want her to stop worrying about me and the kids. We'll do just fine. I want her to rest and recuperate. Tell her to lie back and enjoy being waited on for a change…to pretend she's on vacation."

"Some vacation," Roy muttered.

"I know. I take it that Chris is still there with you?"

"You bet he is. I don't know what I would have done without that boy this afternoon. He was right there helping me with Freda as calm as you please just like he was a growed up man and knew exactly what to do. I was downright impressed by the way he kept his head and all. That son of yours is growing up real fast.''

"I know.''

"I never realized it until we was helpin' to get Freda in my truck, but that dang kid is almost as tall as I am,'' Roy said, his amazement plain. "When did that happen?''

"I noticed the same thing a day or so ago, Roy. I guess that's what happens when you keep feedin' 'em.''

"I keep threat'ning to put a brick on his head, but it don't seem to do much good.''

Bret looked at his watch. "How much longer do you intend to stay at the hospital?''

"Until the doctor tells me what these last X rays show. Then I'll take the kid out and buy him something to eat before we head home.''

Bret massaged his forehead, absently noting a headache he hadn't been aware of until now. "Sounds like a good plan to me.''

"At least we managed to get that tree set in its stand before Freda fell. Maybe you and the girls can get the thing decorated and help keep 'em entertained that way. They were real upset over Freda, you know.''

"Yes, I know. But they handled everything very well. Brenda's feeding them now.'' He sighed, resigned to the inevitable. "Yeah, you're right. I guess I'll get up in the attic and find those decorations.''

"Fine. Then we'll be seeing you after a while.''

"Tell Freda I'm really sorry about the accident.

Tell her I'll be up to see her in the morning once I get the kids off to school.''

Bret hung up and stared at the phone. A broken leg, at least. Maybe something even more serious. Why did something like this have to happen? It didn't make any sense. None of it. Now Freda was in the hospital, suffering, and he was here at home trying to figure out what to do next.

The three older ones were in school during the day, at least until Christmas break. He would just have to take Travis around the ranch with him, or postpone his work until he could find someone to come in and look after the boy.

Who could he find, especially at this time of year? Everybody was busy with their own families.

He dropped his head into his hand and sat there at the desk, trying not to feel his weariness. He still had to get upstairs and find those blasted decorations, help the kids decorate the tree, give Travis his bath and make sure the girls got to bed at a decent hour.

''Oh, Patti,'' he whispered. ''I need you so much.''

As though aware of Bret's feelings, Rex padded into the office and rested his head on Bret's knee.

Bret straightened and looked down at the dog. ''Did you come in here to comfort me?''

The dog thumped his tail.

''Freda's the one who needs some comforting, poor thing. The rest of us are doing just fine.''

He wasn't at all sure Rex looked convinced, which

wasn't surprising, since Bret didn't know exactly what he was going to do without a housekeeper.

He would just have to take it a day at a time rather than worry about a future over which he had no control. He pushed himself out of the chair and stroked Rex.

"C'mon, old man. We both need to get a move on. We've got a full evening ahead of us."

Bret headed toward the hall bathroom to wash up before finding out what Brenda had made them for supper.

As soon as supper was finished and the kitchen cleaned, Brenda offered to give Travis his bath while Bret found the decorations. Something had happened where his two oldest children were concerned, Bret realized as he pulled the ladder to the attic down from the ceiling and began to climb. Freda's accident had caused him to look at Chris and Brenda in a new light. Both of them had stepped in to help—Chris assisting Roy in getting Freda to the hospital and Brenda looking after the younger children.

They'd shown a surprising maturity that deeply touched him. Brenda was attempting to keep to a familiar routine in order not to alarm Sally and Travis any more than was absolutely necessary.

Bret knew that he could do no less. He was actually thankful to have the tree to trim, which should keep the children occupied until their bedtime.

Once he was in the attic, Bret mentally blessed Freda for keeping the storage area neat and orderly. The Christmas decorations were labeled and waiting in one of the corners. He carefully stacked the boxes and managed to get down both flights of stairs without mishap.

By the time the children came back downstairs from getting their baths and dressing for bed, he'd tested and strung the lights.

"We always have hot chocolate when we decorate the tree," Sally said pointedly. "Can we make some hot chocolate?"

"Uh, well—I'm not sure if we have the time to—"

"Don't worry about it, Dad," Brenda said. "I've got it ready to heat." She grinned at him, looking calm and in control of the situation. "I'll get it ready while you ride herd on these two."

He began to sort through the boxes, opening them and arranging them around the tree.

"Oh, Daddy, look!" he heard Sally say behind him. "Our angel! Isn't she beeootiful?"

Bret glanced down at the battered box that continued to hold the Christmas tree angel. Her dress no longer stood out quite so stiff and shiny. Her wavy hair could stand a good brushing, but her deep blue gaze was as potent as ever. He'd never before or since seen a doll with so much character in her face. The little angel remained a symbol for Bret of another lifetime…a time when he'd been young…a time when he'd actually believed in happy ever after.

He was glad Patti had insisted they keep their angel. She stirred bittersweet memories, but the memories were a part of who he was.

He watched Sally reverently lift the little angel from the box and carefully smooth her dress where it had been mussed from being packed away for the past year. Sally looked up and saw him watching her. She smiled and once again he saw Patti's smile in their daughter's face.

"Here, Daddy."

He took the angel even while he said, "Not yet, honey. Remember we put her on the tree the very last thing, after everything else is hung, just before we turn on the lights." He didn't point out to her that he'd already made sure all the lights were working first.

He glanced down at the angel in his hands. He couldn't seem to take his gaze away from her while the children quickly hung their treasures from Christmases past. He carefully smoothed wisps of hair away from her cheek before gathering the soft fluff of hair in his hand in an effort to subdue some of the curls.

She had such a wise look, as if she understood him and the pain that he perpetually carried in his heart. Bret knew he must be losing his wits to have such a strong reaction to a doll, even if she was supposed to be an angel!

He placed the angel on the mantel and turned to help Travis. Picking him up, Bret pointed out some of the higher branches that still needed decorating.

"Dad?" Brenda asked, carrying a tray with cups into the room and setting them down on the coffee table. "Did you find out how Freda's doing and when Chris is coming home?"

"Chris probably won't be home until late. He and Roy plan to wait at the hospital until the doctor finishes with all his tests."

"Was her leg broken?" Sally asked.

"'Fraid so, sugar," Bret replied.

"Well, who's supposed to look after us?" Sally asked. "What are we going to do without Freda?"

Bret readjusted Travis's weight on his hip, handed him a tiny rocking horse and waited while small hands arranged the ornament to a three-year-old's satisfaction before he answered. "It seems to me that we managed quite well last summer when Freda went to visit her sister for a few days, didn't we? None of you starved to death."

Brenda giggled. "Maybe so, Dad. But you really looked silly wrapped up in Freda's apron making pancakes."

Sally chimed in. "And you got real mad that time when you burned the biscuits you'd made for supper."

Bret forced himself to smile at the girls, recognizing their teasing was a way to lighten the atmosphere. "Okay, so maybe I need a little more practice. This will be a good time. According to the weather report, it's going to be too bad for me to work outdoors for the new few days, anyway." He looked down at his son who was still in his arms. "Travis and I'll find something to keep us busy, won't we, pardner?"

"Will Freda be here for Christmas?" Travis asked.

Since Travis seldom spoke they all looked at him in surprise.

Bret hugged his son a little closer to his chest. "I hope so, son, but it's too soon to tell just yet."

"School's out next Friday, Dad."

"I know, Brenda."

"Then we'll be here all day long for two weeks," Sally pointed out.

"I know."

There wasn't much to add to the conversation and for the next few minutes each of them concentrated on the tree.

Eventually, Brenda said in a subdued voice, "I wish we could go see Freda and let her know how much we miss her and how sorry we are she got hurt."

"Maybe we can, sweetheart," Bret replied. "I'll talk to the doctor tomorrow to see when he thinks she can have visitors." He glanced at the clock. "In the meantime, it's way past time for you to go to bed. School isn't out for the holidays yet."

"But Dad—"

"We have to—"

Brenda and Sally spoke at once, but it was Travis who was the most emphatic.

"You forgot the angel," he said with a great deal of indignation.

Bret stepped back from the tree and studied it. All

the ornaments were hung…everything was in place…except for the angel.

"Sorry, gang," he muttered, leaning over and setting his pajama-clad son on the floor. He reached for the angel and carefully smoothed her dress and hair once more, then stepped on a nearby footstool so that he could reach the top of the tree.

With an ease from years of practice he attached the angel to the tree so that she faced the room. Then he climbed down from the footstool, walked over and turned off the overhead light, leaving the room in shadows. He returned to the tree and flipped on the switch.

The tree immediately came to life with a multitude of tiny lights flickering and twinkling among the scented branches.

"Oooh," Travis sighed softly. The girls took each of his hands and stared at the tree in awe.

Finally Brenda said, "I wish Chris could have been here. This is the first Christmas he hasn't helped us decorate the tree."

"I know, honey," Bret replied. "I miss him, too, but Roy says he was a real help today. At least he helped to choose the tree." He was silent for several moments, as they enjoyed the magical sight before them. His gaze returned to the angel who presided over the tree like a benevolent reigning monarch.

She'd been a part of this family for as long as there had been a family. Somehow having her with them once again gave him a sense of peace and a degree of normalcy to the unusual day. Nothing seemed quite as bad as before.

Brenda was the first to turn away, still holding Travis's hand. "You want me to put Travis to bed, Dad?"

"Thank you, honey, but Travis and I'll manage just fine, won't we?" Bret replied, smiling at his son. He held out his hand to Travis, who took it with a nod.

Spending time with Travis was always a pleasure to Bret. He enjoyed looking at the world through a three-year-old's eyes. The girls were patient with their little brother, but he didn't want them to feel overwhelmed with the responsibility of looking after him.

No matter how tired or sore Bret was each evening he made a point of spending the last hour of Travis's day with the boy.

His youngest scampered up the stairs, no doubt racing ahead to find a story for Bret to read to him while the girls chattered about school as they left the room. Bret decided to leave the tree lights on for Chris when he came in. Roy would probably wait until morning to give him an updated report from the hospital. Bret knew he wouldn't sleep until he heard Chris come in, anyway.

By the time Bret heard Chris come up the stairs, Travis had fallen asleep—his giraffe tucked next to him.

Pausing in the doorway of his own room, Bret watched his oldest son come down the hallway toward him. Roy was right. Chris was growing fast, and not only in height. He was losing his boy-child look. His face appeared to be changing—his features looked sharper and more defined.

"How's it going, Dad?" he asked, following Bret into the room and sprawling out on the bed with a sigh.

Bret began to unbutton his shirt. "All right. How's Freda?"

"She was asleep when we left. The doctor gave her something for the pain. She's got a nasty sprain in her left ankle—probably caused when she tried to stop her fall—as well as a broken right leg. I was glad they gave her something. I could tell she was really hurting when we took her in, but she wouldn't complain."

"Did the doctor have any idea when she'd be able to leave the hospital?"

"He wants to keep her at least a week, maybe longer. He said they may put her leg in traction because—" He paused because Travis was trotting down the hallway toward them.

"I thought you were asleep," Bret said gruffly, shaking his head.

Travis ignored him and made a beeline for his brother. "The angel's here," Travis announced to Chris, crawling up on the bed beside him.

Chris glanced at Bret with a question in his eyes.

"We spent the evening decorating the tree," Bret explained.

Understanding flared in Chris's eyes. "Oh! So the

angel's here, is she?" he asked Travis, pulling him over to hug him. "Were you glad to see her?"

Travis nodded vigorously. "She always talks to me."

Chris's eyes met his dad's before he smiled at Travis and said, "I know, Travis. She used to talk to me, too."

Travis frowned. "Doesn't she talk to you anymore?"

Chris thought about that for a moment. "Good question. Maybe I haven't been listening as close as I used to," he admitted.

"C'mon, son," Bret said, picking Travis up and carrying him back to his bedroom. "It's way past your bedtime." He tucked him into bed once more, gave him a kiss and closed the door behind him.

He found Chris waiting for him in the hallway.

"What are we going to do now, Dad?"

"We'll manage somehow, son. I'll keep Travis with me. You and the girls are old enough to look after yourselves."

"I was really scared today. I mean, everything happened so fast. We heard Freda give a surprised cry, then we heard a big thump and pans clattering." He shook his head. "I was really glad Roy was here."

"Me, too. I'm also glad you were able to get the tree. At least it helped to keep the younger ones occupied tonight."

"Were you able to finish checking all the fences?"

"The worst ones, I think. The rest will have to

wait." He patted his son's shoulder. "Things will work out. You'll see." He looked at his watch. "You're going to have a short night, son. Morning's going to come awful early for you."

Chris smiled at Bret, his eyes shadowed with concern. "I could stay home and help you if you'd like."

Bret shook his head. "We'll be fine, but I appreciate the offer. Good night, Chris," he said, turning away before Chris could glimpse the emotion he was feeling. His oldest son was no longer a child. He was rapidly becoming a fine young man. Wasn't it too soon? Did he have to grow up quite so fast?

Bret went back into his bedroom and finished undressing. Stripping out of his work clothes, he went into his bathroom for a shower. The hot spray felt wonderful to his sore muscles.

"You'd be proud of our children, Patti," he whispered, now that he was alone. "They handled today's emergency just fine."

He'd gotten in the habit of talking to Patti at times when his mind was in a turmoil. It seemed to help him sort through everything going on inside his head. He'd fill her in on his day, share with her his concerns about the ranch and the children.

Some folks would consider him crazy. They were probably right. But somehow he felt closer to her that way. By reviewing his day in this manner he sometimes saw solutions that he might have otherwise overlooked.

He was drying off when he remembered Travis's

remark about the angel talking to him. Kids could say some of the most unexpected things. They must be born with a wild imagination.

All the children talked to Travis about his mother in an effort to make her real to the boy. Bret had placed a framed photograph of Patti beside Travis's bed. He wasn't certain how much Travis understood what had happened to his mother. Bret hadn't wanted Travis to feel as though he were to blame for the loss of Patti. The doctor had been careful to explain to Bret and the three older children that her heart might have stopped whether she'd been in labor or not.

Bret reentered his bedroom and slipped on a clean pair of jeans. He zipped them, but didn't bother with the button since he was only going downstairs to make sure Chris had locked up when he came in. He'd forgotten to ask him if he'd looked in on the tree. Not that it mattered. Chris could always see it tomorrow. In the meanwhile Bret wanted to make certain the lights were turned off.

The house still retained the heat of the previous days' warm weather, although with this new cold front, he'd better make sure the thermostat on the furnace was set to come on.

Silently Bret made his way down the hallway, pausing only long enough to make certain the children were all in bed. Even Chris's light was out.

Bret went downstairs, found the back door locked and the thermostat set. He decided to set up the coffeepot, so that it would brew early in the morning. He'd have to get the children off to school before doing his regular chores. A fresh cup of coffee first thing would help to keep him going.

He paused in the doorway and gave the kitchen a last glance before he headed down the hallway to the living room. When he reached the doorway he came to an abrupt halt, staring at the figure in front of the fireplace with total disbelief.

A young woman stood on the braided rug, looking around the room with interest. From the light given off by the tree, he would guess her to be in her twenties. She was slim, with white-blond hair wrapped in a coil on her neck. She looked to be of average height and wore jeans, a plaid shirt and sensible low-heel shoes.

For a few moments he was too stunned to say anything. The woman hadn't noticed him. She was too busy studying the furnishings, running her hand along the polished wood of the mantel and delicately stroking the clock that sat there.

A sudden burst of anger shoved him into action. Bret flicked on the overhead light, its brightness almost blinding after the muted light from the tree. The woman spun around with a gasp, her hand going to her throat.

His smile was grim with satisfaction. Obviously he'd startled her as much as she had startled him.

"Who are you and how in blazes did you get in here?" he growled, not caring how intimidating he sounded.

She took a quick breath before she gave him a dazzling smile. "I'm Noelle."

Chapter Two

Noelle could feel her heart racing in her chest, which felt very strange to her. But then, at the moment everything felt strange.

She looked at Bret with a sense of uncertainty that she strove to hide, unsure about what she should say or do next.

He stood there staring at her in disbelief.

She couldn't blame him. She hadn't known exactly how to appear and it was now obvious that she hadn't quite worked out the finer points of her new role in the Bishop family's life.

Noelle had waited until they all went upstairs before she privately assumed human form. She was glad she'd waited. Finding herself inside a body adapted specifically for earth and gravity was quite a shock!

She had taken a couple of breaths, then released

them and smiled. Air...she was taking in oxygen. Other sensations had captured her attention in a confusing array...sounds...and scents...and sights.

She had closed her eyes and waited for a sense of equilibrium. She'd thought she understood how human beings functioned, but she was rapidly adjusting all her perceptions now that her reality had changed so radically. She felt heavy—and more than a little sluggish—now that she had weight and substance.

She had stood before the twinkling Christmas tree and studied the small doll at the top. She could scarcely believe she used to exist in that tiny body. In comparison, she now felt like a giant...awkward and a little unsure of how to navigate her new body in a physical world.

Another unexpected gift was her heightened awareness. She'd always thought she understood human senses...until now. Everything was so much... so much *more* than she had expected. She'd inhaled, taking in the intoxicating smell of fresh pine and scented candles. She could even smell a whiff of freshly baked breads and cookies from earlier in the day.

Not only her sense of smell had intensified. Lights and colors glittered and sparkled as though with a special life. She'd tilted her head with delight and listened to the ticking of the clock on the mantel and the gentle creaks of the house.

She'd been fascinated by her surroundings: the comfortably rumpled furniture, the wall hangings, the touches that made a dwelling a home for those who lived there. She had clasped her hands and sighed. Oh, this was going to be so much fun! She just knew that she and the family would—

That's when Bret had turned on the bright lights and interrupted her thoughts with his demand to know who she was and how she'd gotten inside.

His deep male voice had almost stopped her heart from taking another beat! She stared at the man standing so belligerently in the doorway of the room.

Even if his words hadn't startled her, the overhead light would have. Its sudden brilliance almost blinded her with its glare.

Bret looked considerably different to her human eyes than her angelic ones. From her new perspective she could see that he was tall and very well built. Her conclusion was easy to reach since he wore very little clothing to hinder a thorough visual inspection of his body.

She found her reaction to him as startling as anything that had happened to her thus far. She couldn't seem to take her eyes off the broad expanse of his bare chest, which was covered with an intriguing design of soft curls. His arms and shoulders were strongly muscled and his hands, which rested on his hips near the low-slung waist of his jeans—his unbuttoned jeans—were well shaped and very capable looking. She could almost feel their callused roughness on her skin.

What a strange reaction!

Noelle blinked and tried to pull her attention back

to his question. She smiled, hoping to soothe the anger she could feel washing toward her.

"I'm Noelle," she repeated, hoping to show him that she was no threat to him or his family, but he didn't appear to be reassured.

"That doesn't tell me a blasted thing! How did you get in here?" he demanded.

She gave a quick glance toward the tree before she said, "I knocked, but I guess nobody heard me, so I just came inside and waited." She looked out the window, shivering at the sound of the wind and steady rain.

"Like hell you did! The door was locked!"

She nodded. "Yes. I locked it when I came in."

He paused, thinking about her quiet explanation. Maybe Chris had forgotten to lock the door. Still—

"What are you doing here?"

She gave him another quick smile, feeling his anger easing slightly. "I was in town and heard what happened to Freda. I thought I would offer to fill in for her until she could return."

Noelle had an almost overpowering desire to assure him that she'd had nothing to do with Freda's accident, but of course he wouldn't understand. Perhaps later, when all the events unfolded, he would—

Before Bret could say anything more she asked, "How is Freda? Was she badly hurt?"

"Bad enough, but that's not the issue here. I've never seen you before. You're obviously not a local. How did you hear about the accident?"

This was the tough part. She had no experience

with falsehoods. Then again, she couldn't very well explain to him who she was or why she was here. He'd have her hauled away and hospitalized. There was no help for it. Thankful that her supervisor had offered a plausible story, she said, "I'm from California. I came to visit my aunt, Ida Schulz. We were in town shopping today when we heard the news." She gave him her most innocent look. "Aunt Ida suggested I offer my services, so...here I am." Once again she smiled.

Ida Schulz lived on a remote ranch and rarely came to town. Noelle's supervisor felt that Ida was sufficiently removed from the scene not to be available to refute Noelle's story.

She waited for Bret's response. It wasn't long in coming.

"How did you get here? I didn't hear a car."

"One of Ida's hands drove me out here. Perhaps the storm muffled the sound of his truck. He waited until he saw me come into the house before he left."

As though finally becoming aware that he was still standing in the doorway, Bret walked fully into the room, coming to a halt a few feet in front of Noelle. Running his hand through his hair with frustration, he growled, "Look, I'm sorry you had to come all this way for nothing. You should have called first. We'll do just fine until Freda's better, so there's no need for you to..." His words slowed when he got a good look at her for the first time. "...fill...in." He stared at her in bemusement. He forgot what he'd been saying. He forgot everything but the presence of the woman standing little more than an arm's reach from him. Her eyes were a startling blue, but it wasn't the color that he found so mesmerizing. No. It was something else, something he couldn't define. There was a sense of familiarity, as though he'd looked into those eyes many times and had seen the wisdom there…the peace and the serenity.

He kept staring at her, feeling the same peace and serenity steal over him, so that he could feel his muscles relax, his body unwind, his mind cease its racing.

He lost track of time while he studied the woman before him until he was jolted back into awareness once again by the sudden realization that he wasn't dressed. Feeling at a distinct disadvantage and blaming her for her unannounced entry into his home, he regained his emotional balance and control. He could feel his anger mounting once again. How dare this woman—this stranger!—come waltzing in here without notice and surprise a man in his own home. He felt like a fool standing there in his own home embarrassed because he wasn't wearing a shirt and socks.

"I don't understand any of this," he muttered, "and I don't like it. Nobody walks into a stranger's house like you've just done and offers to go to work." He crossed his arms over his bare chest. "I want to know what's going on and what you're doing here!"

"You don't believe me?" she asked faintly.

He stared at her for a long moment in silence,

trying to decide what he believed. The woman looked young and innocent, wide-eyed and harmless.

Harmless? Not likely. A woman as attractive as she was couldn't be as naive as she was pretending to be. Bret groaned, running his hand through his hair, and took another step toward her.

She stood her ground, watching him.

Why, she wasn't afraid of him! How strange. She should be. After all, he towered over her, outweighed her by more than a hundred pounds. He could hurt her badly without even trying.

He stopped when he was a few inches from her. She had not moved. However, when she looked up at him, she blinked as though surprised to see the difference in their sizes.

Yeah, lady, he thought. *You'd better blink. And you'd better start using your head.*

"Look, whoever you are, I—"

"Noelle," she said in a quiet voice.

"Noelle," he repeated sharply. "I suppose I should thank you for—"

"Oh, you don't have to thank me! I'm delighted to be able to help you. I promise I won't be a bother. I can—"

"You don't understand. I can't have you stay here. It just wouldn't look right."

She stared up at him. "It wouldn't look right?" she repeated, puzzled.

"No! You're too young and too attractive to be staying here with—"

She burst into laughter. ''Oh, that doesn't matter to me.''

He couldn't take his eyes off her face. What was happening to him? How could he be so drawn to this strange young woman? How could he feel as though he knew her when he'd never seen her before in his life? He certainly wouldn't forget having met someone like her.

She took his hand and patted it gently for all the world as though he were Rex. ''It's going to be all right. You'll see.''

Rex. Where was Rex and why hadn't he warned them of an intruder? He jerked his hand free and looked around for the dog. ''Where's Rex? What did you do with him? Why didn't he—''

Responding to his name being called, Rex wandered into the room, yawning, as though he'd just been pulled out of deep sleep. He blinked bleary-eyed at Bret, silently questioning why his name had been mentioned.

Bret felt a momentary relief that the old dog was all right. ''Some watchdog you are,'' he said gruffly, watching the animal amble toward him. ''Why didn't you let me know she was here?''

Rex stopped and looked at Bret, then at Noelle. Slowly his tail began to wag. He gave a sharp *woof!* and trotted to her side, whining.

Bret watched in shock and amazement as Noelle knelt beside the dog and buried her head in his coat, her arms around him. ''Hi, there, fella. It's good to see you. How're you doing?''

Bret couldn't believe what he was seeing. Rex was not a friendly dog. He was fiercely protective of the family and avoided everyone else. He tolerated Freda and Roy as though understanding the necessity for their being on the ranch but had little to do with them.

Bret had never seen Rex act this way before. He didn't know what to think.

Once again he ran his hand through his hair, wanting only to see the end of this rather harrowing day. "Look," he said, his voice echoing his irritation. "I don't know what's going on here but it's late...too late to drive you clear across the county to Ida's place. You can sleep in Freda's room tonight, okay? I'll figure a way to get you home tomorrow. Come on, I'll show you where Freda's room is located."

Bret spun on his heel and strode out the door, feeling as if he were in some strange dimension. Maybe this was another dream and he'd wake up soon to find himself in bed. Nothing made sense anymore.

He walked across the kitchen and opened a door, revealing a bedroom with its own small bath. He glanced over his shoulder and saw that Noelle had followed him, Rex staying close beside her.

Noelle peered around him at the neat room and its carefully made up bed. "This looks fine to me. Thank you."

He turned away, then paused and looked back at her. "Look," he said, "I'm sorry if I've been abrupt with you. It's just that I've had a rough day and finding you here so unexpectedly like that was a little unnerving.''

''I understand.''

''The thing is, we really don't need any help. I've managed on my own with the kids before. I can do it again. I appreciate your concern. Tell Ida I thank her for sending you, but it really wasn't necessary.''

She touched him on the arm and once again he felt a strange peace settle over him. ''Why don't you get some rest, Mr. Bishop. Things will look better in the morning. You need some sleep, that's all.''

She had a point, one with which he was too tired to argue. He nodded and started across the kitchen. He paused in the doorway to the hallway and looked back. She stood watching him, Rex by her side.

''C'mon on, Rex. Go back to your bed,'' he called to the dog. Rex generally slept on the rug in Bret's office.

Rex just looked at him and blinked before he leaned against Noelle and sighed.

''I'll see that he goes to bed.''

A strange woman comes into his house—God only knows how—and ends up sending him to bed with a promise to look after his dog?

Bret refused to think about it any longer. He was going to sleep.

Noelle let out a pent-up sigh of relief when she heard Bret's door close upstairs. He was really upset, something that she hadn't counted on when she'd made her plans.

Absently she patted Rex before turning and going into Freda's room.

Whether or not Bret wanted to admit it, Noelle knew she was needed here. The children needed her. So did their father.

Hadn't he realized how much he'd cut himself off from his emotions? It was only around the children that he allowed himself to feel anything. The rest of the time he locked himself behind a wall of indifference.

Well, at least she was here now. The first crucial step had been taken. She would have to face the next step tomorrow morning.

Noelle looked around the tidy room, wondering what she should do next. Her stomach growled, startling her. She rubbed the offending noisemaker with wonder. So this was what hunger felt like…as though she had an empty spot in her middle.

She understood empty spots, of course. Bret, whether he understood or not, was also hungry. He had lots of empty spots that needed to be filled. She hoped to make him aware of them between now and Christmas.

In the meantime, she might as well enjoy all that her new assignment had to offer. She went back to the kitchen to explore while Rex watched her.

She checked out the cupboards, the pantry and the refrigerator, sampling the different fare, fascinated by the different tastes. Being human was quite an experience, one she intended to fully explore.

After she ate, she tried out the shower in Freda's

bathroom, another new sensation she found exhila-
rating as well as surprisingly relaxing. After her
shower she returned to the bedroom and looked
around her. She would need some clothes.

No sooner had she thought of it than the idea man-
ifested itself in the form of a packed suitcase that
appeared open on the bed, with clothes neatly folded
inside.

"Thank you," she murmured absently, searching
for a nightgown. Whoever had packed for her had a
strange sense of humor, she decided, pulling out a
nightshirt with Garfield on the front. She sat down
at the dresser and pulled the pins from her hair, then
took her time brushing out the long strands. After
dividing it into three parts and plaiting a single braid,
Noelle had started toward the bed when she sensed
a new presence in the room.

She glanced toward the door and smiled. A tor-
toise-shell-colored cat sat watching her with round,
unblinking eyes. Noelle recognized her immediately.
Sally's cat was not supposed to be in the house but
whenever Sally thought she could get away with
smuggling her inside without Bret's knowledge, she
did so. Obviously tonight was no exception.

Noelle also knew that Rex detested the cat and that
the feeling was mutual. She looked around and saw
that Rex had fallen asleep on the rug beside her bed,
looking as though he was down for the final count.

"Would you like to go outside, Mischief?" she
whispered, waiting to see what the cat would do
when she spotted Rex.

Mischief continued to stare at Noelle without blinking.

"Ah. You prefer the warm, dry house, do you?"

Mischief majestically stalked into the room and headed toward the bed. Rex roused, raising his head and eyeing his natural enemy. The two of them froze, their gazes locked in looks of unveiled hostility.

Noelle shook her head and sighed. "Oh, really, you two. We can't have this kind of behavior, you know. It really is time to learn some tolerance." She walked over and stroked each one of them, murmuring to them.

Eventually Rex lowered his head back on his paws and closed his eyes, while Mischief ignored his presence and leaped lightly onto the extra blanket folded at the foot of the bed. She turned around twice, then lay down in a furry ball, purring her approval.

"Yes, that's much better," Noelle said to them both before looking at Mischief. "Wouldn't you prefer to sleep with Sally?" she asked, sitting down beside the cat and lightly stroking her.

She paused, her fingers sensitively following the contours of the animal's body. "I see. Well, perhaps you're right in coming to me. I'll keep you safe."

With that Noelle turned out the light and slipped into bed.

The soft mattress felt wonderful. She hadn't realized how exhausting it was to manuever all this weight around. No wonder humans needed several hours of sleep each night. It felt wonderful to stretch and relax her muscles.

She sighed contentedly, feeling very pleased with herself. She'd done it. She was actually here snuggled down in bed, preparing herself for sleep. What fun!

Of course she still had some work to do where Bret was concerned. She'd known he was going to be a tough one to convince. Somewhere he'd gotten the idea that he had to do everything on his own without help.

She smiled sleepily to herself. He'd learn, oh, yes, he would. She was going to enjoy teaching him.

The next time Noelle opened her eyes she realized it was morning, although the sky had not lightened as yet. A soft whine and the thumping of a tail caught her attention.

"Good morning to you, too, Rex," she murmured. "Yes, I suppose it is time for us to be up, isn't it?" She wasted no time in getting out of bed and dressing, although for the moment she left her hair in the long braid. "Would you like to go outside?" she whispered.

Rex's tail whipped back and forth behind him. With a grin on her face she went into the kitchen, unlocked the door and let the German shepherd outside.

Noelle stood on the the porch and looked around. The storm from the evening before had passed, leaving a clear sky that was brightening as she watched. What a fascinating spectacle to see the stars begin to fade and warm color tint the eastern horizon.

With a smile on her lips she turned and went back into the house. Since it was too early for anyone to be awake, she took her time and explored all the downstairs rooms. Looking around she saw scuffed floors and battered furniture, tired decorations, abandoned toys and clothes that needed mending.

Poor Freda had had her hands full trying to keep up with everything and still have time to care for the family. She deserved her rest. Noelle was pleased to know that Freda's guardians were looking after her, helping her adjust to her change in circumstances.

She finished her inspection by returning to her room to make the bed and finish unpacking her clothes. She found Mischief in the closet.

"Ah, so there you are. I see you fared well during the night, my friend." She touched the soft fur behind the cat's ear and rubbed gently. "You picked a safe, quiet place and I won't disturb you."

Leaving the door to the closet partially opened, she turned away, wondering how Bret was going to deal with his next decision. Yes, he certainly had his hands full.

She returned to the kitchen, discovered the coffee was ready to brew, turned the machine on and decided to start breakfast, knowing the family would be getting up before much longer.

The biscuits were in the oven and the bacon was frying on the stove when she heard someone on the stairs. She turned and waited for her first visitor.

Travis appeared in the kitchen doorway rubbing his eyes. His hair was tousled, his pajamas rumpled and his slippers were on the wrong feet. He clutched a rather battered-looking stuffed giraffe.

"Good morning, Travis. You're up early."

Still half asleep, he started toward her. "I smelled something good cooking and it woke me up. I was—" He realized for the first time that Noelle wasn't Freda. His eyes seemed to grow in his face. She removed the bacon, wrapping it in absorbent paper towels, then went over to the table and sat down.

Travis still stood frozen in the middle of the floor.

She smiled at him and held out her hand.

Slowly, like a sleepwalker, he moved toward her. "It's you," he breathed in awe.

"Yes."

"I di'nt know you was real."

"I am."

He stopped when he reached her side. "Can I touch you?"

"Yes, you may."

He stuck out his forefinger and carefully placed it on her denim-clad knee. "W-w-o-o-w-w," he whispered. "You *are* real, you really and truly are." He reached up and touched her braid, stroking it. "I like your hair better hanging loose."

"I wear it that way when I'm all dressed up, but when I'm working around the house, I need it out of my way."

He walked around her. "Where are your wings—and your halo?"

"I only wear those for formal occasions as well."

"Oh."

He came around in front of her again. "Do you have a name?"

"It's Noelle."

"Noelle," he repeated, his lips curving. "That's a pretty name."

"Thank you."

He leaned his elbow on her knee and casually crossed one foot over the other. "Do you know my mother?"

Tenderly she brushed his silky hair off of his face. "Yes, Travis, I do. She's a very special lady."

"She's an angel, too, you know," he confided.

"Is she?"

"Uh-huh. My daddy told me. Is she going to come see us, too?"

Noelle swallowed. "No, Travis. I'm afraid not."

He straightened, patting her knee. "It's okay. I know she's pretty busy. I never knew her," he added matter-of-factly, "so I thought maybe I could see her."

"She visits you whenever she can, mostly when you sleep."

He grinned. "An' Chris and Brenda and Sally, too?"

"Them, too," she agreed.

"And Dad? He really misses her, I think. Sometimes when he's in my room he stares at my picture of her and looks sad."

She could think of nothing to say to that, so instead she asked, "Are you ready to eat?"

"Mmm, yes," he replied, rubbing his stomach.

"Would you like some oatmeal, or an egg or—?"

He looked at the biscuits. "One of those, and some bacon and I guess an egg."

She leaned over and hugged him. "Coming right up," she said, getting up and going to the refrigerator.

"Are you going to take care of us until Freda comes back?"

"I'll be here for a little while, yes."

"That's good." He climbed up into his chair and watched her, his arms folded around his giraffe.

"What's your giraffe's name?"

"Harvey."

"Oh. Did you name him?"

"Uh-uh. My daddy gave him to me a long, long time ago."

"So your dad named him."

"Nope. Harvey named hisself. He jus' tole me it."

"Oh, of course. Silly of me to forget we pick our own names."

"Yeah, only I forgot about picking mine. They had to teached it to me again when I could finally remember."

Noelle placed his breakfast in front of Travis and sat down across from him to eat her own in companionable silence. They heard a door open upstairs, another door close, a shower come on, and one of the girl's voices.

Travis looked over at Noelle, his eyes sparkling. "Boy! Are they going to be surprised to find you here!" He finished his milk and slid down out of his chair. "I'm going to go tell 'em," he said, racing off.

The family members would be down shortly. She'd better get the rest of their breakfast ready for them. She was sorry Patti wasn't there, too. For a brief moment of longing, she wished her stay wasn't going to be so short.

She was here now, she reminded herself, and she definitely had her work cut out for her.

She cleared the table of her dishes and went back to fixing breakfast.

Bret smelled the fresh coffee, frying bacon, warm biscuits and smiled in his sleep. All of it smelled so good, especially the coffee. He wanted a cup…but not enough to let go of the woman he held in his arms. The swaying rustle of palm trees and the gentle swish of nearby water added to the sense of paradise he'd found in her arms. He stroked his hand over her hair, feeling the silkiness ripple beneath his palm as he smoothed his hand over her shoulder, lingered, then moved down until he could cup her breast.

She sighed and he could feel her lips brush against his mouth just as he—

"Dad? Aren't you up yet?" Chris's adolescent voice jolted Bret into immediate wakefulness. Wild-eyed he stared around him in alarm, relieved to discover that his son hadn't caught him on a beach with a blond-haired, haunting blue-eyed woman in his arms.

It was a dream, that's all it was. He'd just been

dreaming about…about…a face popped into his mind and he groaned.

"Dad?" His door swung open.

Bret jerked up in bed, trying to look awake. "Yeah, I'm here. Guess I must've forgotten to set my alarm."

Chris looked at his dad, then back over his shoulder. "Well, if you're still in bed, who's downstairs making breakfast?"

Now that the door was open the aroma of coffee wafted in even stronger, along with the smell of biscuits and bacon, causing his mouth to water.

Bret yawned. "How'd you know it wasn't me?"

"Because your door was still closed. It's always open unless you're asleep," he absently explained. "So what's going on? Who's downstairs?"

"Ida Schulz's niece arrived late last night. Said she'd heard about Freda and offered to help out for a few days."

"No kidding? Ida Schulz? I never knew she had a niece."

"Neither did I. Guess you learn something new every day."

"So how old is she? Is she good-looking?" Chris turned away as though to take a peek.

Bret grinned. "Too old for you, buddy. Since when have you been so interested in what a woman looks like?"

His son shot him a purely masculine expression that spoke volumes. "See you downstairs, Dad," he finally said with a lopsided grin before he turned around and disappeared down the hall.

Bret was shaving when he heard Travis calling him. "Daddy! Daddy, where are you?"

"In here, son," he said. "What's the matter?" He leaned around the door into the bedroom in time to see his youngest child bolt around the corner, his eyes sparkling with excitement.

"Did you see her, Daddy? Did you see? It's the angel! She's come to look after us. She's never done that before!"

Bret paused in his shaving. "The angel?"

Travis bobbed his head vigorously. "Our angel. You know. She's in our kitchen and—"

"Oh! You must be talking about Noelle." He knelt beside his pajama-clad son. "Honey, Noelle isn't an angel, although I suppose her showing up at such a time could be considered a godsend."

"Oh, yes, she is. She tol' me so." Travis's bottom lip edged out belligerently.

"She must not have understood what—"

"Daddy!" Sally cried, sounding distraught. She came running into the bedroom and came to a skidding halt beside Travis in the bathroom doorway, her hair standing in uncombed peaks all over her head. "Daddy! I can't find Mischief anywhere! Have you seen her?"

Bret straightened to his full height and frowned down at his daughter. "Are you telling me that you let Mischief in the house when you know she isn't supposed to be in here?"

"I *had* to let her in last night," she replied, dramatically. "It was wet and cold outside and she had nowhere to sleep—"

"Except in the warm barn curled up in the soft hay," he reminded her sternly.

Sally's shoulders drooped. "But, Daddy, something's wrong with her. I couldn't get her to eat last night and she kept pacing back and forth, crying. I couldn't throw her out in the cold. She seemed a little better when I put her in my room, but when I woke up this morning, she was gone! Do you think she's died?" Her large gray eyes stared up at him, desolate.

How did they learn how to do that at such an early age? Bret wondered.

"I doubt very much if she died, Sally. Mischief looked perfectly healthy the last time I saw her. Have you checked everywhere downstairs?"

"Downstairs? Oh, she wouldn't go downstairs. She hates Rex, remember?"

"I don't know what to tell you, Sally, except that you need to go eat so you won't be late for school."

Sally walked away, carrying the weight of the world on her delicate shoulders.

Bret turned back to Travis. "C'mon, sport. We need to get you dressed. From the looks of that pajama top, you've already had your breakfast."

Travis smiled sweetly at his father. "Noelle's a real good cooker, Daddy."

"I'm glad to hear it, son," he said. "Let me finish

shaving and I'll be in your room in a few minutes to help you dress."

When Bret walked into the kitchen Noelle was the only one there. "Mornin'," he muttered to the woman standing at the stove, her back to him. He strode over to the counter and poured himself a cup of coffee.

She turned around, smiling at him. "Good morning," she replied, and carried a plate of perfectly basted eggs to the table and set it at his place. "Help yourself to the bacon and biscuits."

He couldn't resist taking a sip of the savory coffee before he cleared his throat and said, "Look, you didn't have to make breakfast this morning. I'm perfectly capable of looking after this family. I just happened to oversleep this morning. Otherwise I would have—"

"Oh, but I've enjoyed it. This is what I came to do, to help out wherever I'm needed." She looked past his shoulder and smiled. "Good morning."

Bret heard Chris say, "Mornin'," his voice cracking slightly, before he circled the table and sat down across from him. Bret noted that his son—who normally paid no attention to what he looked like—had carefully combed his hair and put on a freshly ironed shirt. When Chris's gaze met his father's, Bret lifted his brow slightly and watched his eldest child blush a fiery red.

Bret had almost finished his breakfast when he was interrupted by a wail coming from Sally in another room. "Daddy, I can't find her *anywhere!*"

He glanced around in time to see the tragic face of his youngest daughter, still in her pajamas, having gone nowhere near a hairbrush since his last glimpse of her.

"Sally, go get dressed or you're going to be late for school. The cat will show up sooner or later, you can depend on it. She's a survivor and she knows how to take care of herself."

"The cat?" Noelle repeated. "Are you looking for your cat?" Everyone looked around at her in surprise. She grinned and silently motioned Sally to follow her into Freda's room. Chris immediately followed. Reluctantly, Bret shoved his chair back and joined the parade.

From the doorway he watched Noelle tiptoe to the closet and widen the opening. There, on a couple of blankets lay Mischief with four tiny lumps of fur beside her, none of them the same color. When it came to romance, Mischief obviously lived up to her name.

Sally fell on her knees in front of the cat. "Oh, Mischief, look at you! A Christmas present for each one of us. Aren't you the sweetest thing?"

The cat arched her neck so that Sally could scratch her behind her ear in the prescribed manner while Bret attempted damage control. "Now wait just a minute, Sally. Four more cats around here are the very last things we need."

Chris peered over Sally's shoulder and grinned. "Look at that one. All black except for white-tipped toes. I'll call it Lucifer."

"I want the striped one. It looks like a ferocious tiger, doesn't it, Chris?" Sally whispered. "That's what I'll call it. Tiger."

"What 'cha looking at?" Travis wanted to know, pushing past his dad into the room.

Bret sighed, knowing when he was on the losing side of an argument.

"Kitties!" Travis exclaimed, dashing to get a closer look.

"Shh!" Sally and Chris echoed.

"Don't scare 'em," Chris went on. "Or she'll move 'em somewhere else and we won't be able to find them."

"Heaven forbid," Bret grumbled. He happened to glance at Noelle and saw a sympathetic look in her eyes. He turned and went back for another fortifying cup of coffee. Unfortunately for his digestion, he could still hear the conversation in the other room.

"The tiger-striped one is mine," Sally was explaining to her awestruck little brother, "and the black one is Chris's. Which one of the other two do you want?"

Normally Bret was a logical man. He considered himself totally rational. But the past several hours had been far from normal and for a brief moment he actually found himself blaming Noelle for the fact that Mischief had decided to present the family with four kittens just before Christmas.

Being—on the whole—a fair person, Bret admitted to himself that Noelle could certainly cook up a mean bunch of biscuits. What she had done with the eggs and bacon was almost mystical. He forced himself to be fair. Noelle was no more to blame for Freda's fall than she was for those blasted kittens.

The children chattered over their breakfast, filling in all the exciting details to Brenda when she arrived downstairs.

Bret noticed that all of them were chatting with Noelle as though they were old friends. Children continued to amaze him. They had taken her presence in stride, adapting to a new order of things without a grumble. They were already gathering up their books, putting on their coats, getting ready to leave, the whole time chatting with Noelle as though she'd always been a part of their family circle.

Not that their attitudes made any difference to the outcome of the situation.

She could not stay and that was the end of it. Just as soon as the older ones left for school he would set her straight. He would—

Travis walked over to Noelle and said, "I hope you're going to stay with us for a long, long time."

Bret and the children stared with varying degrees of disbelief. Travis was quiet. Travis took a long time to warm up to people. Even with people he knew, Travis was aloof. Seeing his son with his arms entwined around the woman who Bret had fully intended to send away shook him. What was going on here? How had she managed to bewitch his son?

"Are you going to tell me some more stories? Will we get to—"

"Travis?"

Travis looked around at his father.

"I'm afraid you must have confused Noelle with someone else. I don't believe you know—"

"Yep, I do!" His son nodded with emphasis, then reluctantly let go of Noelle's waist. "She's the angel."

Chris paused in shoving his foot into his boot. "The what?"

Big people could certainly act dumb, sometimes. Travis put his hands on his hips, unconsciously mimicking one of his father's habitual poses, and said in a very patient voice, "She's the angel…you know." He waved his arm toward the living room. "She comes to visit every year!" He spun back to her. "But I like you best when you're just like real people." He threw his arms around her again in a big bear hug.

Bret shook his head, dumbfounded. Not so his vocal children.

"Wow! Travis is right. She *does* look like the Christmas angel," Chris said in awe.

"I knew you looked familiar!" Brenda exclaimed.

"Wait until I tell my friends," Sally added, her eyes wide.

"Whoa, whoa, wait a minute." Bret finally found his voice. "I don't care who she looks like, or who she reminds you of, this is Noelle, Ida Schulz's niece." He glared at his younger daughter. "If you go spouting to your friends that an angel cooked your breakfast, they're going to have you taking all kinds of mental tests."

Noelle hadn't said anything. Now she leaned down and whispered something in Travis's ear. He nodded, relaxed his hold on her and scampered out of the room.

Chris broke the silence. "We've gotta go. The bus will be here shortly." He turned to Noelle. "Thanks for breakfast. It was great."

Travis returned with one of his small trucks and perched on one of the chairs. Bret tried to think of something to say. His son looked very content. Was there really a good reason to drag him outside in the cold when he could stay here with Noelle? He knew he didn't want her here, but he had to look at the larger picture. He had to decide what was best for Travis, as well.

He wished he knew what to do. He wished he knew what to say. Since she hadn't sat down since he came downstairs, he asked, "Aren't you going to eat?"

Noelle chuckled. "I already ate. There's something about the air this time of year that's given me quite an appetite."

"I didn't know angels got hungry," Travis said.

Noelle acted as though his comment was perfectly natural. She didn't smirk or smile in a patronizing way. Bret appreciated her tact. He wouldn't have wanted her to hurt Travis's feelings. Instead, she slid into one of the vacated chairs and propped her chin on her palm. "Normally angels don't get hungry," she admitted. "It depends on what they have to do and where they're working."

Travis nodded very seriously. "I'm glad you've come to work here. We can have lots and lots of talks, just like before, right?"

Bret had never seen such a loving smile on anyone's face when Noelle nodded, and said, "I'm glad to be here. We'll have some wonderful talks while I'm here."

Yes, she had neatly cut the ground right out from under him. If he sent her away now, Travis would be upset. Why had she encouraged his son to think she was some kind of angel, anyway? Granted, he could see a resemblance between her and the angel at the top of their Christmas tree...the same color eyes and hair, the same slender build. But this woman was far from an angel! She knew exactly what she was doing when she flashed those eyes so provocatively at him, the way she was now.

"More coffee?" she asked.

Right. That may be what she said, but it wasn't what she was thinking. Why, every time she looked at him, he felt the jolt all the way down to his toes. "No. I've got work to do." He walked over and put on his coat. He grabbed his hat and pulled the brim down low over his eyes.

Deciding to put his son to the test, he looked over at Travis. "Do you want to come help me with my chores today, son? I could use some extra hands feeding the animals."

"Could Noelle come, too?" Travis asked, his eyes shining.

"Well, I don't think—"

"I'd love to!" she said. "I haven't had a chance
to be around animals for...oh, a long, long time."
She met Bret's glance with equally shining eyes.

Well, that little experiment certainly blew up in
his face. Why did he feel like such a grouch? What
possible difference did it make to him whether she
stayed or not?

Silly question.

He didn't want to be reminded of her or the
dreams he'd had about her all night. Having her stay
here at the ranch would be too much of a strain. She
meant well, no doubt, but she just didn't understand
that—

"I'll clean the breakfast dishes and be ready to go
whenever you are."

Travis scooted out of his chair and darted out into
the hallway, his footsteps echoing on the stairs. "I
left my coat upstairs," he called. "I'll be right
back."

Bret looked at Noelle, once again feeling power-
less over the events around him. He pulled off his
hat and began to turn it between his fingers. "Look,
I— uh—"

"Oh, please don't thank me. I want to thank *you*
for the opportunity to be with you and your family
for the next few days. It's literally a dream come true
for me. I feel very blessed."

"I'm sure you find it strange that Travis thinks
you're the Christmas angel. The thing is, that, well—
he's—"

"He's wonderful! Bright, full of life and so very

innocent. He's delightful and you must be very proud of him.''

Bret absently studied his mangled hat through sightless eyes. ''Yeah, I am.'' He forced himself to meet her gaze. ''His mother died when he was born. He was like a miracle God gave me when He took Patti. None of us in the family would have been the same without Travis.''

''I'll watch over him very carefully, Mr. Bishop.''

The title caught him off guard, reminding him that she had called him that last night. Nobody called him Mr. Once again she'd managed to make him feel uncomfortable. He didn't like the feeling. Not at all.

''My name is Bret,'' he muttered, hearing the ungracious tone and not being able to do a blasted thing about it. He knew he was telling her more than his first name. He was also agreeing that she could stay at the ranch with him and the children until Freda could return.

He knew he was making a big mistake. He just didn't know how to get out of it. He felt as though fate had jockeyed him into some kind of corner where he couldn't get out. He didn't know exactly how it had happened and he was bewildered by the whole sequence of events.

When she didn't say anything in response, he turned toward the hallway. ''I'll go help Travis find his coat. We'll be down in a few minutes.''

''Bret?'' she said to his back.

He stiffened, feeling his name on her tongue like

a caress down his spine. He forced himself to turn around and face her. "Yes?"

"It's going to be okay. I promise."

"I'm sure you really believe that, but I don't agree with you. Human nature being what it is and all, I think we're both making a big mistake here. If we were smart, we'd make up some excuse why you can't stay."

She looked startled. "Human nature?" she echoed, wonder in her voice.

Impatient, he said, "Yeah! Human nature. You know. Man. Woman. Male. Female. Birds. Bees. All that kind of stuff. I'm a normal red-blooded American male, lady, with my fair share of needs. I've managed to handle my situation because I've kept myself too busy to give it much thought. Plus I haven't allowed myself to spend much time with any women that might remind me of what I've been missing. You moving in here is going to change all of that."

If anything, her eyes grew lovelier as they continued to stare at him. "Are you saying that you're attracted to me?"

She sounded absolutely astonished, which ticked him off something terrible. "What's the matter with you, don't you ever look in a mirror? Of course I'm attracted to you! I'm not dead, dammit! I thought all those feelings died along with Patti and I'm telling you the truth, I'm not at all happy about finding out they're still alive and kicking, rarin' to go!"

Noelle became very still, as though she were listening to something only she could hear. The echo of *his* voice still rang in the room and once again he felt foolish to have made such an outburst in front of this woman.

What was it about her that made him so uncomfortably self-conscious?

He spun away and started toward the hallway once again.

"I'm attracted to you, as well," she said softly, which effectively stopped him in his tracks. In fact, he felt paralyzed. Was she out of her mind, making such an admission? He forced himself to face her once more.

"Hasn't anyone ever warned you that it's dangerous to be too honest?" he growled.

"No."

"Then let me be the first."

"I shouldn't have told you how I feel?"

"You got that right."

"Even if it's the truth?"

"Especially if it's the truth!"

"I don't understand."

He shoved his hand through his hair, feeling his blood pressure mount. "Where have you spent your life, in a convent?"

She smiled. "Close."

"Well, then you'd better smarten up fast, or some guy's going to come along and take advantage of all that sweet innocence of yours."

"You wouldn't."

"I'm not the only guy around."

She smiled. "But you'll protect me from those others, so I'm safe enough."

"Maybe so, but who's going to protect you from me?" Once again she looked puzzled. Bret muttered beneath his breath, then shook his head. How could he explain something he couldn't fully understand himself? "Forget it. I've got to go help Travis."

He was already in the hallway when he distinctly heard her say in a voice just above a whisper, "I enjoyed our time on the beach together, Bret Bishop."

A wave of dizziness swept over him. How could the woman possibly have known about his dream?

Chapter Three

"I understand Ida Schulz's niece is helping you at home these days," Freda said. "How is she working out for you?"

Bret had just arrived at the hospital a few minutes before. Rather than give an immediate answer, he looked around the room, then walked over to one of the chairs. Settling into its depths, he stretched his long legs in front of him, crossing his ankles with a sigh. "Okay, I guess," he muttered, staring at the toes of his scuffed boots.

"Now there's some real enthusiasm for you," she said after a moment, when she realized he wasn't going to volunteer anything more. "What's the matter, afraid I'll get my feelings hurt to hear how well she's taking care of everything?"

He glanced up at her. "I miss you, Freda."

"I miss you, too, Bret. And I miss the kids."

"Life was a lot less complicated when you were at home with us."

She shifted slightly, trying to find a comfortable position. After four days in that infernal bed, she was ready to get out of there. "What's causing you problems now?"

He lifted his shoulders in a shrug. "I don't know how to describe it exactly. Things are different these days. Noelle seems to have taken over."

"And you resent that?"

"Not exactly. I'm just puzzled by it all." He glanced up, giving her a halfhearted smile. "Travis insists she's our Christmas tree angel come to life."

"Yes. He was all excited about her visit when Roy brought them in yesterday." She eyed his pensive expression and said, "I don't see any harm in his believing she's an angel, do you, Bret?"

As though he could no longer sit still, Bret straightened and leaned his elbows on his knees, staring at the floor between them. "At this point, I'm too confused to know what to think," he finally said. He looked up at her, his pain evident. "When Patti died, I wanted to die, too. If I hadn't had the children I wouldn't have made it through these last few years. Even with the children, I've been too busy to think about anything but getting through each day."

"And now?"

"Now all I seem to think about is a slip of a girl who seems to have wrapped my kids in some kind of magical cloak. They seem so happy these days.

They don't argue as much, they're so helpful around the place, I'm constantly amazed."

Freda started laughing.

"What's so funny?"

"Well, I would say that you're finally waking up and noticing the world around you."

"What's that supposed to mean?"

"It's Christmastime, Bret. The children have always behaved themselves around Christmas, hoping that their behavior will encourage you to get everything on their list."

"You think that's all this is?"

"What I think is that in the past you've kept yourself aloof from Christmas. You've let me take the kids shopping, you've had Roy pick up the special gifts they find under the tree. You did everything you could to ignore the whole business."

"I guess that was a lot to ask of you and Roy."

"That's not my point. My point is that you've encased your feelings in some kind of deep freeze... until now."

"You think so?"

"Oh, yes. I see a definite thawing going on." She smiled. "Chris says Noelle is one awesome babe."

Bret blinked. "Awesome babe? What's that supposed to mean?"

"I took it to mean he's impressed with her looks."

He fidgeted a moment before saying, "The kid's got good taste."

"Definitely thawing, I would say," she murmured. "It's time you let Patti go, Bret. She wouldn't have wanted to see you like this, all grim and uptight about everything. What I remember about Patti is how she could always get you to see the humor in every situation. One of your problems recently is that you take life too seriously."

He met her gaze without smiling. "Life *is* serious, Freda."

"Actually, life is too *important* to be taken seriously, Bret. Life is meant to be enjoyed…each and every moment. I believe the reason Noelle has come into your life…and the children's lives…is to remind you of how much life has to offer, to shake you out of your rut, to make you look at your life."

"Noelle came into our lives because Ida Schulz told her to come help us out after you fell."

"Ah, Bret. Must you be so literal?"

"Well, I certainly don't see her visit as some kind of miracle. I'll admit that it was a help to me that she happened to be visiting from California, and that she heard about—"

"God works in mysterious ways, his wonders to perform."

He raised a brow. "You think God sent her?"

"I wouldn't be at all surprised."

"Well, if that's the case, I'm in deep trouble because I've been having some unheavenly reactions to her."

"No doubt you're reacting like a normal, red-blooded human being who's been living too long without a companion. It's all right to admit that you get lonely, you know."

"I haven't had time to think about it."

"You haven't *wanted* to think about it, which is why you've kept yourself so busy, burying yourself out on that ranch and refusing to take part in anything."

"So what do you think I should do?"

"Join in the celebration of Christmas. Be a part of it all. Allow yourself to feel again, to believe again."

He shook his head. "I'm not a kid any longer, Freda."

"Sometimes I wonder if the children aren't the wise ones. They accept—with gratitude and without questioning—all the good things in life. Perhaps we could learn from their example."

"I'm surprised you can say that considering that you're lying here in a hospital with a broken leg."

She smiled. "I'm here to tell you that it's been downright good for me. I've discovered several things about myself and my life while I've been forced to lie here. It isn't so bad to take time out to reflect about life. I found that I'm not indispensable. You and the children have been doing quite well without me. I discovered that I'm enjoying having some time to myself where I can catch up on my reading and such." She watched him closely as she said, "You know, my sister still wants me to go to Austin when I get out of here."

"You were planning to spend Christmas with her, anyway. Does the doctor think you can be released by then?"

"Oh, I think so. He's pleased with my progress.

I've got to learn to get around on crutches first, and I can't do that until my sprained ankle gets a little better.''

"You're certainly cheerful about the whole thing.''

She smiled, her eyes twinkling. ''I always believe that things work out the way they're supposed to. I already see a lot of good coming out of my accident.''

"If you say so.''

"Think about taking the kids Christmas shopping, Bret. Get out there with them and look at everything. Listen to the music, watch the people, catch the holiday spirit.''

"Hah! Now that *would* be a miracle.''

"I happen to believe in them, myself.''

He got up and leaned over the bed, hugging her. ''Thanks for the pep talk, Freda. I appreciate your comments and concern.''

"You're going to do just fine, Bret. I know you will.''

"Wish I had your faith.''

"Eventually you probably will.''

On the drive home Bret thought about his conversation with Freda. Perhaps she was right about his having put his emotions in a deep freeze. He loved his kids but he wasn't sure how much he showed them his love. He couldn't remember the last time he'd done anything with them, just for fun.

He hadn't realized how self-absorbed he'd been, totally wrapped up in his own misery.

The first thing that had happened to him after Noelle's arrival was the realization that he wasn't a eunuch! The dream he'd had the first night had certainly made that fact clear. He'd had trouble looking at her for the rest of the day without being reminded of all that his subconscious had him doing with her.

He hadn't had the courage to ask her what she'd meant about enjoying their time on the beach together. Had he had some kind of mental lapse and actually told her? He shook his head, wishing he understood what was going on at his house these days.

Like it or not, he found himself working closer around the house, stopping more often to check on Travis, even though he quickly learned how much Travis enjoyed his new friend.

Then there were those times when he'd catch her looking at him and their gazes would lock until he felt as though he was going to drown in those deep blue eyes. Somehow she made him feel as though he had no secrets from her. Normally he would be upset to think he was so easily read and understood, but with Noelle, he almost felt a sense of relief.

He drove into the ranch and followed the lane to the house, reminding himself to call Ida Schulz and thank her for sending Noelle to them.

At dusk the house looked like something on a calendar, or maybe a Christmas card. The building itself was a mellowed gray and the bright glow of golden color from the downstairs windows beckoned any weary traveler to come inside and find comfort. He wasn't certain what it was about the house that made it so different. He couldn't believe that Noelle's presence could contribute to the overall restful quality but he couldn't deny noticing some of the changes.

In the four days she'd been there he could see the effect she'd had on the children. There seemed to be more laughter in the house since she came. Travis had turned into a chatterbox, giggling and repeating stories she'd told him.

And what stories! He'd never before heard of such a powerful imagination as this woman had. She admitted that she seldom watched television and he guessed he'd have to accept that since he'd never seen any program to match her tales.

In addition to the changes he'd seen in the children, he'd also noticed that the house appeared brighter...almost newer, especially the old linoleum in the kitchen. When he'd mentioned the difference, Noelle explained that she had found a new cleansing agent that brought back the original color and shine to the old covering.

The oak floors in the rest of the house looked as if they'd been refinished and buffed so fine he could almost see his reflection in them, causing the thick area rugs to look like colorful islands floating on a polished sea.

The sofa in the living room had lost its sagging appearance, and new throw pillows had added bright color to the room.

Whenever he commented on some change, Noelle made light of her efforts, so he hadn't bothered to mention that his clothes had never looked brighter or cleaner. He either found them neatly folded in his drawers or hanging with precision and precise pleats in his closet.

Bret stepped up on the back porch and let himself into the kitchen. As usual, the room was spotless and gleaming, but he could still smell the savory remains of supper. She'd set large helpings aside, no doubt for him, and he intended to eat every bite as soon as he washed up.

He paused in the hallway because he heard Noelle's voice. It sounded as though she was in the middle of one of her stirring sagas. Without giving his actions much thought, Bret sank onto the bottom step of the stairway to listen.

"...so when the train started up the steep grade the engine had trouble pulling all that weight up the hill, which meant the train was forced to go slower and slower," she was saying.

"I know, I know," Sally interrupted, obviously excited. "That's how that mean ol' robber could jump on, isn't it? He didn't have to make the driver—"

"The engineer—" Chris interjected smoothly.

"Yeah—the engineer—slow down, 'cause he could get on without anybody noticing."

"But wouldn't one of the train guards see him?" Brenda asked.

"Maybe he made himself invisible," Travis suggested gravely.

"Oh, Travis," Sally began, "People can't—"

"Shh! Let Noelle go on," Brenda snapped.

Silence reigned for a telling moment before Noelle continued.

"The robber knew exactly where the guards were stationed. He waited until the perfect moment to leave the boulders he'd used for cover and raced toward the train. He leaped for the train and grabbed on to one of the metal steps that led to the top of the baggage car. He scrambled to get his feet on another one so that he could—"

"Are you trying to glamorize the profession of train robbery, by any chance?" Bret interrupted from where he now stood, leaning against the doorjamb, his arms folded across his chest.

"Daddy, you're home!" Sally announced.

"Hey, Dad, did you see Freda?" Chris asked.

"Dad, Noelle said you might take us shopping tomorrow," Brenda said, catching him off guard. How had Noelle known that he'd considered going this year? Brenda was still talking. "I told her that you usually had Roy or Freda take us but she said to ask you, anyway. Will you?"

Travis grabbed him around the knees and said, "Don't you want to hear about what happened to the train robber?"

He looked over the children's heads to where Noelle sat in the middle of the sofa. The children had been clustered around her, listening intently. A small fire danced in the fireplace, giving off a rosy glow.

The most surprising addition was Rex stretched out asleep in front of the fire while Mischief sat nearby, ignoring his presence while she fastidiously groomed herself.

He'd found a very domestic scene, one that was rarely enacted in this house. Somehow this woman had managed to captivate all four of the children with her tale, a tough job with such a wide range of ages.

"How was the last day of school?" he asked, hoping to buy himself some time before facing all their questions.

Brenda beamed. "Oh, Dad, I aced my test this morning. You know, I didn't really understand the theory behind the equations. I felt like such a dunce because the teacher had explained it over and over, but somehow it just didn't make sense to me. When I showed Noelle my homework she immediately saw where I was confused." Brenda glanced at Noelle. "Somehow she explained it in a way that made the whole thing seem so simple. I was trying to make something hard out of it!" She laughed. "Even the teacher was surprised when he saw my test score."

Sally interrupted. "Since there's no school tomorrow, can we go to town and do some Christmas shopping?" she asked, her eyes bright. "I've had some great ideas for gifts lately. Freda isn't here to take us. Don't you want to?" She took his hand and looked up at him with soulful eyes, filled with pleading. "It'll be fun, Daddy. You'll have a good time, really you will. Can we go?"

If this child did not find a lucrative calling on either stage or screen he would be very much surprised. The look, the tone, the body language—she could give lessons.

Bret stared down at his youngest daughter and sighed. First Freda, then Noelle, now this. He knew when he was beaten. "All right, gang. I'll take you shopping."

He and Patti used to go to Austin each year. He couldn't face going to the same stores, doing the same things they used to do together. However, there were other places to go, places that didn't hold painful memories.

"Why don't we drive in to San Antonio tomorrow and make a day of it?"

"San Antonio!"

"Really?"

"Oh, boy!"

"Yippee!"

With everybody talking at once he didn't try to respond except to the little guy who had him by the knees. He glanced down at Travis. "Do you want to go to San Antonio?"

"Uh-huh. Will I get to see Santa?"

"More than likely," Bret replied, remembering when the older children had been young enough to be excited by the thought of seeing Santa Claus.

"Good, 'cause I gotta talk to him," Travis said, sounding very serious.

Bret knelt down beside his youngest. "You do?"

"Uh-huh."

"Do you plan on telling him what you want for Christmas?"

"Uh-huh."

"What *do* you want?"

"I can't tell you. It's a secret."

"But you can tell Santa?"

"Course! How else is he gonna know?"

"Good point."

Noelle came over to them and, as though she'd been doing it for years, brushed a wisp of Bret's hair off his forehead. "You look tired," she said in a soothing voice. "Have you eaten?"

He jerked his head away from her as though she'd burned him with her touch, and straightened from his kneeling position beside Travis. "I'll eat in a few minutes."

She clasped her hands behind her like a small child whose fingers had been slapped, but she didn't drop her gaze. "I'll warm supper for you."

He turned away and started up the stairs. Without looking around he spoke over his shoulder, "Don't bother. I'm sure it's fine the way it is."

Bret reached his room and closed the door before leaning heavily against it. What was wrong with him! She'd merely brushed her fingers against him and he'd felt a charge of electricity shoot all through his body, as though he'd touched a hot-wired fence!

He was acting like a fool—a lovesick fool who'd never been around an attractive woman before.

He'd better eat and get to bed early tonight. He'd need every ounce of energy he could muster tomorrow to deal with the shopping expedition.

After washing up, he returned downstairs. When

he walked into the kitchen his place was set, fresh coffee scented the air and Noelle waited to fill a plate for him.

"You didn't have to go to all this trouble for me," he began, politely.

"It was no trouble," she replied, equally polite.

Uncomfortable with the need to apologize, he managed to blurt out, "Look, I didn't mean to be rude earlier. You just startled me, that's all."

She clasped her hands in front of her and gave a brief nod. "I understand. Some people don't like to be touched. It won't happen again."

He sat down and within moments she set a full plate of steaming food in front of him. "It isn't that I mind being touched, exactly...." he said slowly, searching for words.

"It's me, isn't it?"

She'd sat down across from him and watched him with those mesmerizing blue eyes of hers.

He sighed. "You've gotta admit this is an unusual situation."

Her grin was full of mischief. "It certainly is!"

He relaxed a little, now that he realized she wasn't going to take offense. One bite of food told him that as usual, she'd prepared a heavenly meal. He gave up all pretense of conversation and applied his entire attention to the meal in front of him until his plate was clean and he was sipping a fresh cup of coffee.

"There is one thing I'd like to caution you about," he began in a mellow tone, feeling immeasurably better now that he had a full stomach.

Her eyes met his gaze calmly and she waited to hear what he had to say, a personality trait he'd come to recognize in her. She never appeared defensive or unsure of herself. He couldn't remember ever having known anyone who seemed as comfortable with herself as Noelle. Even if he was going to reprimand her—which in this case came close to what he had in mind—she didn't appear anxious or disturbed about what he might say.

"I couldn't help but hear you telling the kids about that train robber earlier. You were making him out to be some kind of hero, eluding the guards and everything."

"Oh, he was far from a hero. He was a very stubborn individual, determined to ignore any helpful advice about his choice of livelihood."

He smiled at her prim tone of voice. "You talk like you knew him."

"In a manner of speaking."

"Except that people don't go jumping on Amtrak and attempting to rob the baggage cars."

Thoughtfully, she nodded. "That's true."

"You've got a rich imagination, you know. Have you ever thought about writing some of your tales down? People might enjoy reading about some of these characters you've been talking about. But you'd have to make it plain that they aren't real people. You'd also have to explain how good generally triumphs over evil, no matter how glamorous the bad guys seem to be at times."

Her smile sparkled and lights seemed to dance in

her eyes. "So you understand that, do you? That's wonderful."

"What?"

"Nothing, really. I guess I was thinking out loud. If you had let me finish my story, I would have told the children what happened to the bank robber."

"He got caught and ended up in jail?"

She shook her head. "Worse. He didn't get caught and he spent his life running, never being able to trust anyone, never being able to have friends or loved ones, or a family. Never learning how to live." She sighed. "It was a very sad life. Such a waste…especially since it didn't have to turn out that way."

"Was this some movie you once saw?"

She glanced at him in surprise. "Oh, no. I mean, I heard about him from members of my family."

"Oh."

She straightened, and placed her hands on the table. "About tomorrow," she reminded him.

He rolled his eyes. "How could I forget. I've taken advantage of Freda's and Roy's generosity enough. I'm embarrassed that I didn't realize that sooner."

"Don't you ever take the children Christmas shopping?"

"Not if I can help it and I've generally managed to be unavailable each year. Talking to Freda today helped me see how selfish I've been with my time."

"The children were telling me about their visit with her. She sounds like a warm and caring person."

"Yes, she is. She's been a good friend to me through everything."

"I'm glad."

He shifted in his chair. "The truth is, this is always a tough time of year for me. Patti always looked forward to Christmas…decorating the house… planning all sorts of gifts…baking… teaching the children all the time-honored stories. Once she was gone, all the joy left."

"I wonder why? The season is all about experiencing the joy of love and fellowship. She left so much that could remind you of her and her love. The children have shared with me so many wonderful things they remember about their mother. She's very real to them and always will be. She left you a legacy of love, you know. But you have to claim it before you can fully experience it."

He stared at her for an interminable amount of time before he asked, "How old are you?"

She blinked. "What possible difference does that make?"

"Because some of the things you say surprise me, that's all. It's as though you've lived a long life filled with all kinds of experiences and from those experiences you've drawn some fairly profound insights. But you're too young to have experienced very much."

"I don't think of age very much. I suppose I consider it more of an attitude rather than a fixed number."

"An attitude, huh? Then I feel about eighty years

old today, too old for all this exuberance and enthusiasm.'' He rubbed the back of his neck. ''But I want my kids to be happy and I'll do whatever I can to help make this a fun time for them.''

''You're a very loving father, Bret. You've done a great job with your children.''

He could actually feel his ears burning with embarrassment. ''I make all kinds of mistakes with them every day.''

''So? Don't you think they need to see that fathers don't have to be perfect? You also show them that each of them is very important to you. You aren't afraid to show your love for them. You're also willing to admit your mistakes when you make them. How can they not find you endearing?''

''They need more than I can give them, though. They need their mother.''

''I believe they've come to terms with her loss better than you have, Bret. They're getting on with their lives while you're still looking back, wishing for what was rather than accepting what is.''

''Maybe so. Maybe I don't know *how* to get on with my life.''

''That's because you haven't tried. You need to get out more. You need to socialize, find some nice woman to date, enjoy being—''

''There! You're doing it again!''

She looked startled. ''Doing what?''

''Talking like you're some old woman. I don't—''

''Dad?''

Bret glanced up at Chris who'd just come in the back door.

"Yes, son?"

"Roy was just telling me that he's planning to go shopping tomorrow, too. Would it be all right with you if the girls and I went with him? He said he'd take us to San Antonio and we could meet you all there later."

Bret smiled at his oldest son. "Are you saying that you don't want to see Santa this year, Chris?"

Chris laughed. "Well, it won't break my heart if I miss standing in line for hours like we had to do last year. Besides, Roy lets us shop on our own so our gifts are a surprise to everybody."

"And you think I'll insist on tagging along behind you, is that it?"

Chris looked startled, then concerned. He walked over to the table and stopped beside his dad. "I guess I wasn't thinking, was I? Does it sound like we don't want you to go? It isn't that at all! It's just that we've kinda set up a routine with Roy, that's all. But, hey. It's no problem. I think it's great you've volunteered to take us. We can all go in together and make a day of it. It will be just like old—" He paused, then swallowed and looked away.

"I like your idea just fine, son. You and the girls go with Roy. Noelle and I will take Travis with us and we'll meet you at a designated place and time."

Chris's eyes met Bret's. "You sure you don't mind?"

"I'm positive." He didn't drop his gaze.

Chris gave a sigh of relief. "That's great, Dad. I know we'll have a good time tomorrow. Having you there will make it even more special."

The room seemed to fill with silence after Chris went upstairs. Bret wasn't sure what to do or say. Noelle quietly gathered his dishes and washed them, then began putting them away.

"I hadn't realized how protective the children have been of my feelings," Bret finally said.

"They love you very much," Noelle replied, standing on tiptoe to put one of the serving bowls away, her back to him.

"It's bad enough that they had to lose their mother without worrying about the remaining parent, as well. That's a lot to push off on a child."

"Children are strong. Otherwise they'd never survive."

Bret slid down into his chair, his legs stretched out in front of him. "Patti used to say that every child was born with at least one guardian angel making certain they would be safe."

"You don't believe that?"

He gave her a wistful smile. "Wouldn't it be a great world if that were true? Babies wouldn't be born addicted to whatever their mothers' choice of drug was...they wouldn't be born with physical defects...they wouldn't be born in parts of the world where they'll probably starve to death before they reach school age."

"You think that guardian angels could prevent all of that?"

He raised his brows. "Don't you?"

"Not all angels are capable of performing those kinds of miracles. I like to think that the angels guard those little babies as much as they are able, comforting them, helping them to feel safe and loved, preparing them for a better place, regardless of what eventually happens to them."

"I'd like to believe that, too," Bret admitted. "I can scarcely remember those first months after Patti died, but somehow Travis managed to survive anyway. I must have cared for him and loved him, but I don't remember much of it. It's almost like I was in some kind of fog, or a bad dream."

"It's time to wake up, Bret."

He glanced up and saw that she was standing beside him. He gave her a lopsided smile and obeying an impulse, snaked his arm around her and pulled her down on his lap. She would have slid down the length of his legs if he hadn't caught her with his other arm. Before he could quite believe what he'd done, Bret discovered he had one arm wrapped around Noelle's hips, the other around her waist, and she was lying along his chest and shoulder.

Slowly he straightened in the chair, keeping a firm grasp on the woman in his arms. She felt good there. Very good. For the first time in a long, long time, he felt alive.

"I'm awake, Noelle," he murmured, his voice rumbling deep in his chest.

He could see that he had caught her totally unprepared, which pleased him considerably. She seemed to know so damned much about so many things, but there was one area where she didn't know diddly... and he was just about to show her!

"Uh, Bret, I don't think—" she began, pushing herself away from him slightly.

He wasn't having any part of her retreat. She was now resting squarely on his thighs, which freed up one of his arms. He tilted her chin up with his thumb.

She smelled tantalizingly feminine and his body no longer felt eighty years old. He tilted his head slightly and kissed her.

He'd been right. She didn't know a blamed thing about kissing, but that was fine. He had plenty of time and he was a very patient instructor.

Her mouth felt so soft. He watched her eyelids flutter, then close. When she gave a tiny sigh he used the opportunity to touch his tongue to her lips, edging her mouth gradually open until he could explore more fully. He increased the pressure, enjoying the pleasure of holding her close, feeling her respond to him. He allowed his hand to slide along her neck and throat downward until it came to rest cupping her breast.

Yes! She felt just the way he had dreamed she would, her breast filling his palm as though made with him in mind. He could feel her heart beating so rapidly her chest shook.

She was so innocent and he was taking advantage of her.

That thought washed over him like a sudden cold and drenching rain. Reluctantly he forced himself to move his hand until it safely circled her waist once more. He even tried to end the kiss, but even his strong willpower couldn't overcome the intensity of their shared experience.

When he finally released her, he buried his face in her hair and shuddered with the depth of his overwhelming desire for her.

She clung to him and he was thankful that he hadn't frightened her with his strong reaction to the kiss. He was a grown man and he should have known better. But he was also human, and no one short of a saint could have withstood the temptation that Noelle presented to him.

As soon as she stirred, he released the pressure of his arms around her. She pulled away until she could look into his face. "I didn't know," she said with wonder.

"You didn't know what?"

"How it felt. I had no idea what happens…I mean the way we react to each other." Her eyes were wide. "Kisses are pretty potent stuff, aren't they?"

He grinned. Did she have any idea how adorable she looked perched on his lap, her hair all mussed, discussing the ramifications of their first kiss?

"They can be, yes," he replied, still grinning.

"I had no idea."

"Are you telling me you've never been kissed?"

"Not like that," she replied emphatically.

"Are you beginning to understand why I was concerned about your staying here?"

She looked at him warily. "Why? Do you intend to do that again?"

He laughed. He couldn't help it. She looked like one of the tiny kittens whose fur had just been rubbed the wrong way.

"Not if you don't want me to, of course. I'd never force myself on you. But I got a distinct impression that you didn't mind that kiss at all, and that you wouldn't argue if I proposed another one."

She thought about that for a moment, then smiled, obviously delighted with her conclusion. "You're right. I didn't mind it at all and I'd very much like to enjoy another one." Without waiting to see his response she closed her eyes, wrapped her arms around his neck and kissed him with a burst of innocent enthusiasm.

Chapter Four

"Why didn't somebody tell me what it's like? I had no idea, no warning, nothing to prepare me. I—"

"*Noelle—*"

"By the way, how old am I?"

"*You're ageless. Noelle—*"

"That's what I thought. I mean, if I'd ever bothered to give it a thought. But all of a sudden I'm thinking about such things—earthly things—a great deal. Like, how old I am, and how I look, and if Bret finds me attractive—he certainly kisses me like he finds me attractive—and I find him very attractive. I can't believe how attractive. I mean, the most subtle things about him start my heart racing as though I've been running for hours. Take his hair, for instance. I find myself spending hours of my day while I'm cleaning house or washing clothes or preparing meals, wondering exactly how you'd describe his hair. It's so thick and it's all these different colors, like taffy and wheat and cinnamon and straw. Straw. I never would have thought that straw was a beautiful color but oh, on Bret it looks wonderful, really amazingly so.

"And his eyes. I can't stop gazing into his eyes. At first I thought they were brown. Well, maybe a light brown. Then I realized they were the same exact, identical color of well-aged whiskey—almost like topaz, but with swirling depths in them. They even change color according to his mood. When he's tired they're golden and when he's angry they get darker, almost like they're flashing sparks. Sometimes, when he looks at me a certain way, they go all liquid and molten. That look makes me go weak in my knees. It really does. I've heard the expression many times but I've never experienced the feeling before. I'm telling you right now, it's the weirdest feeling I've had in a long time. Let's face it, I've just gotten used to having knees and now they're already acting up on me.

"The thing is, I don't know what to do. Well, of course I know what I'm supposed to be doing. My assignment was all very clear and concise. And it isn't as though I haven't always loved Bret because I have. But this is different. I mean, really different. And it's confusing me. I've been daydreaming around the house, rerunning the dreams he has about me every night, trying to imagine what it would feel like if he really were doing those things to me. I'm telling you here and now being human isn't anything like I thought it was at all.''

"What did you think it was like?"

"Going around making really stupid mistakes, needing somebody to guide you through them. Well, from my new perspective, they don't look so stupid, and most of all they don't look like mistakes.''

"Would you care to give me an example?"

She thought for a moment. "Well, the other day Travis told me that he wished that I would stay with them all year-round instead of just during the Christmas season. He said that he wished I could be his mommy.''

"Not a very surprising wish for a young child who has never had a mother."

"I know. Before I took on human form, I would have quickly explained how that wasn't possible, how it was only through a special dispensation that I had been allowed to materialize for him at all.''

"You didn't tell him that?"

She hung her head. "No.''

"What did you tell him?"

She lifted her chin and stared at her supervisor. "I told him I wished I could be his mommy, too.''

Noelle waited for an explosion at the very least. She had done some unangelic things before, she'd managed to get into some pretty tumultuous situations before, but never had she made such an out and out earthly remark.

She waited for a response. She waited for what seemed forever. For that matter, it could have been forever since there was no measurement of time in this dimension. So she wasn't certain if a few minutes or an eternity passed before her supervisor responded.

"I see."

Those two words seemed to circle her as though they had taken on their own form, becoming special entities capable of independent action.

What had she expected...a reprimand? Some form of judgment? Chastisement? Maybe she'd been on earth too long. She was already beginning to react like a human being, waiting for a lightning bolt to strike her.

"The thing is, I don't know what to do. I'm really confused."

"Are you looking for guidance?"

"Oh, yes! That's exactly what I want."

"You need only to ask, surely you haven't forgotten?"

"I know that I've made a positive change in the children's lives. In addition, Freda is getting a much needed rest and an opportunity to review what she's doing with her life and whether she wishes to continue her present path.

"As for Bret...well, I think he's beginning to see how he'd cut himself off from the world these past three years. How he'd retreated into himself, giving only what was demanded of him.

"Now he's beginning to feel again, to notice the world around him. He's, uh, well, he's realizing certain things are lacking in his life—like female companionship and physical closeness. He's discovered that he's in the prime of his life and that he could have so much more if he decided to reach out for what he wants.''

"Then you are doing your job well, I would say.''

"Except that he wants to reach out to me."

"For physical closeness and female companionship?''

"Exactly."

"Surely you can arrange for him to meet some eligible women before you leave, women with whom he would have something in common, perhaps a woman who's been unable to have a family of her own and would feel blessed to find a ready-made one waiting for her.''

"I suppose so."

"Do I detect a certain lack of enthusiasm in your tone?''

"Yes. That's exactly why I'm so confused. I know what needs to be done. I know I'm capable of bringing about the situations needed for him to have a varied selection from which to choose. The problem is, I don't want him to fall in love with someone else."

There. She had finally put her feelings into words.

"You prefer to see him the way he was before you came into his life?''

"Not at all. It's just that I want to be the one with whom he falls in love."

"Given your present circumstances, I can understand why you might feel that way. It's perfectly nat-

ural and normal for a human being to have such yearnings. Once Christmas arrives and you return to your original form those strange human yearnings will no longer be with you. You will be able to regain your objectivity in the matter."

"Are you certain of that?"

Her supervisor smiled. *"Have I ever lied to you?"*

"Of course not. Please forgive my doubts."

"There's nothing to forgive, of course. I can see tremendous growth in you since you embarked on this latest assignment. You're doing splendidly."

"It feels more like I've gone backward. I used to have such a clear vision of what I was supposed to be doing in relation to everyone around me. Now, I don't have a clue of where I am."

"I believe we do our greatest growing during that period when we seem not to know anything. Perhaps that is our greatest lesson—to understand how very little we know. What is important is that we do what needs to be done in a timely fashion. I would say that you are on schedule, wouldn't you?"

"Christmas is only a week away. I have seven days."

"An eternity to some."

"Thank you for listening to me."

"I am always here for you, just as my counselor is always here for me, and so forth and so on. No one has to be alone unless he or she so chooses."

"Bret doesn't understand how alone he's been, how he hasn't bothered to ask for help or guidance. He would laugh at the idea of being alone while raising four children, not to mention having Freda and Roy around most of the time. As far as that goes, Bret doesn't believe in angels, which is amusing when you think about it.''

"Whether you recognize it or not, you are making great changes in this man's life. He will never again be quite the same man he was before you appeared before him."

"That works both ways. I'll never forget Bret, either. Never.''

Chapter Five

Roy tapped on the kitchen door while the family was eating breakfast the next morning. Noelle quickly opened the door since she had just stepped to the counter nearby for the coffeepot. "Good morning, Roy," she said, smiling at the tall, thin cowboy. "Would you like some coffee?"

Stepping inside, Roy raked his hat off his head with his hand, and nodded shyly. "Sounds good, ma'am."

"Chris tells me you still plan to go Christmas shopping today," Bret said, eyeing Roy with a half smile on his face. "You're a real glutton for punishment, aren't you."

"Well, I kinda like taking the kids every year. It's become sort of a tradition with me. They're my family, you know. We've got a regular thing going."

"Since I promised Travis I would take him to see

Santa this year, why don't you take Chris and the girls in the Bronco and Noelle, Travis and I'll go in the truck." He named one of the newer malls in San Antonio and said, "We'll plan on meeting at Santa's Village about four o'clock. Will that give everybody enough time to see everything they want to see?"

A chorus of affirmatives almost deafened him. He could see the excitement building as the children all exchanged glances.

Noelle looked at Travis. "Is that all right with you? If you stay with your Dad and me?"

He nodded vigorously. "Yep."

Bret ruffled his youngest son's hair. "This will be a new experience for us, won't it, young'un? We've never gone shopping together for Christmas."

Travis's smile was cherubic. "It's because Noelle's coming, too."

Bret glanced over at Noelle and saw her cheeks flaming. Slowly Bret acknowledged, "You're probably right. Guess Noelle's caused a lot of changes since she arrived, hasn't she?"

"Uh-huh. I think we should keep her."

With a speculative glance at her flushed cheeks Bret replied, "You think so?" When he caught her eye, he winked.

Obviously flustered, Noelle gathered up the dishes on the table and carried them to the sink.

The room soon emptied of the children, who'd gone upstairs to finish dressing. Bret shook his head and said, "I don't know how four children manage to sound like a hundred-voice chorus. It's kind of nice to have a few minutes of peace.''

Absently he watched Noelle move around the room until everything had been washed and put away. His gaze followed her as she went into Freda's room and closed the door.

Roy lowered his voice. "Have you noticed something strange about Noelle?''

"Strange?''

"Yeah. Well, different maybe.''

"Not particularly. Have you?''

"Well, for one thing, she never seems to get tired. She's on the go every time I see her, and she's always in a good mood. Now I never knowed a woman to be in a good mood *all* the time. By and large, I find women to be kinda moody. It's a little distracting to me to see somebody so blamed cheerful all the time. It kinda makes me wonder what she's up to.''

Bret carefully hid his smile. "Do you have any ideas on the subject?''

"Well, I've been wondering if she's trying to take over Freda's job.''

Bret lifted his cup and took a swallow of coffee, trying to gain some time to think of what to say.

Roy went on. "Have you asked her how long she intends to stay?''

"Not in so many words. She said she'd come to help out while Freda was in the hospital, that's all.''

"Have you noticed how she's managed to wrap those kids of yours around her little finger? Why, they about fall all over themselves being helpful and respectful."

"Let me get this straight, Roy. Are you saying that this woman has aroused your suspicions by being too good?"

Roy thought about that for a minute. "You gotta admit it ain't real natural."

"Do you think she has an ulterior motive? Other than possibly taking Freda's job, of course."

"That'd be bad enough."

"You're missing Freda, I take it."

Roy's ears glowed red. "Well, I guess I've gotten used to her ways. A fella doesn't like change in his life, you know? I prefer a set routine, something I can count on."

"Do you think Noelle's undependable? Untrustworthy? What?"

Roy scratched his ear and frowned, thinking. "I just don't want to see you and the children hurt, that's all."

"It may be my imagination, but the kids have seemed much happier since she arrived."

Roy leaned on the table and looked at Bret from beneath his bushy brows. "They ain't the only ones. I actually heard *you* laugh the other day."

"You didn't! Why, Roy, I'm shocked."

"You gotta admit that it takes some gittin' used to."

Bret's smile slowly faded. "You're right, Roy. I guess I hadn't noticed the number of changes that have occurred recently. I haven't been one to laugh very much these past few years.''

"Don't suppose you found much to laugh about.''

"That's true.''

Roy nodded, still thinking through the subject very carefully. "So maybe, in that respect, having Miss Noelle come to stay a spell's been good for you.''

"You think so?''

After a long moment, Roy said, "I reckon I do. I guess not every change is necessarily bad.''

"There's a positive thought, Roy. Very positive. I'll keep it in mind.'' He pushed back his chair. "Guess we'd better get ready for this big shopping trip.''

"That's one of the things I've been talking about. You always found fifteen good reasons why you was always too busy to go into town during Christmas season. Now you seem almost eager.''

Bret sighed and lightly tapped Roy on the shoulder with his fist. "I can't begin to explain it, myself. It must be the Christmas season…maybe it's contagious and I've just now caught it.''

Bret left the room and headed up the stairs, thinking about their conversation. He met the three older children clattering down the steps, and got hugs from his daughters and a casual wave from his oldest son. He glanced into Travis's room on his way past, and abruptly halted. Travis was sitting on the side of his bed, holding the framed picture of Patti.

"Something wrong?'' he asked casually, leaning against the doorjamb.

Travis looked up. "No. I was just talkin' to Mommy. 'Splaining stuff to her."

"I see."

"Are we ready to go?"

"Just about. You're looking pretty sharp there, fella. Did you get dressed on your own?"

"Mostly. Sally helped me with my boots 'cause sometimes I get 'em on the wrong feet."

"You did a fine job."

"I wanted to look good for Santa."

"He's bound to be impressed." He turned away. "I'll see you downstairs." Bret went into his room, wondering what exactly Travis had needed to "'splain" to Patti.

He also wondered how he was going to get through today without revealing how hard it was to become a part of the Christmas scene. He was doing everything he could to release the past without letting those around him know how difficult it was for him.

Roy was right. Noelle had made it much easier for him. She had a way of looking at him as though she could see deep down into his soul...to the place where his most private feelings were stored. How could someone who appeared so young and naive continue to project so much warmth, empathy and caring? At times it was all he could do not to gather her in his arms and just hold her close, knowing how good he'd feel.

The problem with taking Noelle in his arms and holding her as he'd done last night was the fact that he forgot all about her empathy and caring and was

immediately made aware of her womanly warmth
and how blasted good she felt in his embrace.

He didn't want to take advantage of their situation
but after last night he knew the temptations were
steadily mounting.

By the time Bret returned downstairs Roy and the
older children had already left. Noelle and Travis
waited patiently for him in the kitchen.

"Sorry to take so long," Bret said sheepishly.

Travis took his hand. "It's okay, Daddy. Don't be
scared in the big stores. I'll hold your hand so you
don't get losted."

"I appreciate that, son."

Travis beamed up at him. "'Course it helps to
have an angel along, you know."

Bret raised his brow slightly. "Good point. I'm
obviously in good hands today." He reached down
and picked up Travis. "Let's hit the road, pardner."
He paused in the doorway and held the door open
for Noelle. She looked up at him and smiled. His
heart lunged in his chest like a spooked mustang and
raced at an alarming rate.

Over a simple smile?

He gave his head a sharp shake, reminding himself
that he wasn't some adolescent kid with a schoolboy
crush. Now he had to convince his body of the fact.

Bret hadn't been to San Antonio in several
months. For that matter, he hadn't been anywhere
other than the ranch and the small town nearby where

he bought supplies. Forcing himself out today made him realize how limited he'd been.

When they came in on the northern outskirts of the city, the traffic had picked up considerably, a strong reminder of why he avoided big cities during the holiday season. He reminded himself that there was no hurry, they had most of the day, and eventually edged into the lane he needed to exit for the mall.

The mall had been designed to cater to large crowds so the parking lot was immense. However, they circled for almost twenty minutes before he happened to spot the flash of backup lights of a vehicle just ahead. With a muttered comment, he waited until the elderly couple pulled out, then whipped into the available space.

"Wow! I didn't ever think we'd find a place, did you, Daddy?"

"I was beginning to wonder, myself." He glanced at Noelle—who had kept Travis entertained during the two-hour drive from the ranch—and smiled.

Once again her response made his heart kick into overdrive.

As soon as they reached the mall itself the piped music echoed all around them. Bret almost groaned aloud. Travis skipped along between them, holding each of their hands. His eyes were shining as he took in all the tinseled splendor.

"When are we going to see Santa?"

Bret gave Noelle a knowing look. "I have a hunch we'd better put that first on our list."

They had no trouble finding Santa. All they had to watch for was the long line of small children eager to talk and have their pictures taken with the man.

"Poor dear," Bret heard Noelle mutter.

"Who?"

She glanced down at Travis who was hopping from one foot to the other, chattering with a little girl in line behind them. She nodded to the man in the Santa suit. "He's really not enjoying the job. What a shame that he chose to take it."

Bret looked around the large rotunda at the crowd of people. "Who could enjoy something like this?"

She looked surprised. "To be able to speak to each child, to hear their fondest hopes and dreams? I would imagine that many people would." She looked away. "I know I enjoy it very much."

"But you've only had to listen to the four at home."

She chuckled. "That's true."

"Besides. How do you know he isn't enjoying himself? He's handling the children very professionally, I would say."

"He's very good. His heart's just not in it."

"And you can tell that from here, of course."

She nodded. "Just as I can tell that your heart isn't in this shopping expedition. Tell me, why did you agree to come?"

He looked down into her mesmerizing eyes for a long time before he murmured, "I'm not sure. It felt like the right thing to do at the time."

"I'm glad you did. Perhaps it will change your attitude about Christmas."

"What, exactly, is my attitude?"

She looked surprised. "You just want to get it over with as quickly and painlessly as possible."

"Do you do mind reading acts in addition to looking after households?"

"Bret, I don't know exactly how to break this to you, but even your three-year-old son knows how you feel about Christmas."

"That obvious, huh?"

"That obvious."

"And here I've been patting myself on the back all the way to San Antonio, congratulating myself on how well I've hidden my feelings."

Her spontaneous cascade of laughter caught him off guard. She rocked with hilarity, leaving him bemused. In the first place, he didn't particularly appreciate being the object of her amusement, but more startling to him was the sound of her musical laughter. The people in line were glancing at her and smiling at her unrestrained enjoyment of the moment.

Sheepishly Bret chuckled, finally seeing the absurdity in the situation, which set her off again. He began to laugh in earnest, for no reason other than it felt good. He'd long since forgotten the last time he'd found something to laugh about. The shocked look on his son's face was a silent reminder that in all likelihood Bret hadn't laughed with wholesome enjoyment since Travis was born.

"What's so funny, Daddy?"

Noelle did a commendable job of regaining control. Only her eyes still danced with laughter.

"We were just being silly," he replied, still grinning.

"I didn't know that daddies could be silly, just like kids."

Bret's gaze met Noelle's. "I guess I kinda forgot that myself, son."

When it became Travis's turn to talk with Santa he gave Noelle a brief, panicked look. She immediately knelt beside him and whispered into his ear. He nodded and his features relaxed. She gave him a quick hug and he turned away from her, walking over to Santa with quiet dignity.

Bret couldn't hear what he was saying, but he could certainly see his son's earnestness.

"Do you know what it is he wants for Christmas?" Bret asked.

"Yes."

When she didn't say anything more, Bret verbally nudged her by saying, "Aren't you going to tell me?"

"No." Her smile took any sting out of the quiet response.

"It's going to be tough for me to see that he gets it if I don't know what he wants."

"I'm sure he'll tell you in his own good time."

"I don't think so. He wouldn't tell me the last time we discussed it."

"Perhaps he didn't find the timing to be the best."

"Are you telling me that a three-year-old has the knowledge and intelligence to plan strategy?"

"It's an instinctive form of survival. He's watched how his older brother and sisters manage to get what they want from you. They know when to leave you alone—when you're tired and hungry or upset about something. They also know when to approach you…when you're well fed and in an expansive mood."

"I had no idea I was so easy to read."

"Your children know that you are all they have, therefore you've assumed a position of major importance in their existence. They instinctively know that it is mandatory for them to understand you well."

Travis came bounding over to them and said, "When do we eat?"

Noelle laughed. "I can see you have your priorities straight."

It was over a sandwich in the food court section of the mall that Bret said to Travis, "Tell us about your visit with Santa."

Travis swallowed, then took a sip from his straw before he said, "I liked him, even though he wasn't the real Santa."

Bret eyed him warily. "He wasn't?"

Travis looked at his dad in disgust. "'Course not. The real Santa doesn't have time to sit around and talk to people this close to Christmas. But he told me that he'd be sure to pass my message on to the real Santa."

Bret refused to meet Noelle's eyes. "That's com-

forting to know." After a few more minutes of silence while they finished their meals, he asked, "So
what was your message?"

This time Travis wouldn't meet his father's eyes.
"I can't tell. It's a secret." He looked at Bret with
a wide-eyed gaze. "But I think you'll like it,
Daddy."

Bret sat back. "Me? I thought we were talking
about what *you* want for Christmas?"

Travis looked like a mischievous cherub. "It's for
both of us...all of us...the whole family!"

Now Bret did look at Noelle but her attention
seemed to be fully caught by something beyond their
table. Whatever was going on, he'd need to get some
answers soon.

By the time they met Roy and the other children
Bret felt as though he'd been pulled through a knot-
hole backward. Where did everyone get their energy?
The noise and the crowd had given him a headache.
He was too used to the solitude of wide open spaces
to ever get used to the turmoil swirling around him.

Roy spoke up. "I've been thinkin', boss. Why
don't you let me take Travis and the kids back with
me. We'll stop and eat on the way home and maybe
drop by to see Freda for a while. That'll give you
and Noelle some time to yourselves."

Bret was surprised at the suggestion. He was more
surprised at the eager expressions worn by all his
children. They must really miss Freda.

"I suppose so, Roy." He glanced down at Noelle.
"What do you say?"

"Whatever we do is fine with me. I'm along for the ride."

And so it was that Bret found himself having dinner with Noelle some time later at a restaurant overlooking the river in downtown San Antonio, a restaurant Roy had suggested.

"What a beautiful view," she was saying, staring out the window.

"Have you ever visited San Antonio before?"

She shook her head, smiling.

"So what do you think of the city?"

Her eyes sparkled. "I'm fascinated by everything. This is such an exciting time of the year."

"How do you generally spend your Christmases? Do you go home?"

After a brief hesitation, she nodded. "Yes...at home."

He smiled. "Well, you've made our Christmas season much more joyous this year. I'm not certain what we would have done without you."

"I feel very blessed. The time seems to have rushed by. There's only a few more days until Christmas."

"We haven't talked about that, have we...I mean, how long you've been here, and your salary—"

"Oh, please!" Noelle looked quite distressed. "I can't accept money for helping you. I have all that I need. Perhaps Freda—"

He took her hand. "I've already reassured Freda that all her bills are taken care of. She knows how much I value her. She will never do without anything as long as I'm able to look after her.''

Her smile trembled with sweetness. ''I'm so glad.''

''You are?''

She blinked. ''Yes, of course. I'm touched to know she means so much to you. You're a very honorable man.''

It was his turn to sit back in surprise. ''Me? What have I done?''

''Still care about those around you, despite the pain you've been experiencing.''

He looked at her for a long while without saying anything. When he did, his voice sounded gruff to his ears. ''Speaking of being honorable, I need to apologize to you.''

''For what?''

''For my behavior last night. I shouldn't have grabbed you the way I did…and I sure shouldn't have kissed you.'' He fought not to squirm like a schoolboy confessing to the authorities. ''I had no business taking advantage of you. You're a guest in my home and deserve my respect.'' When he finally forced himself to look up from the coffee sitting in front of him all he saw in her face was curiosity. ''What's wrong?''

''I'm afraid I don't understand. By kissing me you showed me disrespect?''

He couldn't think of how to respond. She looked honestly curious, rather than offended or disapproving. Didn't she understand anything about men? His thoughts unerringly raced back to the kiss…to the second kiss that she had initiated. A ripple of awareness ran over him. She might have seemed inexperienced during their first kiss but as for the second one…whatever she might have lacked in experience she certainly made up for in enthusiasm.

He shook the disturbing memories away. "What I'm trying to do is to reassure you that it won't happen again. I promise."

Darned if she didn't look disappointed! This conversation wasn't going the way he'd expected. He didn't know what to say.

She didn't help matters any. She reached across the table and touched the back of his hand with her fingertips. "I enjoyed kissing you, Bret Bishop. Please don't apologize. If you prefer not to kiss me again, I can accept that, but you did nothing wrong."

His hand tingled where she touched him and he was having trouble getting his tongue to come unglued from the top of his mouth when he heard his name being called in a light, feminine voice.

"Bret? Bret Bishop! Is it you?"

He glanced around, then stood with a grin. "Gina Sweeney! I don't believe it." He held out his hand. "I haven't seen you in a coon's age. How are you?"

She took his proffered hand in both of hers and said, "It's Montgomery, now, although I've been divorced from Hal for almost four years." Gina's face shone with pleasure. "My, but it's good to see you after all this time. When I looked across the room I couldn't believe my eyes."

Bret turned and said, "Noelle, I want you to meet Gina. We went all the way through school together, from the first grade until we graduated from high school." He shook his head in wonder. "I haven't seen you since graduation, which has been—"

She laughingly interrupted. "More years than I want to admit to." She offered her hand to Noelle. "I'm very pleased to meet you. Noelle. Such an unusual name, but it seems perfect for you, somehow."

Bret looked to the table where Gina had been and saw another couple. Before he could ask, she explained, "I'm visiting friends here in San Antonio. They've been after me to come see them for so long. I haven't been back to Texas in years. Finally I decided on the spur-of-the-moment to fly down and visit for a few days."

He motioned to a chair. "Well, sit down for a minute. Let me find out what you've been doing."

Gracefully she slid into the chair he offered. "I've been working in the court system in a county just north of Nashville for several years. Hal's an attorney there. We had an amicable divorce, which made it so much more comfortable to stay on there. I really love my work."

"Do you have any children?"

"One...a girl." She looked at the two of them and asked, "Do you and Noelle have children?"

"Oh, we—" Noelle began to say when Bret cut in.

"We have four—two of each."

"Still ranching?"

"Of course. That's all the Bishops know how to do."

She shook her head. "Better you than me. I could hardly wait to get out of ranching country." She grinned. "Give me city lights any day."

After a few minutes of discussing old classmates and their possible whereabouts, Gina said, "Well, it's been wonderful running into you like this. If you ever get to Tennessee be sure to contact me."

Since she'd already given him her address and phone number, he nodded. As soon as she left their table Bret looked at Noelle and smiled. "Are you ready to go?"

"Whenever you are." She stood and he helped her with her jacket. After paying the waiter, Bret took her hand and led her out of the restaurant into the cool night.

Once outside they walked to the truck in silence. Noelle waited until they left the city limits before she spoke.

"Bret?"

"Hmm?"

"Why did you let your friend think that you and I were married?"

He was quiet for a moment, thinking. "I don't know, really. I guess because I didn't think it really mattered to the conversation."

"But she's single."

"Yeah, so she said."

"And you're single."

"So?"

"Haven't you given any thought to the possibility that you might marry again someday?"

Another long silence ensued. "Now that you mention it," he drawled, "maybe the thought has crossed my mind once or twice recently, why?"

"Well, Gina was obviously happy to see you and I thought—"

When her voice dwindled to nothing, he prompted, "You thought—?"

She heard amusement in his voice. "Well, it just seems to me that maybe you'd want to follow up on your friendship."

"Tell me something, Miss Noelle, are you trying to play matchmaker for me?"

"Oh! Well, no. Not exactly."

"I'm glad to hear it. You know, I'd much prefer to decide for myself who I'd like to spend my time with."

"Of course."

He glanced at her from the corner of his eye. The glow from the dash offered enough light for him to see her heightened color. "How about you? Have you ever given any thought to getting married?"

"Me?" She sounded shocked. "Of course not! What I mean is, I—uh—well, have my career to think about and—" She coughed and gave up.

"Your career. I see. I certainly hope your helping us here hasn't delayed any of your plans."

"Oh, no," she quickly replied. "My career is all about helping people wherever I can, so this was all part of— What I mean is, I was just glad to be able to help you,'' she finished lamely.

"You know, I realize that I haven't had much time to visit with you since you arrived. Why don't you tell me more about yourself."

"All right."

When she didn't say anything more he waited, and waited, and finally started laughing.

"Did I say something funny?"

"Not at all. What was funny was that you didn't say anything. Most people who agree to talk about themselves don't sit in silence."

"Oh! I'm sorry. I was waiting to find out what you wanted to know about me."

"Have you always lived in California?"

"No."

"Do you visit Ida often?"

"No."

"Come on, Noelle. I need a little help here."

"I guess I don't know what it is you're interested in learning about me. I feel as though you know the truly important things about me. I enjoy children. I love to cook. Living in the country is the closest thing to heaven I know.…"

"Then you really are content at the ranch."

She turned and looked at him, her face glowing. "Oh, yes, more than I can possibly say."

Something deep inside him seemed to splinter, shift and break loose. Freda was right. His emotions were definitely coming out of the deep freeze…they were melting like ice in a spring thaw.

He reached over, took her hand and carefully placed it on his thigh, then rested his hand on top.

They rode that way in silence for the rest of the way home.

Chapter Six

By the time they reached the ranch the house was dark except for a muted glow coming from the living room. Bret parked the truck in the large shed beside the barn, then went around and helped Noelle down from the big vehicle.

Instead of going toward the back door, however, he led her along the driveway until they reached the front of the house where he paused. From there they could see through the living-room window into the warmth of the room beyond.

"The tree looks so festive all lit up like that, doesn't it?" he murmured. "I've never really taken the time to look at it before tonight."

She stood beside him and saw the love and attention that draped and surrounded the tree, each and every ornament carefully chosen over the years by a family's tradition. "It's lovely."

He gave her hand a gentle squeeze, then led her up the steps to the front door, which was seldom used. They found Roy asleep on the sofa, the television flickering its late-night movie. The quiet closing of the door alerted Roy to their arrival and he sat up and yawned. "Did ya have a good time?"

"Yes," Noelle answered softly. "You were right. The view of the river was well worth seeing." She glanced up at Bret. "Thank you for taking me."

Roy coughed. "Well, guess I'd better get home."

"How was Freda?"

"Oh, she's looking good…seemed tickled to see us. Said she'd missed all the ruckus of getting ready for the holidays and all."

"Has the doctor told her when she could leave the hospital?"

"Well, he said it would definitely be in time for Christmas, providing she doesn't try to get around on that leg anytime soon. He's insisting she take it easy and get plenty of rest. Guess her sister intends to make sure she does." Roy looked at Noelle. "You planning to be here through the holidays?"

"Well, I'll be able to stay until—"

Bret interrupted, saying, "We haven't had a chance to discuss it, Roy."

Roy got the message. "Well, I'll see you in the mornin'," he said, picking up his hat and settling it on his head.

Bret followed him to the door and locked up after him. He returned to the living room, where Noelle stood gazing at the tree, a wistful smile on her face.

"Noelle?"

She turned and looked at him.

As though drawn by a magnet, Bret moved closer until he was close enough to touch her. He brushed her cheek with the back of his hand. Her skin was so smooth, smoother than anything else he could name. Her complexion was so fair—like ivory—with just a hint of color tinting her cheekbones. However, it was her eyes—deep blue surrounded by a fringe of thick lashes—that tugged a deep response from somewhere inside of him.

He forgot what he had intended to say. Instead, he murmured, "Travis is right."

"About what?"

"You really do look like the Christmas angel. They must have modeled her after you."

She smiled, but didn't say anything.

Carefully, as though she were made of porcelain and could easily break, he slipped his arms around her waist. "I know what I said earlier, and I hate to break a promise, but I don't think I'm strong enough to leave this room without kissing you."

She went up on tiptoe and placed her hands trustingly against his chest. "I'd like that...very much."

A strong surge of protectiveness swept over him even while he took what she offered without hesitation. She felt so natural there, as though she'd found her home in his arms.

He brushed his lips against hers, wanting to savor each sensation, wanting to relish the moment. He could feel her quivering, causing him to stroke her

spine in a soothing gesture of comfort. Then he lost
all sense of thought or awareness of anything other
than their blending.

Eventually he scooped her up in his arms and settled down on the sofa with her draped across his lap.
He took his time exploring each tiny new discovery
about her…her delicate waist, the gentle curve of her
hips. Meanwhile he continued to press kisses on her
face and neck and down to the opening of her blouse.

Her fluttering fingers touched his face, danced
through his hair, shyly caressed his chest until he
thought he might explode with desire for her.

Bret forced himself to lift his head away from her.
He drew several deep breaths, still holding her close
to him, before he allowed his head to lean against
the sofa's backrest.

When he opened his eyes and looked at her she
was watching him with a solemn scrutiny he found
captivating.

"You don't enjoy kissing me?"

He couldn't hide his smile. "On the contrary. I
enjoy it very much."

"Then why do you feel guilty for doing something
you enjoy?"

Her discernment never ceased to amaze him. "I
don't want to take advantage of you."

"You've done nothing that I haven't allowed."

He sighed. "I know this will sound crazy, but I
feel as though I'm cheating on Patti."

"I can understand that. You've treated Patti's absence in your life as temporary. Somewhere you've harbored the feeling that she will be back.''

''I know better.''

''Your rational mind, perhaps.''

''But you're right. I haven't wanted to be around another woman…until you came. I feel as though someone turned on a light for me and made me look into all the dark corners of my mind. I can see what I've been doing to myself by not accepting her loss.'' He looked down at Noelle. ''You've been that light for me.''

''I'm so glad, Bret. You deserve so much happiness. You're a good man, a caring father. It's time for you to accept all the good things that life has to offer.''

''Does that include you?''

She looked startled. Carefully she replied, ''I'm not certain that I understand what you mean.''

''Then you are much too innocent and naive for your own good. Roy knows what's been happening to me. From the way the children made themselves so willingly scarce tonight, I have a hunch they see it, too.'' He placed a kiss on the tip of her nose, on each cheek, and finally gave her a lingering kiss on the mouth. ''I don't want you to disappear out of my life now that I've met you. I want you to stay here with me…with us.''

''I'm afraid that won't be possible,'' she began before he effectively stopped her rebuttal with another long, lingering kiss that seemed to effectively distract her. At least for the moment. Eventually she continued, but on an entirely different subject, he decided. "Christmas season is a magical time, a time when miracles can and often do occur."

He smiled. "I suppose you're right. I feel like I experienced a miracle when you showed up here at the ranch just when we needed you."

"Exactly. I feel very blessed to be here." She stroked his cheek wistfully before she continued. "However, the magic ends on Christmas Day. It reaches its peak at midnight on Christmas Eve. I'll be gone by the next day."

"Nonsense. There's no reason to believe that you can't stay as long as you wish. If you have another job, send them your resignation. Better yet, call and resign now."

"I'm afraid it isn't quite that simple. There are some professions that are considered lifetime callings."

"Perhaps if you explained that—" He paused, realizing what she had just now admitted. "You don't want to stay. That's it, isn't it? You knew when you arrived that you would only be here until Christmas."

"It isn't a question of what I want. It's a question of what I'm allowed to do."

His eyes narrowed. "Are you telling me that I was right? You're really from some religious order?" Hastily lifting her off his lap he set her beside him. "Well, why in the world didn't you say so. How could you let me be kissing and loving you when—"

Her peals of laughter effectively interrupted him.

"No, no. It's nothing like that...well, not exactly. It's just that—" She paused, resting her head lightly in her palm, thinking. Finally she looked up at him and sighed. "I really don't know how I can explain. You'll just have to take my word for it that I will only be able to stay until Christmas, then I must go. But we'll be able to enjoy each other during the time I'm here."

"So you're saying I should accept the miracle of your presence without wanting more."

"Exactly."

"Since having you here has made such a tremendous difference in all our lives, I don't suppose I have cause for complaint." He stood and pulled her up to stand beside him. "I'd sound terribly ungrateful not to accept what's been so graciously offered to us." He kissed her again before saying, "It's late. You'd better turn in while I see to the lights and make sure everything's locked up."

With a slight smile she turned away and left the room. Bret stayed and stared at the tree. The little angel looked tired tonight. Her wand was drooping and her halo had a slight dip in it.

"Patti," he whispered, "you always said I was the most stubborn cuss you'd ever known. I guess you're right. I hung on to your memory for so long, making myself so miserable. The fact is, I almost enjoyed wallowing in my misery. If you'd been here, you would have kicked my rear for acting that way.

"Having Noelle visit has been a miracle, all right. It was like having her hand me a pair of glasses that,

once I put them on, made me see what I was doing
to myself and the children. You know that I'll never
forget you, Patti. I see you in our children every day.
We had a wonderful life together. You were my
youth.

"I have a chance now to have another life, not
better, just different, because I'm different. I know
that it'll take some convincing on my part to get
Noelle to consider spending her life here on the ranch
with me and the children. I don't know how much
influence you have on that side, but I'd appreciate it
if you'd put in a good word for me."

He stood there for a long time lost in thought before finally turning off the lights, securing the house
and quietly climbing the steps to his empty room.

He wanted to believe in miracles very badly. If
this was the reason for them he'd like to apply for
one.

Bret fell asleep, thinking of Noelle. Once asleep,
he dreamed of her, a normal occurrence for him during the past several nights.

As soon as Noelle woke the next morning, she got
up and hurried to the window, knowing that something was different. The ground was covered with a
blanket of snow several inches thick. She found the
view enchanting. Although it was barely daylight,
she hurriedly dressed, found appropriate boots,
gloves and a cap, and quietly slipped outside to mar-
vel at the new landscape.

Curiously she touched the snow, awed by its lightness. Then she scooped some up with her hands and touched it with her tongue. She shivered at the iciness and tossed the snow back to the ground, its cold already coming through her woolen gloves.

She walked toward the barn, then turned and looked at her footprints in the snow. What fun to have experienced Mother Nature's grand performance. The sky continued to lighten and sunlight set the snow to sparkling like the Milky Way on a moonless night...all glittery and shiny, winking and blinking with light and color. No one had ever mentioned bright specks of color in snow...all the colors of the rainbow. Fascinating, simply fascinating.

"Mornin', Miss Noelle," Roy said on his way to the barn from his cabin. "You're up mighty early."

She turned and gave him her version of a sparkling smile. "Oh, yes. When I saw that it had snowed last night, I couldn't wait to come outside and get a closer look."

"Guess you don't get much snow in California." He looked around them and said, "Even though it means extra work for us here—to make sure the livestock makes it through this cold snap—I've always been kinda partial to days like this. The wind is still so the snow clings to every surface."

Noelle walked over to where he stood and saw how each ordinary ranch implement left outside was now decorated with a trim line of snow. "I imagine the sun will melt it fairly quickly."

"Yes, ma'am."

She started to turn away, then paused. "I need to

go start breakfast. You're welcome to join us, you know.''

''Thank ya, but I already ate. I might come in for some coffee once I've looked after the animals, though.''

Noelle reached the porch in time to meet Bret on his way outside. ''What are you doing up so early?''

She laughed. ''I couldn't resist getting a closer look at the new snow.'' He looked so good, standing there in his sheepskin-lined denim jacket, with his Stetson pulled low over his eyes.

He glanced out over the ranch yard, no doubt noting the footprints she and Roy had made, then dropped his gaze down to her. ''I'll need to check the rest of the livestock and take hay to them after breakfast. Would you like to come along?''

''I'd like that.''

''Good.'' He touched his forefinger to the curled brim of his hat. ''I'll be back in time for breakfast.''

When she went inside she discovered that Bret had already started the coffee. Quickly she began to find the necessary ingredients to feed the Bishop clan a warm and nutritious breakfast.

She had just taken the biscuits out of the oven when she heard someone come in. She turned around and saw Travis, still in his pajamas and slippers. He shuffled into the room, still not completely awake.

''Good morning, sleepyhead. How are you this morning?''

He looked at her with wide eyes, his bottom lip

quivering. "I had a bad dream," he said in a husky voice.

Noelle immediately walked over and sat down at the table, then beckoned him to join her. When he reached her side, she hoisted him onto her lap and wrapped her arms around him.

He smelled of scented soap and floral shampoo and warm little boy. She hugged him to her and said, "Tell me about your dream, honey."

He sighed and allowed his head to relax against her chest. "I woke up and it was Christmas and there were lots and lots of presents but nobody was there but me. I didn't want to be by myself. It was scary."

"Well, I don't think anything like that will happen to you, sweetie. You've got your daddy, your brother, your sisters and Roy and Freda who all love you and will be around for you so you won't ever have to be alone."

He lifted his head and looked at her. "Will you be here?"

She smiled. "I'm always here for Christmas, remember?"

"On the tree. But I like it better when you're grown-up size and you feed us and things."

"I like it, too, but I won't be able to stay this way. Remember I explained to you about the magic? I'll still be able to talk with you and hear what you tell me each and every year, but I don't think I'll be able to cook for you and look after you."

"Why?"

"Well, eventually I'll have other work...angel kind of work."

"Why can't an angel work in the kitchen?"

She laughed. "Believe me, Travis, people who work in kitchens and prepare food for others are definitely angels, every one of them." She tried to find words to explain. "You see, I'm a novice angel, which means that I'm learning how to be a full-fledged angel. There's still a lot of things I have to learn, so it's like I'm still going to school."

"You know enough for me. And I want you to stay here and be my mommy."

"Oh, Travis, I know. You told Santa you wanted a mommy for Christmas."

"Yes, but it's you I want, not just any mommy."

"That's the nicest thing anyone has ever said to me, did you know that? If it were possible, I'd love to stay here and be your mommy. I can't think of anything I'd like better."

"Can't you be going to angel school while you're being my mommy?"

"I don't think that's quite the way it works." She rocked him, wishing she had the wisdom needed to help this little boy. He relaxed against her, content to be in her arms.

The first thing Bret saw when he opened the door was Travis cuddled in Noelle's arms. Her fair head rested against his black curls. Despite the difference in their coloring, they could easily have been mistaken as mother and son. There was so much love shining from each face. Travis looked so contented in Noelle's arms and she looked very natural holding him.

It was one of those moments when everything seemed to come together for Bret. He loved this woman, loved her with a maturity and a passion that almost frightened him. He didn't want to think about what it would mean to let her leave them. He needed her. Travis needed her. The older children did, as well. Somehow he would have to figure a way to convince her to stay.

He stamped the snow off his boots and came into the kitchen, closing the door behind him. Travis and Noelle looked up at him and smiled, the same trusting innocence shining in each face. Something grabbed at his heart and he was humbled by the love he saw.

Noelle helped Travis off her lap, then went to the stove. "I'll have your eggs for you in a few moments," she said. "Travis and I were chatting and I lost track of the time."

Bret hung his hat and coat on hooks beside the door, then strode over and swung his son up in his arms. "I didn't expect to see you up this early. It seemed like a good morning to stay tucked under the covers for a while."

Travis grinned. "I know."

"As long as you're here, you might as well have breakfast with me and keep me company."

Noelle joined them and they were finishing up when Roy came in. "Thought I'd take you up on that offer of a hot cup of coffee." He took off his leather gloves and briskly rubbed his hands together. "Brrr! Looks like old man winter's getting serious out there."

"I'm taking Noelle with me to check on the rest of the livestock. Do you suppose you can hang around the house for a while, just to keep an eye on things?" His gaze touched Travis before returning to Roy.

"Can't think of anything I'd like more than to build up a big ol' fire in that fireplace. Would ya like to help me, ol' fella?" he asked Travis.

"Can I help carry the wood, too?"

"If you get the right kind of clothes on. Wouldn't want you to get sick this close to Christmas."

Travis slipped away from the table and rushed upstairs. Once he was gone, Roy looked at Bret, glanced at Noelle, then looked back to Bret. "There's something I've been needing to tell you, boss, but I haven't quite known how to bring it up. Seems to me this is as good a time as any."

"That sounds a little ominous, Roy. Don't tell me you're thinking about quitting here, 'cause if you are, I want a chance to convince you otherwise."

Roy grinned. "No. It ain't that. I don't think I'll ever be able to get too far away from your young'uns. They feel like mine."

"Then I'm sure I can handle anything else you might decide to spring on me."

"Well, maybe. Then again…" His slow speech became even slower before he stopped completely, scratching his ear. "I had a little talk with Freda last night after the kids went in to see her. Well, the thing is, I guess I've pretty much taken Freda for granted. I mean, we've known each other for years…been friends and all…but the day she was hurt really got me to thinking. I can't remember a time when I've been so scared. I could see she was in a lot of pain and there wasn't anything I could do for her. That's when it hit me how much Freda means to me. When I got around to telling her how I felt she seemed real surprised—but happy, too—like she felt the same way." He gave Bret a sheepish grin and said, "So there's a good possibility that when Freda returns to the ranch she'll be my wife and live with me."

"I couldn't be happier for you, Roy. I'll admit I'm surprised. I had no idea there was anything in the wind of that nature, but you couldn't do any better than Freda."

Roy cut his eyes over at Noelle once again before saying to Bret, "I just thought that you might want to know how things stand and all, in case you were thinking about making plans of your own."

Bret nodded, biting down hard to keep from smiling. "That's really decent of you, Roy, keeping my interests in mind like that. I want you to know that I appreciate it." He glanced at Noelle. "I need to get moving. I have quite a lot of ground to cover today." Then he smiled innocently.

"Let me clear the table and get my coat. I'll be ready to go in a few minutes."

The men discussed what needed to be done over the next few days and Noelle cleared the table before going into her room to gather her hastily discarded outerwear. She could feel the pressure building all around her. First the children, then Bret, now Roy. She'd never seen such a transparent bunch of matchmakers in her life.

This wasn't what she'd had in mind when she asked to come into the family to help them during this particular season. She hadn't understood how quickly she would get involved in their lives and heartaches. She hadn't understood how strongly she would grow attached to them.

She hadn't known how deeply she would fall in love with Bret Bishop. Unfortunately there wasn't a thing she could do to remedy the outcome of their present situation.

Chapter Seven

By the time Bret and Noelle reached the gate that would take them off the track to where the cattle were, the sun had melted much of the snow. Only patches dotted the landscape, giving the area a neglected look as though Mother Nature's party was over and everyone had gone home, leaving the remains of the decorations scattered around.

Noelle waited in the warm truck while Bret got out, unlatched the gate, drove through, stopped and relatched it behind them. She looked around but could see no road.

When he crawled back into the truck, she asked, "What happened to the road?"

He grinned. "There won't be a road from now on."

"Then how do you know where to go?"

"Easy. I know every inch of this place. I've

learned where I can take a truck.'' He patted the steering wheel. ''It's times like now when this particular horsepower comes in handy.'' He glanced over at her and winked. ''Hang on.''

She was glad of the warning. Although Bret seemed to know where he was going, she couldn't see a path anywhere. He drove along an abutment that eventually widened and leveled off.

Once she adjusted to their newest direction, Noelle began to look around, glancing into the brush as they passed. When she saw eyes staring back, she blinked and stared. Adjusting her gaze, she realized that there were deer hidden all around them, watching their progress.

''Bret, look at the deer.''

''I know. Why do you think I'm out here?''

''To feed the deer?''

''To make sure there's enough feed for my cattle after the local wildlife eat. It takes a great deal of feed to keep cattle. Some of my ranch acreage has low vegetation and has to be supplemented during certain seasons.''

Periodically he would stop the truck to unload hay and grain. He seemed to have a regular route because the cattle would be standing around as though waiting for him to show up.

Noelle found the whole procedure fascinating.

During the last stop, she watched Bret kneel beside a small creek bed and study the ground, frowning. When he joined her once again, his mouth looked grim. He turned the truck in a tight circle and started back the way they'd come.

''Is something wrong?''

"Yeah. It looks like my visitor's back."

"Visitor?"

"Several of the ranchers around here have been complaining of seeing cougar tracks on their property, no doubt stalking the cattle. A few weeks ago, I spent the better part of a day tracking him on my property. The blasted thing crossed my boundaries onto another ranch before I got more than a brief glimpse of his tawny coat. He's a cunning devil."

"What are you going to do?"

"Saddle Hercules and get back up here as soon as possible. I've got to find that cat before he destroys any of my livestock."

"Isn't that dangerous?"

"Can be."

"You'll be careful, won't you?"

He gave her a quick glance from the corner of his eye. "Are you worrying about me?"

She could feel herself blushing. "I just want you to be safe."

He grinned. "Guess my guardian angel will have to make sure I don't come to any harm."

"You're teasing me, but I don't care, because you're right. Your guardian angel *will* be with you."

As soon as they returned to the house Noelle went inside the house. Roy and Travis were in the living room.

"Bret said to tell you he spotted cougar tracks and was going out looking for the cat on horseback."

Roy shook his head. "Maybe he'll have more luck finding him today than he did last time. Boy, was he ticked off when that cat disappeared onto a neighboring ranch. He said he'd wasted a whole day following him around.''

"Isn't it dangerous for him to go out on his own like that?"

"No more than any other time, I reckon. Bret's always careful, though. No need to worry about him." Roy picked up his hat. "Guess I'll see you later, then," he said and walked out of the room.

Noelle turned to Travis. "Would you like to help me bake some cookies?"

"Uh-huh."

"Where are Brenda and Sally?"

"They're upstairs, wrapping presents. They made me promise not to go up until they said I could."

"Is Chris with them?"

"Nope. His friend Jamie wanted him to help move firewood over at his place. He'll be back later."

"How did he get over to Jamie's?"

"Jamie's big brother came and got him."

"Well, then we'll get to work and make up a batch of cookies for everybody."

"Can we make 'em look like Christmas trees and angels and bells and stuff?"

"You bet."

Travis trotted by her side into the kitchen.

Bret saddled Hercules and took off on the road he and Noelle had just followed. He knew he needed to take care of the cougar, but what he wanted to do was to stay at the house with Noelle. He wanted to spend as much time as possible with her. Somehow he needed to convince her that they could work out whatever was going on with her. She was obviously

a very loyal person. He couldn't fault that. Loyalty
was an admirable trait.

He would just have to convince her that he deserved her loyalty as well as her present employer.
He smiled to himself, thinking of all the ways he
would enjoy convincing her that she needed to stay
with the Bishop family.

Once he left the main road, he took the horse directly to the last sighting he'd had of the cougar's
tracks, rather than following the trail made by the
truck. There were times when traveling by horseback
could save him miles. This was one of those times.

Dismounting, he knelt and studied the tracks, then
circled the watering hole for any sign. When he came
across tracks leading into the rugged hills, he re-
mounted and slowly followed them, keeping his eyes
trained on the surrounding foliage, as well.

Despite his focus on the cat tracks, Bret lost some
of his concentration because he kept thinking about
Noelle. The unexpected whirr of the deadly rattle-
snake spooked the horse as well as startling Bret.
He'd been leaning forward, peering up into the trees
for a possible sighting of tawny fur when the horse
let out a snort and began to buck.

Feeling like a complete fool for having been
caught unprepared like some greenhorn, Bret had
only an instant to realize that he wasn't going to be
able to stay in the saddle. The world did a crazy tilt
as he sailed over the horse's head. Bret concentrated
on relaxing and rolling with the fall.

It wouldn't be the first time he'd been forcibly
ejected from a saddle, he managed to think before he

came to an abrupt halt as he slammed against the hard ground on his back.

He would have been all right except for some bruising if he hadn't fallen beside a granite upcropping. The jagged ridge of rock caught him behind the ear as his head whipped back from the fall.

One instant he was aware of a whirling blue sky, the next instant pain exploded in his head, turning the blue sky into a fathomless darkness.

By midafternoon Noelle could not keep her eyes away from the kitchen window that overlooked the direction Bret had taken a few hours before. There was still no sign of him. Shouldn't he have found the cougar by now?

She was alone in the kitchen. Travis was upstairs taking his nap, the girls had gone to visit with friends and Chris had returned home to help Roy somewhere on the ranch.

She couldn't quite forget the shiver that had raced over her when she'd watched from this same window as Bret had ridden away earlier. She'd seen him leave the house alone on several occasions before today. She couldn't understand her uneasiness when she'd watched his solitary figure ride out.

The girls returned in time for a late lunch. She fed them and they disappeared upstairs. When she went to check on Travis he was still sound asleep, Rex curled up on the rug beside his bed. Once again she fought her uneasiness. Rex was usually by Bret's side. Perhaps his staying behind was what made the day seem different to her.

Noelle tiptoed over and adjusted Travis's cover before she left the room.

Next, she went into her bedroom and checked the kittens, smiling as they milled around on wobbly legs, batting at each other, their eyes barely opened. She sat back on her heels, remembering how Bret had been so badly outnumbered on the question of whether or not to keep the kittens or to attempt to give them away. All four were now officially members of the Bishop family, each with its own name and owner.

She had a hunch that none of them would be sleeping in the barn.

Noelle returned to the kitchen and peered out the window once again. She couldn't quite shake her restlessness. Her thoughts kept returning to Bret and how lonely he'd looked riding off alone. A brief picture of him flashed into her mind and she froze, frightened. She saw him lying on the ground, his eyes closed, his face almost gray. Hercules stood nearby, restlessly shaking his head. She could almost hear the whuffling sound of the horse and the jingle of the bridle.

Had something happened to Bret?

Unable to stay in the house another moment, she grabbed her coat off the hook and slipped it on, then stepped outside on the porch. The wind had picked up since morning, and it felt icy whipping around the corner of the house.

Worried, she peered up the lane where he'd gone, but she could see nothing.

She was still standing outside when Roy and Chris

drove into the yard in the truck. Giving in to impulse, Noelle went over to the truck.

"Howdy," Roy said, opening the door. "It's a little cold to be standing around outside, ain't it?"

"Roy, I'm worried about Bret."

He glanced around. "Where is he?"

"He left several hours ago to check out those cougar tracks. I haven't seen him since then."

Roy pushed his hat back and scratched his head. "Well, there's nothing unusual about that. A man can spend hours trailing that cat. Bret's been worried about the cussed thing. He's probably decided not to come home until he gets him."

"But what if he's hurt...or something?"

Roy gave her a sharp look. "Whaddaya mean?"

She bit her bottom lip and looked away. Meanwhile Chris had walked around the truck and joined them. He stood there watching her, his gaze intent on her face. She forced herself to look at Chris, to let him see her concern. His face blanched but he showed no other sign.

"Let's go find him, Roy," Chris said quietly.

"Well, son, I can't see where we need to—"

"I do. I think Noelle's right. We need to go find Dad."

Roy looked from one to the other with uneasiness written on his face.

"If you think we should, Chris, of course we'll go. I just didn't want your dad irritated at us for wasting time."

"He'll understand," was all Chris said, turning away. Then he stopped and looked back at Noelle.

He touched her lightly on the shoulder. "He's okay, isn't he?"

She heard the frightened little boy beneath the young man's calm. She closed her eyes, forcing herself not to alarm him more than she already had. On a subconscious level Chris remembered her, remembered who she was, remembered their talks so long ago. She had consciously touched the bond that had been forged between them without fully stopping to think how it would affect him.

"You'll find him," she whispered, nodding. "That's the important thing."

"Did he take Rex with him?"

"No. Rex is upstairs with Travis."

Chris hurried into the house. Within minutes he reappeared with Rex. The dog sniffed the wind, then looked up at Chris. Chris lowered the tailgate of the truck and Rex leaped inside.

Chris crawled into the cab of the truck and said, "Let's go, Roy."

Noelle briefly described to Roy where she and Bret had gone that morning to save Roy and Chris as much time as possible. She stood in the middle of the ranch yard for a long time after they had disappeared from view, praying that they found him before dark, praying that he was all right.

Then she turned and slowly went into the house for the long wait ahead of her.

When she heard the faint sound of a vehicle coming down the lane what seemed to be hours later, Noelle rushed to the door. The rest of the children had been fed and were upstairs. She had explained to them that Roy and Chris had gone to look for Bret, that she was certain he was all right, but that she felt he needed some assistance.

Because she was calm, they were calm. Their trust in her touched her like nothing ever had.

She slipped outside and was waiting on the porch when the truck stopped a few feet away. The gray gloom of late afternoon had sunk into deep shadows. All she could make out was that Rex wasn't alone in the bed of the pickup truck.

Roy hopped out of the cab of the truck and hurried to the back. She followed. "Is he all right?"

"Yeah, I think so. A little groggy, but he recognized us. Last thing he remembered was flying off that blamed horse. He must have hit his head on something. He's got a he—a heck of a knot behind his ear."

Chris had been sitting in the back, allowing his dad to rest against him. Between Roy and Chris they managed to help Bret off the truck.

She could no longer stay away from him. Moving closer, she ran her hands over his face and shoulders. "Bret?"

"I'm okay," he growled in disgust, then promptly made a liar of himself when his knees buckled. Roy and Chris each took an arm and helped him up the front steps.

"Put him in my room. It's closest," she said, running ahead of them and holding the door open.

Bret began to protest but Roy interrupted with, "Don't be a fool, boss. There's no reason for you to climb those steps right now."

As soon as she saw him in the kitchen light she knew that Bret was in pain. His skin was a pasty white and he kept shivering. She hurried into her room and pulled back the covers. She looked at Roy and said, "Help him get out of those cold clothes. I'll make him something hot to drink."

Roy nodded. "Good idea." He looked at Chris. "To be on the safe side, I want you to call Dr. Warner. Have him—"

"No!" Bret said, then winced at the sound. Ruefully he rubbed his head as though apologizing for the noise. "I'll be all right, once I get warm and have something hot inside me."

"I'm sure you will, but I want Warner to look at your head, maybe check your ribs, anyway. It's either that, or I'm hauling you into town, myself. You decide."

Bret stared at Roy for a moment and realized that this was going to be one argument he was going to lose. He sighed. "Do what you want," he replied.

Chris left the room and Roy pulled off Bret's heavy jacket, then eased him to the side of the bed. He methodically pulled off his boots and reached for his belt. "I'm not completely helpless, dammit," Bret growled, pushing Roy's hands away. He stood, swaying, unfastened his jeans and slid them over his hips.

Bret pulled off his shirt and stretched out on the bed. Roy pulled the covers up, found another blanket and added it to the bed. Rex, who had followed them inside the house, lay his head on the side of the bed and looked at Bret in concern.

Noelle returned carrying a large mug of hot liquid. Chris was immediately behind her. She sat down on the edge of the bed and held out the cup.

"Dr. Warner said I was lucky to catch him," Chris said, standing at the end of the bed. "He was on his way out the door. He said he would be right on out here...before he made any other stops."

"It's a waste of his time," Bret muttered, then sipped the reviving tea. He grudgingly admitted to himself that Roy might have a point. He felt very strange at the moment, not to mention humiliated. He couldn't remember the last time he'd been thrown off his horse!

"Did someone bring in Hercules?" he asked, looking up at Roy.

"I'll make sure he gets put away properly. I tied the reins to the saddle. He'll follow us in."

Bret closed his eyes. "Make sure he does." He didn't remember Noelle taking the cup from him.

The next thing he knew Dr. Warner was poking and prodding him. "Ow, Doc," he murmured, feeling probing fingers along his ribs.

"Yeah, I thought so," Dr. Warner replied. "We better tape up these ribs, just in case you may have cracked them."

Roy stood in the door. "Think we should take him to the hospital for X rays?"

Before Bret could protest, Dr. Warner was shaking his head. "There's no need to make him travel that far for tests. The hospital's full. We'd have to send him back home again." He looked up at Noelle. "Don't believe we've met."

"No, sir. I'm Noelle St. Nichols."

The doctor grinned. "Pleased to make your acquaintance. Hope you don't mind filling in for a couple of days looking after this character. He needs to stay in bed and let those ribs rest. He's got a mild concussion, and from the looks of things he spent a little too much time lying around outdoors in this kind of weather." He peered at her over the top of his glasses and she knew he wanted her to understand the seriousness of the situation.

She nodded. "I'll look after him."

"Good." He stood and stepped away from the bed. "I'll give you something to help with his aches and pains. I want you to monitor his temperature. If it starts to climb, call me right away. You got that?"

"Yes, sir."

He smiled. "He's tough, you know. He's gotten banged up a lot more than this since I've known him."

"You keep talking about me like I'm not even here," Bret complained. Noelle looked down at him and smiled. He felt his heart contract at the sweetness of her look. "Are the kids all right?"

She nodded. "Worried about you."

"Tell 'em I'm all right."

"I will."

He looked around the room. "Guess you'll have to sleep upstairs for tonight."

"I don't mind."

The doctor nodded. "I'll give you a call in the morning." Once again he looked at Noelle. "Call me if there are any changes."

"You can count on it."

Bret kept dozing off, so that the time seemed to be moving in jerky, freeze-frame motion. He was alone, then Noelle was there. He was alone, then all four children were there. He'd close his eyes for just a moment, and when he would open them he would be alone once again.

Roy was there. Then he wasn't. He heard voices in the kitchen. Then it was quiet. Chris came in to report that Hercules was safe, dry and fed. Roy mentioned he was going to the hospital to see Freda. He heard the shower going upstairs, footsteps on the stairs, Noelle's voice talking to the children. With a deep sigh, he let go and allowed himself to drift away.

The next time he opened his eyes the house was quiet and the room was dark, except for a tiny nightlight glowing from the adjoining bathroom. For a moment, Bret couldn't figure out where he was. Then he remembered.

He'd gone looking for the cougar…Hercules got spooked…he'd been thrown off. He could feel the pain in his ribs as well as his head. If only his head—

"Here. The doctor said this should help the pain."

Bret opened his eyes and looked up. Noelle stood beside the bed, holding a glass and a capsule. He blinked, then rubbed his eyes. It *was* Noelle, wasn't it?

Absently he took the capsule and swallowed it without taking his eyes off the woman who stood beside the bed. He couldn't have taken his eyes off her if his life depended on it.

She glowed. There was no other term for it. She wore a white robe and her hair was loose around her shoulders. Just above her head was a pulsating, circular light that looked remarkably like a halo. Just past her shoulders he could see the gauzy outline of wings, giant wings that looked capable of lifting her.

"Noelle?" His voice didn't work. He licked his lips and tried again.

"I'm right here, Bret. Try to rest. Dr. Warner said you should be feeling much better by morning."

"Travis was right," he managed to say. "You *are* an angel." He could feel his pulse begin to race and his heart pound.

She nodded.

"I'm not dreaming this, am I?"

"No."

"What are you doing here?"

"Looking after you…and your family."

"I know. What I mean is…you aren't real, are you?"

She smiled. "Of course I'm real."

He reached out and brushed his fingers along her sleeve. She took his hand and held it between both of hers. He had difficulty swallowing. "All those things you said…about other commitments. You're not able to stay here because you're a— You're a— an—"

"That's right. I'm so glad you understand. I didn't like the idea of misleading you about me."

"Understand? How can I understand? This isn't possible." He closed his eyes, opened them, saw she was still there and closed them again. They remained closed. "I know what it is. I have a concussion. The doctor said so. I'm probably delirious. I'm dreaming this whole conversation." He opened his eyes.

Noelle stood beside him in her nightclothes, still holding the empty glass he'd drunk from earlier. The night-light cast a soft glow around her. There was no sign of either a halo or wings.

"How are you feeling?" she asked, placing her palm on his forehead.

"Like I'm losing my mind," he admitted, as though to himself. "I can't tell when I'm awake or asleep."

"It's probably the medication. Don't fight it. Just allow it to work so that you can rest."

His eyes drifted shut. He needed his rest. He was obviously overtired or he would never have dreamed such an impossible scene. Travis's stories about angels had finally gotten to him.

Chapter Eight

Bret opened his eyes and realized that from the light in the room he'd overslept. Again. In the days since his mishap he'd spent more time asleep than awake.

After the first night, he'd been sleeping in his own room. After that memorable night, he hadn't done any more hallucinating about Noelle.

Thank God.

He lay there for a moment, listening. The house was silent of voices, which was unusual in his household. He wondered where the children were. After all, today was Christmas Eve. They were bound to be excited and full of eager energy.

Moving gingerly, he got up and went into the bathroom.

Dr. Warner had come out yesterday and cut off the tape around his chest, but only after extracting a promise from Bret that he wouldn't be doing any heavy lifting.

Now Bret looked into the mirror at his bruised ribs. At least now he could stand under the shower to bathe instead of having to wash around his bandages. The water felt good and he stood there for countless minutes, enjoying the soothing massage.

He also took his time shaving and dressing, refusing to admit to himself that he wasn't looking forward to going downstairs to what he suspected was an empty house.

Over the years he'd sometimes wondered how he would feel to be alone again…completely alone. Sometimes when the kids were fighting with each other, or one of them was sick, or a teacher called with a stern request for a conference, he'd wondered what his life would be like without a family.

This morning he had an uneasy feeling, as though he'd awakened in a different space and time. As though he was now living another kind of life altogether, where he'd never married, or had children—a life where he had chosen to be alone.

That blow on the head had really done a number on his thinking processes.

Bret patted after-shave on his face, dried his hands and headed downstairs. He paused when he reached the bottom of the steps and looked into the living room.

Lights twinkled on the tree. Everything in the room—from the floor to the furniture—had a shim-

mering glow about it. He walked over to the fireplace, where a fire danced with twists of flame.

Someone had decided to move the kittens in closer
to the warmth of the fire. Mischief was curled up
asleep in the basket that had been made into her bed.
Four tiny balls of fur were curled into a pile of multicolored fluff.

He smiled to himself, remembering the argument
he'd lost regarding the latest arrivals. Christmas kittens, he'd been told, were very special and needed
to be treated with respect.

After a moment he went across the hall and into
the kitchen. Something was baking in the oven—
bread, perhaps—giving the room a wonderful scent.
He heard a slight noise from the bedroom off the
kitchen.

"Noelle?"

She appeared in the doorway. "Oh! I didn't hear
you stirring. You must be hungry." She started toward the refrigerator until he stopped her with a light
touch on her shoulder.

"I'm okay. Where is everybody?"

"Roy invited the children to go with him to see
Freda. She's leaving the hospital today. He's planning to drive her to Austin to be with her sister. He
promised the children that they could come."

"When did they leave?"

"Not quite an hour ago."

He glanced outside. The sun shone brightly.
"Doesn't look as though they're going to have the
snow they wanted."

"No."

He walked over to the window and peered out, his hands in his back pockets. Noelle looked at his back for a moment before turning away and finding the ingredients for his breakfast. Soon she had bacon frying, eggs on the griddle and bread in the toaster. She poured him a cup of coffee.

"Is something wrong?" she asked in the continued silence.

He turned away from the window and looked at her. "I suppose you're leaving today, aren't you?"

Suddenly she was busy scooping up the eggs, draining the bacon and buttering the toast. "That's right."

"Is there anything I can say or do to make you change your mind?"

She shook her head without looking up.

He sighed and sat down at the table. Methodically he ate the food in front of him, not really tasting it. When he was through, he said, "It's hard to realize that you've been here two weeks. In some ways, I feel as though I've known you forever. In others, I can't believe two weeks have gone by since you arrived."

She sat down across from him and clasped her hands. "I've enjoyed being here. You have a warm, loving family."

"They deserve so much more than I've given them."

"You've given them love. You've been there whenever they needed you."

"I've been selfish, wrapped up in my own pain."
His eyes met hers. "You've taught me that."

He pushed away from the table. "I want to check
on the animals. Do you need a ride over to Ida's?"

She shook her head.

"Have you already told the kids goodbye?"

"Not yet, but they understand that I have to
leave."

He pulled his jacket on and reached for his hat.
"Guess there isn't much more to say then…except
to thank you for looking after all of us. I wish you
the best of everything."

"Bret?"

"What?"

"I'll be here until late tonight. At least we can
enjoy what time there is together."

He stiffened. "What do you mean?"

She smiled. "If you're leaving you could give me
a kiss goodbye."

Her request obviously startled him. She saw him
tense, his face showing no expression. "Sure," he
muttered in an offhanded manner.

She came to him, went up on her toes and kissed
him sweetly. He stood there, willing himself not to
grab her and beg. Her hands rested on his chest. He
could feel their imprint burning a brand on him.
When she pulled away, her eyes were brimming with
unshed tears.

"Please be happy," she whispered.

He fought for control of his emotions. He swallowed hard, then nodded. "You, too." He jammed

his hat on his head, opened the door and stepped outside.

The sun had fooled him. The air was much colder than he'd expected. He took several deep breaths, willing away the emotion that had threatened to overcome him. He'd managed this far in his life without Noelle. There was no reason to believe he couldn't continue.

After he was finished outside, Bret decided to ride into town and have coffee with some of the other ranchers. He was glad he did because he got some good news. They'd managed to catch the cougar that had been prowling around the countryside. One of the officials from an exotic ranch in the area had shown up and offered to trap the cat and release it in a less populated area.

Bret enjoyed visiting with his friends and neighbors. He felt as though he was seeing them with new eyes. They were a friendly bunch who had made many overtures toward him these past few years to join in their social life. They'd never given up on him, even when he'd been his most surly.

He wasn't sure what had changed his perspective, but he knew that he was looking at his life and the people around him in a new way.

"The family all ready for Christmas?" one of the ranchers asked.

"More than ready," Bret replied.

"Your family sure has seen its share of problems this year, Bishop," another said. "I understand Freda's leaving the hospital today."

"Yes. Roy and the children went to help her get moved."

"I must say you're looking good, considering your mishap."

"I wasn't hurt badly, except for my pride," he admitted.

Everyone laughed.

Nobody asked him about Noelle and he felt reluctant to bring her into the conversation. None of them knew her, anyway, so it didn't really matter.

He was getting into his truck when he spotted a familiar face leaving the post office. On an impulse, Bret decided to go say hello to Ida Schulz.

She was getting into her car when he reached her side.

"Hi, Ida. It's good to see you."

She glanced around in surprise. "Well, hello, Bret. I haven't seen you in a long while. How's Freda?"

"Doing well. She's getting out of the hospital today. Roy and the kids are taking her over to her sister's in Austin. I think they're planning a little celebration for her over there."

"I'm sure she'll appreciate it." She got into the car and closed the door, rolling down the window.

Bret leaned over and said, "I haven't taken the time to thank you for sending your niece out to help when—"

Ida looked at him in surprise. "My what?"

"Your niece... N—"

"You must be mistaken, Bret. I don't have a niece."

He stared at her. "You don't?"

"I've got two nephews, though. They live over near Killeen. My brother's boys."

"No niece," he repeated slowly.

"Nope. Ed was always sorry they didn't have a girl, of course." She looked at her watch. "I hate to rush off like this, Bret, but I've got some more errands to run, plus company coming in and all." She started the car. "You be sure to tell Freda hello for me. Hope she's continuing to improve."

Bret stood there and watched as she pulled out of the parking space, his mind whirling.

Noelle wasn't Ida Schulz's niece, because Ida Schulz didn't have a niece.

Then who in the world was Noelle St. Nichols?

A sudden memory shook him, a memory of the night he had banged his head. She had come to him and she had—

No. There wasn't any way. She couldn't be.

He went back to his truck and started home. He now knew who she wasn't. He was going to find out who she was before the day was over. He wanted some answers.

Bret opened the back door and stepped into the empty kitchen, looking around him. Cakes, pies, cookies and homemade candy lined one of the cabinets. There was enough food there to feed the entire county.

He removed his jacket, hung it beside his hat and continued into the hallway.

He found Noelle in the living room and for a moment could only stare at the scene before him.

She sat on the rug in front of the fire with Rex curled up beside her on one side, Mischief on the other. Mischief eyed the dog from time to time but for the most part she ignored him, instead keeping her attention on the kittens who were venturing out of their basket and exploring their immediate world.

Rex sniffed at one, then blinked when it hissed and turned into a bristling fur ball.

Bret's gaze went from the woman with a soft smile watching the kittens to the tree that sparkled nearby. The little angel on top looked almost new. Her dress was starched and stood away from her, her hair fell in soft waves and curls, looking freshly combed and her wings glimmered in the light.

When he looked back at Noelle she was watching him, waiting.

He walked into the room and sat in his favorite chair before the fire. Rex pushed himself up and came over to him, shoving his nose beneath Bret's hand.

Noelle continued to watch him. She wore the same soft smile on her face she'd had with the animals.

Absently Bret rubbed Rex's ears, wondering what to say…how to begin.

"You aren't Ida Schulz's niece," he finally said in a statement more than a question.

"No," she agreed quietly.

"I want to know who you are."

She tilted her head. "Do you?" There was a hint of doubt in her voice.

"Of course!" he replied with exasperation. "There was no reason to lie to me. You could have just said that you—" He paused, running his hand through his hair, feeling more than a little foolish. "Well, you could have told me the truth—whatever it is. You were passing through town…needed a job…heard about Freda…whatever happened, you could have told me."

She shifted so that she was facing him, her knees pulled up to her chin. "I think that you've always known who I am, Bret, but you couldn't admit it, at least not to yourself…especially not to yourself."

"Now wait a minute. You aren't going to start in with that—" he waved his hand toward the tree "—Christmas tree angel stuff, I hope. I'll admit that you look like her, and I can see where the kids would think that you had come to help us and all, but—"

"But you don't believe in angels."

"Of course not."

"And therefore I can't be an angel."

"Exactly."

"Then who am I?"

He leaned forward in his chair, his elbows resting on his knees. "How should I know? I haven't been able to figure out how you got into the house in the first place. I told myself that Chris forgot to lock the door, but he never forgets something like that. You said someone brought you but there were no tire tracks outside and with the rain that blew in, the ground was soft enough to leave tracks. The only ones I saw were the ones Roy made when he and Chris came home.''

"Why haven't you said something before?"

He shook his head in bewilderment. "I don't know. I guess everything was happening at once and I was having trouble keeping up with all the changes. I remember thinking that you must have walked, but you were dry. Besides, that suitcase would have weighed too much for you to have hauled it any distance at all.''

"An angel could do all of those things, Bret. Appear without getting wet, manifest a suitcase filled with appropriate clothes…''

"But angels aren't *real,* Noelle, can't you understand that? They're just something people make up to help deal with their own fears about life.''

Noelle gracefully unfolded her legs and came to kneel between his knees. "I'm real, Bret, for the next few hours, I'm very real.''

This close he could see the love in her eyes, as well as the compassion and understanding. He felt as though everything he knew about himself, his life and reality was being questioned and tested.

With a groan he pulled her into his arms, cuddling her to him, holding her in such a firm grip that no one would be able to take her from him. "Don't go,'' he whispered, burying his face against her neck, "I don't care who you are, or why you came. I just know that I need you in my life.'' He found her lips and kissed her, putting all of his feelings and yearnings into the kiss.

She twined her arms around his neck, kissing him back, refusing to think of anything more than this moment.

They heard Roy's truck and knew that the children had returned home. "I'm going to stay out of the way for the rest of the afternoon," she whispered. "This is your time with the children. Once they're in bed I'll spend my last hours with you."

Before he could protest, she slipped off his lap. He heard the door to Freda's room close just before the children burst into the house.

The children were filled with enthusiasm. They had stories to tell about Freda and the party her sister had for her. They excitedly showed Bret the gifts they'd gotten to open while they were there and how pleased Freda was with what they had given her.

For the rest of the afternoon and early evening, Bret kept busy with the children. They all trooped outside to feed the animals their special Christmas Eve meals, and Chris pointed out to Travis the stars that Santa used to navigate on his flight from the North Pole. When they returned inside Bret found the CD of Christmas songs he'd bought in San Antonio. He played it and the children sang along with gusto.

Chris and Sally coaxed Travis upstairs to take his bath and to get ready for bed while Brenda helped Bret to get the stockings to be hung near the fireplace ready for Santa's visit.

"Could I help fill them, Daddy?" she asked.

He grinned. "And ruin Santa's fun? No way."

"Ah, Daddy. I know it's you."

He sat down on the sofa and hugged her. "Don't you ever get too old to believe in Santa, honey. He's as real as you and me."

"Really? Then he's like Noelle? He can really come and visit on Christmas, even though he's just an angel or spirit or something?"

Bret grew still as he looked at his oldest daughter. "Is that what Noelle did?"

She frowned. "Well, sure. That's what she said."

"When was that?"

"The first day she was here. She explained that she would only be able to stay until Christmas."

"So that's why no one is surprised that she's leaving."

Brenda smiled. "She won't be *gone,* Daddy." She pointed. "She'll be right there." She looked up and smiled at the angel. "She made this year's Christmas extra special, didn't she?"

"Yes, honey. Very special." He looked around the room, avoiding her gaze. "You'd better get to bed, yourself."

Brenda gave Bret a hug. "Good night, Daddy. Merry Christmas."

"Merry Christmas, baby," he replied.

He followed her upstairs, told Travis a long, involved story that eventually put him sound asleep, peeked in at the girls, then paused in Chris's doorway.

His son was in bed with earphones on. When he saw his dad, he pulled off the headset and shut off the radio. "It's a little early for me to go to sleep," he explained with a grin.

"I know. I'm surprised that Brenda and Sally are already asleep."

"Well, they had a full day, helping with Freda and all. It was kind of fun, like Freda and her family are a part of our family."

"Has Roy mentioned how long Freda intends to stay in Austin?"

Chris grinned. "If Roy has his way, he's going to haul her off to get married as soon as Christmas is over."

"So he's told you about his plans, has he?"

"Yeah, but he didn't have to. I mean, a blind man could have figured out what was going on with him. You should have seen him the day Freda fell. You would have thought he'd caused the accident on purpose."

Bret leaned against the doorjamb. "I'm glad they've admitted how they feel."

"Me, too." He cleared his throat. "Speaking of feelings, Dad. Your feelings for Noelle have been fairly obvious. Did you mention to her how you felt about her?"

"I tried, but it didn't do much good. For whatever reasons, she's made it clear she couldn't stay around here. Besides, why would she want to?"

"Maybe because she loves you…and us, too."

Bret tilted his head slightly and looked at his son.

"Aren't you going to try to convince me that Noelle isn't really Ida Schulz's niece? That she's an angel?"

Chris's gaze remained steady. "Why should I do a thing like that?"

"Well, I'm glad there's somebody in this family who isn't caught up in all this Christmas magic stuff. I was beginning to think I'd lost my mind."

"All I'm saying is that I think you should have told her how you felt."

"I asked her to stay."

"That isn't the same thing as telling her how you feel."

"Sure it is. I want her around."

"Why?"

"Because."

"Because, why?"

Bret could feel his frustration grow. He used to have these kinds of conversations with Chris when he was Travis's age. He counted to ten in silence before he said, "This is a pointless conversation. I'll talk to you in the morning."

"Why don't you want to admit that you love her, Dad? There's nothing wrong with that, you know. Admitting how you feel might make all the difference in the world."

"Good night, Chris," Bret said, straightening.

"Good night, Dad," Chris cheerfully replied. "Merry Christmas."

"Smart-alec kid," Bret muttered to himself, returning downstairs. He had enough to keep him busy tonight without listening to Chris's crackpot advice.

He pulled a set of keys off one of the hooks in the kitchen and went over to Roy's cabin. Roy had already told him he wouldn't be back tonight. As he had done every year, Bret had stored the gifts he set out beneath the tree at Roy's place, where the children wouldn't find them. He let himself into the place, gathered up the boxes, and returned to the house, quietly letting himself back in.

He found Noelle waiting for him. She took some of the presents and helped to arrange them around the tree, then helped him fill the long red felt stockings with fruit, nuts and candy.

"Thank you for helping me," he said when they were through.

"I enjoyed it."

He took her hand and led her to the sofa, then sat down beside her. "Would it make a difference to your leaving if I told you how much I love you, Noelle?" he asked. "I want to marry you," he finally admitted aloud.

Tears made her eyes shine, reflecting the lights from the tree. "There is nothing I would like more, Bret, but I don't have that choice. I have to leave at midnight."

"How? How can you leave? Do you expect me to take you somewhere? Or do you have someone coming to pick you up?"

"No. I'll leave the way I came." She smiled with a hint of sadness. "In a blink of an eye...now you see me...now you don't."

"Like an angel."

"Yes."

He sighed. "This isn't funny, Noelle."

"I know."

"I'm not a child."

"You've forgotten the wisdom of childhood. You've forgotten how to believe."

He lifted his brows incredulously. "You mean you would stay if I'd believe you were an angel? Is this some kind of test?"

"I don't have any control over getting to stay, Bret. I would stay if I could, believe me. There's nothing more I could want than to spend a lifetime with you and the children." She leaned her head against his shoulder. "It's just that I have other commitments that I must honor."

"My loving you doesn't matter, is that it?"

"Your loving me is the greatest gift I could receive."

"Will you ever come back?"

"I don't know. If possible, I'd like to come back."

He glanced up to the top of the tree. "At Christmas?"

"Perhaps. We'll see."

He pulled a small package out of his pocket. "Here's something I want you to have," he said, offering the gaily wrapped gift to her.

Her eyes had misted over so much that Noelle was having trouble seeing. When she finally managed to open the gift she felt the lump in her throat grow. A heart locket hung on a thin gold chain. She opened it and found a picture of Bret on one side and a picture of the children on the other.

"I know it sounds corny to say, but I want you to carry the thought of us in your heart, no matter where you go."

Tears trickled down her cheeks. "I love you, Bret Bishop. I love you with all my heart. If there was any way I could, I would stay here with you. I would be your wife and love and cherish your children...if I could."

Her sincerity and her pain were too obvious to doubt. He could only nod.

She kissed him with love and longing, with an almost desperate intensity, until the almost silent chiming of the mantel clock called them both back to the present...and reality.

With a final kiss she broke away from him. "Goodbye, my love. God bless you."

One moment he had his arms around her, the next moment he was alone in the room, wondering what had happened. Had he been sleeping? Was he awake even now?

Bret looked around the room. The tree still sparkled with light, music played in the background, presents were piled high all around it, long, red felt stockings were stuffed for each child and the tiny angel at the top of the tree watched him with compassion.

He shook his head, got up and went all through the house. Each child was asleep, the cat and her kittens were down for the count, even Rex merely opened one eye before shutting it with a sigh.

Freda's bedroom was neat and orderly, and unoccupied.

The refrigerator and pantry were stocked full of food for the next day. Everything was ready for Christmas.

Only one change had taken place...Noelle was gone.

Bret knew he needed to go upstairs to try to get some sleep. The children would be up by dawn, insisting on getting him downstairs to open gifts.

However, Bret returned to the living room knowing this was one night when he'd be unable to sleep. Instead, he went into the kitchen and made coffee, then found a bottle of brandy and carried them into the living room. He sat down on the sofa, so that he could look at the tree and the angel at the top.

He didn't understand what had happened but he did understand the miracle that had occurred in his own heart. Somehow his appreciation of life had been given back to him. For the first time in over three years, he felt whole again.

The music played softly in the background. The scent of vanilla and cinnamon and bayberry filled the air. The only light in the room came from the tree. He leaned back, took a deep breath and relaxed. Occasionally he sipped on his coffee, enjoying the blend of flavors, and absorbed the sights, scents and celebration of this time of year.

In the quiet of the night, on this very special night,

Bret acknowledged to himself how much Noelle had given to him. He would always love her.

He relived the times they had spent together...the mall in San Antonio, dinner along the river. He remembered all that she had told him.

Once again he looked up at the tree. "If there's such a thing as Christmas magic, then I ask that Noelle be returned to us, that we be given the opportunity to live together and to love together."

His eyes blurred and he closed them, wiping the unexpected moisture away. He was really losing his grip on reality, sitting there talking to himself as though there really was a Santa, a Christmas angel, a magical time of year.

Bret set his cup down and rested his head against the back of the sofa, knowing he needed to get some sleep. The kids would be up early in the morning, eager to—

He felt something brush against his hand. No doubt Mischief had decided to look for some attention. Lazily he opened his eyes—and stared in disbelief.

A brilliant light filled the room, almost blinding him. He blinked a couple of times before he could see anything. The light seemed to be centered immediately in front of him.

He felt more than heard a voice say, *"You may not believe in us, but we believe in you. We have done what we could to protect and guide you. Now you ask that one of us join you in your dimension, giving up her studies with us. This is highly unor-*

thodox, but because she is willing to forgo her train-
ing with us at this time, we allow the choice to be
hers.''

The light gradually diminished until the tiny lights
of the tree were all that illuminated the living room.
Bret stared at his cup of coffee, wondering how much
brandy he'd put in there.

What was the matter with him? Had he fallen
asleep? He looked around the room. The kittens were
asleep in their basket. He didn't know where Mischief was.

Bret forced himself to get up, turn off the lights,
and go upstairs.

Maybe he'd better have Dr. Warner take a look at
him the next time he was in town. His eyes and his
hearing were definitely acting up on him.

Chapter Nine

He'd just closed his eyes, or so it seemed, when the door to his bedroom opened and the whispers and giggles moved to the side of his bed.

"Dad! C'mon, it's time to get up. It's time to open our presents!"

Bret squinted through swollen eyelids at Travis and sighed. Of course it was time. It certainly wasn't Travis's fault that his dad seemed to be having some kind of a hallucinatory midlife crisis.

With a groan Bret sat up and looked at Sally and Brenda, hovering nearby. "Did you wake him up?" he growled.

Brenda giggled. "No. He woke *us* up."

"Figures," Bret muttered. "All right. Give me a minute and I'll be downstairs."

As soon as they left he threw the covers back and went into the bathroom. After splashing water over his face several times he returned to the bedroom and got dressed. He didn't take time to shower or shave. He could do that after the kids enjoyed the results of all these weeks of anticipation.

He was the last one downstairs. Out of habit he turned on the tree lights and glanced up at the top.

The angel was gone. Before he could register the shock he felt, Travis said, "What happened to Noelle?"

The other three children looked up and gasped. Instead of an angel, a bright star glowed at the top of the tree, as though lit from inside.

Sally jumped up. "What did you do with her?" she demanded to know of her father.

Brenda said, "Dad, how could you?"

Chris said, "I don't understand."

Bret exchanged a glance with his bewildered son. "*You* don't understand! Believe me, neither do I!"

A tinkling chuckle caught their attention. They all turned to the hallway and gaped at the young woman standing there. She walked into the room, smiling. "It's simple, really. The angel is gone." She smiled at each of them, but her gaze lingered on Bret. "I hope you don't mind if I'm here to take her place."

"Noelle?" Chris asked, his adolescent voice cracking halfway through her name.

She nodded. "Yes."

Travis threw himself at her, his arms clutched around her waist. "You didn't go away. You stayed here!"

Her gaze stayed steady as she continued to look at Bret. "If you still want me, I can stay here."

If he was dreaming, Bret didn't ever want to wake up. The fact that his children also saw her reassured him tremendously. He paused in front of her, unable to stop grinning. Taking her hand in his, he said, "You came back."

"Yes."

"How?"

"They offered me the position permanently if I wanted it."

"Then you aren't—"

"Well, it isn't as though I was fired or anything, but I did lose access to certain powers in order to stay here full-time."

He kissed her palm. "You were willing to give up so much for me...for all of us?"

Her smile dazzled him with its brilliance. "I kept the most important thing. Love is too important to ever allow any to be wasted. We'll all share in that love and it will grow and grow. Maybe our love will help others to better understand."

He hugged her to him, while Travis still clung to her. Chris, Brenda and Sally joined them.

The Bishop children had a mother once again... and daddy had his angel.

* * * * *

The Merry Matchmakers

Helen R. Myers

For Mrs. Ethel Jane Keyser
(Retired schoolteacher, Baltimore, Maryland)
With gratitude and love for the friendship, the many
hand-stitched memories and for setting a graceful
example of how to live life to the fullest.

Chapter One

"C'mon, Dad...don't say you're too tired. We did better on this week's video. And it's shorter!"

Read Archer sent his son a sidelong look, convinced he couldn't be that lucky. Sure he'd sat through last Saturday night's entire tape, but only because he'd been startled with Ricky and Molly's announcement that they'd come up with a way to help him find them a new mother.

At first he'd reasoned that if it stopped them from watching so much TV, and got them out into the fresh air a bit more, he could suffer through the results of their efforts. Maybe even get a laugh or two out of the thing. But that was before he'd realized they considered anything—correction, *anyone*—an improvement over the way things were now. He wasn't up to dealing with that emotional blow again. Not tonight when he was already bone tired, and feeling like the last guy on earth likely to be voted as single father of the year.

"You know, the more I think about it, the more doubtful I am about you two borrowing Billy's camera, kids. Are you sure Mr. and Mrs. Johnson know about that?"

"Yes, Dad. I told you last week."

There was a gentle rebuke in his eldest's voice, and as Read belatedly remembered the conversation, he cleared his throat. "Well, I'm telling you again. If you accidentally broke or lost it, I'd be obliged to buy a replacement, and I don't have that kind of money to throw away on luxuries for us, let alone for someone else."

His son scowled at him. "That's not it. You just don't want to meet anyone."

"'Cuz you can't 'ford no wimmen," Molly piped in, looking proud to be able to add to the conversation.

Read paused at scraping the stubborn remains of tuna and macaroni from the bottom of the casserole dish. His words sounded particularly crass coming out of his four-year-old's mouth. "I wish you'd listen that well when I tell you to eat your food while it's still warm, Missy."

Molly brushed aside a tangle of curls to eye the small mountain of mush that remained on her plate. "It's okay, Daddy. Warm don't make it taste no better."

Hell. What did you do when your kids were not only funny, but embarrassingly correct? After fourteen months of trying to be both father and mother to them, he may have learned how not to turn their underwear pink or blue in the wash, but his cooking still left much to be desired. But that didn't mean he wanted to think about getting involved in another re-lationship.

"Smarty-pants," he muttered, repressing most of his smile. "Then eat up so I can get these dishes done before midnight." Sunday was his one day to catch up on sleep, and he cherished that extra hour in bed.

"If she finishes, *then* will you watch the video?" Ricky asked, ever persistent. "Please, Dad?"

Read reached deep to try to make the boy understand. "Son...I thought we talked about this. Your mom was special and she would be hard to replace. Taking pictures of ladies around town isn't— First of all, they're strangers, and I told you last week that it wasn't polite to ask strangers personal questions like, 'Are you married?' and 'How old are you?'"

"We didn't this time, Daddy! We behaved really good."

"Is that so?" Read considered Molly's innocent face and wondered why he wasn't convinced. "What did you ask?"

"If they liked little girls." His daughter beamed and wriggled in her chair, clearly delighted with her inventiveness. "And every single one said yes!"

"Uh-uh!" Ricky adamantly shook his head. Like his sister, he had chestnut hair that gleamed with gold streaks under the fluorescent kitchen light, and although his was arrow straight, it was in bad need of a trim, just as his sister's was desperate for a brushing. "The last one didn't say anything of the kind!"

Molly pouted. "That's 'cuz you made her sad."

"Oh, great." Read looked from his four-year-old to his eight-and-a-half-year-old. "Who did you upset?"

"We don't know. But she was real pretty." Molly ignored her brother's dirty look. "She was my favorite 'cuz she looked like Snow White."

Ricky snorted. "She did not, dummy. Snow White didn't have hair anywhere near as long as that."

"Hey!" Read pointed the nylon scrubber at him. "No names. Besides, who just got a D on his last spelling test?"

"Yeah, big shot! And, anyway, she had black hair and white skin like Snow White, so there." After making a face at her brother, Molly sobered. "But you know what, Daddy? It was when she asked Ricky his name and he said Ricky Read Archer, that she got this funny look on her face. She asked if you were our daddy, and *that's* when she got sad."

Her brother groaned in frustration. "Don't you get it? She was sad because she *knew* Dad, but she didn't know about Mom going to heaven."

Read tried to match the description of the woman with his recollection of the various people he knew in the area, but without success. Of course, while Berryfield, Massachusetts, wasn't the smallest town west of Worcester, it was hardly a metropolis, either. The kids could have run into someone he'd done some custom work for awhile back.

"Did she happen to say where she lived?" he asked both of his offspring.

Although they signaled that she hadn't, Molly added, "She did say she'd been away for a long time."

Something inside Read tightened, while unwelcome images flashed before his eyes. He tried to ignore them—after all, he knew better than to think *she* would ever come back—but some devil's advocate in the most resolute part of his mind wouldn't leave him in peace. He heard himself ask, "Are you sure you didn't get the lady's name?"

"We didn't get a chance," Ricky told him. "She left right after that. You're not mad, are you? We didn't mean to say anything wrong."

"I know." Nevertheless, Read had to put down the dish he was holding because his hands were shaking.

"You sure don't look like you mean that."

On impulse he snatched up the towel on his shoulder and began drying his hands. "Let me have the tape, son."

Molly uttered a panicky sound. "Now? Wait a minute, Daddy! I'm not finished."

"I just need to see something," he replied, as she scooped up a spoonful of food and shoveled it into her little mouth. He touched her soft curls absently on his way to the living room. This couldn't wait. He had to make sure he was wrong about his hunch.

"Did you say the last one?" he asked his boy, as he put the cassette into the VCR machine.

Ricky handed him the remote control unit. "Yeah. It's about halfway through the tape."

Read fast-forwarded the tape and thought it nothing short of ironic that he stopped at the instant the kids focused on the woman. She'd paused to look into a store window, and when she turned and smiled into the camera, Read felt his heart skip a beat…then another…and another. Stunned, he lowered himself to the nearest seat—the coffee table.

Ten years. He hadn't seen her in an entire decade. Sometimes he went days, a week without thinking of her, or feeling the hollowness, the ache, her leaving had caused. Life had gone on. And yet he couldn't believe that she could be back, and he hadn't somehow known.

Don't do this, fool. You didn't want to know.

No, he hadn't. He'd worked hard to get on with his life, to build something good and solid for himself. He'd succeeded, too.

Then why's your pulse going nuts and your palms getting sweaty?

God, he felt like such a fraud. Just looking at her was a betrayal to Gwenn.

Those eyes… Slightly sloe-shaped and midnight dark, they seemed to look straight into his, immediately ensnaring him with a look that was as sad as it was startled. Those eyes were ancient in a face that remained incredibly youthful and lovely. She always had possessed a quality of gentleness and femininity, but that expression in her eyes told him that life hadn't left her unmarred. He didn't want to even begin thinking about what had happened. And yet another part of him wanted to reach through the television screen, to feel again her soft skin, and watch her eyes fill with emotion for him. For *him*.

"Damn."

"What is it, Dad? Is it true—you know her?"

He knew her. Read stopped the tape, and canned laughter from a popular but mindless sitcom filled the room. Oh, yes, he knew her.

"Dad?" Ricky frowned. "Why did you stop? You haven't even heard her talk yet."

That was the point. As it was, the memory of her

voice filled his head and made the room, his past, feel as if it was all closing in on him, crushing him.

"Dad?"

He handed the buttons to his son and rose. "Watch whatever you want. I need to finish up in the kitchen."

It was an abrupt rejection, and he could sense his son's bewilderment and hurt; however, he couldn't do anything about that right now. Certainly not pretend. Before he could deal with anyone else's feelings, he needed time to get hold of his own.

Marina watched the middle-aged man return from his painstaking tour of the first floor of her house. "What do you think, Mr. Fields? Is my idea feasible?"

"Oh, yes, Miss Davidov." Every few steps he scribbled something else on his pad. "I think we could do an extremely satisfactory job for you as far as the structural changes are concerned. This is a wonderfully built old house. Terrific foundation, good solid walls... I don't foresee any difficulty in getting you the connecting effect from room to room you want on this floor. But when it comes to the specialty items... Well, let me be honest. I can get you bookcases, cabinets, shelving...you name it. But for a house of this quality I think you'd be doing yourself an injustice with settling for factory-made products.

"First of all there's the obvious look of mixing and matching. You want to stay with pieces that will fit the authenticity of the house's grand style. Outside, people see the brick and stonework, the century-old trees, the formal garden—why, this is one of the landmarks of Berryfield. Once people know they can come inside and they see the authentic hardwood floors, the sweeping staircase, all extraordinary detail work everywhere... Well, simply put, you don't want to destroy the effect with mass-produced items.''

Marina nodded, glad she'd called the building contractor. He'd been recommended to her by the agency that had been watching over the property. The man did seem to have a good feel for the house. ''What do you suggest?''

''Custom work. A craftsman who'll respect the project he's taking on and provide an even tone with real wood—and I don't mean pine—to make proper display points for your merchandise.''

''You have someone in your firm who can do this?''

''No. To be honest, I can't afford someone like that full-time. Berryfield's economy is solid enough, thanks to being so close to a number of fine colleges, but these days people buy homes wanting built-in microwaves and extra bathrooms. A master carpenter's talents get wasted on installing prefab cabinetry and securing baseboards. But I can refer you to someone.''

''Very good.''

''He would be glad for the work. He lost his wife not long ago, and between funeral expenses and raising two young children, things haven't been easy for them.''

Marina thought of the children she'd met downtown this morning. Her insides gave a strange little jolt.

Surely not...?

But she found herself holding her breath as the contractor reached into his billfold and took out a business card, found herself amazed that her hands didn't shake as she accepted it and read the name. His name.

"Read Archer."

"That's right. You'll find he's quite the individualist, stubborn as hell about his work and sometimes a bit too proud for his own good. But a finer craftsman doesn't exist around here. I use him, myself, as often as I can."

Despite her jangling nerves, it pleased her to hear Read praised so highly. "I seem to remember the name somehow...."

"Could be. He's lived here all his life, and his folks used to operate a little general store near the high school you said you'd briefly attended. Maybe that's the connection. After he got out of the service, Read handled their deliveries until his folks got killed in an auto accident."

Poor Read! "I had no idea," she murmured, struggling to quickly come to terms with that revelation. The accident must have occurred shortly after her father had decided they should leave Berryfield. Once again she wished she'd been able to correspond with someone back here, but she knew the mail could never have kept up with them—or slipped past her father.

"It was sad," the contractor said, his expression grim. "Read sold the business and signed up for some woodworking classes at the college, thinking he'd learn some kind of trade. It turned out that he was a natural. His instructor found him an old guy in

Worcester who was a magician with wood, and the rest is history. You give Read a call. He won't disappoint you.''

That remained to be seen. But Marina thanked the man as she slipped the card into the pocket of her cardigan sweater, and for the remainder of the meeting, she listened to him go over figures and schedules.

''All right, Mr. Fields,'' she said, once he lifted his eyebrows to indicate the final decision was in her hands. ''I'd like to open at least the front parlor to the public by early November, and more rooms by Thanksgiving, although I know there would still be noise and some traffic from your people. How soon can you start?''

''Well, a few weeks isn't much time, so we'd better get in here Monday morning. Will eight o'clock be good for you?''

''Perfect.''

''Thank you, Miss Davidov, and welcome back to Berryfield,'' the man said warmly, shaking her hand. ''I've often thought this was too fine a house to be standing empty, and I'm sure the business venture you're planning will be a big hit around here.''

''Until Monday, Mr. Fields.'' But as she closed the front door after him, Marina's smile grew skeptical. She knew that—at least in the beginning—people would come strictly out of curiosity, to inspect Dmitri Davidov's daughter and the house where the eccentric Russian pianist-composer had worked while hiding from the world. Nothing more.

She reached into her pocket and drew out the business card the contractor had given her. This had to be a sign that what she'd done was right. Or was she trying to fool herself? Tomorrow she must find out, Sunday or not. She would contact Read then. She had no choice, since she had to be here for Mr. Fields's people on Monday.

"Tomorrow..." Would Read even speak to her? Only time would tell.

Read awoke to the sound of voices. Laughter and voices, he amended, wincing at a particularly loud squeal of giggles. *Jeesh...* His Molly could shatter beer mugs at two thousand paces.

He blindly reached for his alarm clock, then peered at it through the slit of his right eye. It was almost nine. He had to forgive the kids for getting restless. By now he should at least be out of the shower and on his way to mixing some pancake batter.

If he was lucky, they'd grown tired of waiting, maybe put some frozen waffles in the toaster or something. Then he remembered that they'd melted the insides of the toaster over a week ago and he hadn't yet had the chance to replace the small appliance.

"Up and at 'em," he muttered, kicking off an already tangled sheet and blanket.

Less than five minutes later he was dragging a crewneck sweater over yesterday's jeans and shuffling down the hallway. He wanted coffee and another nap, not necessarily in that order. But some interesting, if disconcerting, smells rising from below quickly canceled those ideas.

Dare he hope the kids had been watching some cooking channels for a change instead of cartoons?

Right, Archer. And you're going to get a Christmas present that doesn't have to get taped to the fridge.

"He inhales cholesterol," he heard Ricky declare from the kitchen. "Don't be stingy on the margarine for his pancakes or we'll have to pay."

"Pay? I don't think I understand," a soft, feminine voice replied.

"You know, *chores,* like walking the dog and cleaning the bird feeders." Molly made that sound like a life sentence on a chain gang. "Mommy loved birds and we have lots and lots of feeders, but none of us 'member to keep 'em filled."

"I see. It sounds as if you two work hard to earn your keep around here," the woman told them, sounding politely amused.

"You don't know the half of it," Ricky intoned.

But Read barely heard him. It was the woman his psyche had locked on to like some precision radar detector. That voice almost made him miss the last two steps on the stairs.

His knees were weak and his mouth bone-dry by the time he reached the kitchen doorway and saw the cozy picture of domesticity she made with his kids. It was her, all right; ten years or ten times ten, he would have recognized her anywhere.

Heaven help him.

It wasn't fair that she looked so good, even better than she'd appeared in the video. Dear God, he didn't need this.

"Hello, Read. It's good to see you. As you can see, I've intruded."

Yes, that was her way—to admit to everything, anything, leaving him with nothing to protest. All he could do was nod, circle her as if he suspected her of being a hallucination and back up to the coffeepot where a mug was already set out for him. That annoyed him, too. How was a man supposed to enjoy his anger when she'd thought of every courtesy and convenience?

He turned away from her to pour himself a full dose of the steaming brew. His hand shook. "Naturally," he muttered under his breath.

"Pardon?"

"When did you get back into town?" He tried to look casual as he returned to the entryway to use the doorjamb for support. It definitely made a sturdier spine than his, which at the moment felt ready to betray him.

"Tuesday, but I'm afraid I'll be unpacking for days to come." She glanced toward the table. "I hope you don't mind that I helped the children. They said they were starving."

"I'll bet they did." He eyed his two innocents. "And how did you two escape your chains and jimmy the basement door lock?" he said to them.

His son and daughter merely offered beatific smiles. It was Marina who exhibited unease. Bowing her head, she scooped the next batch of pancakes onto the platter that already held sausages and bacon.

"You're angry."

"Why should I be angry? I find it perfectly reasonable to have someone disappear out of my life. Vanish without a word of goodbye or go to hell, then wake up one Sunday ten years later and find her charming my kids in my own kitchen."

Molly clapped her hands with glee. "Daddy has to put a quarter in the oops jar," she sang, skipping to the pantry beside the refrigerator. She brought out an old mayonnaise jar and carefully set the half-full glass on the counter between him and Marina. "You said the H word, Daddy." She explained to Marina, "When he says a bad word, he has to put in a quarter, and when he fills it up, we get to have lunch anywhere we want."

Marina eyed the jar and then his daughter. Her lips twitched. "It looks as if you dine out frequently."

Molly nodded and grinned. "Uh-huh. 'Cuz the H and D words are his favorites. C'mon, Daddy. Pay up." She extended her tiny hand.

Read sipped his coffee and briefly reflected on how much simpler his world had been when he'd been single and his only responsibility was an aquarium occupied by a few dozen goldfish. Realizing that seemed a lifetime ago, he dug into his pocket and gave her the coin. "Now go wash your hands and sit down, Miss Mouth. You're about to eat."

"How do they like their eggs?" Marina asked him.

He found it incredible that her voice still bore a faint trace of the Russian accent that had intrigued him from the beginning. He would have thought she would have lost it by now. She was American by birth, having been born to parents who had defected from what had been the Soviet Union just in the nick of time for her arrival. But most of all it was her femininity that got to him, triggered memories of how it used to feel to hold her close to his heart and dream of the future he'd wanted to build for her, with her.

A sharp pain within his chest surprised him, and he stiffened against it. "No eggs. They'll do good to finish what you already have there."

"What about you?"

Did she think he could swallow anything while she was under his roof? ''All I want is to know why you're doing this.''

''The children asked me.''

He lifted both eyebrows this time. ''They phoned you and asked you to come over and make them breakfast?''

''I came over to talk to you. This…just happened.''

Marina carried the platter to the table, already set by Ricky. The smile she gave him made his son stare as if she was presenting him with his own personal rainbow. Read understood the boy's reaction only too well; he'd felt poleaxed, too, the first time she smiled at him.

''What do we have to talk about?'' he asked, feeling abruptly older and more than a little empty inside.

As the children attacked the food, she crossed over to him. She looked like a heroine from a Gothic novel in her black dress, which covered her from neck to wrist to matching suede boots. The palm-size silver cross dangling from a heavy chain to her narrow waist emphasized the dramatic bone structure of her heritage. But most dramatic was her wonderful hair; like onyx, it fell free nearly to her waist. It was a far different style to the braids wrapped tightly around her head that her father had preferred she wear.

''Read…my father passed away last month.'' She stopped no more than a yard from him. ''Perhaps the news was carried locally on TV?''

''I wouldn't know.'' Unlike his children, he rarely had the time or interest in watching television. And he didn't plan on offering any condolences, either.

Dmitri Davidov had hated his guts, and by the time the world-renowned pianist and composer had left Berryfield, taking his daughter with him, Read had reciprocated those feelings. In spades.

By her expression, it was clear Marina wasn't about to question his quick denial. "He caught a cold in Budapest," she told him instead. "We took a train to Paris, and by the time we arrived, his condition had deteriorated. Pneumonia set in. I still can't believe he's gone."

She gripped the Russian Orthodox cross and looked away for a moment. Even so, Read could see her fight back tears, and had to lower his gaze to his coffee to keep from weakening and doing something stupid.

"So you're here to sell the house." That was a good thing. Let it change hands. It had stood long enough as an embarrassing testament to his youth and naïveté.

"Sell? Why, no."

"No?"

"I told you, I've moved back to Berryfield."

She'd mentioned unpacking. That didn't necessarily mean she was staying permanently.

After delicately wiping at the corners of her eyes, she wrapped her arms around her waist and managed a proud smile. "I'm going to be a businesswoman."

He was so bowled over by the revelation about her intention to stay on, the rest was slow to register. "What kind of— Doing what?"

"Marina's going to turn her house into a Christmas store, Daddy!"

Read had just enough composure left to shoot his daughter a look of mild rebuke. "It's Miss Davidov to you, young lady, and this is grown-up talk. You keep your nose in that plate.''

"Yeah, like an anteater," Ricky said, chortling.

"Daddy!" Molly pointed at her brother.

"That's enough—both of you." Read gestured their guest toward the hallway. "Would you mind?" Without waiting for her to respond, he led the way.

In the entry hall, he discreetly kicked one of Ricky's dirty socks as close to the steps as possible and ran a hand over his hair. "What are they talking about?"

"A shop based solely on Christmas items, doesn't that sound fun? The idea came to me several times over the years. You see, we traveled a great deal, and while my father was in a practice session or in meetings, I had hours of free time on my hands. You can only tour museums so often and for so long. At least that's how it was for me," she said with a self-deprecating grimace. "So I explored the specialty shops next. They were an escape for me—a fantasy world, especially around the holidays. Then it came to me that there might be others like me, people who, for one reason or another, might have missed out on such delights. Do you think I'm right?"

"Beats me."

Marina's hopeful expression waned. But after a few seconds she continued determinedly. "In any case, over the past month I've been talking to artisans and craftsmen, and I've purchased a modest inventory to stock at least one room in the house. Enough to open right after Halloween."

She lifted her chin. Read thought the subtle movement gave her a regal air that a Bolshoi ballerina would have envied. "And?" he demanded, increasingly uncomfortable because he sensed there was more. Much more.

"In the meantime I've hired a contractor to make some structural alterations."

Read couldn't believe what he was hearing. She did sound serious. "What kind of alterations?"

"Connecting the rooms…closing off the kitchen… creating an office area behind the checkout counter. That sort of thing. I plan to turn the entire first floor into a store, Read."

It didn't make sense, but he was beginning to feel hunted, and that made him angry. His memories were tough enough to cope with. Did she have to move back and rub salt in those old wounds?

"Don't tell me your daddy didn't leave you with enough money to live in the fashion to which you'd grown accustomed?" he muttered, more unhappy than ever that she'd returned.

It came as no surprise to see her blanch, even draw back. She might be American by birth, but she certainly wasn't liberated. An American woman might even have taken a swing at him, but all Marina did was study him with those haunting eyes and clench her hands more tightly. "You're more bitter than I anticipated. I thought…I'd told myself that if I could come here and explain—"

"The time for explanations was ten years ago. You didn't bother. You just left."

"But I had no choice."

"Didn't you?" Realizing how intense he sounded, he forced himself to relax, even shrug. "In any case it no longer matters. The question is what do you want from me?''

For an instant she looked as if she might not tell him, might snatch up her wrap from the chair behind her and race out the front door. Then she moistened her lips and said, ''Your professional services. Mr. Fields recommended you to me. For the shelving and various display furnishings. He said you were the best craftsman he knew. Someone who would understand and enhance the architecture.'' She waved her hand in a way that denoted confusion, helplessness. ''I had no idea of your profession, Read. This is all a coincidence.''

''And that little performance with my kids yesterday was a coincidence, too?''

''Performance?'' She sighed. ''Read. You once said I would have to wear a burlap sack over my head to win a hand of poker. Do you think I've changed that much?''

He *thought* he should never have gotten out of bed. He thought he was a fool to have listened to her for as long as he already had. Aware only that he wanted this fiasco to be over, he shook his head. ''It's no good.''

''But, Read—''

''I can't help you, all right?''

She tilted her head and eyed him sadly. ''Can't or won't?''

He forced the words out before he lost his conviction. ''It doesn't matter. What does is that you don't belong here.''

Chapter Two

Marina didn't quite succeed in repressing a shiver, but then she'd never been treated to such bitter rejection before, either. Even when the Soviet Union had ceased to exist and her father had agreed to return to his homeland to do a series of concerts, they both had been treated with the utmost respect and affection, not any of the cool disdain and suspicion they'd feared. That it should be Read who exposed her to the worse side of human behavior was unbearable.

Afraid he might see how badly he'd hurt her, she spun around, snatched up her cape and rushed out of the house. It was a miracle that she didn't topple down the steps in her haste to get away, and she made it nearly a half block before she grew aware of the nip in the early October air. Only then did she pause long enough to slip her cape over her shoulders.

For the first time since stepping back on American soil, she wished she owned a car. Her father had never seen the need to have one, nor had he ever obtained a license himself. While living here in town, they'd relied on the elderly couple who'd cared for the house and property if they'd needed transportation. And she didn't need a car because Berryfield wasn't so large as to be inaccessible by foot. Her house was only a few blocks away. But thanks to Read's behavior, she suddenly felt as if there were eyes peering out at her from behind every curtained and shaded window. Dear heaven, the last thing she wanted to do was become as paranoid as her father about being watched.

Still, she was on her own now, and the Pedersons were long gone. A management company had been in charge of keeping the house in good order, and she'd just ended that arrangement. She needed to do something about getting a driver's license and a vehicle as soon as possible. She never wanted to endure this kind of embarrassment again.

Oh, Read. How could he have said what he did? She couldn't believe it. She had hoped, in spite of the unorthodox way they'd parted ten years ago, that he'd somehow understood what had happened. That they—

Well, there was no sense in dwelling on what had been now. Clearly, she'd lost more than her father. She'd lost the only real friend she'd ever had, too. Read had left no doubt that not only didn't he want to help her with the house, he didn't want any contact with her at all.

When she reached her house, she quickly unlocked the front door, bolted it behind herself, reset the security system and slumped against the heavy door. Gone was the excitement and anticipation she'd felt earlier. Suddenly, she was exhausted and so alone. The huge house was utterly void of the joy and laughter she'd experienced while around Read's children.

She could almost hear her father's rich baritone chiding her, "But this is who we are, Marina. Why do you fight it and me? Wasn't I was right about *him?* He's not for you."

"*Ochin' zhahl',* Papa. I'm so sorry."

So many hopes shattered. So many dreams turned to ash. What was she going to do?

By Monday morning she was still wondering.

Not surprisingly, it had been difficult getting through the rest of the weekend, although she enjoyed being back in the house. She might not want such silence and solitude to represent her life now, but she was used to being alone. She'd grown up understanding her father's need for having absolute silence while he practiced and composed. Even Mrs. Pederson had been forced to work under the sternest restrictions, because her father hadn't tolerated strangers "lurking and snooping about and making a racket." As a result, Marina had often done much of the housework herself.

Her homecoming had changed nothing in that respect. While the management company had hired someone to prepare the house for her return, the woman had been restricted to only certain rooms. As a result, Marina had much work ahead of her. It was also no surprise that despite all the physical labor, her mind focused on her troubles, and the disappointment and worrying took their toll.

Throughout the night she tossed and turned, struggling through disturbing dreams and more than one nightmare. By five o'clock Monday morning she threw back the part of the down comforter and sheet that hadn't already slid to the floor and took a long, rejuvenating shower. Afterward she dabbed on the foundation she used on only special occasions to hide the shadows under her eyes, a little blush, a brighter lipstick than usual and headed downstairs. She felt nowhere near terrific, but she had come to a decision.

She was determined not to let Read's anger control her for another moment. She also knew she couldn't let him change her plans for the future.

Her clothes helped give her a bit of a lift. She'd dressed in one of her new pants outfits, a deep chocolate brown with the tunic sweater boldly accented in black and gold. Pants had been forbidden by her father; he'd seen them as unseemly attire for a proper young lady. But she liked the way the slim slacks emphasized the length of her legs, and the hint of gold thread in the sweater added a touch of luster to pale skin she thought needed more help than usual this morning.

She finished securing her hair over her right shoulder with a black velvet ribbon just as she arrived in the kitchen. After flipping on all three light switches, she turned on the new portable radio she'd placed by the wall telephone. It was set to an easy-listening station. Not exactly pop rock by any stretch of the imagination, which won a crooked smile from her, but some changes took longer than others. Besides, she needed to be able to hear herself think.

Once she put on some water to boil for *cháhy*—or tea, as she was trying to start thinking of it, now that she didn't have to talk, write and think in her father's native tongue—she opened the leather-bound notebook she'd left on the counter last night. On the top page of the tablet she considered the drawing she'd sketched of the house—the way she hoped it would appear by Christmas. It wasn't a professional job by any means; she'd never had any training in art. But she was rather pleased with the winter-wonderland effect she'd achieved by inking in all the garland and ribbon bows she planned to drape along the waist-high stone wall that fenced in the three-acre property. That and the lights to be strung over dozens and dozens of the shrubs and evergreens would provide a fairy-tale quality to the estate, which possessed a surreal quality, anyway.

She imagined how children would soon press their noses against car windows as their parents drove them past the house, the same way she used to gaze longingly at decorated houses when she was a child. Although hardly cruel, her father hadn't believed in that aspect of the holiday; he'd seen that as "offensively commercial," and preferred a more spiritual approach to the holidays.

But this wonderful house all but cried out for more. It wouldn't for long, though, not if she had anything to say about things. And she did. That was the wonder of it. Despite the deep sadness she felt for the loss of her father, there was an undeniable sense of excitement and freedom, too.

The boiling water got her attention. She poured it into the fine china cup and saucer she'd set out on the counter last night, and let the tea steep, thoughtfully eyeing the next page, where she'd drawn the inside floor plans. If only Read had given her a chance to show him these. But he hadn't been in the mood to think about anyone else but himself, and she couldn't blame him for that. When she left ten years ago, she'd hurt him terribly.

Theirs had been an unexpected, wondrous romance that ended before it really had a chance to fully blossom. She'd been fresh out of high school, a private, restricted one. Read had just finished four years in the air force and was helping his parents at their small grocery store. They met when bad weather brought him with a delivery to the house.

He'd arrived in dripping-wet leather and denim, a breathtaking example of American masculinity, leaving her as dumbstruck as if she'd never been alone with a man in her life—which she hadn't. Her strict and protected upbringing hadn't prepared Marina for someone so physical and direct as Read.

No, her heart never stood a chance. He swept her off her feet with the kind of bold romance she'd only glimpsed when sneaking a few minutes of television, or one of the cherished novels that were so difficult to keep from her father. Within weeks she'd found herself wildly in love with a man five years her senior age-wise, and a lifetime older in experience. Small wonder that when her father discovered what had been going on behind his back, he accepted the first offer to travel that came along. Thereafter, he kept a grueling pace until his death last month.

Ten years of globe-trotting…and Read couldn't know how she'd been helpless to do anything about it. Well, not at first. Not when it mattered.

But Read hadn't suffered long, had he? Marina removed the tea bag from her cup, added a cube of sugar and stirred thoughtfully. Ricky told her he would be nine soon, and that delightful imp, Molly, was four. The reality of them meant Read had met someone and married her not long after *she* left Berryfield; so what right did he have to treat her as if she'd ruined his life? At least he had two adorable children to love. She had no one.

With or without his help, somehow she would go on. She wasn't a child any longer, but twenty-eight, an independent woman, both emotionally and financially. If she didn't make her own happiness, she had no one to blame but herself.

She was repeating that warning a few hours later when she heard the buzzer that announced Mr. Fields and his crew had arrived at the front gates. Drawing a deep breath, she pressed the button that let them enter and prepared herself to take the first step in achieving at least a few of her goals.

"I thought I would stay with the boys this first day," Mr. Fields said, after shaking her hand. "Thereafter, I'll be in and out, but I'll put my best foreman in charge, who just happens to be my son. However, if at any time you have a question he can't answer, or a complaint, don't you hesitate to call me."

Marina liked the middle-aged man's earnestness, just as she'd liked his honest face the other day when they first talked. After letting him introduce her to the crew, she drew him aside to tell him of her bad news.

"Mr. Archer turned me down, Mr. Fields."

"You're kidding!"

"I wish I was."

Phil Fields pushed his baseball cap off his forehead. "But this project is perfect for him—and he's always been eager for more business."

"Well, apparently not as much as you thought." Definitely not her business.

"Let me call him. There must be some misunderstanding."

As he started for the kitchen phone, Marina touched his arm. "Wait. I haven't told you— You should know something first." She took a deep breath to compose herself, and gather her courage. Embarrassing as it would be, she had to tell him. It wouldn't be fair to put Read on the spot, regardless of how disappointed she was with his behavior. "It turns out that we know each other," she blurted out. Belatedly, she realized that suggested more than she wanted to share. "Knew each other."

As expected, the contractor eyed her owlishly from behind his thick glasses. "No kidding?"

"When you first mentioned his name, I recognized it, of course. But I had no idea he'd gone into carpentry and— Oh, dear, this is embarrassing."

"Now, now." Mr. Fields patted her hand. "Surely there's nothing to be embarrassed about. After all, you were quite young when you left here."

"True. But...all I can say, Mr. Fields, is that our reunion wasn't what you would call pleasant."

The man thrust out his barrel-like chest. "Was he rude to you? If he was, I'll straighten him out, you can put money on that."

"Please, no. He's made his decision and I have to honor it."

"But if he won't do the job—"

"Then you'll have to recommend someone else."

Phil Fields spread his arms wide. "There isn't anyone else. Not anyone who doesn't have to drive from way out of town, which in bad weather means not showing up at all, which then delays progress and might affect your ability to open on schedule." He scratched at his encroaching bald spot. "I always anticipate problems, but I can't say I expected anything like this."

"Surely something else can be arranged?"

He shot her a droll look. "You can go away for six months, while I bring in slower, possibly less-talented people. Sure, the situation's not impossible. But is that the desirable solution? That's something only you can decide."

True. And it was a decision Marina had no problem making. "Mr. Fields, do you have any idea what it's like to live out of a suitcase, week after week, month after month? To have no permanent home, nowhere you feel absolutely comfortable and relaxed? Always having to rely on someone to deliver food to you, clean clothes, clean sheets for the bed? Never knowing your neighbors, let alone establishing long-term friendships?"

The contractor tugged at his ear and wrinkled his nose. "Well, if you had my neighbors, that wouldn't sound half-bad." But after the gentle teasing, he quickly added, "I know what you're driving at, Ms. Davidov. I'm just not sure I can guarantee you a best-of-all-worlds scenario."

"Understood, Mr. Fields, but I'm not leaving my home again. One room. I can establish The Christmas

House with just one room. Look.'' She picked up the
notebook that was never too far out of her reach these
days. "If necessary, I can take some furniture from
the study and elsewhere to use as display tables. But
if your men could make me some kind of shelving,
that would be a wonderful start.''

The contractor grimaced. "Ms. Davidov, if we
were talking about any other room, maybe we could
work something out. But not that one. The first impression people get upon entering this house should
be one of class and distinction, and it's a bright room.
You can't have anything but the best, and none of my
men could create work to compare with your furnishings.''

His impassioned speech made Marina smile. "Your
sensitivity to the house and my father's reputation as
a perfectionist is touching, Mr. Fields. But you should
know that he often had to settle for less than perfect
behind the scenes to achieve a goal before an audi-
ence. Out-of-tune pianos in practice halls, borrowed
clothes because luggage had been lost, performances
in buildings with horrible lighting and even worse
acoustics… This would be just another of those hur-
dles, as far as I'm concerned.''

But Phil Fields clearly would have none of that.
"That's a generous attitude, Ms. Davidov. Only it's
not going to make you like those shelves any better
if my guys do them.''

"Then don't do them,'' came a baritone pro-
nouncement from the doorway.

Read watched Marina's reaction. He had to admit
he enjoyed the shock and confusion in her eyes, even

if he didn't quite trust the innocence all that seemed to enhance.

"I thought you turned the lady down," Phil Fields said, recovering enough to draw himself to his full height and glare up at him.

Having worked with the older man for several years, Read knew when to disregard a businessman's blustering. "Maybe I changed my mind."

While the contractor considered that, he noted the surprise and pleasure that played across Marina's face. She looked lovely this morning, and whether he wanted her to or not, she spawned a deep-seated hunger in him that he hadn't felt in a long time.

"Are you saying you've reconsidered?" his sometime business associate demanded.

He didn't bother taking his gaze off Marina. "I think that's something between Ms. Davidov and myself. Can we talk?" he added directly to her.

She managed a nod, then murmured something soothing to Phil that he couldn't hear. Although the elderly man didn't look happy about being left out, he deferentially stepped back to let her lead Read from the room. Read followed, drinking in the sight of her lithe figure, her glorious hair, her feminine walk. He became so preoccupied, he didn't realize where she was taking him until they reached the regal study that he guessed had been her father's hermitage.

"Nothing like rubbing it in," he muttered under his breath.

The room was a designer's dream, fit for a prince—tapestry-covered walls, the finest woodwork, yards of bookcases and furnishings that belonged in a museum. But it wasn't exactly a study, for in the place of a stately desk stood the grand piano. Elegant though it was, Read hated it on sight, because it represented what he had lost when Marina left him. All the more reason to resent her for bringing him here.

"This may not be the room to have this discussion," he said, feeling a new rigidness in his body as she closed the solid French doors behind them.

"It's the most soundproof in the house."

Did she think he'd come here to cause a scene? Hardly, although in all honesty he'd come without having decided what he did hope to achieve. As his gaze once again drifted over her, he decided some of the possibilities were better left in the furthermost recesses of his mind. Shrugging at her comment, he began wandering around the room.

He paused by a side table to admire the wood carving of a bear, then moved on to a hand-painted commode and around the piano to consider the view of the grounds. But he couldn't relax. Dmitri Davidov remained too much of a presence here.

"Will you keep that?" he asked abruptly, turning to nod at the piano. To him it would always resemble a great black predator.

"Yes. For now." Marina approached the highly polished instrument, but did not touch it. "Someday I may donate it to a conservatory, or perhaps a museum. Several have mentioned they would like to have it."

"You don't want to play it yourself?"

"I can't play."

That revelation stunned him. "Can't?"

"No. Besides being a perfectionist, my father was wholly competitive. He could never have dealt with the possibility that I could have a natural talent—or worse, had no talent at all.''

''That's...twisted.''

''That's focus.''

Absolutely no emotion showed on her face, leaving her as visually perfect but remote as a mannequin. Read didn't like the effect at all. ''How can you defend him?''

''I'm not. I'm explaining who he was. His weren't necessarily admirable traits, especially not to people who have never experienced such passion. But without them, I'm not sure art would exist in the form we've come to know it.'' Her look held challenge. ''You're reported to be a painstaking craftsman. Surely you know what it's like to be fixated to the point of obsession.''

Did she really want an answer to that? Read doubted it. Rather than respond, he eyed the piano with new loathing. ''If I were you, I'd get a chain saw and turn the damned thing into a lawn chair.''

That won a brief laugh from her. ''The thought did cross my mind...when I was thirteen. But he chose that weekend to compose an adagio for me. It was a strange experience to hear something so exquisite played on something I resented so. In a matter of moments his piano became a friend rather than an enemy to me. A few years later I heard Candice Bergen reminisce about her father and the odd relationship she'd shared with him and his puppet, Charlie McCarthy. I realized there were other people who could parallel in a way what my life was like.''

It was an interesting admission, and Read knew it was just the tip of the iceberg regarding her complicated relationship with her father and his work. But he knew he couldn't listen to too much more without having to deal with the danger of caring again. He thought of a safe question. "Will you let the public in here?"

"Not as I would the other rooms, no."

"That might be best. If you make this one of the display rooms, you'll have heck trying to keep the kids from hammering out 'Chopsticks' on it. Wouldn't that have the old man rolling over in his grave?"

"It can be locked. I did think of turning it into a small museum," Marina said, eyeing the room thoughtfully. "Maybe setting out some photos, his awards…that sort of thing."

"Berryfield's answer to the Smithsonian?"

Marina's disappointment in his sarcasm was palpable across the few yards that separated them. "I don't blame you for being bitter."

"Is that supposed to make me feel better or kinder toward your father?"

"No. But you should restrict your anger to me, and not blame my heritage."

"That's all right. I have plenty of animosity to go around."

Her wince was fleeting, but poignant. "Read. I'd hoped I hadn't hurt you too deeply. I survived those first weeks by convincing myself that I'd overestimated how you felt about me."

"Maybe I should have tried that technique. You look as if the process agreed with you."

But that wasn't true, either. She looked about as substantial as a puff of smoke. On top of that, if she'd slept more than a few hours since he'd all but bitten her head off yesterday, no one would be more surprised than him.

Ashamed, Read turned away to stare outside at the evergreen garden that looked straight out of *Alice in Wonderland.* "Why did you come back?" he demanded, for the second time in so many days, but this time without his previous resentment.

"This is my house now. The only home I've ever really had."

"It's a piece of property...one you turned your back on for almost a decade."

"But I never forgot it," she replied, a slight tremor in her voice. "Never. If you believe otherwise, then you know me less than I thought. I may have spent most of my life living out of a suitcase, but I always hoped to return here."

"Why not sell the place and start over somewhere else?"

"Would you prefer me to do that?"

"It doesn't matter what I think." He knew he sounded like a petulant five-year-old and silently swore at himself for the weakness...and his lack of honesty.

Even so, she caught on to him. "Suppose you tell me why you are here, Read?"

"Beats me."

"Just passing by, is that it?"

His grunt was more of a growl. "I wanted you to know that you ruined what was left of my weekend."

"So you thought you'd come by and ruin my week."

Her calm, quiet observation held just enough mockery to finish making him feel like a heel. Needing her to understand, he did an about-face. "My kids aren't speaking to me. They think I chased you off."

"You did."

"But you know why."

She shook her head, her expression sympathetic. "That was a decade ago, Read. Ancient history. I'm not expecting anything from you on a personal level."

"Aren't you?"

He watched her lift her clasped hands to her lips. With her clear dark eyes and black hair, she reminded him of a young Madonna. But Marina Davidov wasn't that innocent. He'd been stung deeply once for making that mistake, but never again.

"Oh, Read," Marina said, as if his renewed resolve was written on his face. "You think I knew what my father was planning?"

"Yes. You had to. You couldn't have disappeared so quickly without being aware that something was up."

Her laugh was brief and more than a little hard. "Oh, really? Let me give you a crash course in Russian culture. Secrecy is ingrained, Read. The people are extremely insecure, and they find it difficult, if not distasteful, to admit to an error. So they go through life playing everything very close to the chest. On top of that they're extremely superstitious— another reason not to verbalize too much before acting.

"The night my father and mother defected from the Soviet Union, for example," she said, looking as if she'd experienced the event herself, "they'd been in Moscow for a concert honoring the new ambassador from the United States. My father didn't even tell my mother that he'd decided they were to leave the Soviet Union until that morning. In a matter of hours after his performance, they were under U.S. diplomatic protection and being rushed to the West.''

Read felt a pang of sympathy for Davidov's wife, who, he knew from previous talks with Marina, had been pregnant with their only child at the time. What kind of man did that to a woman he was supposed to love and trust above anyone else?

"Are you saying when you left it was all his idea, too?" he asked Marina with a frown.

"When I told him about you...about us, he barely said a word. Two nights later, when I was supposed to meet you for your friend's Christmas party, he informed me that he'd accepted an invitation to play in England and that we were to leave immediately. He'd actually packed for me while I was at the library.''

His heart pounded with remembered fury and hurt. Read clenched the hands he'd thrust into his jacket pockets. "You couldn't take a second to call and tell me?"

"He'd already removed the phones."

"What about sending me a note or letter?"

"I tried. He found them."

She said it so calmly, without apology or accusation, as if announcing a sheet of cookies had been burned in a too-hot oven and needed to be thrown out. It made what she said all the more impossible for Read to deal with. Where was this Russian passion he'd heard so much about? Where was *her* fury and grief?

As if picking up on his thoughts, Marina shook her head. "You have a son going on nine years old, Read. Exactly how long did *you* brood over my abrupt departure?"

She had him there. He lowered his gaze to the expensive-looking rug between them. "Things... happened."

"They always do."

"Look," he muttered, needing no help in beating himself up for what he did. "Gwenn was a nice girl. And she deserved better than what she got from me, but I tried to make her happy."

To his surprise Marina looked sympathetic. "I hope you loved her."

"I learned to. Later."

"How did she die?"

"She'd had a stroke during her labor with Molly. She had another fourteen months ago. This time she didn't pull through."

Marina wrapped her arms around her waist. "How sad for the children."

"But not for me, eh?"

"It's obvious you won't accept my sympathy or anything else if I offered it, Read. But even I can see your children need more attention than they're getting."

"I'm not neglecting my kids."

"I didn't say you were."

"Just keeping a roof over our heads and them clothed is a full-time job."

"Undoubtedly." She eyed him for another long moment. "And that's why you're here, is that it?"

He exhaled, glad to have that behind him. "I can't

afford to continue letting my personal feelings interfere with what I know is best for Ricky and Molly.''

"At least you're big enough to put their welfare ahead of your personal feelings.''

"I always have—and will.''

Twin spots of color spread in Marina's cheeks. "Read, I don't want to make this a painful experience. I'd hoped after I had a chance to explain about the past that you and I could be…well, at least cordial to one another.''

Cordial? Did people actually speak that way in the circles she traveled in? If so, it was just another reminder of how wrong they'd been for each other, mismatched from the beginning. Her father had done them both a favor. So why did he still feel such anger?

"I don't know if that will be possible,'' he replied, owing her the truth.

Marina bowed her head. "I see. Would you be happier if we communicated through Mr. Fields?''

He could imagine what the rest of the men working for the contractor would say to that, not to mention Fields himself. "It wouldn't work. No, if we do this—and I do mean *if*—we'd have to learn to deal with each other directly.''

"I would like us to try.'' When she lifted her gaze to his, that truth shimmered in her thick-lashed eyes. "Mr. Fields does say you're the man for the job.''

Aware he was becoming mesmerized, he had to swallow to find his voice. "Then I suppose you'd better show me around and tell me what you had in mind, and I'll…I'll let you know if that's feasible or not.''

Chapter Three

Where to start? Despite his agreement to at least listen to her plan, Marina was intimidated by Read's unmistakably resentful attitude. She hadn't expected this to be easy—no, that wasn't true, either. In her dreams she'd imagined quite a different reunion for them. But she'd thought she was prepared to at least sell her idea to him, if not herself. Win him over business-wise. The realization that he would be looking at everything from a dubious, and worse, critical standpoint had her doubting her ability to achieve even the slightest point with him.

"I should start by telling you why I want to create The Christmas House," she began, leading the way into the large circular foyer.

"You already did. During your travels, you spent your time in shops to alleviate your boredom," he replied, his tone indifferent. "You think a college-orientated town like Berryfield will have enough frustrated housewives who share that kind of feminine malaise.''

So, he wasn't through wanting to punish her. Marina clasped her hands more tightly and faced him again. ''Not quite. I want to do this because we never celebrated holidays. Do you understand what that's like for a child? To grow up without the magic of knowing your birthday is special? To make excuses to classmates for not participating in seasonal celebrations? There is a joy in giving, but it was a late discovery for me. There is a grace in learning to receive, but I'm still trying to discover it.''

Although the muscles along his jaw worked, Read's expression remained stony. ''Why didn't you? Your father didn't ascribe to any Iron Curtain political dogma, did he?''

''I told you, he believed in his music. Anything that detracted from it was either discouraged or simply rejected.''

Read's look held doubt. ''You're serious? No Christmas trees or Easter Bunny?''

It hurt that he'd forgotten, because she had explained it to him once. Back then. ''No dressing up for Halloween or exchanging Valentine cards with friends. No Thanksgiving dinner to celebrate the country that had given us sanctuary and a standard of living that would never have been possible in the old country.'' She winced inwardly at that expression. It was one of her father's, and underscored how ingrained his influence remained in her life.

Read was silent for several long seconds. ''I knew

he'd been strict, but what you're describing is closer to imprisonment.''

"Words and definitions." Marina shrugged, avoiding his direct but troubled blue-gray eyes. "He was my father. That was my life and it wasn't conventional. What does it matter now? It's today I care about. This house—" she spread her arms as if it was possible to embrace the place "—understands. Like me, it's been locked up and empty for too long. It's endured too much silence despite all the music, and many more temper tantrums. It wants and deserves to hear children…laughter. It yearns for *life*.''

Read stared, his look cautious, dubious. "I'm not sure I understand all that.''

"Of course you don't," she replied, almost sympathetic. "You were born with freedom. People who are can't conceptualize what it's like to live without it or understand how precious it is. But I do…and a good part of why I'm doing this with the house is to give myself the childhood I missed. I know I must do that if I'm to get on with my life.''

"It sounds as if you have a lot of territory to cover," Read said, his voice not unkind.

She smiled at that verbal olive branch. "I know. Come look." She continued to where she'd placed her folder and showed him the handful of brochures, photographs and notes. "This is just the first group of artisans I'll be dealing with. I want you to see these, the kind of things I'll be displaying, so that when you tour the house, you can tell me if what I'm asking for makes sense, or if there's a better way to display the items.''

"I'm not sure I would be any good.''

Marina decided to ignore that. "This is the angel tree," she said, opening to the photograph of the huge Norfolk pine filled with every kind of crystal, porcelain and wooden angel imaginable. "I'm not sure what kind of tree I'll use, but I thought I'd set it here in the middle of the foyer on this round table, so that people see it almost as soon as they enter the house. Then I wanted the walls lined with display tables and armoirs that I can fill with the items that are on the tree."

Read looked from the picture to the old English table and its distance to the walls. "Isn't that too far away? The idea of displaying stock is fine, but maybe of other items. If this was something I was planning, I'd put the decorations on the tree beneath this table. Use some kind of heavy cover to protect this table first. Maybe taffeta in gold, or a plaid, and then circle the floor with large copper and brass buckets around the table to hold your inventory. Or baskets, something like that. It'll keep people from getting too close to the tree and the table and accidentally knocking anything down."

"I like that." Encouraged, Marina showed him the parlor and the sketch she'd made of how she wanted it to appear after Mr. Fields's people cut the doorway from the parlor to the formal dining room. "I've asked for the parlor to be done first. This will have another display table in the center, and whatever else you can think of to show off the bulk of what I'll have to offer this year. Of course, if you think there's time to do more…?"

"Exactly how long do you think it takes to make a piece of furniture?"

Marina touched his arm. "I didn't mean to offend you, Read."

His gaze fell to where she had her hand, and he eased away from her. "Never mind."

"No, really. I didn't mean to sound as if I thought it was something you could do like a paint-by-number picture. That's why I asked for someone with your talent to help me." Despite the knot in her stomach at his reaction to her, she forced herself to go on. "Why don't you tell me what's feasible?"

He bowed his head. His hair, shades fairer than his children's, caught the chandelier light bringing out flashes of gold. Its thickness and health made Marina yearn to touch it again as she used to during those stolen moments when he held her close to his heart.

"Well, maybe I can do something." He gestured toward the parlor. "Let me actually walk through the rooms."

Taking hope from that, Marina led him to the large coat closet she wanted transformed into a checkout area. Then they went to the formal living room, where sheets still covered the furniture, but the French influence was unmistakable.

"I wanted to rearrange this room, get rid of several pieces that I could use elsewhere and put up several trees. I'm calling this the Ornament Room. Except for the angel tree, most of the ornaments I'll carry will be stocked here. Later the parlor will be for my most collectible, one-of-a-kind items."

"Are the couch and chairs among the items going?"

"No. I want to leave them to make the room look like a real living room."

Read lifted eyebrows much darker than his hair. "About two weeks of three-foot-tall urchins traipsing through the place, and it should look plenty real."

She'd thought about that, but she planned to have attendants in each room eventually and hoped to keep damage under control. As she explained that to him, she drew out the drawing she'd sketched of the final results she wanted. "Do you see the railing around the trees? I want to be able to hang custom-made stockings on these while using them to keep people from taking the ornaments off the tree."

"Securing the railings may be a challenge."

"You can't nail them to the floor?"

His expression turned stunned. "This is real hardwood! Do you know how expensive it is—and you want to make holes in it?"

As he crouched to move aside a Moroccan rug and examine the floor more closely, Marina bent over him. "But it's not as if this is going to be temporary. The railing will stay."

"Confident, aren't you?"

"Yes. Do you have a problem with that?"

"It's not my money you're throwing away."

The nerve of the man! "Why are you assuming that I'm going to fail?"

Read rose swiftly, and unaware of how close she was, bumped into her with the full force of his powerful body. Fortunately, his reflexes remained as excellent as she remembered, and he saved her just as she began to topple backward into the furniture, or maybe onto the floor.

He pulled her toward him and used his body to steady her. "Damn my clumsy— I'm sorry."

"It's okay. I shouldn't have, uh..." She couldn't finish because their close proximity made her too aware of him, his stormy eyes, his firm mouth, his even firmer body.

"I should have been more careful," he told her gruffly.

"No, I was crowding you."

Something angry flickered in his eyes. "Do you have to be so agreeable all the time?"

She couldn't believe his reaction. "Would you be happier if I hit you, or maybe just fired you and threw you out?"

"Yeah. Then I could leave here with a clean conscience."

"You can anyway."

"Yeah. Right."

"What's stopping you?"

"Those Bambi eyes of yours," he muttered, his fingers tightening slightly. "The thought of you falling into the hands of some crook who'd ultimately take advantage of you and your inexperience in this area—which shows big-time."

"Is that all?"

"Don't push it, Marina."

But his gaze had lowered to her mouth, and she saw something familiar and exciting in his eyes that she had seen before. Something that filled her dreams for years, and that she had yearned for for too long.

She lifted her chin, yielding to a recklessness that was new to her. "Is it?"

"Not quite," he replied, an instant before claiming her mouth with his.

He didn't want to kiss her. She could feel his anger

and resentment, even as his lips pressed against hers
and his heat seeped into her. But what made Marina's
heart sing was that he couldn't seem to help himself.
Overjoyed with that knowledge, she wrapped her
arms around his neck and gave herself up to the emotions that had known no outlet for a decade.

He groaned and forced her lips apart, crushed her
closer to him. It was as if he was trying to make up
for all the lost time in a few explosive seconds, and
although she wanted his hunger and passion, wanted
his eagerness and energy, she didn't have his experience. That didn't matter to her, but it made an obvious and profound impression on him.

He jerked back his head and frowned at her. "My
God...it's not possible."

"What?" she asked, a little dizzy.

"You're twenty-eight, for pity's sake. Where's
your sense of self-preservation?"

"I don't understand."

"You don't have any experience with men, do
you?"

She couldn't resist reaching up to that wonderful
mouth she ached to feel again. "I have what you
taught me."

He swore under his breath. "That's not funny."

"It wasn't meant to be," Marina replied, seeing no
reason not to be utterly truthful. "I told you, I've
lived a different life than most women, Read. The
only man who's ever held me like this is you. The
only man to have ever kissed me as if he wanted to
share the very air that fills my lungs is *you*."

"Stop it."

"You want me to lie?"

As if he was fighting his own will, he shifted one hand to cup her face. "I want you to quit sounding as if you think we can pick up where we left off."

"I know that's impossible."

"It is."

Only his fingers kept moving restlessly; he caressed her cheek and inched toward her hair. His gaze continued to roam hungrily over her face.

"It *is,* damn it." And yet he lowered his head and closed his mouth over hers again.

This next kiss was less angry, but that made the ardent assault all the more breathtaking. This time Marina caught a glimpse of Read's grief, the frustration and the desire that had never been consummated. It broke her heart, and she tried to show him that she'd grieved, too; that she'd missed him and the promise of what had blossomed so briefly between them.

With a deep-throated groan, he tore his mouth from hers and forced her to arm's distance. "No more."

Although Marina needed to grip his forearms to steady herself, her voice came calm and sure. "Why not? I like the way you kiss me. I always have."

"That doesn't matter. It can't!"

He almost yelled the protest. As the desperate sound echoed in the room, Read closed his eyes and raked his hands through his hair. Marina would have loved to offer him the consolation of her embrace, to reassure him that she understood his nervousness and doubt. She'd dealt with her own share, only to come to the conclusion that it was saner, healthier, to trust what was in her heart.

"Look," he said quietly, "this was a mistake. It won't happen again."

Not "mustn't," not "can't," but "won't." His resolve stung. It was so foreign from the intimacy they'd just shared, Marina was sure she must have heard incorrectly, and yet his expression told the terrible truth—Read regretted giving in to whatever had driven him to touch her.

"There's a streak of cruelty in you that I don't remember being there before," she whispered, feeling as if she was bleeding from an internal wound.

His jaw worked. "I'm not cruel. I'm just a realist."

"And you flirt with euphemisms."

With an exasperated look, he let her go, spun away from her to gesture around him. "All right, you want it in black and white? Look at this place. It's practically a castle."

"It's a large house. Stately, maybe, but hardly a castle."

"Because you've been in some, haven't you?"

She didn't like what he was driving at. "I can't deny that."

"Well, I haven't."

"Suggesting what?"

"Gold and tin, Marina. Diamonds and glass. Silk and polyester. Take your pick of the contrasts," Read declared, his tone hardening. "It all boils down to the same thing. We're polar opposites. To try to pretend that we're not is asking for trouble, not to mention grief that neither one of us needs or wants. Maybe I was too young and dumb—and, okay, hooked on you—before to acknowledge it, but I've had years to wise up and see things the way they really are."

His rejection had Marina clutching the notebook to her chest like a shield. "But I'm not asking you for anything except your expertise in woodworking and the friendship we once shared. Do you want me to pretend I don't miss it?"

"We weren't friends, we were falling in love," he insisted, stiffening. "We would have become lovers if you hadn't left."

If…if…if… "I told you, I had no control over what—"

"I *know*," he all but roared. "But you did leave, and that changed everything."

Marina quickly bit her lower lip to keep it from trembling. "How true…and your son Ricky is clear evidence of that."

"Leave him out of this," Read snapped. His chest rose and fell, his eyes blazed. "It's today that matters."

"How convenient. If I came back penniless and emotionally broken, someone with a bad case of co-dependency, I suppose you would have greeted me more warmly?"

Although there was a moment of guilt in his eyes, he had no trouble rebounding. "This is nuts. You don't want to hear anything I have to say."

"On the contrary, I'm very interested." Marina took a step closer. "Most of all I'm interested in why you're here if all you want to do is insult and hurt me."

"Damn it all, Marina—"

Someone cleared his throat behind her. She spun around to see a man close to her age take off his baseball cap and approach her. Twin dimples punctuated an apologetic but warm smile. A nice-looking man, one she knew she'd never met before.

"Excuse me for interrupting, Read, Ms. Davidov. I'm Seth Fields—my father thought I should introduce myself since I'll be supervising when he can't be here."

So this was Phil Fields's son. His timing couldn't be worse. Not only was Marina not in the mood to have to deal with meeting another new face—no matter how hard she worked at it, meeting new people remained difficult for her—but she was embarrassed by what he might have heard pass between her and Read. Only the fact that she had to keep Read from knowing how deeply he was upsetting her made her return the man's smile and offer her hand.

"Hello, Mr. Fields. I'm very glad to have you and your father handling this project for me."

"Please, make it Seth."

He crossed to her, trim, attractive and cheerful— so American, she thought, feeling anything but herself. It was ridiculous, since she'd been born here, too. But her life had been so different than the lives of everyone she came in contact with. Would the day ever come when she didn't always feel like an outsider?

"Seth it is," she replied, avoiding his admiring look. "I'm Marina—and apparently you know Read Archer."

"From way back. He was the hero of Berryfield High the year I started playing freshman football. How's it going, Read?"

"Fine."

Seth was inches shorter than Read, and his hair was

almost as dark as hers, but his cheerful demeanor gave him a bright aura. In contrast, Read seemed sulky.

"Dad said something about you doing the custom work here?"

Read's gaze swung briefly to Marina. "We're discussing that now."

"So I heard. Need any help? I'm a great arbitrator."

"No."

The message behind Read's curt reply was unmistakable, and Seth was clearly not slow. "Then I'm interrupting. Excuse me, I won't take more than a minute of your time. Marina, I just wanted to add that if you have any questions or problems, please don't hesitate to let me know."

"That's very kind, Seth. You seem as conscientious and thorough as your father."

"I better be." He beamed. "Or he'll fire me." He raised a hand in parting and backed from the room. "I'll touch base again later. Marina, I'd like to show you some paint color charts."

"Wonderful," Marina replied, nodding.

Read watched the younger man withdraw, disturbed by his reaction to him, as much as Fields's to Marina. Seth was right; they'd known each other for years. In all that time he'd never had one negative thought about the guy. But the red tide of jealousy that swept through him when Seth's gaze had zeroed in on Marina and his smile had turned as goofy as a teenager's was just another sign to Read that he was probably incapable of behaving objectively around this woman. How he wished she'd stayed away.

"You were saying?"

Marina had turned to him. Her expression was composed, patient; she looked as if she had no idea what she'd done. More than likely, she didn't. He was no whiz at female psychology—Gwenn had pointed that out to him more than once when he'd failed to be sensitive to her moods—but he didn't need to be an expert to know Marina didn't have the capability of acting like a vamp. If she came off as feminine and alluring, it was because that's exactly who she was. That made what had to be said all the more difficult.

"We can't go back."

He hated seeing the flinch at the corners of her eyes, realizing how deep her hurt went. Despite his own hurt, his past anger and present resentment, he still felt for her and believed she was too soft for her own good. How in the world did she hope to open and operate a business, function in the real world, when only minutes ago she'd told him that her past ten years had been as incubated an existence as the first eighteen?

"Read...believe me when I say that more than anything, I have no desire to go backward in time. The very reason that I'm doing this is to go on, to live *my* life, mistakes or no mistakes *my* way."

That was the problem. *Her* way seemed to be to torment him with memories of what they'd once had. He needed to make her refocus elsewhere. "Are you prepared to face the possibility that this—venture might not work out?"

"Are you speaking as an impartial observer, or someone who doesn't know how to admit a project might be too much for him?''

When had she become a politician? The suspiciousness he understood; the day they'd met she'd reminded him of a scared little rabbit ready to slam the door in his face and hide. There were still traces of that wary girl in her. But there was a new stoicism and resolve that hadn't been there before. He had a feeling she already knew what he was up to and wasn't about to let him get away with too much.

"I'm speaking as someone who knows what it is to lose…everything that matters.''

She studied him in prolonged silence, and too late he realized why. He hadn't meant for his words to have a double meaning, but he couldn't take them back now.

"Anything worthwhile has its risks and its cost,'' she finally told him.

"Fine.'' There was nothing to be gained from continuing to argue with her. He could see his only solution was to give her an estimate that even she couldn't afford. That would settle things, and he could go away and lick his wounds. "Show me the rest and let's get this over with.''

She led him to the formal dining room, as big as his kitchen and living room combined. Read couldn't help but admire the exceptional detail work in the room from the monogrammed, slipcovered chairs to the pier glass at the head of the table, to the multitiered chandelier, to the plaster scroll trim along the baseboards and ceilings. The table could easily seat twenty, and there was enough china in the hutch for twice as many. It had to be the most formal room in the house. "What do you want to do with all this?" he asked, truly at a loss.

"Burn it and start over?"

Certain he'd heard incorrectly, he spun around to focus on her. "Pardon?"

She grimaced. "It's cold and stuffy. I've always hated this room. The windows are fine." She pointed to the wall of floor-to-ceiling glass that ran the length of the room and provided a southern view of the spectacular grounds. "And I like the mirror over the fireplace, but the rest…"

Heaven help him, but the forlorn expression on her face made it impossible to resist asking. "Does it bring back unhappy memories?"

"Of other places, other dinners. Constantly dining with strangers. Eating foods that more often than not didn't agree with you." She shook her head. "We never ate in here. My father took most of his meals in his workroom, or in the kitchen with me if he was relaxed and in the mood for company."

"And who did you eat with the rest of the time?" Read asked in spite of himself.

"No one."

The image of her alone brought an unwelcome pang. "Didn't you have a housekeeper? I distinctly remember someone—"

"Mrs. Pederson always left in the afternoon after her chores to be with her husband, Donald, back in the garage apartment."

By exposing how lonely she'd been, she was chiseling away at his armor and resolve as successfully as if she was using a power drill. More lonely than she'd admitted to him before. Back then she'd confessed that she had trouble making friends because she was shy. At school her classmates thought she was a snob. But she'd liked the teachers. If only one of them could have helped her escape her father's suffocating hold on her. If only *he'd* been given more time…

He cleared his throat and struggled to concentrate on the room. "Next to turning everything into kindling, what did you have in mind?"

"This is where I'd like to show local crafts if I can find enough artisans who are willing—things like nutcrackers, rocking horses, teddy bears, vine and pine reindeers…"

"What will you do with that?" Read pointed to the table.

"I'll offer it to the college, or ask if they know someone who has a need for it."

Quite a gift. He was beginning to understand that her financial situation had to be even healthier than he'd thought, which made him feel gloomier than ever. Maybe as a younger man he'd been too lovesick to see that he could never make her happy, but it was clear now that he didn't have a hope in hell of making an heiress like Marina happy.

To ease the tension those thoughts brought, he wandered around the room. Ironically he could begin to see a hint of what she had in mind for the place, and that made him feel all the grimmer.

If successful, The Christmas House would be a stunning place. However, such an endeavor would require a great deal of work to set up, let alone manage.

Too much for one slight woman. Even if she had help, she would have her hands full. That spawned the first hopeful thought he'd had all day—if she was tied up with her business, she wouldn't have time to focus on him—or what had been.

"Read...are you going to help me?"

Not "take the job" but "help." He almost groaned, because he wanted, needed her to keep thinking of him as someone she would hire. He'd already compromised himself when he'd kissed her. What would it be like if he had to face her every few days? Could he keep his hands to himself? Ten years ago he'd walked around in a daze at the mere thought of tasting her sweet lips again. His appetite was far stronger now, and it had been denied for a long time.

Marina's smile waned. "We always come back to the past, don't we?"

"Afraid so."

"Do you hate me so much—"

"Let's leave hate out of this." If he couldn't explain his feelings to himself, how could he hope to tell her?

"All right. What else can I say, Read? How can I get you to take this project? Will reminding you about your children help? Mr. Fields said—"

"I'll just bet he did. Well, you can skip that part, too," he muttered, shoving his hands into the pockets of his jacket. "The trouble with living in one community your entire life is that too many damned people like to stick their noses in your business." Damn it, he didn't need her to tell him that he would be a fool to turn her down because of a broken heart and stung pride.

But she was right again. He needed the work. The kids deserved better. No matter what his personal problems were with Marina, he had to think of them first.

"Can you afford me?" he asked, allowing himself a little arrogance.

Marina arched a fine eyebrow. "Name your price."

Chapter Four

He told her yes. But in the days that followed, Marina wondered if she hadn't made a mistake by working so hard to get Read to take her on as a client.

It proved more difficult than she'd anticipated to do anything that required concentration when he was in the house, and for several days she couldn't have avoided him if she'd tried. There was measuring to do, and decisions to be made regarding various wood and stain choices on the pieces of furniture she wanted him to make. She'd known her input would be required, of course, but she'd hoped the tone of their meetings would be more professional, if not congenial. Instead, the tension began as palpable and grew steadily worse.

On the morning he planned to purchase some of the material he would be needing, he stopped at the house first, expecting her to drop everything so he could immediately review his notes and her color choices. He criticized every decision she made, then waited with visible impatience if she took too long to select an alternate.

No one was more relieved than she was when those daily visits ceased. As it was, he left her nerves frayed and her sleep disturbed. Not even the kindness of Phil Fields and his son, Seth, who quickly picked up on the situation and tried to run interference, had eased those awkward moments with Read. She began to wonder if she'd made a mistake hiring him, and wondered if she should ask Phil to recommend someone else.

Then Seth helped her direct her focus elsewhere. "Are you going to be opening the gates for the kids to come trick-or-treating on Halloween?" he asked one afternoon as she picked up a brilliant red maple leaf from the driveway.

She hadn't heard him come out to get something from his truck. "It hadn't crossed my mind. I've been rather preoccupied with Christmas."

"It might be a way to spread the word about your plans for the house. At the least it would get your mind off, er, the business, while you're waiting for us to finish the front room."

He was too nice to actually mention Read, but she saw the concern in his dark eyes. An invitation, too. Grateful for both, she thanked him, and quickly learned he was a sanity saver.

Naturally, having never celebrated the festivity herself, she didn't have a clue as to what to do or where to find decorations. Seth volunteered to drive her around town to see other people's decorations, then took her to several nurseries that stocked what she needed.

She bought dried cornstalks, then bound and stacked them on each side of the front gate, then bought more to design her own scarecrows. When dressing them became a problem, Seth cheerfully took up a collection of old work clothes from among his employees. Next she bought square bales of hay and dozens of pumpkins, which she scattered artistically on and around them. Seth told her that was a good start, but delighted her by painting comical or silly faces on a few.

When he suggested flowers for the long-neglected flower beds, she couldn't resist, although she felt guilty taking so much of Seth's time. "Are you sure you aren't going to get into trouble with your father?" she asked him, as he drove her to yet another garden center.

"He understands that you don't drive," Seth replied with a shrug. "Besides, he likes you. And he knows I do, too." When she failed to respond to that, he teased, "I particularly like the way you talk. You roll your *R*s and emphasize the *CH* more than Americans usually do, and you have a tendency to say *een* instead of *in*."

"It's because we spoke nothing but Russian when my father was alive," Marina told him, once again embarrassed that she stood out as an oddity in her own country.

"Hey, I'm not making fun of you. I think it's sexy."

She couldn't deny it did her ego good to be thought of that way, but it also warned her that she mustn't encourage Seth too much. She couldn't respond to him the way she sensed he wanted, and she didn't want to hurt him by giving him false hope. That was why, when later she realized she needed more plants, she had the nursery deliver her order.

She planted every color of chrysanthemum and pansy available—white, gold, rust, yellow and purple. Once she got them planted, she was caught up in the fever and brought in more pumpkins to line the driveway, all the way to the front door where additional mums and pansies were already filling great copper and brass urns.

"Do you think the children will get the message that they're welcome here?" she asked Phil Fields late one afternoon, as she walked him out to his truck.

He ran his hands over his belly, swollen from the homemade borscht and bread she'd prepared for him and his workers as a thank-you for their kindness to her. "Well, they should. The place looks like a park, as nice as anywhere in town."

With that encouragement, she ordered a taxi a few days later when Phil's crew left for the day, and purchased an assortment of every candy available. Everything that would have appealed to her if she'd been the one going on that night of door-to-door adventuring.

She was paying the taxi and hoisting two full shopping bags from the back of the cab when Read arrived in his pickup truck. Already exhausted from a day of cleaning and other chores, she sighed, wondering if she was going to have to face yet another round of censure from him. She didn't have the energy to fight anymore.

"You take a taxi to shop?" he asked, staring incredulously after the cab as he emerged from his truck.

Once again she repeated her explanation. "I don't have a driver's license."

"Everyone has a driver's license."

"Read."

Her whispered plea reached him with surprising speed. "Excuse me. I'd forgotten that you're different."

The words were by no means meant as an apology, and the sardonic tone annoyed her. "There's also no more Archer grocery store with a deliveryman."

"Thank heaven for small favors," he muttered under his breath. But he did nod at the bags. "Let me have them so you can unlock the door."

"Thank you. I'm quickly discovering that candy weighs more than my schoolbooks used to, and there was a time I believed nothing was heavier or more dull than science and math texts."

As she started up the sidewalk, she heard Read stop in his tracks. Curious, she turned in time to see him staring into the bags.

"This is all candy? What for?"

"Halloween."

"You took a taxi to go shopping for *candy?*"

Trying not to lose her temper completely, Marina went on to unlock the dead bolt and pushed open the front door. "How else was I supposed to get it? That's how I do all of my errands." She decided not to share the news about Seth's helpfulness. Heaven knows what he would find to criticize there, and it was none of his business. "But I am going to sign up for driving lessons as soon as I can leave the premises knowing I won't be needed for an hour or so." She'd been thinking that through for days now, and found the idea of having her own car exciting—although she became terrified when she thought of actually going through the process of purchasing one.

"There's no school near here," Read said, breaking into her thoughts. "The closest is a good hour away."

Marina shrugged. "If it can't be helped, it can't be helped."

"Hell. I'll teach you."

"What?" She stared at him as he passed her and headed for the kitchen. She shut the door and followed.

"I said I'll teach you. You need to learn, and whoever has to drive out here to pick you up for lessons will charge you an arm and a leg just for travel expenses, so I'll teach you. Look at it as my gesture to the community," he added, setting the bags on the center island in the kitchen.

Marina lingered in the doorway of the huge room. "Why?" she demanded simply.

"Because I have a reputation around here as a safe driver."

"Not good enough."

"Believe me, the way most of the people drive in this town, that's a lot."

"You're purposely ignoring my point. Need I remind you that you don't want to spend any more time around me than you have to? What's changed?"

"Nothing."

Maybe he could make a stranger believe that, but not her. When she didn't comment any further, he scowled at her.

"Don't make a big deal out of it. You need to learn, I have a conscience. Isn't that enough?"

The thought of being the beneficiary of that conscience would have made her feel better if it wasn't already putting a trapped look on his face. Dear heaven, he confused her.

"You'll have to let me pay you for your time."

Something dark and violent flared in his eyes. "Don't even think of it. I said I'd do it and that's that."

"But—"

"Change the subject, Marina."

Yes, he was a strange man…and he proved a tougher taskmaster. She realized *that* during her first lesson three days later.

On Saturday he picked her up just before noon, dropped the children off at the movies for a matinee—despite their protests and assurances that they wouldn't mind coming along—then drove to the outskirts of town, away from traffic congestion, where they changed places. Marina quickly learned that few people if anyone could please him.

"Don't talk, just listen. The speed limit is thirty-five, that doesn't mean going fifteen is going to make you brownie points with the officer who'll test you. It's just as dangerous to go too slow as it is to go too fast. Don't assume. Stop and look both ways. Don't change lanes without signaling."

It was a great deal to remember, and she made a mistake quickly. Several of them.

"You're too close to the car in front of you!

"Exactly what do you think a blinking red light means?

"Watch out for the— *Curb.*"

By the time she pulled into the driveway, she was so close to tears, she barely managed to get the truck stopped before leaping from it and running inside. She ignored his shout after her, and then the pounding on the front door, which she'd bolted and leaned against while choking back sobs.

When she heard him leave, she stumbled up the circular staircase to her room and threw herself on her bed, the tears coming fast and furious. Miserable wretch of a man! What right did he have to treat her as if she was still a child, or worse, stupid! What had she done except try her best? She should never have let him talk her into this arrangement. He didn't want to help, he wanted to punish her!

Minutes later the phone rang. She refused to answer it, knowing who it had to be. She'd given Read her number, but she had no intention of talking to him because she couldn't imagine him apologizing and she didn't think she could bear another judgmental remark from someone who'd meant so much to her.

For days afterward, she lived in fear that he might come by and make a scene, but he didn't. When a whole week passed and there was no sign of him, Marina finally relaxed to where she returned to her daily routine, tackling the chore of cleaning the huge house, cooking lunch for the workmen and handling whatever issue came up regarding her fledgling business. The focus on getting her driver's license was put aside for the moment. Maybe the theory of getting back on a horse after you were thrown worked for some, but she wanted some quiet, stress-free time before she tried again.

On Halloween morning, which fell on Saturday, she rose with excitement and dressed in a cashmere tunic the color of fresh pumpkin and black leggings. Adding a vibrant scarf with multicolored fall leaves and copper-and-gold threading, she slipped on gold hoops and practically danced down the stairs. Her mood was a far cry from last week's, and for good reason—today she would get to show the townspeople of Berryfield that the Davidov estate was no longer that curious, closed place it had been for years.

Throughout the day she busied herself filling bowls of candy, then moving them from spot to spot in the foyer. Seth had already told her that trick-or-treating began later in the afternoon, with the younger children arriving just before dusk and the older ones later. Although she was impatient for that time to come, she happily carved several jack-o'-lanterns from some of the biggest pumpkins in her yard, set in sconces with candles and placed them around the front door.

At four o'clock she opened the gates, and at five she switched on the floodlights to highlight her decorations and offer a welcoming path to the front door. Then she turned on the music she'd bought, tapes of comical or melodramatic tunes and Hollywood special-effects soundtracks that were more humorous than spooky to her. She could just imagine how it would have offended her father. He would probably have ripped the tapes to shreds and gone to bed with a bottle of pills to nurse one of his frequent headaches.

At six, she began standing guard at the window nearest the door, wondering if the gates had somehow swung shut in the wind. But there was no wind tonight, and when she rechecked, there was nothing wrong with her doorbell, either. However, she had yet to have her first visitor.

By seven o'clock she turned off the tape player and began blowing out the nearly burned-out candles in the pumpkins. She didn't need anyone to tell her that no one would be coming trick-or-treating to her house.

What had she done wrong? Her decorations were wonderful, her property well lit. She'd tried to do everything she could think of to welcome people.

Too disappointed to focus on anything else, she got her coat and keys. There was no sense staying put and getting herself worked up and upset; she would take a walk and see where the children *were* going.

She headed toward downtown, only a few blocks from her house. Traffic was light, and there were enough houses and streetlights to make her feel comfortable about being alone at this hour. Once or twice she saw a car pause and a load of children rush out and run up to someone's front door. Her chest tightened with envy at the adults enjoying the giggles and yells of children who rushed from one house to the next.

But it was when she approached Berryfield Elementary School that she saw real traffic. Dozens and dozens of cars were parked near the gym, and music and the roar of laughter, screams and chatter rushed out at her whenever the heavy doors swung open and people both tall and small came out. Most of the children were in costume, and each one carried either a plastic pumpkin or a shopping sack filled to the brim with goodies.

As Marina wondered what was going on and whether she should venture inside, the door burst open again and an adorable small lion emerged. Blinded by an overlong mane, it missed the top stair and dove forward. Despite the candy launching at her like missiles, Marina lurched forward to save the child.

In the next instant the door opened again and Read exited with Ricky. "Molly!"

Between the shock of seeing Read again and being knocked to her knees in order to catch hold of the little girl, Marina was left momentarily breathless. Truth be known, she wasn't sure what hurt more, the bruising concrete or having to acknowledge Read's presence. However, the latter was delayed as he hoisted the child off her by the scruff of her neck.

"Young lady, what did I tell you about running off without me?"

"Daddy! You don't pick up a lion this way!"

"You do if she's a mischievous squirt who doesn't behave."

Set on her feet, Molly pushed back the hood of her costume and looked up indignantly, only to spot Marina. "Marina! Look, Daddy," she cried, pointing with her pumpkin, spilling several more pieces of candy. "It's Marina!"

Shoving the container into her father's hands, she spun to Marina and wrapped her arms around her neck. Still on her knees, Marina hugged the child, breathing in the scent of bubble gum, popcorn and the various wonderful smells she linked with childhood.

"Hello, little lion," she murmured, trying to ignore the pang in her heart that was every bit as strong as the sting in her knees.

"Do you like my costume?"

"I've never seen anything grander."

"Did you hear, Daddy?"

Behind them, Read remained silent, but stooped to pick up the dropped goodies. It was Ricky who descended to join them.

"Hi, Marina! What're you doing here?"

"Well, I—"

"Did you see all that I got?" Molly cried, eager to chat.

"And you know what else? They had a magic forest this year with marshmallow mushrooms and licorice vines and whole bunches of other stuff—and you know what? You could eat it! The haunted cave was the best," Ricky added, his face bearing the dark slashes of paint that she'd noticed in magazine ads that football players wear. An oversize jersey with a single digit completed his costume. "You climb up this fake rock and slide down a dark tunnel into a pool full of rubber snakes. Then you wait for girls to come down and scare them to pieces."

Molly shook her head vehemently, her oversize cub ears wiggling like watery pancakes. "Not me! I was too little. Daddy said I shouldn't go."

Having no idea what they were talking about, Marina looked at Read. He'd finished collecting his daughter's treats, and there was no missing that his silence was as speaking as the children's enthusiasm.

"Is this a school party of some kind?" she asked.

"Halloween Fest. More and more parents feel it's safer to bring their kids to some organized and supervised function like this than take chances having their kids on the street taking candy from strangers."

Was that why no one had come to her place? She could have saved herself considerable disappointment if *someone* had told her. After sending him a cool look, she focused on the children. "I didn't realize." Struggling to her feet, she summoned a smile for the children. "So obviously you two had a wonderful time?"

"Yeah, and now we're going to the ice-cream store, right, Daddy?" Molly cried, hopping up and down with unbridled excitement.

"Guess so," Read murmured. "Since you won't be happy until you have a tummy ache." But he was watching Marina and frowning. "What's wrong? Did you hurt yourself?"

"Not really. I just stumbled when I caught Molly."

Clearly not believing her, he passed Molly's bucket to Ricky and came down to join her on the bottom stair. Without asking for permission he stooped to inspect her legs. "The material's not ripped, but that doesn't mean you're not bleeding."

"It's just a bump. I'll be fine."

"There could be tendon or ligament damage."

"I'm *fine*." Didn't he understand that she didn't want him touching her? His closeness just reminded her of how insensitive he'd been the other day, and she would be darned if she would cry before him again.

"Maybe you'll feel better after some ice cream," Molly said, her voice tiny and sad.

The statement caught her by surprise and she stared. "Oh, I—"

"Uh, Marina doesn't—" Read said at the same moment.

Ricky stepped forward and grabbed her hand. "Yes, come!"

"Then it'll be a real party, not just us." Molly brushed her tousled curls aside to look up at her father. "Daddy, do you have money for her to have ice cream, too?"

Read looked up into the star-filled sky. Marina would have chuckled at his comical reaction to the child's unabashed honesty if they'd been on more pleasant terms. As it was, she felt obliged to be gracious.

"That's very generous, Molly and Ricky, but I was only out for a short walk. It wasn't my intention to intrude."

"You can be *my* date," Ricky interjected, patting his jacket pocket. "I have a whole month's allowance saved."

Just as Marina sent the boy a loving smile, Read laid a hand on his shoulder.

"That's nice, son, but I said this was my treat, remember?" His gaze sought Marina's. "You're welcome to join us."

"I don't want to," she whispered as low as possible so only he would hear.

"I know...and I know why. And all I can say is that I'm sorry."

"This isn't fair, Read."

"No. So don't come for me." He glanced at his children, who stood by watching them in confusion and worry. "Come for my kids."

"All right."

Read barely registered Marina's reply before Molly whooped and took off running into the parking lot. With a shout of rebuke, her older brother gave chase. That left Read and Marina to bring up the rear. As she turned, he noticed her wince, and he took hold of her arm. Immediately she stiffened.

"Marina, don't."

"You knew what I was doing for Halloween. You could have warned me. Why didn't you?"

"Because if I had been wrong and people had swarmed to your place with their kids, you would have seen me as a party pooper."

"Ah…and you're happy with being only a semi-party-pooper?"

She'd made her point. Again. But this time his annoyance was only secondary to his chagrin. "I'm sorry I let you go through so much trouble for nothing."

A strange smile curved her lips. "Oddly enough the experience wasn't wasted. I enjoyed the preparations, and that's how I realized they were part of what the festivities are about."

"Keep it up, you're going to put us all to shame."

"I'm just trying to learn."

They'd reached the truck. Read unlocked the passenger side and Ricky and Molly climbed into the back seat. As Marina got in front, Read realized that despite his concern for her fall, despite his shame for his earlier behavior, he really was glad that she'd agreed to come with them. How to communicate that was another story.

There was no chance to say anything during the drive to the Polar Express, the ice-cream shop in the center of town. Molly was her talkative self, and Ricky seemed to have been bitten by the chatterbox bug, as well.

"I'm gonna have the biggest hot-fudge sundae," Molly declared, shortly after updating Marina on what else she'd consumed at the Halloween Fest.

"Yeah, right," Ricky replied with a senior sibling's disdain. "You couldn't eat half of one if Dad kept you on bread and water for a week."

"Can so! I'll eat two if I want."

"Good idea," Read drawled. "Then we'll have to roll you home. I've always wanted my very own roly-poly girl."

"Daddy!" Molly squealed, covering her face but clearly delighted with her father's teasing.

"Dad, can I get the Cliffhanger?"

As Read groaned, Marina glanced from him to Ricky and asked, "What's the Cliffhanger?"

"It's the biggest dessert on earth," Ricky crowed. "You start with this big ol' brownie, and then stack all this Rocky Road ice cream on top, then whipped cream, then marshmallow and chocolate sauce, and nuts and a cherry."

"And you have to try to eat it before it falls all over the table and everyone around you," Read added as an aside.

Ricky echoed his father's earlier protest. "Aw, Dad, it's neat. Marina, you should try one, too."

"Well, as exciting as it sounds, unless this is an

all-night establishment, I'm not sure I could eat a whole one in a single sitting. Would you believe that in my whole life I only remember one scoop of vanilla on a cone?''

''What?'' both Ricky and Molly gasped.

Whispers of ''unreal'' and ''awful'' drifted from the back seat. Marina chuckled. ''Actually, it's a marvelous memory. I got to watch the woman make it before my very eyes after a day of hiking in the Alps. It tasted what I imagined clouds must taste like.''

''No, they taste like cotton candy,'' Ricky said, all seriousness.

''Oh, dear. Well, I've never tasted that.''

''Daddy!'' Molly leaned forward against her seat belt. ''Marina's never tasted cotton candy!''

''As far as I know I still have twenty-twenty hearing, pumpkin.''

''But, Daddy—the circus is coming soon and you said we could go. Maybe Marina can come with us. They have cotton candy at the circus.''

''The circus isn't until nearly summer, honey.''

''Is that right after Valentine's Day?''

Read shot Marina an apologetic look. ''We don't usually tell time by holidays where you receive gifts.'' That's all he needed, to have her think he raised his kids to be materialistic. As it was, they were inching dangerously close to that matchmaking scheme again—just when he'd begun to hope they were cured. To change the subject he suggested, ''How about singing Marina the song you learned tonight.''

Instead they told dreadful knock-knock jokes that Marina couldn't possibly have found entertaining.

And yet somehow she laughed—and not polite laughter, either. No, she actually seemed to find them funny.

After Read parked in front of the store and he and Marina followed the children inside, he couldn't resist wiping away the tear of laughter he spotted at the corner of her left eye. "Don't spoil them. You'll make them impossible to live with."

"You're very lucky," she replied, drawing away from him slightly. "They're born charmers."

"They don't get it from me, do they?"

Inside they found that the kids had claimed their favorite booth, the one in the corner by the window that looked out at the park. Next to studying the picture menu, they enjoyed eyeing the pond in the middle of the park best. A family of ducks lived there, thoroughly spoiled by the community. But what surprised Read was that both kids were in the same side of the booth. Usually they gravitated to opposite sides. "Girl cooties," was Ricky's typical judgment. "Boy crud," was Molly's. Read knew why they'd suddenly abandoned their sibling rivalry, and it confirmed his suspicion that Marina was once again their prime "Mommy" target. He had to figure out how to stop them before they embarrassed her.

"Are you planning to deal with getting ice cream and whatnot on that game shirt?" he asked his son, nodding from him to his accident-prone daughter.

"Sure, Dad. No problem. I'll take care of her."

Read couldn't help but raise an eyebrow. His boy's casual acceptance was nowhere near the way he usually reacted, but he wasn't about to make a production out of this in front of Marina. Clearing his throat, he invited her to take her seat in the booth. Maybe it would make things easier, he thought, as he slid in beside her. If they didn't have to sit across from one another, their eyes wouldn't keep locking, their knees wouldn't keep bumping, and maybe he could swallow something without feeling as if he had to force it past a closed drawbridge in his throat.

But it didn't take long to realize that no matter what their seating arrangement, his size made a booth problematic. Instead of their knees bumping, their thighs touched. Instead of getting to stare into her eyes, he had to deal with their arms rubbing. And her hair kept wrapping itself around him like fingers, making him wish it was his bare flesh it was caressing. He could tell Marina noticed, too, because the prettiest blush rose and stayed permanently in her cheeks.

"Sorry," he murmured, shifting yet again after they'd placed their order.

"It's all right." But once again Marina tried to sweep her ebony mane over her left shoulder.

Molly stared with unabashed wonder. "How long do you think it'd take me to get my hair that long, Marina?"

"Oh, another year or so. But you may not like it. It takes a great deal of brushing."

"That's okay. Daddy likes to do that, don't you, Daddy?"

"Absolutely." He nodded, careful to keep a poker face. "Next to sticking my arm down a lion's throat, I can't think of anything more fun."

The children got a big kick out of that. But Marina eyed Molly with continued interest.

"I have a silver comb and brush set that had been

my mother's. If you'd like to visit me sometime, we can use it to do your hair.''

"Can I, Daddy?'' Molly gushed, clasping her hands prettily.

Read thought of a few choice things he wanted to tell Marina. ''We'll see. Miss Davidov doesn't realize what a pest you can be.''

"I'd be happy to watch her, Dad,'' Ricky said, focusing on rolling and unrolling his napkin. ''You know, kinda like baby-sitting. But you wouldn't have to pay me anything.''

Rather than answer, Read turned to Marina. ''These are not my children. I think they're pod people from Mars. They must have assumed Ricky and Molly's identity.'' Then as everyone giggled, he leaned across the table and softly demanded, ''Whoever you are, bring my kids back! I miss not hearing them blowing out my eardrums, and wheedling me for favors and treats.''

"Daddy, it's us,'' Molly said, patting his hand. ''We're just being friends with Marina 'cuz she doesn't have any, right, Marina?''

"Exactly…thank you very much. Both of you,'' she said to the children. ''And I want you to know you're welcome to visit anytime.''

Read sobered. He knew Marina meant well. He also realized she had to be lonely in that big place she lived in. However, she didn't realize what such invitations would do to his kids. And him. One day she would meet someone of her own kind, start her own family. Neither he nor his children needed any more heartbreak in their lives.

As the waitress brought their order and the children

exclaimed over theirs, Marina leaned closer to him, as if she'd sensed his unrest.

"You needn't look so grim. I don't intend to upset your life."

That's what she thought, he brooded. She already had. She had for years.

Chapter Five

Under the circumstances, Read wouldn't hear of not driving Marina home, and the trip to her house was far more quiet. Full and sleepy, the children slumped in the back seat, contentedly looking out their windows, clutching their collection of Halloween treats. Their only sounds were yawns and an occasional soft humming of a favorite song. Like Marina, Read didn't say a word the entire way.

When he pulled into her driveway and saw all the decorations, though, he experienced another pang of guilt for not having told her something about Berryfield. ''I'll walk you to the door,'' he murmured upon stopping. He had to at least do that.

Leaving the engine idling so the heater would keep the children warm, he listened to Marina whisper goodbyes to them. Then he waited for her to round the truck and followed her up the walkway.

''I'm glad you're not limping,'' he told her. ''How do you feel?''

"A little sore, but fine."

The place was well lit; nevertheless, when she unlocked the door, she immediately reached inside to key in a code to adjust the alarm system. That underscored how alone she was here.

"Would you like me to look around before I go?"

"It's not necessary," she said, running her finger along a series of green lights. She faced him again. "It's a good security system. Thank you for tonight, Read."

He shook his head. He knew full well he didn't deserve her gratitude.

"Yes. Thank you for being so kind to me."

She made him feel like a heel. "You're very easy to be kind to."

"Does that mean you don't hate me anymore?"

The lights above and behind her created a nimbus around her head, and Read knew she'd never looked more beautiful to him. "I never hated you, Marina. I tried, but…I just hurt." Hurt because he'd lost her. Hurt still because he could never have her.

"Me, too. How do we make it stop?"

He didn't know. All he understood was that he wanted to kiss her, to take her in his arms and hold her tight, until the aching stopped. The problem was that tempting himself would only bring worse pain…and heartache to his children.

After a long moment he simply shook his head and began backing away. "I don't know if we ever will."

"I don't know if we ever will."

Marina blinked at Phil Fields. His words were so

much like what Read said a few days ago, that for a moment she lost track of time and what they'd been conversing about. "Excuse me?"

"Finish with our pumpkins. At our house, my wife just wraps some lights around them and they become part of the Christmas decorations." He chuckled and gestured in a way that encompassed the entire yard. "The thing is that they're definitely part of Thanksgiving, so why not leave everything as it is, and enjoy it? Folks don't actually decorate for Christmas until then anyway."

Before she could respond, Read's pickup pulled into the driveway. Marina's heart gave an excited leap. "Uh…thank you, Mr. Fields. I think I'll follow your advice."

"Of course, when you are ready to put up your Christmas stuff, you just let Seth know," the contractor added, following her gaze. "He'd be glad to help you out. We wouldn't want you overloading any fuses or anything. Well…looks as if Archer's as good as his word. He told me yesterday that he would have a piece or two to deliver to you soon."

That was more than he'd said to her. In fact Marina hadn't heard from him since Halloween, to be exact. She followed Phil to Read's truck, hoping her excitement didn't show too much.

Read exited and nodded to the contractor, then her.

"Good to see you," Phil said, slapping him on the back and beaming at the round table in the bed of the truck. "That's a beauty."

"It is, Read," Marina added, impressed at the gleaming creation. "It will look wonderful in the front room."

"Glad you like it."

He spoke politely, but his eyes avoided hers. When he quickly asked Phil to help him carry the table inside, Marina was left to simply stand by and listen to a conversation that centered around sports. Her only chance to say anything else was after she showed them how she wanted the piece set in the parlor. Right after they set down the table, Phil got called into another room by one of his men, leaving her alone with Read.

"Did you bring an invoice so I can write you a check?" She wanted to know if it had been Phil's presence that had made him hesitant about talking to her.

"It's in the truck, but there's no rush. I have some shelves to put up, too. Just ignore me, because I'll be a while."

Pretend he wasn't there? Impossible. However, she understood what he was telling her; he wanted their relationship to get back on a more professional basis. With a slow nod, she murmured, "Call if you need me," and withdrew.

She spent the day going through a new shipment of inventory, more of the crystal angels she planned to hang on the artificial tree she had just set in the foyer earlier that morning. The detail work of making tiny price tags and attaching them to each item proved painstaking, and Marina was surprised when—after hearing the doorbell—she glanced at her watch and realized it was after three o'clock.

She experienced another surprise when she discovered Molly and Ricky were her callers. "Why, this is a wonderful surprise!"

"After I picked up Molly at day care, I realized I forgot my key this morning. We can't get into the house," Ricky told her, looking anything but regretful. "Dad said he'd be here today, so we thought we'd come get his."

"I thought you said she would ask us to stay, Ricky?" Molly asked, gazing at her brother with great confusion.

"Absolutely, because you've been doing a great deal of walking. Come in, both of you." She hugged them one by one and added a kiss for Molly's wind-reddened cheek.

"I thought I recognized your voice," Read said from behind her. She turned to see him frowning. "What are you guys doing here?"

Ricky explained again—only this time he looked less confident about his story. Read's expression told Marina he didn't buy it for a second.

"Uh-huh. Your key that you keep in your wallet, right?"

"Uh…I left my wallet home, too. It was a real bummer, 'cuz I missed lunch and everything," his son replied, sliding a look to his sister. "Listen, Dad, we can wait for you. We don't mind, do we, Molly?"

Although the little girl shook her head in vigorous agreement, Read narrowed his eyes. "Oh, no, you don't. You aren't going to bother Miss Davidov—"

Marina was glad for the opening. "They're no bother at all. Besides, Read, didn't you hear him? He has to be starved. They probably both are."

"Thirsty," Molly said, sticking out a tongue as pink as her cheeks and proceeding to pant like a puppy.

"Heaven save me from impostors," Read growled.

But Marina caught the twinkle in his eyes and the twitch around his mouth. She herded the children toward the kitchen. "Why don't you come with me. I have some of the prettiest cookies you've ever seen that an acquaintance sent from Europe. I bet they would taste especially good with some hot chocolate."

"All right!" the children cried in unison.

First, however, Marina helped them off with their jackets and hung them over the banister at the foot of the stairs. She smiled as they oohed and aahed over what she'd been working on.

"Wait until you see the tree finished—all of the house," she told them.

"I wish we could," Ricky replied, adding an adult sigh. "But Dad's not likely to let us back."

"Why do you say that?"

"We've known him a long time. You can tell by his face."

They were a delight. "We'll have to figure something out," she told them. Once Read saw how well the children behaved here, and how much she enjoyed their company, surely he would change his mind. Brightening, she clapped her hands together. "Why don't we turn this into a tea party? Without the tea, of course."

"Then how can it be a tea party?" Molly demanded, her face scrunched into a pixie's frown.

"I'll show you."

She had them help her arrange bar stools around the center island, and then brought out French lace place mats and silverware. Molly's eyes went wide when she saw the china with the gold trim. Marina let Ricky help her carry things, chuckling to herself as he moved as if carrying explosives.

She let them both light a set of candles for their centerpiece with a lighter, and then arrange the cookies on a crystal platter. Marina supervised, while heating the milk for their drinks. Through it all, she entertained them with stories about the items they held.

"Those dishes once belonged to cousins of the Czar of Russia. Isn't it wonderful how the firebird's tail becomes the handle of the cup?"

"I thought it was a peacock," Ricky said, eyeing his more closely.

"The firebird is a favorite creature in Russian fairy tales. Molly, that candelabra was a gift to my father from the Countess Molinari. She lives in Venice."

"You knowed a countess?" the little girl gasped. "That's almost as good as a princess! Did she live in a castle? Was she scary to talk to?"

"A villa. It's not quite as big as a castle, and the countess was very sweet and—*normal* is the word you'd probably understand best—just like you and me."

"Wow, what kind of marshmallows is that?" Ricky asked as she shut off the mixer.

After pouring the hot chocolate into the cups he'd brought her, she scooped a large dollop of the white froth on top of each. "Whipped cream. I'm afraid I'm temporarily out of marshmallows, but I think you'll find this a tasty substitute."

He didn't look convinced. However, he was the perfect young gentleman, helping her carry the drinks to the counter. Then they all took their seats.

"Do you eat like this all the time?" Molly whispered, her gaze winsome as she surveyed their bounty.

Marina knew she had to answer carefully. She didn't want Read's children to get the wrong impression. "Well, what do we have here?" she began thoughtfully. "Milk and cookies. But presentation makes it look more special, doesn't it? A pretty cup and a lit candle…"

"Tell me about it," Ricky replied. "We get chipped plastic served on vinyl—when Dad remembers place mats. It's nothing like this." He looked at the cookies. "Um…can we taste now?"

"Absolutely." Marina invited him and Molly both to help themselves. "Why don't you tell me what your favorite foods are?"

"Mac'roni and cheese!"

"Hot dogs and fries!"

"Oh, dear," Marina replied, laughing behind her cup. "Would you believe I've never tasted either?"

"You must've had a strange life," Molly offered, breaking open her cookie to lick the coffee cream inside.

"Well…different."

"What did you eat?" Ricky asked her, reaching for a chocolate-dipped wafer.

"It depends where we were. For instance Russian cooking, which my father preferred, is fairly plain and filling. Caviar…sturgeon eggs," she explained, when she realized they hadn't heard of it before.

Both children screwed up their faces.

"Also boiled eggs. Herring."

"At the same time?" Molly mumbled, her mouth full.

Marina grinned. "It's an acquired taste. But what's interesting is that the eggs are peeled and often marinated in red beet juice. Can you imagine having Easter eggs year-round?"

Ricky shook his head and admitted that wasn't a bad idea. "But I can't even imagine trying herring."

"It's an acquired taste. I'd bet you'd like the blintzes, though."

"What are they?"

Marina used both hands to create a big circle. "Large pancakes that you fill up with all sorts of things like cottage cheese, sour cream and jam."

"I guess that wouldn't be too bad," Molly murmured. "But I think I like mac'roni better."

Grinning, Marina replied, "Maybe next time you can come over we'll try that."

"Promise?"

"Don't get greedy," Read said from the doorway.

Marina almost spilled her drink, and despite the tone in his voice that warned her that he was a bit annoyed, she managed a bright, "Hello. Did you change your mind about joining us?"

"Uh—no. I was just concerned that they were making pests of themselves."

"Not us, Daddy!"

"We're doing good, Dad, aren't we, Marina?"

Nodding to both Ricky and Molly, she turned to their father. "We're having a lovely time, Read. Come, have a cookie at least. You won't compromise your principles by having one cookie." She was teasing him, but gently.

"No, thanks. I just wanted you to know I'm done for now, and to tell the kids that we'll be leaving in ten minutes or so. As soon as I collect my tools."

"But, Daddy, we just started," Molly cried. "Look—the candles aren't even melted yet!"

Marina bit her lower lip to keep from laughing. Oh, Read's child was a treasure; both of them were. She could see that this little party meant as much to them as it did to her. She hoped Read could, too, and wasn't so closed-minded and resentful toward *her* as to discount that.

As if she'd spoken out loud, he turned back toward the door. "Why don't you just let me know when you're done, and I'll check on a few things with Ph—Mr. Fields."

He left before Marina could think of a way to stop him. As the door swung shut, she felt a small hand touch hers.

"Don't be sad," Molly coaxed. "He gets like that if he really likes you."

"Excuse me?" Marina said, with a brief, embarrassed laugh.

"Yeah," Ricky seconded. "He tries to pretend he doesn't care, but you can tell he does."

"Really? I suppose you have to know him better to be able to tell."

"Yeah." Molly nodded sagely. "We've known him all our life."

"Oh, Molly…I do like you. I like you both very, very much."

When Read heard Marina's soft, melodious laugh, he was reminded of the old saying about listening in on others' conversations. He deserved this, all right. Never mind that he was trying to do the right thing and not take advantage of her; any guy less responsible and principled would be working overtime to make her remember how close they'd been ten years ago. Anyone else would have gone in for the kill with a line like, "For old times' sake," and be visualizing a cozy future for himself. But not him.

He had his pride. Regardless of how badly his kids wanted a new mother, he needed to be the one who would provide for his family. No matter what Marina said or did to try to convince him that her wealth didn't mean much to her, he knew it was all she knew; therefore it had to count. All that fancy dishware and silver was perfect proof of it.

Grim but resolute, he sought relief by throwing himself into his work. He spent long hours in his garage workshop, pausing only to prepare the kids' meals, check Ricky's homework and supervise their baths before he tucked them into bed. Afterward, he returned to the shop to continue. Now that he had the parlor ready, he was working on the railing for the living room display.

His kids were no help at all. At every opportunity they tormented him with anecdotes about Marina, or with questions.

"D'you know what, Daddy? She can ride horses," Molly gushed, her expression rapt. "Not cowboy horses like on TV, but like a lady where you wear gloves and hats and shiny black boots. She's gonna show me pictures someday."

"There was this monster kinda pot on the counter, Dad, only real fancy," came Ricky's interjection. "I thought it was where she kept her dad's ashes or something, but she told me it's a—a sammy something. Oh, yeah, a samovar. Bet you didn't know I knew any Russian. Know what it's used for? Tea. Cool, huh? And she showed me the cups they use. They're glass in these neat silver holders. Marina said next time we come over she would show us how it worked.''

''Daddy, d'you have any friends in Europe? I sure did like those cookies.''

''I feel sorry for her being in that big house all by herself. Do you suppose she gets lonely, Dad?''

On and on it went. A conspiracy. Read knew what his kids were up to; their plan was to drive him out of his mind. But he did manage to stay away from Marina's for nearly another full week. Only, inevitably, it came time to deliver the railing.

He arrived one morning when Marina was saying goodbye to a middle-aged woman in a fur-lined suit. The elegant woman managed to pass within inches of him, yet ignored him as if he didn't exist. Drolly amused, Read watched her slink into a low barracuda of a car and drive away.

''That's Mrs. Danforth-Wellington,'' Marina said, joining him at his truck. ''She's the president of the ladies' art league.''

''Not exactly the friendly type.''

''Yes…and I think I did something unwise by turning down her invitation to join the organization.''

Read lifted an eyebrow. ''Sounds smart to me if she's representative of the rest of the group.''

''But it came to me afterward that she knows a

great number of people who could help get the word out about The Christmas House.''

That earned her a stare from him. She looked particularly mature and stunning in a deep red dress that he guessed might be cashmere. With its high collar secured at the side of the throat by a pearl button, and matching pearl studs running along the left side of the dress, she stood as a strong representative of her ancestors. But what she'd just said…

''You'd suffer the company of snobs like that to sell a few ornaments?''

Her gorgeous brown eyes lit with gold fire. ''Thank you for sharing your feelings about my business, Read. If you'll excuse me, Seth is waiting for me. He's trying to get his people to finish up today, and he needs me to okay something. I don't want to delay him any more than I already have.''

As he watched her walk away, her high heels clicking lightly on the sidewalk, Read had to fight the urge to run after her and apologize. Lord knows, he deserved her cold shoulder and more. Since when did he belittle anyone else's efforts to make a go of a business? His inner conflict over the woman was turning him into someone he no longer recognized.

But didn't she see? He knew people like Mrs. What's-her-name; they always managed to get more than they gave. He'd experienced that when his parents owned their business, and even today in his own. He suspected the woman wanted Marina's celebrity, but it was doubtful she would ever come here to shop, no matter what she promised.

Shaking his head, he began carrying the first set of railings inside. Marina had been so preoccupied with her visitor that she'd ignored what he'd brought. That hurt *his* feelings; but once inside the living room, he saw how much work she'd done since the last time he'd been here, and that changed his attitude to one of shame.

"I wanted to have the trees up so that you could install the railings without having to worry about how to maneuver around them," Marina said, coming in behind him. She paused beside him and touched the gleaming, walnut-stained wood. "This is lovely. You were right about the shade. It's going to blend in well."

"Yeah. If you'd gone any lighter, things might have looked too... Marina." He considered her profile and felt his heart clench at the sight of her sad smile. "Marina, I was a jerk about what I said."

"No, you're right. I'm an amateur, and all this might be a pipe dream. But, Read, try to understand— the only way I survived the loneliness and longing all these years has been by dreaming."

She was turning him inside out. It was all he could do not to sweep her into his arms to relieve his frustration and pain. His mouth was dry from wanting to taste hers again.

He swallowed hard. "At some point we have to stop. We have to look at the world the way it really is."

"Grow up, you mean?"

Her dry tone of voice had him glancing at her again. "I'm not suggesting you're immature. Just..."

"Idealistic." Marina tilted her head and studied him with greater curiosity. "How can you have two beautiful children like yours and not be the same way? Their future lies in your ability to hope for a better world for them."

"That's different."

"How convenient to think so."

He uttered a guttural sound. "Believe me, it's neither convenient nor easy."

To his amazement she smiled.

"What's so funny?"

"I'm realizing what a liar you are."

Before he could respond, she quickly, lightly touched her lips to the corner of his mouth. Even as he reached for her, he sensed her stiffening. Following her gaze over his shoulder, he saw Seth leaving the room.

"Excuse me," Marina murmured, and went after him.

What the hell...? Read wondered.

Marina hurried after Seth. She'd thought they'd finished their business. She'd approved the hardware for the doors on the office behind the checkout counter. The final bill would be mailed by his father. There had been no reason for him to seek her out; instead he'd walked in on a personal moment between her and Read, and the expression on his face told her that she needed to speak with him.

"Seth." She caught up with him outside.

He stopped on the walk and frowned. "It's cold. You shouldn't be out here without a coat."

"Will you come inside with me so we can talk?"

"It's not necessary, Marina. You don't owe me an explanation."

"Seth." She pleaded to him with her eyes. "I'm sorry for not being more clear about Read."

"I should have guessed." He shrugged and offered a sheepish smile. "You can't blame a guy for hoping."

"I do like you."

"I like you, too. But I'm beginning to think our friend Archer isn't playing with a full deck of cards." Seth nodded toward the house. "What's his problem? Would you like to talk about it?"

"It's a long, complicated story, and it barely makes sense to me. I'm not sure I could explain it to you, nor would it be fair to Read to talk about him behind his back."

Seth whistled softly. "Tell him for me that he's a fool if he lets you slip through his fingers."

"Read doesn't pay a great deal of attention to what I say."

"Would you like me to offer him some advice?" Seth asked, his eyes twinkling despite his sad smile.

"Thank you, but no."

"Going to take your chances on wearing him down with gentleness?" He sighed and shook his head. "I wish you luck, Marina. That's a brick wall you're dealing with."

"I know, Seth." But what she couldn't tell him was that she loved that stubborn man. Until she could learn to stop caring, all she could do was hope he stopped rejecting what she instinctively knew he felt for her.

Read struggled to ignore his curiosity about Seth and Marina the rest of the morning and well into the afternoon. He was two-thirds of the way through with the installation of the railing when he heard a commotion at the other side of the house. Then there was the brief stampede of small feet. "Hi, Daddy!"

"Hey, Dad."

He spun around and whipped off the protective glasses he'd been using during drilling. "What's this?"

"We came to see Marina," Molly said, aiming a wet smack on his left cheek. She waved a cut-and-paste picture inches before his nose. "I wanted to bring her the turkey I made today. You don't mind if I give her the first one instead of you, do you, Daddy? She don't have any little kids to make pictures for her 'frigerator."

"Doesn't," he said automatically. "She *doesn't* have any kids. And it's *re*frigerator."

Ricky put a protective arm around his sister. "Don't be so hard on her, Dad. She knows. She's just excited to be here. Uh...the railing looks good."

Read sat down on the floor and pinched the bridge of his nose. His not-yet-nine-year-old son was using psychology on *him?* This was perfect. He looked over their wind-tousled heads to see Marina in the doorway. She'd changed into a pants and sweater outfit in blue and green, and her smile made it clear she was as happy to see his kids as they were to be here.

"I suppose now that you're here you'll want to hang around until I'm ready to leave?" he drawled, already knowing the answer. He knew Ricky had a key; he'd checked with his son this morning.

"On account I broke my shoe, Daddy." Molly

lifted her foot, showing him the snapped lace on her hot pink sneakers. "The sidewalk tripped me."

"Ah." Read looked from the tiny foot to Marina. "Now I'm supposed to ask you if this is infringing on your time."

"It's not," she said sweetly. "We're going to start bringing ornaments and things into the front room after we have a snack. Can we get you anything?"

Aspirin. He was developing a headache, because he knew full well what she was doing. "No, thanks." He did, however, give each of his children meaningful looks. "Now hear this—behave."

For almost half an hour things were fairly quiet. It made him wonder what they were up to in the kitchen. But then a short time later he began hearing squeals and loud voices. Since he was finished with his work for this visit, he followed the sounds to the front parlor where he found his son, daughter and Marina sitting on the floor surrounded by boxes upon boxes of ornaments and gift items.

"This is the most *beautiful*." Molly reverently stroked a porcelain reindeer wearing a fine gold chain with a tiny bell hanging from its neck.

"You said that about the bear ornament," Ricky chided, wearing a necklace of price tag labels.

"That's because I didn't see this one yet. Do you think this is Dancer or Prancer, Marina?" the little girl asked, once again stroking the sleek figurine.

About to answer, Marina spotted him. "Oops, I think we concerned your father again."

"No, I—" Read heard the subtle teasing in her voice and changed his mind. She was right; he had charged in here to look for an excuse to end their visit. He'd been about to punish them because of his inability to reconcile his feelings with her. "I thought you might like to see how the finished product looks," he said quickly before he could change his mind.

Marina brightened. "Let's go look! I could use some advice about setting up some things."

The children rose with care, more care than Read had ever seen them use around their own possessions, let alone anyone else's. Then Molly bolted for him and asked for a piggyback ride. Glad not to be left out of this scenario despite their obvious manipulation of him, he crouched to let her hop on and carried her to the next room. Ricky raced ahead and screeched to a halt before the semicircle of trees inside the new wooden barricade.

"Wow! This is so cool, it's just like a penned-in forest!"

"The finish is still setting, Rick," Read warned quietly. "Be careful."

The boy looked ready to climb onto it, and gingerly backed off. "Sure, Dad. You did good."

"Think so? Thanks. I'm pleasantly pleased myself."

"It is wonderful, Read. Thank you." Marina stopped beside him. "It's exactly what I had in mind."

He couldn't see how. Actually, all he could focus on was that her arm was touching his. It was a reminder of the whispery caress she'd bestowed upon him earlier...and the way she'd taken off after Seth. What had happened between them? What was she up to now?

He cleared his throat. "Are you sure this is what you wanted?"

"Exactly what I wanted! Can't you see it—the trees decorated, baskets of ornaments against the railing and stockings hanging from the posts?"

"Sure sounds like a lot of work, Marina," Ricky said, nodding as if he could see it. "Especially since you said you would be interviewing soon for help. That takes time, too. Me'n Molly could help you until you found some grown-ups, if you wanted us to."

Read laid a hand on his son's shoulder, knowing exactly what the boy was up to; after all, it was only yesterday that he'd overheard him agree with his sister that Marina was "the one." "Now, Rick, Marina doesn't need any—"

"Ricky, that's a marvelous idea," Marina cried before he could get the rest of his explanation out. "You wouldn't mind? But one thing—I certainly would insist on paying you for your time."

As she looked from one excited child to the other, Read set his hands to his hips. "Wait a minute."

"I'm serious," Marina assured him. "It's a wonderful idea, and why shouldn't the children get compensated for their time and efforts?" She beamed at them. "It'll be good practice for when you're grown, not to mention coming in handy for Christmas shopping."

Read couldn't bring himself to argue with her logic. Everything she said was reasonable, except that when he looked down the road and saw his children spending more time with her, *him* spending more time with her, it triggered all the old pains and angsts.

"Please, Daddy? It's about Christmas," Molly murmured, her lower lip beginning to protrude.

He sighed and threw up his hands. "Okay! Fine! I know when I'm outnumbered." Then he wagged a finger at a grinning Ricky. "But if this intrudes on homework—"

"It won't, Dad. Cross my heart."

As Molly clapped and jumped up and down with glee, Marina mouthed thank-you to him. Their gazes clung even after he realized he should look away.

This couldn't work. His mind kept telling him so. But another part of him took too much pleasure and strength from the moment. Just being with her gave him something rare and fulfilling. If he wasn't careful, it was going to turn into full-fledged need.

He didn't quite succeed in matching her smile, but he managed a quiet, "You're welcome."

Chapter Six

Marina could hardly wait for Ricky and Molly to ring her doorbell the next afternoon. Their enthusiasm for what she was doing with the house compounded her own, making her feel as excited as a child again. Not surprisingly, their arrival was noisy.

She welcomed them with bear hugs and listened to them simultaneously tell about their day as she helped them off with their coats. Then it was on to the kitchen for a snack.

"I can't tell you how glad I am to have your help," she told them, when they finally descended on the mass of boxes, garlands and bows in the living room. "The truth is I never expected to have this much of the house ready for decorating this season.

"Ricky, your job is going to be to mark the price tags for these hand-painted nutcracker ornaments," she said, indicating the sheets of adhesive price stickers and the pen she'd set out on the pretty Victorian desk. "Then you can stick one on the back of each, okay?"

"Wow!" he said, picking up one and inspecting it more closely. "They have moving parts and no two are the same!"

"What's my job, Marina?" Molly asked, bouncing like a spring toy.

"First, you have to help me give this place a little atmosphere. Do you think you can reach that switch on the wall by that last tree?" she asked, pointing.

When Molly hopped and successfully flipped up the switch, every tree in the room lit with hundreds and hundreds of delicate white lights. The children clapped and cheered, and Marina had her reward for a morning's intensive labor getting each string placed to suit her.

"Now a little music," she said to Molly, handing her a cassette that advertised favorite children's Christmas songs that she'd found last week. She showed the child how to place it in the portable stereo she'd brought from the kitchen, and how to turn it on.

As "Jingle Bells" began playing, she pointed next to a mountain of artificial pine garland piled on one side of the room. "There's no putting this off any longer," she said, pretending to be overwhelmed by the prospect of their next task. "We have to get all that garland hung."

Molly gaped. "There must be miles of it!"

But as they set to work, she could tell the child felt very important about her responsibility. So did Ricky.

They began working on the railing first. Every few yards, Marina had Molly run over to the couch, where dozens of red velvet bows were neatly stacked, and they secured a bow to the garland. They finished just as Ricky completed his project.

Marina let them hang several of the ornaments on the first tree. She already had a three-foot-tall stepladder for the higher spots, and supervised when they were on it. Then she had them carefully fill a garland-trimmed basket with wooden soldiers, and they placed it outside the railing for easy access by customers.

"What's next?" Molly said, her eyes glowing with pleasure.

"Well, maybe you should help me decide." Marina tapped her chin and pretended she couldn't make up her mind. "Should we put up these lovely silver bugles with the red ribbons from England, or those Scandinavian rocking horses?"

"Bugles!" Ricky shouted.

"Horsies!" Molly cried.

With a laugh, Marina said, "On second thought, maybe both will work." She pointed to the boxes of ornaments she'd already marked, and helped them start adding those to the tree.

"I hope you won't get so tired of this that you won't want to decorate your own tree," she told them, as she held the ladder for Ricky.

"No way," Ricky assured her. "Because last year all we had was a dinky one, and a dumb old wreath on the door."

"Yeah," Molly echoed mournfully. "No lights or nothin'."

Marina didn't know how to respond to that. She hadn't brought up the subject to remind them of unhappy moments or to snoop into their family life. But she found the revelation disheartening. Of course, she could understand Read's reason for disappointing the children; he could still have been mourning the loss of Gwenn, been tired, or perhaps needing to budget at that time. Did the children understand that?

"Let me ask you this," she began, carrying a basket to Molly for the ornaments she'd already labeled. "Did you enjoy being with your dad any less on Christmas morning?"

Molly looked as if she'd been asked if Santa Claus was really a fraud. "'Course not. Daddy's all we have."

"So then you had the most important part of the holiday."

"Guess so." Molly eyed her from beneath curling lashes. "But this is funner."

"Do you know that in European countries such as Holland, Germany and England they celebrate St. Nicholas Day, which is a few weeks earlier than our Christmas?"

"What do they do?" Molly asked, looking intrigued with the idea of another holiday.

"Children place their shoes by the fireplace, adding a carrot to them or a handful of hay for St. Nick's horse like we do cookies and milk for Santa Claus."

"And he leaves toys in their shoes?" the little girl asked, a bit confused. "They can't be very big ones."

"He brings sweets like *lebkuchen,* gingerbread and honey cakes. And fruit. You wouldn't think that's much, would you?"

Both children wrinkled their noses. Molly murmured, "I don't even know what most of that stuff is."

"The point is that for some poorer families, it's all the Christmas they have." She saw them ponder that thought.

"I guess you're saying that we don't have it so bad," Ricky murmured, his expression glum.

Marina didn't want him to think she didn't sympathize with their situation. "All I'm suggesting is that you'll be happier if you don't think of your life as being more or less than someone else's. Try to find joy in sharing moments with people you care about."

"Like this?"

"It depends. Are you having a good time?"

"Yeah."

"Then this is a little bit of Christmas. You see? We're making our own happiness. It's one of the best lessons I've learned in all the years I've spent traveling and watching other people and other cultures."

They worked, and chatted, and sang...and lost track of time. When the doorbell rang, Marina glanced out the window and saw it was close to dusk. That identified her caller.

"You wouldn't by any chance know where I can find two deserters about so big," he drawled, indicating the children's heights the moment she opened the door to him. "They used to live a few blocks from here, but I guess they've forgotten that."

With an apologetic smile, Marina invited him in. "It's my fault, Read. I know I should have sent them home half an hour ago, but..."

"I know. You were all having such a great time, you forgot to look out one of the dozens of windows in this place."

Sarcasm and all, he looked wonderful, like a lumberjack in the red plaid shirt and jeans that he wore beneath a heavy denim jacket. There were deeper fine lines around his eyes indicating fatigue, and his hair looked both windblown and hand mussed, but his rugged, masculine appeal affected her as strongly as ever.

Marina shut the door, aware of her heart pounding. "Did I make you stop in the middle of something important? Oh, dear...if I had my license already, I could have saved you the trip by driving them home."

He gave her a look that suggested she could have spared them the reminder of their failure there. "With what? You don't have a car, either." Muttering about children caring for children, he peered into the parlor. "So where are they?"

"In the living room. That was uncalled-for, Read. I'm not a child."

He paused, his gaze drifting over her black jumpsuit. "You're right, you're something far more dangerous—a beautiful, loving woman who lives in a fairy-tale house. Exactly how am I supposed to compete when you've enchanted my children?"

"You're their father. You don't have to."

With a skeptical look, he headed for the living room. Marina followed, thinking about what he'd said. His words would have been thrilling, except that he hadn't said them to compliment her. It didn't help that when they entered the room, she saw it as he must—that it was beginning to resemble the fairy tale he'd mentioned.

The children didn't notice them at first. Like merry elves they worked to adjust ornaments on a tree, their sweet smiles as bright as the lights framing them.

About to tell them it was time to go, Marina felt Read's touch on her arm.

She turned to see him relax against the doorjamb, but it was his expression that made her breath catch in her throat. There was such a tenderness in him, a look of such hope for his children in his eyes. It made them radiate with warmth and softened a mouth that was usually hard, sensual but hard. In that instant, if she wasn't already in love with him, she would have fallen all over again.

"Have they been working like that all afternoon?" he asked, keeping his voice low.

"Yes. Why?"

"At home they usually bicker and tease."

Now that he'd mentioned it, she realized he was right; she hadn't heard them fuss or criticize each other the way she, too, had heard on occasion. It had her breaking into a smile. "It's the magic of the season taking its effect."

"It's some kind of magic," he murmured, shifting his gaze to her.

His move brought them close, so close Marina could see herself reflected in his eyes. His breath was warm on her face. Once they used to stand like this and talk of the wonder of finding each other, and what they could do to arrange for an hour more, thirty minutes, ten. It was heaven to experience it again.

"Lovely Marina." He lifted a hand to touch her cheek. "You're turning me inside out."

"Why fight this, *us*, so, Read?"

"Because somebody has to keep their head and be reasonable." As Marina began to protest, he moved his thumb to her lips. "No. Not tonight. Let's not argue. I want them to have this moment," he said, nodding to the children.

Just then Molly spotted him and shrieked. "Daddy! Look at what we did!"

Read caressed Marina's cheek one more time before he crossed the room, stooping just in time to catch his youngest as she launched herself at him. He lifted her high before settling her on his hip and hid a momentary rush of emotion by burying his face in the sweet warmth of her soft neck. She giggled and squirmed, but she smelled wonderfully of the bubble bath she'd used last night and something with butterscotch that Marina must have given them here. The brief communion helped take the edge off the loneliness that ate at him.

"What's the matter, Daddy? You feel sad."

Kids. They had better instincts than any adult he'd ever met. "Oh, yeah? So how does sad feel?"

"You're holding tighter and you stand real straight."

Despite the feeling that a boulder had lodged in his throat, Read growled, "The better to nibble some chicken neck, my dear," and playfully pretended he was doing just that. After listening to her squeal in delight for several seconds, he finally relented to her squirming attempts to break free and set her down. "Well, haven't you two been busy? When I first walked in here, I wasn't sure you weren't a couple of Santa's elves who'd lost their way from the North Pole."

"I priced all of those," Ricky said, pointing to his achievement.

"Bet your hand's sore." Proud, Read squeezed his son's shoulder. "I hardly recognize the room from the other day. You're all doing very well. You guys tired?"

"Not a bit. We could work another couple hours if Marina wants us to."

His son shot her a hopeful look. Read understood the adoration as much as the plea to intercede on their behalf.

"If I had my license and a car, I would happily drive you home to save your father another trip," she assured him, with an apologetic smile. "But as it is, I'm afraid you're out of luck."

At that moment the tape deck shut off and Read was left with Marina's words echoing in his ears. Guilt lashed at him sharply, and for good reason. He knew he'd pushed her into letting him give her lessons in the first place, and then used that opportunity to punish her for old hurts.

"How are the lessons going?" he asked with proper chagrin.

Marina grimaced. "I haven't had the time to call an agency and set up an appointment for lessons. Between taking care of things here, I've also started interviewing for sales help."

He knew she was busy, but doubted that was the only reason. "Are you sure you aren't feeling a little beat-up, too, because of what I did?" He supposed he deserved her stunned look. Hadn't he asked her only moments ago not to bring up anything that would upset the children?

Her gaze strayed to the children before flicking to him with confusion. "Read?"

"Let's try again."

"But you said... I don't want to—"

"I know. This is on my shoulders. Let's try again."

She didn't look convinced and seemed hesitant about his motives. Worse, his children were looking from him to her with increasing confusion and worry; they picked up on tension faster than he gave them credit. They deserved a break, too.

"You need that driver's license and I want to help. Consider it a thank-you for what you're doing for Ricky and Molly."

At least the children seemed to like that idea. Probably because they thought it meant even more access to Marina.

"You could teach both of us at the same time, Dad," Ricky declared. "It's not that long before I get my permit."

Read smiled. "Don't rush things."

"Well, if Ricky goes, can I?" Molly asked, tugging at her father's jeans.

Read touched his fingers to his lips to quiet them both. "Grown-ups talking here, okay?" Then he raised his gaze to Marina.

"I won't pretend to understand what you're doing," she told him at last.

He nodded. "I don't blame you, but I know this is fair and right. We could practice an hour right after I drop off the kids at school and day care."

"Aw," Ricky said, crossing his arms and pouting. "We want to come along."

"Not this time," Read replied, not taking his eyes off Marina. "Do we have a deal?"

"All right. I'll see you tomorrow."

* * *

The next morning he pulled into the driveway and found Marina waiting for him. She looked as if she had doubts about her decision—lovely and sophisticated in a royal blue jacket over a slim black dress, but hardly enthusiastic. Read gave her a wry smile as he climbed out and held the door for her to slip behind the steering wheel.

"Don't look as if you expect me to turn into a snarling bear if you blink."

"Give me a few minutes to convince myself that this isn't a figment of my imagination and I won't."

He nodded as he shut her door, then circled to the passenger side. "I deserve that," he said, settling beside her. Trying not to pay too much attention to her legs, he secured his seat belt. "You don't need to remind me that I've failed at finding a happy medium when it comes to dealing with people."

"I think we have that in common."

"You? You've always gotten along with everyone." Except him—and he was beginning to realize that was as much his fault as anyone's.

"As long as I kept to my role as obedient daughter and subordinate female."

That jarred him out of his silent brooding. "Who do you want to be?"

"I'm still trying to find out, that's the point. It's only been a few months since my father died and I declared my independence, Read. Don't you realize I'm like a freshly hatched egg?" Marina sighed as she explored the shape and strength of the steering wheel. "In Russia—at least the Russia my father knew and based all his judgments on—girls were raised by the seen-and-not-heard philosophy. I know that sounds archaic to you, but being demure was a refinement.''

''But that's not who you are?'' he asked, realizing they'd never talked in this depth before.

''I'm polite, not a doormat. I believe in manners.''

''At the cost of speaking your mind?''

''Once…yes. When I was a minor. My father was legally responsible for me, and I lived in his house. Now I still believe respect is important, but for different reasons. And I accept that I'm responsible for my actions.''

''I haven't shown you the good manners I should.''

''No. But I understand why.''

Read wondered if she really did. He shook his head. ''Gwenn would never have tolerated what you have. As sunny-natured as she was, she didn't suffer fools for long.''

''Read, you've succeeded in thoroughly confusing me. What am I supposed to say to something like that? What do you want from me?''

He wished he knew. Maybe he couldn't believe that they had a chance in hell of being happy due to their vastly different backgrounds and situations, but at least he could accept that what was in the past, his anger, was over and done with. It was time to move on.

His children adored her. She had already begun to enrich their lives, and it was clear they could only become better people for knowing her. He couldn't see himself remarrying in the foreseeable future, not even in the distant future—who was ever going to replace Marina in his heart? But maybe she could give to his children what he couldn't possibly accept for himself.

"Could we find some medium for friendship?" he asked with a humility he'd never thought himself capable of. "Let's get you that driver's license. You need it. I want to help you get it. Can that be enough?"

To his surprise Marina didn't reply, and instead started the truck's engine. Read watched her as she made a neat U-turn in her driveway, wondering what she was thinking. Several emotions played over her face, not the least of which were annoyance and disappointment. But he noticed determination, too—and something very feminine that worried him.

When she'd followed his brief direction and turned left out of the driveway, away from town, all without saying a word, he couldn't resist muttering, "Okay, out with it. What's going on in that busy little head of yours?"

"Tell me about Gwenn."

"Marina…"

"You said you wanted to be friends. Friends talk about their lives, their families."

Read groaned. She was going to do exactly what he wanted to avoid—talk about the past. But he'd set himself up for this by that stupid friendship line. "What do you want to know?"

"Where did you two meet?"

"She'd come into the store with her mother. Her mother knew my mother."

"Ah."

"What's that supposed to mean?"

"Mothers. They're a powerful ingredient in relationships. I often wonder if things would have turned out differently if my mother had been alive. So your mother and her mother arranged for you two to date?''

''This is America,'' he reminded her, though a little too defensively. ''We asked each other.''

''You came to this conclusion at the same time?'' She shot him a quick look. ''You mean like it was for us?''

''Eyes on the road.'' Read folded his arms across his chest, not at all pleased with this subject. He had no intention of telling her it wasn't anything *close* to the way it was with them, the lightning bolt of recognition and attraction. The almost feverish need to be in some physical contact, as if their very survival depended on it. The yearning and sweet, sweet passion... ''She asked me out,'' he snapped, reluctantly admitting what would only complicate things. ''I turned her down at first. It was only a few weeks after you left. I was blue and didn't want to see anyone, okay? My mother overheard and bullied me into giving her a call. The rest is history. Satisfied?''

''*Zamichahtil'na.*''

''And what's that supposed to mean?''

''Quite remarkable. Out of that you had a son a short time later.''

''A year, Marina. A little more than—and you were gone. *Gone.*''

She nodded slowly as if accepting that, but Read noticed she blinked a great deal, too. He prayed she wouldn't cry. He prayed harder that he wouldn't have to remind her about the stop sign ahead.

Braking, she came to a complete halt, looked both

ways and then proceeded with caution. "I was in Paris the spring your son was born," she said quietly. "They say it's the city for lovers, but I stayed in my hotel room refusing to even look out a window, because the man I wanted as my lover, the only one I wanted, was an ocean away."

His teeth should have pulverized from the way he clenched them together. Maybe he deserved this, but he wished she would stop. "What good does it do to hurt me, Marina?" he asked when he couldn't keep quiet any longer. "I'm sorry, too. But life turned out differently."

"Yes. Very." She drove to where he'd directed her last time, to practice parallel parking. "I wonder if I could build up the courage to ask someone out."

He had to look out his passenger window so she wouldn't see him close his eyes against the pain. "You won't know until you try," he said without inflection. "Only one thing—don't practice on me."

He was grateful that he'd mentioned only an hour-long session, because after that Marina didn't speak to him again except to ask for directions, and the silence soon gave him a skull-numbing headache.

He couldn't complain about her driving, though. She proved to be the model of decorum—she kept to the speed limit, didn't miss a stop sign and *did* avoid every curb. Even so, on top of the headache, by the time they pulled into her driveway, his nerves were all wearing combat boots and stomping grapes in his stomach. Because she'd been suddenly turned into the robot she'd been for her father for so many years.

"That was good. Excellent," he told her, his palms

damp. "You won't need more than a few hours before you'll be ready for your test." He envied her her shell of composure, but at the same time it troubled him. What would it take to shatter it?

"Thank you." She ran her hands around the steering wheel. "It felt good. Do you think I might be ready to buy myself a car for Christmas?"

Of all the things she might have brought up, that was the least expected. And it wasn't *by* Christmas, but *for*. Did that mean something deeper or was he reading too much into it? God, he couldn't bear it if he discovered she'd never received a Christmas gift in her life. But she had so many gorgeous clothes. On the other hand it would be just like her old man to dress her like a doll but never offer gifts from his heart. One thing he'd learned early on—Dmitri Davidov *owned* his daughter; he *loved* his music.

His throat raw, he managed, "If that's what you want. If you like, I could go with you to a dealership."

She nodded. "Yes, please. I wouldn't know if I was being taken advantage of or not. I promise I'll take up as little of your time as possible."

She was killing him. As she fumbled with her seat belt, Read brushed her hands away, released the catch and pulled her across the seat. When he saw the startled question in her eyes, he murmured, "Forgive me," and closed his lips over hers.

A soft sound rose from her throat. Was it protest or pleasure? He couldn't tell, and more important he didn't let it matter. He was too desperate to experience the pleasure of her, her warmth and vulnerability to him. And yet when she trembled at his deepening, searching kiss, then wrapped her arms around his neck, he could have wept with relief and gratitude for her acceptance. They had lost something precious. This was a blossom on the grave of what had been.

Murmuring her name, he coaxed her lips wider, drank in her soft sigh as greedily as he did the nectar from her lips and tongue. He showed her with his the dance he craved to experience with his entire body, but never would.

The kiss went on and on, bringing his body to a fever pitch and testing his endurance. By the time he forced himself to set her back on her side of the truck, Read had to swallow several times against an ache that was not only pounding in his throat but throughout his body.

"I should apologize for that," he said gruffly. "But it would be a lie."

"All right."

And to his amazement she smiled. It was a shaky smile, but he found it unsettling, nonetheless.

"What do you mean, 'all right'?"

"You're a fraud, Read," she murmured. "You care."

He considered trying to deny it, then felt even more shame. "It won't change what I've already told you," he muttered instead.

"If you say so." But she was all but beaming as she opened her door. "Do I get another lesson tomorrow?"

Not quite comfortable with the way she'd worded that, Read knew that even if he'd wanted to, he couldn't back down now. "Same time, unless you have something else planned?"

"I have an interview at eleven, but that won't interfere. I'll be ready."

Maybe *she* would be, Read thought as he watched her hurry up the front walkway, but he wasn't so sure about himself. Her words echoed in his mind, as sweetly taunting as the memory of her mouth, pliant and giving under his.

"Man, you are asking for trouble," he muttered as he made a three-point turn. "What's *wrong* with you?"

Chapter Seven

A cold front blew in earlier than expected the next day, bringing rain, and Read phoned to cancel Marina's driving lesson. She would have been depressed, except that he promised the children could still come later, guaranteeing that she would see him. What's more, despite his cautious tone, there had been a gruff tenderness in his voice.

Feeling more optimistic than she had in days, she held the interviews with prospective sales clerks as scheduled. The two ladies turned out to be such a delightful pair—sisters-in-law from a nearby retirement community, who were searching for something to do more than earning extra money—that Marina hired them on the spot. After convincing them to stay, she served tea and the baklava pastries from the recipe a Yugoslavian violinist's wife had shared with her on their last trip to the country before its political unrest.

The day passed so quickly, Mrs. Cotton and Mrs.

Merriweather had barely left before Read dropped off the children. Expecting him to bring up the rear, she was stunned to see him turn and drive out.

"Why didn't your father come in?" she asked the two youngsters as they discarded their wet coats.

"He says he has a bunch of work he has to get back to," Molly offered, giving her a woman-to-woman look.

"I see." No doubt it was true, but Marina wondered how much of his avoidance was a reaction to what had happened yesterday. "Well, he's going to miss our fun, isn't he? Come on, today you two get to practice for St. Lucia's Day."

"What's that?" Ricky asked, rushing ahead to push open the swinging kitchen door.

"It's a Scandinavian holiday on the thirteenth of December when children get to do something special for their parents. Remember when I told you that the best part of holidays is the sharing? Well, this gives children a chance to contribute. And it has a lovely ceremony. I'll show you while we're getting our snack."

She told them about a guest house she stayed in once where Swedish children dressed in white for the event, and girls wore red sashes. "The eldest girl wore a wreath in her hair lit with candles, and after all the children prepared breakfast such as sweet cakes called *saffransbrod* and spicy cookies like *pepparkakor,* she led the processional delivering the treats and fresh coffee to their parents who were still sleeping."

"Oh, breakfast in bed!" Ricky said, automatically retrieving the milk for their hot chocolate. "Why didn't you say so? We do that for Dad on Father's Day."

"But we don't get to dress up," Molly said, fingering a curl. She corkscrewed it around and around her finger. "Since I'm the only girl, would I get to wear the wreath, Marina?"

"That's the way I understand the tradition works."

The children decided they might like to try that celebration. But they agreed that their father would get pretty nervous if they tried to make anything more complicated than tuna on white bread or cereal. After promising to bake them something here and letting them hide it at their house, she led them to the parlor to start work on the Advent wreath displays.

They'd been working for only a short while when, as predicted, the rain changed to sleet. Ricky noticed first and his shout drew them all to the window.

"First snow! First snow!" Molly cried, climbing up on the windowsill.

"Maybe," Ricky murmured, looking hopefully at the sky.

Marina hoped it would change, too. She didn't want to think of Read or anyone else having to travel in this dangerous slush. She almost didn't believe her eyes when his truck turned into the driveway.

Squeals of pleasure from Molly and groans from Ricky had her shushing them and urging them to the front door. As Molly ran before them, Marina put her arm around Read's son.

"What's the matter?"

"He'll make us go home. We're only getting started."

"You can't blame him for worrying."

"But we're fine here. Why can't we stay?"

Marina had an idea, but she couldn't share it. Not in good conscience. "Let's wait and see what he has to say."

He slipped and glided down the sidewalk, winning giggles from his daughter. Molly hugged him the instant he finished stomping his boots on the doormat and crossed the threshold.

"Daddy! Did you come to work, too?"

"A little. I also came to deliver something. Here."

With a sheepish smile, he brought out a wooden sign from under the cover of his jacket. Marina stared at the elegant lettering that read *The Christmas House*.

"It has two sides, so you can hang it out front where traffic will be able to read it as they come from either direction. Of course, I haven't put a finish on it yet. I thought you might want to choose that yourself. And I'll put hooks down at the bottom here, too, in case you want me to make another sign listing your hours." As if suddenly realizing he was rambling, he clammed up.

"Read...I don't believe it," she murmured, reaching out to touch the scrolled borders. "This is fantastic! And perfect!"

Although the children raved, too, he didn't seem convinced. "It's probably not as fancy as what you had in mind...."

"Read, with all the many things there are to remember, the thought of a sign had slipped my mind completely." She took the gift from him and held it up, laughing with delight. "It's the most marvelous thing. My business has a sign!"

"It's much better than the one you made for yourself,'' Ricky assured him. ''That one only says No Credit—Beware of Dog.''

Marina looked from father to son. ''I didn't know you have a dog.''

''We have Raspberry,'' Ricky said, a doleful expression lengthening his face.

Read cleared his throat. ''Raspberry sleeps a great deal. Raspberry ran away from his previous home because he wanted owners who understand he likes to sleep. Not go for walks. Not play ball or fetch the stick. Sleep.''

''I see.'' Marina fought back a grin. ''No wonder I didn't see him when I came to your house that day. And how did he get his name?''

Both Read and Ricky pointed to Molly. But it was Ricky who said, ''When we got him, almost every name we suggested she couldn't pronounce without sputtering raspberries, so Dad said we might as well call him that.''

Clearly delighted with her part in history, Molly hugged her father's leg and giggled. ''Go hang up the sign, Daddy!''

''It's not ready to be hung yet, sweetie.'' He tapped the tip of her nose and winked at her before wrapping his arm around Ricky's shoulders. ''So how are things going here?''

''Fine. We're *really* busy working on Advent wreaths,'' Molly declared, before her brother could answer. ''You know what they are, Daddy?''

''No, sugarplum, I guess I don't.''

''It's a wreath like the one we had on the door last Christmas, only it starts out plain, you know? We're going to have small ones and bigger ones, so people can choose, and then we'll have all these different things to decorate them. You have to have candles, too. Then you hang the wreath from the light or put it on the table, and you sing and eat.''

''My,'' Read murmured, using one ringlet to tickle her upturned face. ''You're just a bubbly brook of information these days.''

''Marina told us the story,'' Ricky interjected quickly. ''Advent starts right after Thanksgiving and you light one candle each Sunday until Christmas. Can we do that, Dad?''

When Marina felt Read's gaze shift to her, she offered an apologetic smile. ''They tend to remember the festivities more than the meaning behind them, but they *are* learning, Read.''

Before he could respond, Molly tugged at his hand. ''Marina said we could choose a wreath each and decorate it the way we wanted as part of our pay.''

''Uh-oh,'' he drawled. ''There go the profits.''

''What you really should know,'' Marina told him, enjoying this gentle side of him, ''is that some people spread the celebration over thirty-seven days.''

''Thirty-seven candles? Does this thing come with a fire extinguisher?''

She laughed. ''Don't worry, I'm recommending they keep it down to the four, and they're promising they'll only light their candles when you're there with them.''

''Thanks. I think.''

Marina turned to the youngsters. ''Why don't you get back to unwrapping those Advent animals and set them on the middle shelf, okay?''

As they charged to the parlor, Read lifted an eyebrow. "Animals?"

"It's the Peaceable Kingdom theme." She hugged her sign to her heart. "Why don't you take off your jacket and join us?"

"Well, I was going to go back to the house. I need to work a bit more. I just thought with this weather..."

"Oh, Read. The children did want to stay a bit longer." She let her eyes telegraph even more appeal.

"It wouldn't be smart to attempt this trip again." He tilted his head toward the outdoors. "I have a feeling in a few hours that mess is going to freeze solid."

"I understand. You're right, of course."

"That also means we'll have to skip another practice tomorrow."

"I've waited this long for my license, what's a few more days?"

It was a rhetorical question that she didn't expect to get answered, but it also left her with nothing more to say. Since he didn't add anything, either, they spent the next several seconds listening to the children chattering away in the next room.

"Uh..." Read abruptly indicated the sign.

"Oh, yes." Marina handed it over. "Read, thank you again. It's wonderful."

"Did you think of a shade you'd prefer?"

"Why don't you choose? You've done such a beautiful job already."

He seemed pleased with that. But a moment later Marina realized he wasn't going to comment on his ideas—or anything else. Silence stretched again.

"Would you like a cup of tea? Coffee?"

He simply shook his head, his gaze resting longer and longer on her.

Marina felt a warm rush sweeping through her. "Read?"

"Hmm?"

"You're staring."

"Sorry."

He turned away and started for the door. About to reach for the knob, Marina followed and touched his arm. He froze and stared at her hand.

"I'll get a shovel from the truck and clean your sidewalk."

"I like when you stare."

"The problem is that I want to do more than stare."

"Then why don't you?"

"The children..."

"Are busy enjoying themselves. They're not paying any attention to us." When he didn't make any comment to that, she wondered what she needed to do to reach him. On impulse she stepped between him and the door and studied him sadly. "Was Gwenn experienced when you met her? Is that it? Don't I have her...appeal?"

"Marina."

"You're right. That was unfair. But she was beautiful, yes?"

"She looked like Molly," he admitted, growing more tense. "She had a kind of perkiness, a cuteness that was..."

"Sexy."

"*Yes,*" he whispered angrily. Dropping the sign on

the chair beside them, he boxed her against the door with his hands. "But you're wrong if you think there's only one kind of sexiness."

"What other kind is there?"

"You know damned well. The kind you have, romantic…exotic…untapped…sweet."

"How can sweet be sexy?"

"You tell me," he said, and fastened his mouth to hers.

His self-control had lasted barely more than twenty-four hours, but Read ignored his sense of failure for the sheer pleasure of touching Marina again. God, she was kitten soft, and the cuddly pink tunic she was wearing only made her softer. How could one innocent woman bring him to this state? He was at the point where he ached through and through when he wasn't near her, and he ached even worse when she tempted him like this.

Her lips parted for him and he greedily took what she offered, then asked for more. No matter what happened, he would never kiss another woman without wanting Marina. The truth seared through his body like the hottest of flames. When she slipped her hands into his jacket to wrap her arms around his waist, he groaned softly and used his body to pin her more firmly against the door. If he could imprint himself on her…if he could, she would be his forever.

And yet he knew restraint. She was so willowy and slight compared to him. He could keep her his prisoner with one hand, but behind his closed lids he imagined using both to explore her. Once he had, and he could still remember every exquisite curve and hollow of her body. She'd trembled with excitement and nervousness, but heaven love her, she'd trusted him so. She did now, but he knew she shouldn't.

Aware he was fast approaching an edge, he dragged his mouth from hers and buried his face in her hair. "You have to let me get out of here. Now."

"I know." But she didn't remove her hands from around his waist.

"The kids will be getting curious if you don't get back in there soon."

"You're right."

She did begin to let go then, but slowly, and first she eased her hands along his sides and ran them over the expanse of his chest. He knew she could feel the tautness of his muscles and the heavy pounding of his heart, caused as much by her provocative touch as the expression of admiration and wonder on her face. She was playing with fire, and even if she didn't know what power she had over him, he did.

With a hoarse whisper of her name, he took hold of her hand and lifted it to his mouth for a brief but passionate kiss, then he swept her up and out of his way. "Go to the children."

"Stay with us. I'll make us dinner."

"I can't. As soon as I get the walk cleared, we need to leave."

"I won't ask you to kiss me again."

That was rich. "You didn't ask me this time."

"You just didn't hear the words…just as you can't take what's already yours."

Heaven help him. "No, sweetheart. That's where your logic hits a giant pothole. I may have been the first guy to make your heart race, but I'm the last one you should set your dreams on. Too many miles on this model, and a heavy mortgage for good measure. I'm nowhere near your class, and the sooner you accept that fact, the less painful this is going to be for all of us.''

Her shattered expression was nearly his undoing.

''Look,'' he said urgently, reaching out to grasp her by her upper arms. ''I don't want to hurt you. I don't want to hurt any of us. So help me. *Help me, Marina.*''

Marina didn't regret having been so honest with Read. She was in love with him. It was inconceivable to try to fall out of love with him. Nor did she agree with his theory about why they couldn't be happy together. But witnessing his anguish touched her deeply.

After a night and a day of soul-searching, while the heavens bestowed them with several inches of sleet followed by a few more of snow, she came to the conclusion that she did not want to become someone he worked to avoid. In addition, she couldn't bear thinking of being denied visits with Molly and Ricky. If she was such a torment to him, then she would help him as he'd asked. Maybe if she became this untouchable creature he thought he could deal with, he would see what an impossible lie that was, too.

At least with the improving weather, her life became busier, and that gave her little time to feel sorry for herself. More stock arrived every day, and she had additional meetings with Mrs. Cotton and Mrs. Merriweather to get them familiar with the house and inventory. Then there were permits to obtain, an accountant to hire and advertising to arrange.

Between the weather and those business commitments she only managed to work in one driving lesson during the week, during which time Read never mentioned their last meeting. It was the only dark cloud and moment of awkwardness in what otherwise proved a satisfying day. Less thrilling was that she saw the children only twice because of her conflicting schedule and Molly catching a cold.

Before she knew it, Thanksgiving loomed. She notified Read that she was ready to open at least the front rooms of The Christmas House—if he could finish putting in the front checkout counter in time. He promised it would be ready Friday. On Thursday evening, excited about seeing Read again, as well as getting this last hurdle to opening out of the way, a disturbing cloud from the past shadowed her anticipation when she received a call from Vladimir Lesko, her father's manager.

On Thursday morning when the doorbell rang, she hurried downstairs, hoping it was Read, hoping they would have a chance to talk. Instead she opened the door to find a tall, elegantly dressed man with unapologetically flirtatious gray eyes and a lazy smile.

"Marina Davidov? I'm Jeremy Cameron. Did Vlad call you about me?"

He had indeed. That was why she'd reached into her closet for one of her more businesslike, mature outfits. She'd chosen a sophisticated cranberry suit with a slim skirt and little gold chains linking the matching gold buttons that she hoped gave her an image of confidence as well as independence.

"Yes." She stepped back to allow the blond-haired man into her home. "But I wish he had given me a bit more warning that you were coming. As you can see, I'm not exactly prepared for guests."

"My fault," he assured her suavely, as he took her hand. "When I get these brainstorms there's no point in trying to stop me. I'm afraid I was quite prepared to do whatever necessary to wear down old Vladimir if he resisted my offer."

"If you knew him better, you would realize that Vladimir never passes up any opportunity to promote my father." Marina withdrew her hand.

"Aha…so you're the hard sell."

"Guilty."

"Delightful," he murmured, his smile deepening.

She indicated his chesterfield overcoat. "If I can take that for you, we'll go to my father's workroom. I'm expecting a—the carpenter to finish in here momentarily, and it's bound to get noisy."

"You're redecorating?" he asked, doing an intensive survey as he put down his leather portfolio and slipped out of his coat.

"In a manner of speaking. I'm turning the house into a specialty shop."

"Charming. I've always admired the entrepreneurial spirit. No doubt your father would be filled with pride."

"He would hate the idea," Marina told him, more than a little amused at his ingratiating demeanor even as she admired his finely tailored gray suit. "So does Vladimir, since I broke the news to him yesterday. He believes I should become a living memorial to my father—and that brings us to why you're here. Why don't we go this way…'' She folded his coat over her arm and led the way to her father's room.

She'd prepared tea, being told that Jeremy Cameron was part English and had finished his education at Oxford. While he took a casual tour of the room, admiring awards, photographs and various memorabilia her father had enjoyed surrounding himself with, Marina prepared his tea English-style for him and Russian-style for herself. She also discreetly studied him, and found him attractive in a polished, cultured way, exactly the type of man her father would approve of, which automatically made her wary.

"This is marvelous," the man said, finally joining her on the couch that faced the piano. "This would be a perfect backdrop for what I had planned."

Over the next few minutes, Marina listened to a summary of Jeremy Cameron's proposal. It was exactly what Vladimir had aspired for her during the reception after her father's funeral. She had turned him down—far too politely, considering his timing—and her instinctive reaction now was one of rejection, as well. Not because it wasn't a good idea; her father deserved the immortalization he would undoubtedly receive. But she had given twenty-eight years to Dmitri Davidov. Who would condemn her for taking some time for herself?

About to tell him so, she heard a sound at the front door. Certain it was Read, Marina excused herself and went to let him in.

Although his eyes reflected deep admiration at her appearance, Read had obviously noticed the strange car in the driveway. It had a pronounced effect on his demeanor.

"I'm coming at a bad time?"

"No, it's all right. Someone is here from Boston. My father's longtime friend and manager, who I've asked to continue overseeing Father's estate, sanctioned an idea and Mr. Cameron is here to explain it to me."

His gaze was sweeping and concerned. "You don't look happy."

"It's just that I thought I wouldn't have to face this so soon."

"Would you like me to come back later?"

"Read, I need that counter." She was about to say more, but she heard footsteps behind her. At the same time she saw Read tense.

She turned. "Jeremy."

"Excuse me if I'm intruding," her guest drawled, glancing from her to Read, "but is there some way I can be of assistance?"

His inspection of Read's work clothes clearly stated that he'd already categorized and rejected him as having limited importance. Marina had only one reaction to that.

"Jeremy Cameron, this is Read Archer, a longtime friend and the craftsman behind the displays for The Christmas House."

To his credit Jeremy recognized his gaffe and recovered quickly. "Archer. Nice work."

Read shook his hand, but offered no response until he refocused on her. "I think I should come back in an hour or two."

"Really, that won't be necessary." She did not want him to leave her. Maybe handling Jeremy Cameron was her responsibility, but just knowing Read was in the house gave her strength.

For a moment he looked as if he might argue. "All right. I'll be as quiet as I can," he said almost gently. "But if I do intrude, you tell me, promise?"

"If she doesn't, I will," Jeremy said, easing his arm around Marina and directing her toward the study. "She has such a soft voice, I'll resent missing a word of what she says."

Marina could only mouth a thank-you at Read before Jeremy closed the doors behind them. However, if she was a little miffed at the television producer's take-charge attitude, she couldn't deny that he was skillful at making amends and could be lethally charming.

"Before you scold me," he told her, holding up a hand and placing another over his heart, "let me state in my defense that I have an irrepressible tendency to protect the fairer sex—I know it's an outdated exercise, but there you are. In fact I have an elderly aunt back in Boston who insists I should be frozen until such time that science figures out what to do with a dinosaur like me. Would you believe she whacks me with her cane whenever I pass through her threshold, simply because she knows I'll upset her with my chivalrous nature before leaving? By the way, she collects fine crystal, and you have an angel in the foyer that I'd love to purchase for her."

It was one of the most expensive items she carried, and she had a feeling he'd recognized that on sight. "Your aunt sounds like a wise lady who's not only fortunate to have a clever nephew, but a generous one."

His grin reflected unabashed pleasure. "I have a feeling she would love you. Maybe I can woo her out here to meet you sometime?"

As they took their seats again, Marina found she was able to smile again. "Please do."

"It's a promise. Now, as for my proposal..."

They talked for almost an hour more. Jeremy gave her several reports and outlines to back up what he had in mind, and a tentative schedule. Marina grabbed on to it as her chief excuse.

"This would be in direct conflict with my own plans for the grand opening of my business," she said, scanning the three-page filming schedule.

"Nothing there is written in stone," he assured her. "We'll work it out. What's not negotiable about the contract is *you*. We must have you or it won't be the same. Look at you—you have the face, the presence. The man's passion speaks through those exotic eyes of yours."

He was very gallant when she walked him out, his portfolio and gift-wrapped angel under one arm. He bowed over her hand and raised it to his lips. "Take your time if you must," he murmured, "but understand that I won't take no for an answer."

When she shut the door, Marina turned to see Read straightening from behind the new counter. She could tell by his set expression that he hadn't missed anything.

"The counter's going to be wonderful."

"Thanks. How did the meeting go?"

She lifted one shoulder. "He wants me to host a

lecture series on my father's work for public and cable television.''

Read whistled softly. ''Congratulations.''

''I turned him down.''

''Good grief—why?''

She couldn't believe he needed to ask her that. ''Haven't you been listening to a word I've been saying all this time? I want to have my life. Mine. Why does everyone constantly insist that I be fed intravenously through his life! *Yes,* I knew him best. But no one is interested in knowing that dark, paranoid and selfish person. They want to hear about the genius who filled concert halls for over forty years and made grown men weep and generations dream with his music. They want to believe that art is a gift without consequence.''

''I didn't mean to upset you.''

''No one means to upset me, Read. But no one is interested in hearing about reality, either.'' Marina laughed, feeling a little paranoid herself. ''All I'm trying to do is find my own worth for being on this planet. I loved my father better than anyone ever will because I understood him. He was brilliant. A blazing star the likes of which we'll never see again. But before I help his public give him his proper place in history, I need to secure my own.''

Chapter Eight

Marina eyed the tray of gingerbread men on the front counter and wondered if she shouldn't carry them back to the kitchen and wrap them as Mrs. Merriweather had first suggested before they dried out much more. It was the Monday before Thanksgiving and nearly noon, but so far they'd only had a trickle of customers.

"Don't worry, dear," Mrs. Merriweather cooed, looking up from where she sat behind the counter knitting in a rattan rocking chair. "Everyone's thinking about turkey dinner and trying to remember to put cranberry sauce on their shopping lists. This town is no different than anywhere else. We don't get serious about Christmas shopping until the last of the turkey has been baked in a casserole."

"I'm sure you're right." But it was difficult not to feel a little anxious. She'd already spent as much as she'd budgeted for this month on advertising, and between renovations and inventory, she'd dipped into her savings as much as she thought wise. If she'd been wrong about the store, she would still be fine. But she didn't want to live off her inheritance, she wanted to add to it for the sake of the family she hoped someday to have.

"Look, here comes a car now," Mrs. Merriweather cried, pointing to the window. "Oh, and another is following it in. See? I told you. Once folks see that open sign out there, curiosity will do the rest."

Marina was glad she'd told Read to go with that simple word and not spend time on hours that might change later. "I'll go and turn on the music again, and tell Mrs. Cotton she can switch on the display of motion Santas," Marina replied, already heading for the living room.

For the next few hours, Marina was kept busy greeting customers, supervising her new employees and answering numerous questions. It was true that there seemed to be a great number of curious people wandering in who were as interested at having a peek at her as they were at browsing through her displays. And while a number of them picked up an ornament or small figurine, no one purchased any of the more elaborate and costly items. It wasn't long before the cash register reflected that.

Her only bright moment came later in the afternoon when Read arrived with Molly and Ricky. "What a nice surprise," she said, bending to catch Molly as she ran into her arms. "I didn't expect to see you today."

"Did you think we wouldn't be here to help cele-brate your first day?" Read asked, as she accepted a hug from Ricky, too. "Besides, I told the kids they could each pick an ornament for the tree. We always put it up right after Thanksgiving dinner."

The mention of the holiday was another reminder of disappointment. She'd thought, hoped, that by now Read would have invited her to join them, but so far he hadn't said a word. The sisters-in-law, Cotton and Merriweather, did, and there'd been a few other more formal invitations, including one from Jeremy Cameron, but as thoughtful and generous as they were, they simply didn't hold the weight an invitation from Read would have.

"That's a wonderful tradition," she told the children, hanging their coats on the employee coatrack. "Well, to start off right, have one of our gingerbread men. Then you need to go in the back and see the newest ornaments from Czechoslovakia. They're mouth-blown and painted. Molly, there's a pink heart I think you'd love, and Ricky, wait until you see the pecan-shell reindeer a local craftsman made. Come on, I'll show you."

They stayed for an hour—long enough to cheer her up and help the rest of the day pass. She didn't even let herself get depressed when they left and Read still hadn't mentioned more about Thanksgiving.

On Tuesday she used the quiet time to straighten up, do the bookkeeping and bake a bit. She also took courage from Mrs. Cotton and Mrs. Merriweather and relented when they suggested they break early for them to take her for her driver's-license test. They reasoned that if they could negotiate a vehicle through Berryfield at their age, surely she had learned enough to do the same.

Less than an hour later she was a legal Massachusetts driver.

To celebrate, the ladies treated her to apple cider and a fresh-baked chocolate-chip cookie at a fresh produce market, and by the time she returned home she was surprisingly exhausted. She turned in early, confident that tomorrow just had to be even better.

By Wednesday Read was tired of being noble, and at least for the moment he talked himself out of every good reason to keep his kids separated from Marina. Even though he'd only begun the armoire for the foyer and had nothing to deliver, he surprised his son and daughter by picking them up after Ricky got out of school and driving over to her place. He had no idea of the excuse he would use to explain their presence, but no sooner did they arrive than it no longer mattered.

They found Marina in the parlor with a tall, elegantly dressed woman who stood stiffly glaring at her. On the floor was a shattered figurine, the largest crystal angel in her beloved display.

"Well, it's your own fault for not having them out of reach of children," the woman declared. "My Teddy never does anything like this at home."

There was a decided strain around Marina's small mouth. "Excuse me, but he intentionally knocked the item off the table. This was after you told him that it was time to leave."

"I see, so now you're not only calling me a liar, but you're suggesting I should pay for that?" The woman grabbed her freckle-faced child's hand. "I certainly will not. Come, Teddy. I have no intention of spending another minute in this—place. There's nothing here Mommy could possibly want.''

Despite having come in at the end of the scene, Read was so angry he wanted to shake the woman until her scrawny neck snapped. Beside him Molly bit back a child's moan of despair at the shattered figurine. Belatedly he recognized it as one she'd spoken of so often, ever since Marina had first unpacked it. He drew her against him and patted her back consolingly, protecting her from the glare he bestowed on the rude woman as she stalked past him out the door with her smiling son in tow.

However, it was Marina who had the bulk of his attention. When the door slammed behind the woman, Marina clapped a hand to her mouth, but there was no holding back the tears that flooded her eyes and poured down her cheeks. Knowing she wouldn't want the children to see her so upset, he touched Ricky's shoulder. ''You know what? I think some of those glass icicles would look pretty good on our tree. Why don't you take your sister and go see if there are any left.''

Exchanging wise glances with him, Ricky nodded. ''Sure, Dad. C'mon, Molly. Dad needs to talk to Marina.''

''But I want to hug her. She's crying.''

''Later. Come *on*.''

Without waiting for his son to coax his daughter from the room, Read went to Marina, carefully led her away from the glass and drew her into his arms. It was exactly what he would have avoided doing under different circumstances, but he knew it was precisely what she needed at the moment.

"How can people be so mean?" she asked, her voice raw from repressed sobs.

"It's an acquired talent."

"D-don't make jokes, Read. He broke the most b-beautiful angel."

He hugged her more closely to him. "I know, sweetheart. I'm sorry. I was only trying to— Heck. I suppose there isn't any way to soften the hurt when something like this happens. I'm just sorry it had to happen to you."

"It had been such a nice day so far. Quiet, so I told Mrs. Cotton and Mrs. Merriweather to wait until Friday's grand opening before they came back in, but there had been a few customers who made nice purchases. Then this horrible woman and her monstrous little boy—"

"Try to put it behind you." Repeatedly, soothingly, he stroked her back. "Maybe this is the worst of it and it will be nothing but good moments from here on out."

"No, it's a sign. I was a fool to think I could make this work. Naive."

"You forgot to add incompetent."

"And stupid."

"Stop it!" Read took firm hold of her upper arms and gave her just enough of a shake to force her to meet his gaze. "You've worked too hard to let one arrogant woman ruin your dreams for you."

"But look—" awkward though it was, she gestured to indicate the empty place "—no one's coming, and that shattered glass represents more than I made all day!"

"It'll get better. Give people time. Grand opening

isn't until Friday, and that's the official start of the Christmas shopping season, as all the experts say.''

''What difference does that make if no one comes *here?*''

He could have laughed at the nonsensical approach to her logic, but knowing how badly that would hurt, he sighed instead, and before he could stop himself let impulse reign. ''You know what you need? You need to get your mind off all this. Have Thanksgiving dinner with us.''

She'd barely had a chance to react when he heard a commotion behind him.

''Yeah!''

Before he could see how his kids had managed to eavesdrop on their conversation, they were attacked from behind. Read was forced to release Marina just in time to keep himself from being impaled by icicles.

''Whoa.'' He eased those from their grasp, leaving them free to swarm her with hugs and pleas.

''It would be so much *fun*,'' Molly gushed, her sweet face adoring. ''You could come early and feed the birdies, and meet Raspberry while he's 'wake and everything!''

''Dad never remembers how to make the stuffing,'' Ricky added. ''You could help him do that.''

''Tell her 'bout the dishes,'' Molly whispered loudly to her brother.

''Oh, yeah—and on Thanksgiving we use paper plates so nobody has to miss the game because of dirty dishes.''

Read covered his face with his hands and rubbed hard. He figured that if he did it long enough he would wake up and this would all be a bad dream.

Who needed the threat of famine and crime when he had his own personal town criers to spread good news around?

"Don't forget about setting the table," he added drolly.

Molly brightened. "Oh, yeah—you could help do that, too!"

With a deep sigh, Read took his chances and faced Marina. "Now you know the way *not* to coax someone to come to dinner."

"It's a wonderful way," Marina insisted.

And it seemed she meant it, because she was laughing instead of crying, and brushing the remaining tears from her cheeks. Read thought that after witnessing Ricky and Molly being born, she was the prettiest sight he'd ever seen.

"Well, what can I do beforehand?" she asked everyone. "What can I bring?"

Read quickly placed a hand over both of his kids' mouths. "Just yourself."

"Then you'll have to take those icicles as my gift to you."

He tried to protest, but she remained adamant, asking only what time she should be there. "Uh…" He had no idea what to tell her. He'd never invited anyone to dinner before. "Tell us what's a good time for you and we'll pick you up."

"Well…oh! I almost forgot—I have the most marvelous news to tell you! I have my license!"

She quickly told them her story about her two senior-citizen employees taking her out yesterday on a lark. At first Read felt a bit cheated, but the more she told them, the brighter her mood became, and the happier he felt for her.

"Then you need a car!"

Whoever said it first, they all ended up agreeing. Read convinced Marina that whether she settled on something that day or not, she needed to take the first step.

Whether it was the situation with her last customer or a growing confidence in herself, Marina surprised him by agreeing. She even insisted on leaving the mess to clean up later, and snatched up her coat and purse to follow them out the door.

"Now, the best way to do this is not to get your hopes up, and don't feel pressured," he told her as they pulled into the dealer's lot a few minutes later.

But to his amazement, an hour later they were exiting the dealership and she was the proud new owner of a sleek white sedan. To Read it looked part space rocket, part shark, and the kind of vehicle that when wrapped around her would turn heads at every stoplight.

"Are you sure about the color?" he'd asked, when she'd first picked it. He thought of all the reasons it would be problematic, like how it got dirty fast and how it would be darned near invisible in fog.

"White is a good color for starting over," she'd replied with a slow, firm nod of her head.

He stopped worrying about her after that. He even managed to keep a smile on his face when she wrote out a check to the salesman for the whole amount of the car. Never mind that he would have asked for what terms the finance company was offering these days, and if they accepted mouthy but healthy kids as collateral.

"Sorry you can't get it until Friday," he told her now, as he started back to her house.

"Me, too." Her laugh reflected her pleasure, and that she was feeling a little dazed about the whole thing, too. "I never thought I'd be anxious for a holiday to be over before, but—" She cast him a mortified look. "Er, I didn't mean that the way it sounded."

He waved away her apology. "Believe me, I know what you're feeling. My first car was a lemon with four previous owners, and I had to work a second job for six months to afford it. But I didn't sleep the night before my father took me to town to pick it up."

"Can we go with you when you get your new car, Marina?" Molly asked from the back seat.

"I hope so—and I hope your father will let you two ride with me back to the house." But while they cheered in the back seat, Marina focused on him. "I was thinking, though…about tomorrow? Don't worry about picking me up. You'll have enough to do as it is. Just tell me what time you usually eat, and I'll be there."

Read wanted to argue about that, but she would hear none of it. Her timing was good, too. It was difficult to manage a shrug when he was turning into her driveway. "Well, as for time…"

"We usually eat before one game and after another," Ricky offered when he hesitated.

"Game?"

Ricky gasped. "The football games. All the best

College Bowl games are on Thanksgiving Day! Haven't you ever watched them before?''

After releasing her seat belt, Marina turned in her seat and shook her head, giving him a very apologetic look. ''Sorry. Is that a terrible confession?''

''Yes!'' the boy replied.

''No!'' Molly declared, leaning forward. ''You come early, though, and you can watch the parade with me.''

Read liked that idea. ''Come when you can, okay?''

The next morning he started glancing out the window for her at eight, willing her to come. By nine he was wondering if he shouldn't call to see if she was all right, if she'd had a change of heart, and would she please let him come pick her up, so he would stop trying to give himself whiplash every time a car drove down the street. At ten a taxi pulled up before the house and the only reason no one heard his great sigh of relief was that the kids were screaming with excitement and charging for the front door.

She looked like a snow queen…a princess at the least. Beneath the coat Ricky helped her remove, she wore a winter white knit dress with seed pearls stitched around a yoke collar and teardrop earrings with matching pearls. There were even seed pearls in the combs holding back the heavy fall of her hair from her face. She looked regal and pure—and she left him with the strongest compulsion to go wash his hands again.

Molly was enraptured, too, and took her immediate

attention by asking to touch the combs. After hanging up the coat, Ricky used the time to tuck in his dress shirt, which Read had been asking him to do for the past two-plus hours. But Marina didn't let them hover and flatter for too long. She'd brought gifts.

"I'm glad you like the combs, Molly, because these are for you," she said, reaching into a shopping sack and bringing out a prettily wrapped tissue-paper parcel. "And the earrings were mine when I was a little girl. You have to promise me that you'll save them for special occasions like this.

"And Ricky," she continued, "this shirt is for you. The man at the store assured me that most of the boys who come in there are fans of this team."

Both of the children were thrilled with their presents, and Read was pleased that he didn't have to remind them to say thank you. As they hugged her, however, he did gently scold. "You weren't supposed to do that, and when did you have time?"

"I was so excited after you dropped me off last night, I phoned for a cab and went out again." She reached into her bag once more and came out with a bottle of wine and another of brandy. "I wasn't quite sure what to bring you."

Read didn't know much about wine, but he whistled at the brandy. "Now you're making me feel terrible. I didn't—"

"You've invited me to be a part of you and your family's celebration," she interjected, bringing out the last item—a bouquet of white flowers. "That means the world to me. Now show me where I can find something to put these in or we're going to have a very wilted centerpiece."

They all directed her to the kitchen. While Read hunted for something that bore a close similarity to a vase, Molly and Ricky tried to introduce Marina to Raspberry. The overweight rusty brown mongrel lay on his side under the kitchen table, and no amount of coaxing succeeded in getting him to do more than lifting one eyelid and giving a single lazy thump of his tail.

"Why do I get the feeling he's waiting for lunch?" Marina asked, joining Read at the sink.

He turned on the tap to start filling the tallest drinking glass he could find. Behind him the kids kept picking up Raspberry's paw and trying to coax him into shaking hands.

"Because you're right. That mutt only knows two locations to move to—under there, and the back stoop where he can soak up the most sunshine. The only time he barks is when someone gets too close to his food bowl." But as he set the glass on the counter so she could begin work, he couldn't resist adding, "You do look lovely." He knew he'd been the one to insist they not get personal again, but denying the words would have been a greater offense.

For an instant her eyes grew soft. Yearning. Then she forced a big smile and theatrically bowed. "Thank you, kind sir. I'm not too early, am I?"

No, he was ten years too late in realizing that dreams were only dreams, and that he'd been damned lucky to have her for the short time he did. He would be even more lucky if she would let him be her friend. He would be the best friend she could ever have. "Nope," he said, matching her smile. "You're perfect."

Once the flowers were arranged and on the table,
Read insisted that Marina join the kids in the living
room. "Just enjoy yourself for a while. I'll be with
you as soon as I finish stuffing the bird and shoving
it in the oven."

Preparations were a little more complicated than
that—there were the potatoes to be peeled and
cooked, and the vegetables to be readied for warm-
ing—but he'd done most everything else earlier, so
he didn't take too long. When he joined them, his
kids were entertaining Marina with stories about holidays past.

"My first parade I ate all snacks and got stuffed,"
Molly informed her, as if reciting a scholastic
achievement. "I got such a tummy ache, I didn't even
eat no dinner for a week, right, Daddy?"

"Well…not quite, but you were one sick puppy."

Marina lifted his daughter onto her lap and adjusted
the child's combs. "I'm so sorry to hear that."

"That's okay. Daddy didn't know nuthin' 'bout
cooking that year. I 'member 'cause Mommy went to
heaven only a little before."

Marina bit her lip and hugged the child. "I'm very
glad to be sharing this Thanksgiving with you, Molly.
All of you."

By the time they sat down to dinner, Read had
already realized that just like in the old days—and
contrary to her privileged background—Marina remained an incredibly easy person to please. She'd
complimented his cheese spread and crackers he set
out for the parade, raved over the show and sighed
over the table Ricky and Molly had already set when
he called them to dinner—paper plates and all.

He couldn't have asked the afternoon to pass more gently. Although he couldn't convince Marina to let the kids do their part in clearing the table, or in drying and putting away the rest of the dishes, he couldn't deny he quickly grew spoiled with having her company. She made any chore easier.

"I have a confession to make," she told him, when the children snuck off to watch TV again.

"Go ahead."

"This is easier than I thought it would be."

"Helping out in the kitchen?" he asked, pretending not to understand. He needed a moment to fight down a rush of panic in case she asked for too much again.

"No, being in your home. The home you shared with another woman."

"I'm glad. After I invited you, I wondered."

"I feel sad for her—and you and the children, of course."

"We're doing all right."

"I can see that. That's why I think I'm getting used to the idea about…well, about what you said."

He stopped scouring dried potato from the bottom of a pot. "You mean about us?"

"Yes. This is better." She tilted her head and her expression became thoughtful. "I think I began realizing that after Jeremy called me the other day."

The mention of Cameron delivered a blow to Read's midsection. He turned aside his head to cough into his sleeve. "Excuse me. Tickle in my throat. I always get it this time of year because of the dry furnace heat." The explanation sounded foolish, even to him. "Um…so Cameron called?"

"To talk to me again about the documentary. At

first I was going to say no, but a few days before Dean Wyman telephoned from the college where my father sometimes lectured. He told me how much the film would mean to their music department.''

"So you changed your mind?"

"Not completely. But I did tell Jeremy that he could bring his aunt out to visit me next week. I know he'll use the opportunity to try to press his point.'' She was silent for a moment. "Do you think he's a man who knows his business?"

He damn well knew *what* he wanted, Read thought darkly, and that was Marina herself. A blind man could have seen it that day the young Brahmin had visited her. But he couldn't tell her that without exposing his true feelings.

"Who am I to judge?" he asked her instead. "He looks to be. He talks it." He shrugged, wishing she wouldn't ask him to give an opinion.

"I value your opinion, Read."

So much for staying out of it. "I'm flattered. I just don't… Sure. I have a hunch he's a powerhouse."

"Dad?"

Read glanced over his shoulder to see Ricky standing in the kitchen doorway. He looked cute with his new T-shirt over his other shirt, but there was something about the militant thrust of his son's chin that had him frowning. "What's up, bud?"

"Could I talk to you for a second?"

He lifted an eyebrow, curious about what his son wanted that couldn't be said in front of Marina. "Okay." Wiping his hands, he excused himself and followed the boy into the hallway. That didn't appear good enough for Ricky, who signaled his sister being within earshot and beckoned him into the washroom. Read really got amused when the kid even shut the door. "Hey, this must be serious."

"It is." His son folded his arms across his skinny chest and glared at him. "Just what are you doing, Dad?"

"About what?"

"With Marina? I heard what you said. Why are you throwing her at that guy?"

He couldn't have been more stunned if his son had told him he'd enlisted in the Marines. "I didn't—"

"You *did*. I came to the kitchen to ask when we were gonna have dessert and I heard you. You're going to let her go out with some other guy, and then she'll get married, and we'll never see her again."

Even as Ricky spoke, the possibility was a picture in Read's mind, but he blocked it out to try to soothe his son's pain. It was obvious the kid wasn't pleased with the prospect. "First of all, you really shouldn't have been eavesdropping. Second, Marina has every right to see whomever she wants."

"She's *ours*. We found her. You never would have. And we were the ones to tell her about you. *We* want her for our mom!"

Read didn't know why he was surprised. Hadn't they done everything but have announcements printed? "It's not that simple, Rick. Marina is... different than us."

His son frowned. "No, she isn't. She's been doing all the stuff we have. She likes us."

"She loves you. And she cares for me. But...she's special." Heaven help him, he couldn't have this conversation. "Why don't we talk about this later when we have more time?"

"Now, Dad."

"Young man, we have a guest."

"Fine. I'll ask her to marry us, myself."

"No, that's one thing you can't do." Drawing in a deep breath, Read crouched to be at eye level with the boy. "Marina's had a different life than most people, Ricky."

"I don't care if she's not American. Molly doesn't, either."

"She is American. She's what they call a first-generation American. That's like the children of the early settlers. And in many ways Marina's life has been similar to those children's in that it's been difficult at times."

Ricky frowned. "Dad, she's rich. She can buy anything she wants whenever she wants."

"Money isn't at the heart of this, and I hope you haven't tried to befriend Marina because you think you might get something out of it."

"Not me!"

"Good." The truth was that finances were an important part of this issue, but his boy didn't need to know his old man had just too much pride for his own good. "What is important here is life. Living. Being overprotected to the point that when you gain your independence, you're vulnerable to making mistakes like settling for something that isn't really right for you."

"But, Dad—"

"No, son. Trust me about this. I care for Marina too much to let her jump into something she knows nothing about. A marriage is a challenge all by itself without adding children into the scenario. Marina deserves—''

The unintended inference behind his words struck him too late.

Ricky paled and took a step back. ''It's because of us?''

''I didn't mean—''

''You did! And you're a liar!''

Chapter Nine

Marina not only heard Ricky's shout, she saw him burst from the room and storm upstairs. A moment later Read brought up the rear. By then she'd reached the kitchen doorway.

"What on earth? Read, what he said..."

"It's my fault."

Molly rushed to them. "What's wrong, Daddy?"

"Nothing serious, sugarplum. Go back and watch your TV."

"But Daddy, I saw Ricky crying when he ran upstairs."

"He'll be fine. I'll go talk to him in a minute."

He should have picked her up. He should have kissed her and soothed her. Instead he raked his hands through his hair and retreated into the kitchen.

Marina took one look at Molly's puckering lower lip and stooped to embrace her. "Baby, it's all right. Why don't you do as your daddy said, and I'll find out what's wrong."

With a mournful backward look, the child went. Marina stood by and watched until she saw that Molly had settled on the couch again.

In the kitchen, she discovered that Read had resumed washing the pots and silverware from their dinner. She wasted no time getting to the point.

"I thought you were going up?"

"In a while."

But his tone suggested otherwise, and there was a stubborn set to his chin that she'd seen duplicated on Ricky's. The message she was getting from all that was too disturbing. And what she hadn't told him yet was that she had heard something.

"He called you a liar. That's hardly nothing."

Read looked shocked at first, then dismayed. But too soon his resolute mask fell back in place. "He misunderstood things, that's all."

"What things?"

Read dropped the scrubber and gripped the edge of the sink. "You, all right? You and me and...us."

"Oh, no." She glanced toward the stairs. Poor child. She could only imagine what Ricky had hoped—the same as she had. But she wanted to be certain. "If what you discussed includes me, don't I have a right to know the details?"

"No. Let him have a few minutes to get used to the idea."

"What idea?"

He exhaled sharply, the sound sheer exasperation. "That things don't always work out the way you want them to. Look, Marina, he and Molly are beginning to think that you were going to take Gwenn's place. Don't tell me that after that day in town when they were taking that video, and asking all those questions, you didn't realize what they had in mind? If not then, then all these weeks when they've been begging and wheedling to spend every spare minute they could with you?"

She did on one level. On another she'd just wanted to give two beautiful children the loving attention all children deserved.

"Read, this is terrible."

"Tell me about it."

"Let me go up to him?"

"No. Things are bad enough as it is."

"That's an awful thing to say."

Suddenly Read spun around and whispered harshly, "It isn't when he already thinks that you're like some treasure he found on a bank of a creek or in some forgotten pocket. Finders keepers. Bingo, he and Molly have a new mommy." He closed his eyes and shook his head. "I just wish I didn't say what I did. The words came out all wrong, and now he thinks..."

"What does he think?"

"I tried to explain to him that not everyone thinks a ready-made family is an asset."

"You didn't. How could you? Today of all days!" She flung down the towel she'd just reached for and started toward the stairs.

Read grabbed her. "Where are you going?"

"To talk to him."

"Absolutely not. Haven't you been listening? You'll only make things worse."

"You've told him something that would be difficult for an older child to comprehend, Read. He's only a little boy!"

But Read's grip grew tighter instead of easing. "He's *my* son, Marina."

He might as well have told her to stay out of his business. The message went straight to her heart and lodged there like a dagger. Staring at the resolute message in his eyes, she shook her head.

"Shame on you, Read. I was childish to try to use Jeremy Cameron to see if I could make you jealous. But I see what you're doing, and that's worse than wrong. It's despicable. If you want to keep a barrier between us, that's your right. But shame on you for using your children as insurance, in case your resolve weakens."

She wrenched her arm free and walked out of the room. She went straight to Molly and hugged her. "Angel? I have to go."

The child immediately wrapped her arms around her neck. "No! Why?"

"I'll explain sometime soon. In the meantime I want you to promise me something. Be sure to tell Ricky that I love him. I love you both, and I want you to know that you're still welcome at The Christmas House anytime, okay?"

"I don't understand. Marina? Marina!"

"Bye, baby."

"Marina!"

She jerked at the sharp sound of her name and saw Mrs. Cotton scowling at her. "Excuse me?"

"What do you mean you won't try these?"

Had she said that? She glanced at the checkbook she'd been working on balancing, then at Mrs. Cotton's round concerned face. In the old woman's hand was a tin box of fudge. "Oh. I didn't realize…"

"I made it myself last night after I got home. I thought about how your treats have caught on so well, and how you've been staying up all hours making them, and the least I could do is give you one evening's rest."

"Why, Mrs. Cotton, how very kind of you." Unfortunately, she had no appetite whatsoever, hadn't had one in days. But not wanting to risk hurting the old woman's feelings twice, she forced herself to take one of the bite-size pieces of candy rolled in crushed nuts. "They look delicious."

"Emily's going to make her famous no-bake fruitcake tonight, so don't you worry about trying to make anything tonight, either. You're getting so pale lately, we're beginning to worry about you."

"I'm fine, really."

"Em just has to stop at the market on the way home and pick up the candied cherries," Mrs. Cotton continued as if she hadn't spoken. "She called me last night and said it was the only thing she lacked. Asked did I think it was all right if she left them out. I told her, 'Em, have you been seasoning everything with rum again? A fruitcake isn't a fruitcake without the cherries!'"

"My goodness, neither of you should be going through so much trouble. This is my responsibility." Touched but concerned, because both Mrs. Cotton and Mrs. Merriweather were already working nearly a full schedule since business had picked up, Marina studied the small woman with the same intensity her employee had examined her. "In fact, I've been going over the books and I can see we can afford to hire another clerk.''

''That's wonderful, dear. The more the merrier. But don't worry about us. Why, we're having a ball. Never felt better in our lives.''

''Well, I want to make sure you stay that way. Do you know of anyone in your neighborhood who's looking for some extra cash for the holidays?''

''You tell me how many bodies you need, sweetie, and I'll bring them along. Our senior-citizen Bible study group is loaded with able souls bored with being put out to pasture. Winnie Livingston strikes me as your best bet, though. She raised nine children and has seventeen grandkids as of this past July Fourth, and she knows how to deal with people of all ages.''

''She sounds perfect. Do you have her phone number by any chance?''

''You just leave that to me.'' Mrs. Cotton set her tin of candies on the front counter. ''She lives across the street from me and I've been telling her all about you. She can't wait to start.''

Bemused, and glad to have her mind off her personal worries for a change, Marina shook her head. ''You're quite something, Mrs. Cotton.''

''I know it, dear. But I look at it this way, why waste time being something you're not? I fought being myself for forty years trying to please Mr. Cotton, only there was no pleasing that old stick-in-the-mud. Now that I'm on my own, I'm letting it all hang out.''

As the silver-haired elf waved and went off to help prepare the rooms for another day's business, Marina looked from her to the candy she had yet to taste, and realized she had more in common with Ruby Cotton than she could have guessed. She was asserting herself, too—only she was being far less successful at it than her new friend.

At least business was no longer a worry. Read had been right about things turning around after Thanksgiving. At least she could give him that.

In the week since she'd seen him, they hadn't spoken. Before her was an updated statement of what he'd built for her, and what he still owed her, along with an estimated schedule as to when he would complete each piece. It had come in the mail yesterday. Considering the way they'd parted on Thanksgiving, she wondered if he would freight her furniture over, as well.

A familiar ache resumed its dull wrenching in her chest. She'd had a brief reprieve from it for a few weeks, but now it was back with a vengeance. She was fast coming to the conclusion that love was meant for a stronger sort than she.

The mere thought of what he was doing to them, all of them, hurt. She missed Molly and Ricky terribly, and she doubted they understood. She lived for the day she would have a chance to explain that it changed nothing about how she felt about them.

About to go back to finishing writing a check, she was interrupted by the ringing telephone. "The Christmas House," she said into the receiver.

"Marina? Jeremy here. How's Berryfield's most beautiful businesswoman?"

"When I see her, I'll ask on your behalf."

He murmured a low, sexy growl. "Wrong answer, dear heart. What's the matter, having a bad day?"

There was an understatement. "I'm fine. How are you, Jeremy?"

"Couldn't be better now that it's only twenty-four hours before I see you again."

Marina's gaze flew to her calendar and she sighed inwardly. She liked Jeremy, his intellect and unapologetic flirtatiousness, but she'd developed a sixth sense for recognizing people intent on control, and wanted as little to do with them as possible. "To be perfectly honest, Jeremy, I'd forgotten. We've been very busy since Friday, and I've completely lost track of time."

He was silent for a moment, as if weighing his options. "What are you telling me? Do you need to postpone tomorrow, or are we talking about a full withdrawal?"

Lord, the man worked fast. One meeting and he made them sound as if they had the most complicated of relationships. Didn't he realize that two in one lifetime was more than enough for anyone?

"Well, let me change my approach," he said, almost cheerfully. "Has Vladimir called you lately?"

She had to think fast to keep up with him. "Um…no, not in a few days." Not since lecturing her for not agreeing on the spot to accept Jeremy's proposal.

"Then let me be the first to congratulate you. He's arranged for your father's complete works to be released as a special CD collection."

"That's…wonderful."

"It's perfect. Between the collection and the documentary, we'll have the media covered for weeks."

"Jeremy—"

"Do you know who I want to direct the film? Marge Thornton, who you'll remember just won an Oscar this year. She's an old school chum, who also happens to be a great devotee of your father's work."

"Jeremy…"

"You're letting yourself get frightened off by the idea that we're talking about a probing interview. That's not what I want from you. You open the program—in front of his piano, perhaps. I see you in a formal gown…black velvet, cut off those glorious shoulders. The camera will adore you. You say a few words, something anecdotal, and that's it as far as on-camera work for you until midway through. It's all off-screen narration until then. Halfway through you're back on-screen in another part of the house, or out in that garden beyond his room—or maybe we'll get the college to let us use one of his old classrooms—then more narration. At the end you stand on the stage at Lincoln Center and look out at the empty seats that he used to fill. You say something about his voice being silent now, but his music will live on forever. Walk offstage and credits roll. Like it?"

She felt as if the room was closing in on her. "You have been giving this considerable thought."

"Believe it. I'm not one to let opportunity slip by me, lovely lady."

"You will this time, Jeremy," she said politely but firmly. "I'm afraid I'm exhausted. I'm already short-handed here, and if I have any free time, I'm going to need it to meet with craftsmen to continue stocking my store. I'm sorry, but that's the way I feel."

"You won't get rid of me that easily. I see star potential written all over you, Marina, and I don't intend to let you slip through my fingers."

But she didn't want to be a star. She wanted her own life…and to live it with the man she loved.

As if she'd conjured him from her imagination, she looked up and saw him standing in the foyer doorway.

He must have come in the back way, and either Mrs. Cotton or Mrs. Merriweather must have let him in. He looked as uncomfortable as she suddenly felt.

"Marina? Did you go to sleep on me?"

"No, I'm here, Jeremy. But someone's come in and I do need to go."

She should have taken pleasure in seeing what saying Jeremy's name did to Read's already grim face. But as she said goodbye and hung up, all she felt was another wrenching inside, and an awareness that her hands had begun to tremble.

"I'm sorry for interrupting."

"You didn't."

He looked wonderful. Tired, and as if he wasn't eating any more than she was, but wonderful anyway. He was wearing work clothes, his rugged denim jacket and dusty, rumpled jeans, and he carried the smell of man and wood about him. It reminded her of how safe and feminine a woman felt in his solid and strong arms.

"I only wanted you to know I've brought the unit for the stuffed animals. But maybe you better look at it before I leave. It wasn't what we'd discussed and you may not want it."

She didn't want to deal with this. She didn't think she had the strength left to pretend she was fine and that life was going on beautifully without him. But what he'd said could mean trouble, and if he had changed the design so that the piece didn't suit her needs, she would rather he take it back now, instead of having to call him back for yet another visit.

Pushing away from her desk and the piece of fudge that remained untouched, she rose and quickly buried her hands deep into the pockets of her lacy white apron which, like Mrs. Cotton and Mrs. Merriweather, she wore over a Victorian white blouse and floor-length Christmas-plaid skirt.

She felt Read's gaze like a physical touch as she approached him. Even though she kept her eyes lowered, her awareness of him brought a familiar heat to her cheeks. She hated her body's betrayal, just as she resented his power over her.

"You look like you stepped out of a fairy tale."

His words were a rough whisper and sounded reluctant. Out of necessity she ignored them. "Where did you put it?"

After a slight hesitation, he replied more heavily, "In the living room. But I think when you have the dining room ready, you might want to put it in there. It needs more room."

Without further comment, she headed for that room. Both Mrs. Cotton and Mrs. Merriweather were there, turning on lights and adjusting displays. When they spotted her and Read, Mrs. Cotton clasped her hands under her double chin.

"Oh, Mr. Archer, the train is the sweetest thing. The children are going to want to climb right in with these cute bears."

Only as she rounded the couch did Marina see what she was talking about. Instead of the oversize treasure chest she'd asked for, he'd created a three-car over-size wooden train. The engine was a bright red with a wonderful brass bell behind its steam stack, the next car a bright yellow, the next a vibrant blue and the last a shiny green.

"And look how the wheels turn," Mrs. Merri-weather said, bending at the waist like a giraffe reach-ing for water to roll it back and forth. "Have you ever seen anything like it?"

Marina didn't have the heart to deny Read the praise he deserved. "It's delightful, Read. Thank you."

"Are you sure? I didn't think about the kids want-ing to pull it through the whole house."

"But a house doesn't become a real home unless it's lived in," she said, remembering having heard that somewhere. She managed a wry smile for him. "However, I have a hunch we're going to get a con-siderable number of requests from parents for the train itself. You may find yourself with more work than you can handle."

"That's all right. I've discovered I have a great deal of free time these days."

Between the sad timbre in his voice and the com-pelling power of his gaze, Marina knew he'd in-trigued both of her keen-sensed employees. To escape their sharp inspection, she gestured for him to follow her to her desk.

"In that case, if you'll give me the statement, I'll write you a check right away."

"I didn't mean that in the way you took it, and I

didn't bring a bill. Molly knocked over a can of varnish on my entire box of invoice forms. I have to go reorder more after I leave here.''

The mention of the child created a lump in her throat. She had to ask, ''How is she?''

''Let me put it this way, the spill is the most recent so-called mishap to get my attention. In the meantime Ricky stays in his room and refuses to come out except to go to school.''

Was he blaming her? Did he think she could help? ''I don't know what to say.''

''There's nothing to say. I brought this on myself. I'll figure out how to undo the pain I caused. I did want to…''

Marina looked up when his words drifted into silence. ''Yes?''

''I wish things could have been different.''

Weary with words, she shook her head. ''I'm not sure whether it's a matter of not believing you, or that I just don't care anymore. In any case, go home, Read. We don't have anything left to say to one another.''

Read spent the rest of the day in a state of deep depression, followed by another and another. A week slipped into two, then three.

There came a point when if he hadn't had his kids to worry about, he knew he would have been at the nearest bar drowning his sorrow in beer. But he was a single parent, and reckless behavior was a luxury he couldn't afford.

Instead he spent hour after hour, day after day in his workshop, more often than not staring at the floor.

The gray slab of concrete aptly resembled the state of his life. Most of the time, he sat and replayed Marina's last words in his mind.

She hated him. Somehow his good intentions had gone awry, causing his efforts to fall into a black hole with them. All he could think of now was that she despised him for what he'd become. What he'd tried to do meant nothing.

He was sitting one afternoon when Ricky and Molly arrived from school. He saw his son go straight into the house without even looking at him. His daughter approached more readily, but still without the zest and love she used to.

When she was close he opened his arms. "Can I have a hug? I need one bad today."

She complied and even added a noisy kiss on his cheek. It made him feel very lucky.

"I made a picture of Marina and us at The Christmas House today." She held it up before his face, almost hitting him in the nose with it. "Can we go see her so I can take it to her?"

Read groaned inwardly. "No, honey. I'm afraid not."

"But Ricky could walk me if you said yes, Daddy. He's good with streets."

"It's not the streets, sugarplum."

"Then what now? It's been forever."

"Marina needs some time alone. She's very busy and—"

"Did you make her mad at you again?"

Ricky's sharp voice jarred him. He looked over Molly's curls to see him standing in the doorway, his hands balled into small fists.

"Son, I know I said that in a few weeks maybe you could go see her, but things haven't worked out the way I'd—"

"You did! You ruined things. You always do!"

He charged from the shop despite Read's call for him to stop. Beside him Molly stood by and eyed him sadly. After several seconds he met her sorrowful gaze and sighed.

"Go ahead. Say it."

"What are we gonna do, Daddy?"

"Go on. We've been fine up until now, haven't we?"

She shook her head. "We don't do so good alone, Daddy. Ricky has to take care of me, 'cause you're out here all the time, and there's nobody to take care of you. We're getting confused, Daddy."

Her soft voice brought the accuracy of their situation home with razor-blade precision, and Read hugged her more tightly. "Ah, sweetheart, I'm sorry. I'm sorry."

"I just don't understand. Why can't Marina be our new mommy?" she whimpered.

"It's grown-up stuff, baby. Hard to explain."

"Did I do something wrong?"

He groaned and pressed a kiss to her smooth forehead. "No, sweet. You're as close to perfect as a little girl can get."

"Well, if Ricky didn't do nothin' and I didn't do nothin', what happened? I love Marina, Daddy. Is she going away like Mommy went away?"

Read swallowed hard. "*No.* Don't even think that. Marina would never leave you, baby. As for the rest, you have to give me some time to think, because I just don't have the answers right now.''

"Well, who do you talk to to get answers, Daddy? Santa?''

"Yeah, maybe Santa, babe.''

Chapter Ten

"Marina, dear, why don't you come with us?" Mrs. Cotton said, lifting her crocheted shawl over her silver bun. She eyed her broodingly as she wound the long, fringe-tipped wrap around and around her neck. "I hate to think of you here all by yourself on Christmas Eve."

"I won't be alone all night," Marina replied, securing a missed button on the old woman's coat. "I'm planning to go to a candlelight service later, remember?"

"Alone," Mrs. Merriweather grumbled, tugging on knit gloves.

"Go to our church with us," Winnie Livingston pleaded, looking up from the boots she was tugging on. In the chandelier light the newest employee's hair matched her pastel blue glasses. "It's mostly half-deaf old people so we sing off-key, but we do have a good time."

Marina managed to smile, grateful for the invitation as she was for the friendship they'd established these past weeks. But she shook her head. "I love that you asked me, ladies. And I promise I will think about your invitation for dinner tomorrow. But I think I'm going to turn in rather early tonight."

It had been a busy day. Because it was Christmas Eve, shoppers had begun arriving the moment Marina had opened the front gates, and the last one had left only minutes ago. It was now almost five o'clock, and Marina was sending her employees home before it grew completely dark outside.

The Christmas House had achieved a successful first season of business. Three months ago this had only been a dream, and they had far to go and a number of adjustments and improvements to make. But despite that, and the heartache, she had good memories, and she wanted to be alone for a while to reflect on them as she went from room to room, turning off all the lights.

Hugging each woman again, she gently coaxed them out the front door and waved as they drove away. When she saw them turning out onto the street, she sighed, retreated into the house and locked the door behind her.

Her mouth ached from smiling; her head ached from making small talk all day. She appreciated the group's concern for her, but she was glad they'd gone home to prepare for their neighborhood gathering that would follow church services. She wanted to be alone, to be with her own thoughts, dwelling on those closest to her heart.

It had been weeks since she'd seen Read. Days

since she'd seen the children. On impulse she'd done some shopping and had gifts for them up in her room, but now she didn't know what to do about them. She'd hoped that they would have come over this week, and she would have presented them then, but that hadn't happened. If she called the house, would Read let her drop them off on her way to the church service? Maybe they weren't even home....

For the next two hours she went through the house double-checking that all the doors were secured, the tree lights and display lights off. Satisfied, she went upstairs and took a long, luxurious bath using some of the contents from the freesia-scented gift basket her new friends had given her. Afterward, she used the matching scented lotion on her skin.

The dress she'd set out on her bed was a black velvet sheath, not nearly as daring as the one Jeremy had described. It reminded her that she had another message from him on her desk. He'd called almost every two or three days to press her about the film, or ask her out—or both. Once the holidays were over and she had more time on her hands, she would have to address the matter of the film. She was beginning to believe she was ready to help give the world its image of the Dmitri Davidov it wanted without feeling like an impostor herself.

As for Jeremy...well, Jeremy was Jeremy. Few women would find him easy to deal with, and she knew now that fate hadn't meant her to try, beyond friendship. She and his aunt had finally met, and she chuckled softly as she remembered how they'd come to that same conclusion. Maybe together they would find the right woman for him. "Get our revenge," Bianca Cameron had whispered conspiratorially.

She stepped into the simple but elegant dress and slipped into the black high heels with the pretty faux-pearl buttons on the front. Adding a choker pearl necklace and studs in her ears, she picked up her evening coat, leather gloves and bag and hesitated by the gifts. There were too many to carry in one trip, not with her coat and things. She started downstairs, thinking she would put her things at the door, get a large shopping bag and—

At the bottom she thought she saw a flash of lights in the window, but she decided it had been a car on the street. About to head for the kitchen where she kept the bags, she backtracked to the phone. She would call Read. Nervous or not, the sooner she got the call behind her, the sooner she would know what to do with the presents.

But when she rang the house there was no answer. She couldn't imagine where they could be, unless he'd treated them to dinner out before taking them to church, too. Her heart beat faster at the thought of seeing them there. Read. Would he acknowledge her or pretend he didn't see her?

A sound caught her attention. It was singing. Carolers?

Delighted, she went to the door and smiled at the sight of two flashlights illuminating two youthful faces, rosy pink from the cold and snow flurries that had begun to fall again. But when she recognized the faces, she gasped.

"On the fourth day of Christmas," they began to sing.

Ricky and Molly? She couldn't believe it! As she pressed her hand to her mouth to hold back a tremulous laugh, they sang through the chorus.

But where was Read? Surely the little imps hadn't slipped from the house on their own without telling him?

As she searched the well-lit grounds for a sign of him, the children began, "On the fifth day of Christmas, my true love gave to me—"

The rest of the stanza was lost to her because at that moment she saw a movement. Barely fighting back a small scream, she saw Read step out from the corner...Read holding out a blue box to her. A small velvet box.

Marina stared at it, then at him. "I don't understand," she murmured, as he stopped before her.

"It's not five of them like the song says," he began, carefully opening the lid. "But if it's the right kind, maybe one ring will do?"

The wall fixture lights picked up the brilliant flash of the solitaire diamond in the slender-banded engagement ring. Its brightness burned Marina's eyes and raised goose bumps all over her body.

"Oh, Read."

"Marina Davidov, will you do me the honor of becoming my wife?"

Could this be a dream? As if in slow motion, she saw him take the ring out of the box and slip the box into his pocket.

"Don't tell me you've forgotten your line?" he asked, as the children rushed closer to watch.

"No, I— I don't understand." But she automatically held out her left hand as he reached for it. Nor did she pull back when he slipped on the ring. "You said—"

"Forget what I said. The truth is that I've stopped running away from the truth. I can't bear the thought of living the rest of my life without you. I love you, Marina. Be my wife?" he asked a little less confidently.

Did he think she needed to think about it? "Yes, yes, yes!" she cried, wrapping her arms around his neck.

He kissed her then, while the children shouted into the night and hopped up and down in glee. Within seconds, she forgot the night's cold bite. If she had Read's strong arms around her, she knew she would never feel cold again.

Suddenly she felt another, smaller pair of arms wrap around her waist. Then another around her hips.

"Hey, don't forget me!" Ricky demanded.

"Me, too!" Molly said, rubbing her cheek against Marina's soft skirt.

Laughing, Read released Marina, and she drew the children inside. While Read shut the door, she hugged and kissed Ricky, and then picked up Molly to do it all again.

"Why do I have a feeling that you two were in on this?" she asked them.

"Because we were!" Ricky announced proudly.

Molly nodded, her curls bouncing every which way. "Yeah, we kept the secret good, huh?"

"Wonderfully good," Marina said, her heart brimming with love. "So good you two merry matchmakers deserve a surprise. Why don't you run upstairs to my room. I think Santa left some early presents for you on my bed.''

No sooner did she set Molly down than the two of them charged for the stairs, whooping with excitement. Marina watched them for a few seconds before feeling Read take hold of her arms.

''How long do you think we have before they charge down here again?'' he murmured, drawing her close.

Once again her body tingled with pleasure. ''A few minutes. I was very bad and spoiled them a great deal.''

''Remind me to punish you later, but right now that sounds like heaven. Let's not waste a second,'' he replied, and locked his mouth to hers.

Now came the kiss she'd been longing for, dreaming of. It soothed the weeks of grief and loneliness, and promised the fulfillment of the passion that had always simmered between them whenever they touched. By the time Read lifted his head to catch his breath, she was clinging to him to keep from melting to the floor.

''Read,'' she whispered, unable to keep from brushing her lips against his again and again. ''I can't believe this.''

''Believe it. I couldn't go on the way things were.'' He stroked his cheek against hers. ''Being a proud and stubborn fool made me miserable and nearly cost me my kids. I not only broke your heart, darling, I broke theirs, too.

''I'm sorry for being prejudiced against your father's success,'' he continued, straightening to gaze deep into her eyes. ''I'm sorry for one minute throwing you at someone else, and then being a jealous fool in the next. I want you to know that I'll try to support whatever you do in honor of your father's memory. I may not be the greatest fan of his kind of music, but I happen to be nuts about his greatest composition.''

After he kissed her again, Marina touched his cheek. ''I am going to tell Jeremy Cameron that I'll do the documentary, Read. It's time, and I think it will do a lot to free me from the past.''

Although he nodded readily, a gleam also entered his eye. ''But would you at least hold off until after the wedding? I don't trust that shark around you.''

''You have nothing to fear from Jeremy, Read,'' Marina murmured, stroking his cheek with the backs of her fingers. ''It's you I want.''

Read's arms tightened around her. ''Sweetheart...''

His next kiss unraveled some of the finer threads of their control. Their hands became more restless, seeking and coaxing; their bodies inched closer and closer, desperately trying to assuage the yearning that strained to be fulfilled.

At last Read buried his face against her throat and crushed her close to hold her still. ''I want you,'' he groaned. ''I want you so much.''

''I want you, too.''

They both sighed and exchanged wry smiles as the sound of small feet on the stairs stopped them from saying anything more. They glanced up to see Ricky and Molly descending with their favorite gifts tucked under their arms.

''Dad, look! Marina gave me a microscope and

there's a neat science kit upstairs, too!'' Ricky declared, his eyes sparkling.

"And I got this angel doll, Daddy. Isn't she beautiful? She has hair just like mine, and I got a comb-and-brush set like Marina's and jewelry!''

As Read lifted an eyebrow at her, Marina went down on her knees to accept the hugs and kisses from each child. "I'm so glad you like your presents.''

"We do,'' Ricky assured her. "But the best of all is that you and Dad are gonna get married. Does that mean we'll get to live here with you?''

Although her heart leaped in joy, Marina forced herself to say quietly, "We'll have to see what your dad says about that.''

He looked from one expectant pair of eyes to another. "Why do I get the feeling that I'm woefully outnumbered?''

They were married on New Year's Eve. When people teased them about the short engagement, Read told them about how he'd suggested they catch a late flight to Las Vegas on Christmas Eve.

Molly was Marina's maid of honor and Ricky walked her down the aisle of the small chapel at the center of town and then stood up as Read's best man. Read invited the Fields family and Marina's guests were her new circle of friends from The Christmas House, who all wept profusely and afterward told her that it was the most romantic ceremony they'd ever witnessed. Jeremy politely declined the invitation to attend, but sent a case of champagne for the reception.

They held the brief reception at The Christmas House, but it wasn't long before Mrs. Cotton took control by handing everyone their coats. She even insisted on having Ricky and Molly spend the night with her.

"Mrs. Merriweather will make her famous caramel popcorn," she told them. "Mrs. Livingston's made brownies that will melt in your mouth, and we've rented a half-dozen Cary Grant movies from the video store."

"Who's Cary Grant?" they heard Molly whisper to Ricky, as the three ladies ushered him and Molly out the front door.

Finally alone, Read turned to Marina. The laughter that had lit his eyes only moments before was quickly replaced with something far more profound and intimate. When he stretched out his hand, Marina went to him eagerly.

"Now…? Or do you need a few minutes?" he asked, stroking her hair.

She smiled. "Now. I've had ten years to get ready for you."

Leaving Raspberry, who slept comfortably before the living room fireplace, they crossed the foyer. About to set her foot on the first stair, Marina felt herself swept off her feet and into Read's arms.

"I don't get to carry you over the threshold," he said, holding her close to his heart, "so if you don't mind…"

How could she possibly have minded? Since Christmas Eve, he was continually doing and saying things that either thrilled her or filled her eyes with tears of heartfelt emotion. Telling him so, she wrapped her arms around his neck and offered him the kiss of promise.

In her bedroom—their bedroom now, because he'd already moved many of his things here—he set her on her feet, and for a moment simply gazed at her with wonder and very male possessiveness.

''You're so beautiful.''

She was glad he liked the wisteria blue silk gown she'd chosen to be wed in. But she believed that he was responsible for any real beauty that he saw in her. ''Make love to me, Read. I ache for you so.''

''Marina. I'll be loving you until I take my last breath.''

And as he framed her face with his hands and kissed her deeply, Read showed her how well he intended to keep his promise.

* * * * *

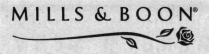

READER SERVICE

The best romantic fiction direct to your door

Our guarantee to you...

The Reader Service involves you in no obligation to purchase, and is truly a service to you!

There are many extra benefits including a free monthly Newsletter with author interviews, book previews and much more.

Your books are sent direct to your door on 14 days no obligation home approval.

We offer huge discounts on selected books exclusively for subscribers.

Plus, we have a dedicated Customer Care team on hand to answer all your queries on
(UK) 0181 288 2888
(Ireland) 01 278 2062.
There is also a 24 hour message facility on this number.